# One Chance, One Moment

### BOOK ONE - THE MANDY STORY

## JUDITH KOHNEN

# Upcoming Books
## by Judith Kohnen

*For the Love of Mandy*
*Whispering Hope*

# One Chance, One Moment

"A Feel Good Romance with Suspenseful Thrills" … "Ms. Kohnen has written a love story that will capture the romantic at heart while weaving thrills throughout the plot—creating 'one' thrilling read."
—*Allbooks Review International*

"… a novel that is impossible to put down. Fans of romance will find themselves absolutely riveted by the story as the suspense and tension becomes as unbearable for the readers as it is for Garry and Mandy."
—*Book Reviewer List*

*To the man who has graced many with his unique gifts;*
*Who has quieted my mind and has stilled my spirit.*
*Thank you, Barry, for inspiring in me*
*the words,*
*the music,*
*the vision.*

# Overture:
## I AM YOUR CHILD

GARRY DANZLO STOOD alone in the middle of the room, surrounded by towering walls that shimmered with gold and platinum records. Facing him were tall sunlit windows that filtered in the last hot rays of the day. But those sunny, ardent rays did little to warm him in the one room of his Bel Air mansion he depended on to make him feel good. His eye flinched at the award plaques that hung neatly in rows on the wall to his right. Each one beamed a wild adventure and held life-changing experiences he would cherish for a lifetime. To his left was a gold Grammy encased in glass, standing radiantly proud on a marble pedestal. And next to it was his beloved piano, as black and grand as the tailored suit he wore.

These were just a few of the visible signs of his extraordinary success—*proof* of his worth. But today, he felt like a tarnished fixture among the shining pieces of his life.

He glanced down at his tanned, gifted hands. One held a glass of brandy firmly; the other was shaking. He slid the shaking hand into his pants pocket, exhaling a calm breath. When he inhaled, the woodsy plum aroma ascended from his glass, luring his tongue to take a swallow. Yet his gaze stayed fixed on the glittering lights in his drink, the reflection of his adventure to paradise stinging his brow.

He moved toward the window, his eyes unfocused on the panoramic view of the splendorous mountains and canyons of California. He dismissed the reflection of himself that stared back at him, avoiding it as usual, for he'd never much cared for his visage. He'd always considered himself *not* handsome. His nose sat large, his chin appearing too short next to his broad shoulders. He thought himself too tall, too thin, and certainly undeserving of a title such as *hunk*. Yet the tabloids called him that. But it was the fame and fortune, he decided, that made one look better, and the talent with which he was blessed that made him the popular man he was today.

He had sought his passion, and he had done so with a passion. Not only was he an award winning musical artist, pianist, composer, and producer of his own music, he'd, surprisingly, become a singer. It was never his intention, for his love was purely in the music—arranging it, writing it. It had been cheaper to sing his own songs than to try and find someone else to do it for him. The next thing he knew, headlines were dubbing him *Young Blue Eyes. The Sinatra of the 80s.*

What an honor. It floored him, even now with 1990 just around the corner.

They said he had charisma. What was that thing anyhow? A gift? A power? The way he saw it, everyone possessed this gift. Everyone had their own personal charm and ability to influence others. It was the blessing he saw for himself: the capacity to grow and be affected, either positively or negatively, by everyone he met. In return, he would possibly give something back of himself. Something good, for he had received such an abundance of good in his thirty-eight years of life, and he felt he owed much to all the people around him—his family, his friends, those he worked with, those he met on a daily basis, his audiences. They had all made him the man he had become.

*Except one.*

Garry took a step back, his eyes dry, burning as the reflection in the window transformed to that of an old man, a worn face with features so like his own—the same deep-set eyes and large ears, the same dent on the right side of his chin when he worked his mouth just so—identical features he'd been unaware of until just days ago. Or perhaps he had denied them, had refused to see them, for they would dredge up a past he wanted to forget.

His desperate attempt to hold back his anger was waning. He swallowed with difficulty and blinked back the moisture pooling in his eyes.

"To you, Father," he whispered, raising his glass to an invisible man. "I am your child, and now a renowned man of the world. Who would've ever imagined that the scrawny Jewish kid from Brooklyn would make it big? Certainly not you. No thanks to you."

2

He downed his drink in one big swallow and welcomed the burning sensation in his throat. The smooth, dry taste of plum and oak in his mouth was pleasant, but then was spoiled by an elder's voice pleading in his head.

*Garry, don't go. Please come back, son! Let me explain.*

His jaw hardened, the hand that was in his pocket now raised and fastened against his temple. The empty glass in his other hand dropped from his fingers and rolled on the plush carpet by his feet.

*Forgive me. Please forgive me, son. I love you. I love you.*

Heat scorched Garry's face, consuming his reserve. *Liar!* his mind shot back. The memory of yesterday's affliction flooded through his senses with a vengeance. *Get out of my face, old man. You make me sick. You betrayed me. Not once, but many times. Just go to hell!*

He tried to calm his ragged breath, to stop that pounding hammer in his chest, but the attempt was futile while the voice of the old man played a broken record in his head—*come back, come back, come back…*

"Damn it!" he muttered between clenched teeth, his fingers digging into his scalp. If he could just squeeze out the gnawing agony, the demon possessing his soul. It cursed him, making him suffer. *For what? My God, for what? For guilt?*

"I didn't kill the old man!" he shouted aloud. "He took his own life! *Dear God… he took his life.*"

Garry's arms fell to his sides, his eyes closing from the horror of it. Only hours ago he'd watched a wooden casket lower into the cold ground. Inside, laid the remains of his father, clothed in linen shrouds and the bloodstained garments found on his body at the time of death—for the blood of an individual is considered by Jewish law to be part of the human being and must be buried with him. As a suicide, he was not to be honored or to receive public recognition. Garry was under no Jewish obligation to mourn or pay special courtesies to his father. No eulogy was written, no traditional burial *Kaddish* recited at the graveside. Nor was *keriah* performed—the rending of one's clothing as an expression of grief for the deceased. Though this custom was generally followed at the graveside, even for suicides, Garry had declined. When he'd returned home and found all the mirrors in the house covered—a traditional practice to avoid vanity and not to diminish the image of God reflected by the recent death—he had ordered them all unsheathed. He was no hypocrite. His Jewish faith had died a long time ago, along with the memories of his father.

*Father. Jonathan Danzlo.*

The name was foreign to him.

Garry had barely been ten years old when his father had left. What he remembered most from that time was his mother's tears and her sleepless nights, when she'd been pregnant with his sister. He had prayed and waited for his father to return. Like a naive child he had hung onto hope for weeks, months, even years. He had sworn he'd never feel that way, nor allow his father to push him over the edge again.

What did the old man expect? *He comes to me after nearly thirty years and I'm not supposed to hate him? I'm supposed to forgive him because he finally found guts enough to confront me? Even then, he couldn't come to me honestly, making me believe he was someone else. For two weeks, he deceived me.*

*Damn you, old man. A charade. It always was with you, wasn't it, Papa? Your weathered and aged appearance paid off for you while I played the fool. Again! And now, your act of suicide has left me staring once again at the end of a broken chain. How many times can one man betray another? And this time, leaving me a hounding vision to haunt me all the days of my life. Well, I'll not be accused of your death!*

Garry slammed his palm against the window pane, blotching out the phantom image. "Nicolas!" he called out. "Nicolas!"

"No need to shout, sir. I'm right behind you."

Garry pivoted, startled by the closeness of the other man's voice. He contemplated the short, plump, and genteel man of sixty-four years, concern etched on a round face.

"I'm fine, Nic," he said, ignoring the other man's unease. "Always at my beck and call, aren't you?" Garry offered a weak smile. "I want you to know how much I appreciate that. You're my favorite assistant. My best butler." He knew Nicolas considered himself a top-ranked household affairs manager, educated in one of the finest international schools for professional butlers. To Garry, Nicolas was both a confidant and friend.

"I'm your only butler, sir. And your appreciation is relayed quite often, thank you. And no, I will not have your car brought around."

Garry blinked. "I've not asked for my car." He watched a crease form on Nicolas' forehead and followed the gray eyes that solicitously spied the empty glass on the floor. "One drink, Nic. That's all I've had. I just want to take the car for a drive. Get out for a while." He paused. "Do you know everything I'm thinking?"

"I hope not, sir. Though you keep me in good practice."

Garry's body was rigid, his mind too tense to find humor in Nicolas' response.

With great effort he forced a teeth-bearing grin. "I'll get the car myself."

He stalked out of the room, hurried through the foyer and headed down the hall past a housekeeper. He heard Nicolas trailing steadily behind on much shorter legs in an earnest attempt to keep up with his pace.

"Sir. Mr. Danzlo, please!" Nicolas shouted as the sleek Alpha Romeo was driven out from its haven. Garry had to slam on the brakes, the little red convertible screeching to a halt just in front of the persistent servant.

"What is it?" Garry asked, his fingers grinding the steering wheel raw.

"Sir…" Nicolas tried to catch his breath. He walked hurriedly to the side of the shiny, waxed car. Garry watched with brittle patience as the older man took time to groom himself, straightening windswept clothes and combing back a gray, thin patch of hair with the palms of two thick hands. Garry scowled.

"Sir," the servant began.

"Speak your mind, Nic, and stop with all the 'sirs.' You know it irritates me."

"I awoke this morning feeling an aura of misgiving," the butler confessed. "I fear something dreadful is forthcoming… if you should leave, sir… I mean, Mr. Danzlo." Nicolas released a breath, his face blushing.

Stunned momentarily, Garry sighed heavily and responded as softly as he possibly could. "I'll be fine, Nicolas. I appreciate your concern, I do, but these *premonitions* of yours… they're getting a little out of hand, old pal. For the most part, you worry for nothing. The last time you predicted something *dreadful* for me, I only lost a button from my favorite suit."

"But, sir, this is different. I really feel—"

"Enough, Nicolas. I need this time alone. You of all people should understand. You know what I've been through. You're the *only* one who knows. I'll be back when I come through the door." Garry put the car in first gear and gave it some gas.

"But, sir," Nicolas bellowed, panting for breath while jogging alongside the car that was pulling away. "Your sister, Miss Melissa! And *Miss Daphne*. All of the guests are expected within the hour for the wake. What shall I tell them, sir?"

But the only response Nicolas received was the squeal of tires as the little red convertible made its way off concrete and headed toward a darkening sky. The promise of a storm was brewing, black clouds following above the vehicle like an omen.

GARRY FELT THE first drop of rain patter on his nose some twenty minutes later. A cool front was forging in. He had just pulled the car onto the interstate, heading east, the wind whistling beneath the vehicle and causing it to sway on the road. The storm would not be missed he realized, but it didn't matter. He needed the storm; he needed to drink from it and cleanse those thoughts that kept thwarting his mind.

*Coward!* it reprimanded viciously. *You couldn't face a house full of people because they all know, don't they? That old man pulled the trigger… because of you.*

A tear stung the corner of his eye as the car raced on, his face numb from the cool October wind. It blew fiercely through him, stronger and wilder as the car sped faster.

Memories flickered through his mind—a lopsided smile, twinkling blue eyes keen with interest, laughter, a pat on the back, the shake of two hands—one smooth and young, talented; and the other dry, aged, calloused. Jake Fayman… brief companion, friend.

Alias. *Liar.*

Moisture blurred his vision. The car lurched, its tires skidding against the shoulder of the road. Garry's body pummeled against the doorframe. He attempted to slide over, jerking the steering wheel left. He bumped and bounced as the car vaulted back on the highway. He straightened in his seat, his heart drumming in his throat. He'd nearly hit a road sign.

*Must stay in control,* he meditated silently. *Get your mind off it, Danzlo. Your mind clear.* He wiped his eyes and inhaled the chilled air. He breathed in its burn. The rain was starting to fall steadily now, dropping like ice upon his skin. He reached forward and pushed the button to close the top over his vehicle. Shivering, he tried to focus his mind on something else.

*New York.* His childhood. The slums of Brooklyn. Those *Brooklyn blues.* In his youth, he could lose those blues with dreams, his imagination taking him beyond the Williamsburg Bridge on the other side of the river. He could see himself surrounded by big city lights and caught in a crowd of strangers where danger, yet excitement always lurked—the New York City rhythm filling his soul, keeping his dreams alive.

He was trying to get the feeling again, but it wouldn't come; somehow lost with the memories of dreams he'd made come true. And yet, one dream stood dormant in his mind. A woman. A faceless illusion, yet real to his senses. She'd stolen into his dreams more than a few times over the past couple of years, a phenomenon of sorts. *A blessing.* For his career had begun to move in exciting directions, new melodies and words sounding in his head. He was creating as never before. The imaginary woman had become his inspiration, a part of his music... *a part of him.*

Like a wisp of wind, she swept his soul, taunting his senses with something unknown that he desperately craved. She was both wicked and beguiling. Disturbing, yet soothing. In his dreams, her stature was almost petite next to his own; her skin, a light bronze. She had hair opaque as the night, and it flowed like honey against his skin, touching his insides with something close to contentment. She sparked his creativity and awakened things in him no true-to-life woman ever had.

His thoughts moved to Daphne. He'd been seeing her for more than a year. It was the longest *intimate* relationship he'd ever had with one woman. Since he'd met her, he'd had an astounding amount of publicity, his success skyrocketing to new heights. Not only was she a marketing genius, she was a real beauty. A classy blonde, tall and graceful, stunning as a rose in winter. And she looked as beautiful, felt as soft, but she never seemed to move him with any kind of intense passion—one stepped gently yet fiercely in love and longing. He supposed he felt *some* type of fierce emotion when he was with her, for the sex was good. It's just that, when away from her, he felt... *he felt he should feel more.*

Was there more? Did he even want more?

The faceless woman suddenly bolted through Garry's mind, seizing his body like a potent charm. *Take me, Garry, I'm here*, her spirit breathed inside him, savoring him like fine wine. He swallowed hard, pushed her back. She wasn't real. Daphne was real.

*Think Daphne... Daphne...*

"HE DID WHAT?" the voice blew haughtily in Nicolas's face. "We confront most of those people on a daily basis. An embarrassment to us all. Sometimes he just doesn't think."

Daphne Dimont turned from the butler with a mixture of horror and disgust on her unblemished face, her back poised regally, her frame tall and slender next to Nicolas' short, stout one. Her tailor-made dress of soft blue-gray enhanced her clear blue eyes. They stared at Melissa with accusation. As if it was her fault.

Melissa Rosten had had just about enough of her brother's very-late, two-faced girlfriend. Couldn't Garry see beyond skin? How she'd love to blotch that fair, expertly-polished-with-makeup face, just one time, or tear down that flawless French knot at the back of her head. So what that the blonde beauty had boosted her brother's fame a couple of notches, put a few more million in his pocket, and she'd done so for free. But there was one thing Melissa knew: Daphne Dimont didn't do anything for free. Her little sugar momma role was sure to backfire in Garry's face one of these days. Try to warn him, and he would get all defensive.

Melissa couldn't worry about that now. Not when her brother was out driving who knows where. Garry had been gone for hours, all the guests long gone, and still no word. She glanced distressingly across the living room at her husband—Dan, his intelligent green eyes kept saying that everything was going to be all right. She envied how he could so easily tune out Daphne. Melissa tried to embrace some warmth from his suave, tawny looks—a young Robert Redford look-alike that had captured her heart nearly twelve years ago. She'd fallen for Dan the first moment Garry had introduced him as his new CEO and manager. He and Garry, the same age, had been twenty-six then; she'd only been seventeen, barely a woman. Yet she had somehow known that this Daniel Rosten would be marrying her. It had taken her eight long years to convince him.

Dan smiled from across the room where he sat on Garry's sofa, his black leather satchel by his side and a mound of paperwork in disarray around him. Melissa took in the handsome curve of his lips, allowing them to send their sweet kisses through her senses. But the feeling was short-lived as his attention went back to his work. She saw his gaze move nonchalantly to his watch, and then back to the documents he'd been signing. His pen rasped in staccato beats across the sheets, matching the subtle jerking visible in his jaw. He could pretend all he wanted, but Melissa knew he was worried just as she was, though not quite on the same level. Garry had a big gig tomorrow night. A lot of money rested on this new project they'd begun. Dan's responsibility was to ensure that everything went all right. The planning and dedication over the past months had been a tremendous amount of work. All had gone smoothly... until *this*.

"Surely he's not upset over that old man's death," Daphne said, brushing a piece of lint from her dress. "How ridiculous would that be?"

Daphne had not only Melissa's attention, but Dan's and Nicolas' as well.

"I mean, it's been twenty-eight years," Daphne added hastily. "Garry would hardly know him, never laid eyes on the man till early yesterday. Isn't that what you told me, Nicolas?"

Nicolas appeared off guard, his right hand pausing in midair holding a handkerchief retrieved from his breast pocket." Yes, Miss Daphne," he replied. "That's what I said, yes." Melissa gazed quizzically at Nicolas as he wiped sweat from his brow.

"Well, I feel nothing for my father," Daphne said with cool indifference, "whoever the bastard was. You can't grieve for someone you don't know, right, Melly? We're living proof."

Melissa tensed at the "we" part in Daphne's statement. And at the nickname Daphne had spoken; she'd told Daphne never to call her that. With a fist at her side, she said between clenched teeth, "Just because you can't feel anything, doesn't mean that I don't... *Daffy!*"

Dan was up from the sofa then, taking his place beside his wife. He laid a calming hand on Melissa's shoulder. "Why don't you go home, Daphne, like the others did? Why bother to come here in the first place? You're four hours late."

Daphne's cheeks grew a shade pinker. "Garry knew I had a... an appointment at noon. I wasn't able to fly to New York last night to attend such a *ridiculously* early funeral this morning, and then fly back in time. However, he did know I was coming later this afternoon."

"You mean later this evening," Dan said.

Daphne averted her attention by maneuvering the matching blue-gray handbag clutched under her arm. "I want to be here for Garry when he comes home," she said a bit shakily, her eyes steady on the purse she now held in one hand. "He may need me." Her gaze lifted to Melissa, and surprisingly, Melissa thought she saw some genuineness sparkling in those clear blue depths. "I do love Garry," Daphne said. "No matter what you think, Melissa. I love him very much."

Melissa suddenly felt ashamed for her previous curt words. She didn't want to dislike Daphne. In fact, she'd always gotten along with everyone.

"We're all upset," Melissa said, decidedly, and then moved toward the large bay window overlooking the drive. She tried to hold back her tears, but that feeling was gnawing at her again. Nicolas had said he'd felt it, too. Something was going to happen. Something bad. But what could they do, except wait? Wait for the phone to ring. Wait, and pray.

THE AIR BLEW warmer against Garry's face, the storm finally over, the top of his small convertible once again laid back. He'd made a pit stop about an hour before in Mesquite, Nevada, just before entering the northwestern corner of Arizona. The time zone had changed there from pacific to Mountain Time. He'd wound his watch up an hour while traveling the twenty-nine mile stretch through Arizona, crossing the Virgin River on his way to the border. He was entering St. George, already six miles into Utah. He supposed he should turn around and head back now. The next exit was just a couple of miles ahead. His mind was feeling more peaceful. He would finally make that call he had promised.

Static began to play loudly on the radio. Garry tried sharpening in a station. An old song came through, his *own* voice sounding through the speakers. A faded memory seized him.

The past was suddenly present.

It was 1981. *The Mirage* in Vegas. It was the first night he'd ever performed in front of an audience of such magnitude. In the front row was his family: his mother, Miriam, and his younger sister, Melissa, cheering him on. The audience consisted mainly of females, enraptured with his songs of love, hope, and heartache. It was on that night that he'd realized he could actually *move* people with his music, touch both sexes, young and old. Watching the cheer on their faces had brought him a great sense of worth. No more struggling years, he had thought. He could finally afford to give his mother a better home, a better life.

His eyes strained through a haze of moving stage lights as his gaze roamed the aisles of many faces. He caught sight of an older man standing alone in the shadows to his right, and then suddenly, the meandering spotlight on the crowd was lit on the lone man—tears falling down his wrinkled cheeks.

Reality surged through Garry like a shard of dry ice. He slammed off the radio, the knob breaking, dropping from his hand to the floorboard. He felt frozen to his seat, heartbeats pounding in his chest.

"My God, it was him. He was there. My father!"

*I love you, son. I love you, son*, a voice echoed in his ears.

Garry's foot fell heavy on the gas pedal, the headlights glittering on the road, blinding his way. But he had to run. Run from that old man's face. It kept haunting him with those tired worn eyes… so sad, pitiful, pleading.

"Dear God!" he cried, his voice howling in the wind to his father. "Am I to believe the lies? That you could *ever* have loved me?" Tears streamed across his face. They burned, wouldn't stop. He desperately tried to wipe them with the back of his hand, to keep the steering wheel steady, to see the stretch of road ahead.

"He begged me," he shouted to himself. "For just *one* chance, *one* moment. He pleaded with me. Yet I turned away. I let him drown in his shame."

The road became oblivion, his foot never easing off the gas as a childhood memory overtook his mind.

*Papa, do you hear me?* the boy shouted from the window one lonely night, all hope gone forever. *I no longer have a father,* he declared, tearing the clothes from his chest, expressing the stabbing finality of their separation. *You're dead in my eyes! Dead! Do you hear me, Papa?*

And then all sight and sound of the inevitable collision with the truck just ahead was gone. Garry could only hear the shot, the one triggering in the old man's hand.

"No! PAPA!" he screamed, his right hand rending the garment over his grieving heart, exposing it for the world to witness the shame that must be written there.

"Murderer! I'm a Murderer!" he cried to the truck he didn't see.

Metal encountered metal with a mighty thunder. Glass reverberated, jangling a crescendo through the sky.

And then came a decrescendo of deadly silence.

# *1.*

# HE DOESN'T CARE, BUT I DO

***Four months later***
***A new home, a different life...***

GARRY DREW IN a breath, the muscle in his right arm contracting as he used his left to reach across the bed to the bedside table. The entire right side of his body was useless. "Nicolas!" he called out, a metallic bell escaping his fingertips and clanging to the floor. He grabbed his head with his left hand while his right one lay limp and crooked against his abdomen.

"Yes, sir," the butler said hurrying into the room. Nicolas gasped wearily as he stood at attention beyond the large mahogany bed. "Are you all right, sir?"

Garry lay lopsided against his pillow, one side of his head mashed against the headboard, the other side padded on a pillow with his right shoulder. "I'll be fine as soon as Melissa and Dan get in here. Where the hell are they? I've been banging on intercom buttons for the past five minutes."

Nicolas paused, eying the telephone lying bottom-side up on the bed, its receiver and cord tangled up in the covers. "I didn't hear, sir. I was taking out the trash." Nicolas reached across Garry to adjust the phone and then placed it conveniently by Garry's hip. Straightening, he said a little breathily, "Your brother-in-law went to town to run a few errands this morning, and then he's picking up your sister from the airport... who has been in Florida for the past couple of days."

"*Days?*" Garry said, his head jerking in horror, his gaze clouding.

"The pills, sir... I think you took one too many the other day. You've been

12

sleeping quite soundly for the past forty-eight hours. But no worry. All is fine. You're fine, I'm fine and,"—Nicolas cleared his throat and nervously glanced at his watch—"and your dear, *loving* sister is soon to be stepping off a plane to give a full report about your new hired... nurse."

Silence grew stifling for the next few seconds as Garry's fury magnified.

"For the last time, Nicolas, I don't *need* a nurse! Why can't Melissa get that through her thick head?" His hoarse rebuttal unleashed a cough he could barely contain. His butler hastened to his side.

"Water!" Garry's voice hacked, his left arm weaving through Nicolas's two attending ones.

"Water!" Nicolas gasped, bolting toward the adjoining bathroom to fetch some.

Garry managed to get a handle on his cough as Nicolas rebounded for the bed with a full glass in hand. "No, something stronger! Bourbon, brandy," Garry said, changing his mind.

Shuffling sideways to do his bid, Nicolas slammed to a halt, water sloshing atop his hand while his round elderly face paled in horror.

"Sir, do you think it wise... I mean, first thing upon awakening, sir. It's not your habit to even drink in the evening let alone, well... anytime at all!"

Nicolas' face was flushed, sweat beading off his forehead. He combed back his thin mass of gray hair with a shaky hand.

"Afraid I'm going to add to your woe, Nicolas, or my own?" Garry winced at intervals as he tried shifting his weight on the bed, a slow attempt to raise himself more fully against the headboard. He sent his butler a sideways glance. "You're right, Nicolas," he said with strained calmness, "I drink only when I really need one. And I really need one... *now*." He paused halfway up the headboard, closing his eyes, his left cheek taut, then twitching.

"Another migraine, sir? I'll go get your pills."

"I don't want pills, Nicolas. I want the drink. Those drugs you've been pushing down my throat are useless... except to cause sleep, obviously. Just get the drink. Please."

"Yes, sir." Nicolas exited the room swiftly, returning moments later with a brandy glass in hand, half-filled with the amber liquid.

Garry reached for the glass with a trembling hand. He raised his gaze to his long-time companion. "I'm sorry," he tried saying, yet his voice creaked with such hoarseness, the words came out coarse, almost unintelligible.

Nicolas lowered his chin, his eyes directed at the floor. "Sir, couldn't I call the doctor? Perhaps—"

"No," Garry said, holding the glass shakily against his lips. He took a large sip of the brandy, half of it dribbling down his chin while the other half drained like fire down his throat. He coughed. "Not another doctor. Not another nurse. I'm telling you, Nicolas, this nurse is leaving like the others."

"But sir, your sister is only trying to help. She loves you. She cares. I... I care, sir."

Garry's eyes flickered as the older man stood poised before him, a look of complete sincerity on his face. Honesty—it was the one thing he most admired about Nicolas, along with his loyalty. Nicolas had kept his secret about Jake Fayman—alias Jonathan Danzlo. And he'd stuck by Garry through the whole wretched experience, before and after the car accident. Nicolas was not only his right arm man, but now his legs, too.

His face softened as he regarded Nicolas with some respect. "I know I—"

His words ceased abruptly by the sight of Melissa coming in through the doorway. Every inch of Garry's skin grew taut as his sister stepped around Nicolas, the older man's eyes widening at her early arrival. Then Nicolas' face transformed, right before Garry's eyes, all bright with pleasure. The butler's thin lips sported a smile as though his ship had just come in.

"I'm ba-ack!" Melissa intoned happily, her chestnut hair bouncing across her sweater clad shoulders. Her heart-shaped face revealed a smile as warm as her peach complexion. She wore a two-piece sweater-top of coral pink, and blue jeans that hugged her petite frame to a tee. She had large almond-shaped eyes like Garry's, and a nose Garry wished he'd been born with.

He glared heatedly into her hazel eyes—she, standing on the balls of her feet, her arms spread childishly wide. Nicolas could smile all he wanted to, but Garry was immune to Melissa's breezy demeanor.

"What? You didn't miss me?" she said, dropping down on her heels. "Maybe I got back *too* early. *Geesch*, and after all that good sleep you had. Dan said it's been the most peaceful, productive two days he's had with you in a long while."

Garry wasn't amused, his surly face as resilient as a sheet of hard rubber.

Nicolas cleared his throat. "I'll be in the kitchen, sir. Call if you need me." Nicolas picked up the bell from the floor, placed it on the small table by the bed and took his leave.

Melissa barely jumped when the bedroom door clicked shut, her smile only slightly wavering as a few seconds passed in deadly silence. Garry eyed her suspiciously as she sauntered slowly toward his bed, that mischievous gleam he knew so well glinting in her eye. "I see you've heard about the new nurse," she said, starting to straighten a jumble of covers at the foot of his bed. "I guarantee she's unlike the others. Yes, indeed. Not like the others."

Garry was about to counter her remark with a caustic response, but her last words rang through in a tone that wasn't quite natural. His gaze zoomed in on that little twitch at the corner of her mouth while her hands steadily smoothed across already neat blankets. His stomach felt queasy. "What have you done this time," he said gruffly. "Spit it out, Sis. God help you if you bring in another two-hundred and forty pound weight lifter—"

"Hey, that was Dan's idea," she said, fists on her hips. "We've both been trying to find the best possible help for you, someone who might make a difference if you'd just let them!" She stomped her foot for effect. "I told you, this one's different. She has... *powers*," she finished lamely, her eyelids flickering.

Garry's brows knit inward, just before they pinned to the top of his head, the outer corners of his face stretched so far his temples ached. He started to hyperventilate.

"Not really powers per se!" Melissa tried remedying. She rushed to his side and placed her cool hands against his hot cheeks. "Breathe a bit slower, Garry, longer breaths." She sat down on the bed beside him and placed her hands in her lap. "Actually, it's something to do with energy. She can manipulate it somehow, you see." Garry's head snapped back and knocked against the headboard. He tried to catch his breath. "It's a mind, body, spirit thing," Melissa said with more excitement. "A form of holistic healing, all very natural. Wait till you meet her. She's really an extraordinary woman—"

"An extraterrestrial is what you mean!" Garry's voice burst out, bristly and cracked. "Good God, Melissa, have you lost your mind? I will not have some strange woman in my home practicing her voodoo on my body!"

In animated distress, Garry's body flailed sideways on the bed, his impaired right side nearly tumbling forward over the mattress. But his sister caught hold of his left shoulder in the nick of time and flipped him safely on his back, despite her petite stature. Garry groaned, one eye narrowed unappreciatively, the left side of his mouth squelched up like a prune.

"It's not voodoo, Garry. And wipe that crazy look off your face. She's not coming to put a spell on you. She's a healer."

"You've got the not coming part right," he said in ragged breaths. His vocal chords were more hoarse than ever and barely audible, but that little quirky smile Melissa smiled—lopsided, cute, annoying—proved she was hearing him just perfectly.

"Oh, she's coming," she assured him, patting him on the head like he was some darling little pup.

He snarled, saying underneath his breath, *"Why can't people just leave me the hell alone."* The last thing he needed or wanted was to have his younger sister directing his life. She'd been trouble since the day she was born—the one who really needed supervision. Just as mischievous at age twenty-nine as she had been at three and thirteen! This was by far her wildest and most daring feat to date—thinking to bring in some new age witch, a hands-on freak to heal his mind, body, and spirit.

*To hell with that!* Solitude, that's all he needed—the reason he'd hired an agent to find him a home away from home, deep in the mountains of Colorado and far from civilization. His life had been swarming with reporters week after week, his picture plastered on every tabloid and newspaper across the country, across the globe. The once great singer/musician had totaled his car and wrecked his career, all in the same night. Now he couldn't play, he couldn't sing, not to mention he was finding it hard to do anything. Stay on the lookout for the next revealing headline— *Danzlo's Biggest Mistake: They Don't Get Larger Than This.*

Was there no peace and privacy in the world?

"Amanda Fields, that's her name," Melissa was saying. "I've got such a good feeling about this one. All these days and nights searching for the right person are finally going to pay off. If you weren't such an obstinate, insufferable grouch, perhaps the other half dozen nurses and therapists I hired wouldn't have walked out on you."

"Because I fired them!" he coughed out, his tonsils flaming.

"Just a few," Melissa said. "The others left on their own free will, and quite happily too."

Garry's shoulder squirmed against the pillow, his left fingers scratching his bare chest in guilty tempo. "Yeah, well, good riddance."

Disappointment dimmed in his sister's eyes. She could always make him feel like a jerk, when he really was a jerk.

"Ah, but this one's a keeper," Melissa said, a changing light brightening her eyes as she pulled the pillow from beneath his head. She fluffed it and shoved it back under his head while he grimaced and growled. "I knew the moment I met her.

She's coming all the way from south Florida."

Garry swallowed with difficulty. "Because demons live in hot places."

Melissa snatched a tissue from a box on the night table. "No, an angel, surely." She slapped the tissue on his chest. "Here, wipe that sweat off your brow. She's not here yet. I think she called it *Reiki*—that thing she does. It's some type of therapeutic touch."

"If you think I'm going to let some old shaman woman rake my body, or whatever it is you say she does with her hands—"

"It's alternative medicine, Garry. Nothing hocus-pocus about it. Some kind of ancient healing art, I think."

The image of an old crone flared red in Garry's head, her gnarled fingers with sharp nails screeching across a magic wand—made of heavy metal, no doubt, the way she was trying to hold on to the thing. Yes, just before she thought to rake those barb-edged nails, and *it* across his body.

"Good grief, Garry, you're looking pale as a ghost and stiff as the dead. Loosen up, stop stressing. I'm not bringing in a sorceress. Give me some credit. This woman is a healthcare professional, a registered nurse who has advanced education in holistic nursing and natural healing. She's worked in a reputable Palm Beach hospital for nearly twelve years. I hear she gives a really good foot massage."

"No one is touching my feet!" A vein throbbed in his forehead as he struggled to cover his right foot, which peeked outside of his sheet.

"I've experienced her work, Garry. Healed me right on the street. The worst case of heartburn I ever had. And all she did was circle her hands over my chest. Within minutes, I'm singing that Alka Seltzer jingle. I ran into her during my business trip in Boca Raton on Monday. She's not even from there, but rather from West Palm Beach. Isn't that wild?"

"Very!" Garry replied, perturbed that Melissa was now pulling up a chair.

"Things just started to fall into place." Melissa plopped into the chair beside him. "I go to my meeting with Kate and what do I find out? Kate knows her!"

Garry shut his eyes, the throb of a migraine pulsing in his head as Melissa continued.

"I rushed through those fashion designs I'd drawn up for Kate. Kate couldn't say enough marvelous things about her friend. But wait, that's not all!"

Melissa bounced in her chair; Garry rubbed his temples.

"I leave Kate's office, take a cab, and I ask, 'God, give me a sign' and lo and behold, around the next corner, a parked car with a license plate that reads

'Amanda1.' *Oh my God! Thank you, thank you,* was all I could say. I contacted her immediately, and by no coincidence, she desperately needed this job—or rather the large sum of money you're offering. And of course, I desperately needed her… or rather, you do."

Garry's eyes popped open. "I don't need anybody! And just how much money are we talking about? I don't remember offering anything. Does Dan know about this crazy idea of yours… about this *hoodoo* nurse woman? I want to talk to him."

Melissa puffed in frustration. "Of course he knows. He trusts me, why can't you? And what difference does it make how much you're paying? You're a multimillionaire. You can afford it. And yes, you do need her. She's coming to fix you."

"There's nothing to fix, nor can be fixed! Besides, I have Nicolas. I'm being fed. My linens are getting changed."

"Yes, poor Nicolas. He's doing all he can do. Oh, and let's not forget Daphne. She's a real help to your integrity and independence, isn't she?"

"I resent that. She cares about me!" Garry's fingers began to scratch at his chest again.

"Right. That's why she's vacationing in Europe right now with *your* money while you lie in bed suffering."

Silence grew for a harsh moment, and then loneliness, wretched and deep. It tore through Garry heavily. Why hadn't he just died the night of the accident? Though it had not been his intention to kill himself, he'd prayed for death in the emergency room, had begged for it. Yet, he was kept alive. And for what? So he could pay for his sins in this living hell?

"Garry…" Melissa's hand reached out and touched his face, just below the small scar that now marred his right cheekbone. "I know something happened that day… something more you're not telling us about our father, about his suicide. I never knew him, but you did and—"

Garry jerked away from her touch, his eyes signaling warning.

"I'm not asking you to tell me, Garry. Only that I'm here to listen when you're ready. I just want my brother back, the one I remember and adore. You've grown so cold and angry, so negative about everything these days. But mostly, I'm concerned about your depression—"

"I'm not depressed! I just want people to leave me alone. Why can't you get that through your head?"

His eyes felt scorched, scratchy and dry like his throat. Not a tear to help moisten them, not since the accident. Not even now, when the urge to cry swelled through him like a tsunami. He watched hurt cross his sister's features, hurt he knew he was responsible for.

"Okay, Garry, I'll leave now."

Melissa rose from her chair and scooted it back toward the wall. She cast one last glance at him, saying. "Amanda Fields *will* arrive tomorrow." She started for the door.

"Okay, so she's a nurse!" Garry said, exasperated, accepting that this woman had qualifications and maybe she wasn't a complete quack. "But I'm not in need of nursing care anymore. I'm not on IVs. I have no open wounds." It was his last attempt to change her mind.

Melissa paused with her hand on the doorknob. "You're right, Garry," she agreed, not bothering to look back at him. "You don't need a nurse anymore. You need a miracle."

# 2.

# BRING ON TOMORROW

*The same day...*
*West Palm Beach, Florida*

AMANDA FIELDS BLINKED away a hot tear, pushing back a wayward strand of dark, silky hair with three slender fingers. She kept her focus on the road as she drove her old white Volkswagen toward her destination. She was determined not to think about the past and all the grief that came with it.

All she'd ever wanted was to love and be loved. Why was that so difficult? To give love and get some back in return? She wanted to receive love as she had so given it for the past ten years. Paul Fields was not her strength, the lover she had always dreamed of, let alone a companion she could confide in and share her secrets with. He was not her support; he was not even her friend. He was just her husband.

His death was a gruesome one. Amanda wanted to forget everything that had happened last year and the lies that had poured out with the investigation of his murder. Paul had ruined his career as a lawyer. His gambling, his fraudulent dealings, and his involvement with corrupt people were revealed during the court trials. For a time, the court pointed fingers at her. Had it not been for Eddie and his brilliant skill as a defense lawyer, she may not have survived it and could've ended up in jail for something she didn't do.

*Eddie Chandler.* The man she could've married instead of Paul. The one man she thought she could always trust, but was afraid to now. Like Paul, he was changed; he held secrets.

All she was sure of was that she was now more mature and wiser, and she would not grieve over mistakes once made. Tomorrow, she may be uncertain of, but it was today that held purpose and chance. Her life was about to change. She'd asked for a miracle and that miracle had come.

*Fifty thousand dollars.* And fifty thousand more if she could get the musician back on his feet and on stage within four weeks.

She could barely believe her luck. But it wasn't luck, and Amanda didn't believe in coincidences. No, this was destiny. Her one chance to make her life right. She had kept faith, and had finally let go and surrendered her worries to the Universe. By releasing her fears once and for all, she'd brought on a blessing beyond her wildest dreams. Surely this was the Law of Attraction in action. Hadn't she taught it to others and seen miracles? She'd neglected to walk her talk, too busy helping others move toward their dreams and goals and not focusing on her own. Instead, she'd drowned in miserable attempts to save a loveless marriage she wanted to believe in. Only, all she was doing was collecting more fears for herself.

Not anymore. This new miracle would not only provide her a chance to get out from deep debt, but it was going to make possible the one thing she wished for *most* in the entire world—the ability to adopt Robbie. She'd have to get approved by the court system to parent the eight-year-old boy—being single was a mark against her—but she'd stay positive.

*For good things come to those who wait,* she told herself. Now, if she could just convince the one she needed to say goodbye to.

She took a deep breath and pulled her old white Volkswagen into the lot of the Delray Home for Disabled Children—Robbie's new home since leaving the hospital three days ago.

The car sputtered and then clattered as she turned off the engine. She waited for peace to follow, and then closed her eyes to gather her courage. A warm and gentle Floridian breeze blew in through the window beside her, invigorating her senses with the smell of orange blossoms. She breathed in its sweet scent while the sound of children's voices and laughter played in her ears and beckoned her eyes open. She searched the many little faces out in the play yard by the old flamingo-colored building. Some pale and quiet, some weak, yet cheerful. Many were wearing leg braces, two on crutches, a few in wheelchairs. Then she spotted him—that one little face she adored. He had not seen her yet, his full attention on a little terrier puppy yelping happily about his feet, its paws bouncing on the metal footrests of Robbie's wheelchair. She was thankful to have a moment to become attuned to his nearness and drink in the sweetness she felt every time she was with him.

She stepped out of the car, feeling more empowered as she made her way to the big iron gate, the boy catching sight of her then, his baby-blue eyes growing big and bright. "She came!" he screamed excitedly to one of the nurses standing by. "She came, I knew she would!"

Amanda's heart quickened as she unlatched the gate to meet the small boy anticipating her approach. He was already wheeling himself toward her. His happy face sent her heart racing and her entire spirit felt enriched with an abundance of gratitude.

"Hi ya, Captain Robbie," she said with a genuine smile. She faced the boy in his wheelchair on the lawn, her right hand in a stern salute. "How's the ole starship holding out, Capt'n?"

"Got things under A-OK control, Starmate," Robbie answered, his lips curling in such an upside down rainbow, it expanded its warm glow throughout her body. "Had some engine trouble for a while," he said with a grave note, one little dimple showing in his cheek, "but I got things all fixed up. It's ready now for blastoff and a quick visit to the Milky Way. I was just waitin' on you."

They both laughed then, celebrating the magical world they'd created together. Amanda couldn't quite remember when these little imaginary starship adventures first began, only that it was early on in their friendship, a relationship that had blossomed quickly during his two-month stay at the hospital. She felt silly at times—a woman of thirty-two years playing imaginary games like a kid; yet it had a way of nourishing and replenishing her energy.

"Didn't you have to work at the hospital today?" he asked, a puzzled expression wrinkling his face. "I thought you were coming tonight. Not that I'm complaining or anything!"

She half smiled, fighting back the pinch of emotion that shifted inside her. The confession of her unexpected visit was gratefully delayed as a nurse stepped toward them.

"You must be Amanda Fields," the nurse said, coming up behind Robbie with the small, sable-haired puppy in one hand. She placed her other hand on Robbie's shoulder. "I believe we talked on the phone this morning."

"She's my most favorite person in the whole world!" Robbie stated proudly, bending his head backward to look at the nurse. "She's a nurse, too, like you, Cathy!"

The dog barked and Cathy chuckled. "So you've told us, Robbie. Why don't you take Amanda over to the big magnolia tree so the both of you can have a nice visit?"

Amanda thanked the nurse silently with a grateful smile. She reached and patted the frisky little dog on the head, receiving a few affectionate licks in reward, and then she wheeled Robbie to a shady spot under the tree. Once there, she parked his chair nice and snug against a white wooden bench and quickly took her seat. Curling close beside him, she threw her arms around his shoulders for a big bear hug, and then grabbed his head so she could plant a half a dozen kisses on his face.

"Ew!" he said, scrunching up his cheeks and laughing all the while.

Her feat achieved, Amanda sat back on the bench and lifted her tanned legs, her flip-flopped feet dangling above the ground. She wiggled her toes in front of her and shrugged her shoulders in delight. "Ah, just what I needed," she said with an enormous smile, her hands slapping in her lap. She looked at Robbie askance and asked, "What's the next galactic spot on our map, Captain?"

"Hey, I didn't get my turn," he said, his eyes still glistening with laughter. Then his expression grew serious. "Captains should always be the first to make strategic maneuvers. It's in the manual."

Her brow arched. It amazed her how intelligent he was. She could even see it—in the intensity of his eye contact and the way he smiled, warm and slow. His olive skin was a bit darker than her own, his hair almost black rather than the dark rich brown she had. His father was of Spanish origin, or so she'd been told. He looked at her now with a stern square jaw.

"I'm afraid that manual didn't consider a sneaky starmate like me," she said with a face just as serious. "I think we should write in a new rule, in case there's another keen starmate like myself adventuring the cosmos."

Robbie burst out laughing. "No, there's not another like you in all the universes, Amanda. You're one of a kind." He patted his hand on her cheek, gazing over at her in child adoration. It brought such an overwhelming feeling inside her that it compelled her hand to move to her chest, lest her heart jump out with joy. She lifted her other hand and placed it against his, the one still warming her skin. She squeezed it more firmly against her cheek.

"And there's no one like you," she said, suddenly filled with emotion. She'd kept her voice from quaking, yet the tremor inside her threatened to break her into little pieces. She brought their hands down to the chair arm and let out a feeble breath, her smile for him, wholehearted, yet very frail.

"Something's wrong, isn't it?" Robbie said, studying her features. A breeze ruffled the dark curls on his head as his fingers began to fidget beneath her own. "I can tell. I can feel it."

Amanda wrapped his hands more securely in hers; their comfort was her courage. "Not really *wrong*," she began, turning in her seat to face him better. "Remember when I told you how we all have a destiny? That sometimes life leads us on different paths, those we need to follow... and what might seem at first bad, might turn into something good?"

"I remember," he said somberly. His right eye started to narrow with wariness. "Bad things happened to me. Then a good thing happened, *you*."

Her focus blurred with tears as she lifted her hands and cupped his face. "Oh, Robbie, you're my good thing too." Then she laid her hands across her chest. She paused and swallowed. "Sometimes we have to step away from the—"

"You have a destiny?" His little hands clenched tightly the arms of his wheelchair. Seeing them was feeling them—the fear, the discomfort mounting inside him. She felt those hands tightening around her heart, strangling the words she needed to say but didn't know how.

"Yes, sweetie, I..."

All she could do was look at him and drink in his worst nightmare.

"You're going away, aren't you?" Tears instantly filled his eyes. "You said you wouldn't leave me. You don't want me anymore. My mama and daddy didn't want me. I don't even know who they are! And I killed Gramma. I killed Gramma!"

"No, Robbie, no!" she said, catching hold of his flinging arms. He responded immediately to her touch, his fingers grasping her, clinging desperately with all of his might.

"Please don't leave me!"

"Shhhh... it's okay," she said next to his face. She kissed his cheeks, his tears. She breathed in his little boy scent, a blend of green apples, puppies, and bubblegum. "I don't want to hear you say that again. You didn't kill your grandmother."

"B-but, but..." he sniffed hard with deep hiccupping sounds, his tearful eyes looking earnestly at hers, "I-I was playing... playing with the... m-matches. I-I knocked over her old oi-oil lamp. I started the fire. And I had to j-jump out the window... and now I can't walk anymore."

"An accident. No one blames you. And certainly not God. He blessed us, remember? He gave us each other."

"B-but you're going away. You promised you *never* would."

Mental numbness seized her mind momentarily. And then came an idea.

"Ah, but some promises are broken for special reasons," she said in a lowered voice. She leaned in, her eyes darting to the left, and then to the right to assure no one else was listening. "This is a very, *very* special reason," she added, her eyes wide for effect. Robbie sat back in his chair and released her, curiosity overtaking the hurt in his eyes. His breath slowed, his lips pursed as she received his rapt attention. "Surely you knew I'd not leave you for long! Only an important secret mission could keep me away from you. A four-week assignment, six at the most—*the chance we've been waiting for.* The one that could possibly make our dream come true."

Robbie sniffed back his tears, rubbing his tear-splotched face with his balled fists. "Our dream? You're coming back for me? We can be a family? I'll come live with you?"

"Well, yeah, that's the plan." She ruffled the soft curls on his head. "What did you think? I'd forget my favorite starship buddy? I'd never find a better commander to search out the yonder galaxies with. Why, we have adventures to take, battles to wage, planets to save. We're the best team that ever traveled the Universe." Amanda shot him a silly *don't cha know!* expression—eyebrows pointed inward, her mouth askew.

Robbie giggled, making one last hiccupping sound. "When do you have to leave? When are you coming back?"

"I... I'll be leaving in the morning," she uttered with a grimace.

"You're leaving too soon!" he cried out.

She sighed. "I know, sweetie, but there's someone who had a bad accident four months ago and is still in need of help. His sister pleaded with me to come as soon as possible."

"Because you're the best nurse in all the world," he said.

Amanda smiled, touched by his sincerity. "Actually, I think my friend Kate— the one I talk about sometimes, remember?—said I have a flair for dealing with difficult patients. This man wants to give up on life. We don't want that, right? We overcome and conquer things. He doesn't want to, so we have to help him."

"We?" Robbie said, eyebrows lifting. "How can *I* help him?"

"Well..." she thought quickly, taking his hands in hers, "when I call and write you, and I tell you about the adventures and troubles I'm having, I need your words of encouragement and thoughts on how I can master plan this mission. At the same time, you'll be helping my patient get better. You *are* captain," she explained, noting a little line furrowing between his brows. "And it was you who got us out of some pretty hectic spots when we were out conquering those awesome creatures in the galaxy. When I leave, you need to stay here and hold down the starship." Robbie nodded, his lips pressed together in a fine line as he attempted to be staunch. "Most of all," she said with a hint of authority, "do what these nurses tell you to do so you can get stronger. And then, some sweet day very soon, they'll let me have you."

"I'll be strong. I promise," he said, looking her in the eye. He sat straight in his chair, chest out, and offered his hand. She smiled and raised her own; they sealed his pledge with a firm handshake.

"Come here, you!" she said, pulling him forward for a big hug and kiss. He held on to her and she him for a very long while. Then they both released each other, and smiled.

"Hey, will you do that thing you do with your hands?" he asked, brows lifting, eyes bright with interest. "So your patient can get better faster like I did."

"Ah, the energy work," she said. She cupped her elbow in one hand and tapped her lips with an index finger. "I don't know," she said in a doubtful chant. "I've been getting some funny vibes about that." She sighed, returning her hands in her lap. "His sister was certainly enthused about my holistic work, but I'm feeling my patient won't be very enthused. Of course I could be wrong."

"But you're usually right," he said with a wide grin.

She shrugged her shoulders, shaking her head. "Not always," she said with a modest smile. "I just hope I can get through to him, and that he's not as difficult as they say he is." She sighed. "But yes, I'll be doing that 'thing' I do if he lets me. Everything depends on him. He has to accept the healing first. Meanwhile, you could send him some healing. You know, like I showed you. I promise it will make it all the way to Colorado. Do you know where Colorado is?"

"It's out West where the cowboys and Indians are!" he said, excited. "This man you're going to take care of… is he a cowboy? Maybe he was thrown off his horse! Maybe his Indian friend wasn't there to help him! Maybe they were attacked by—"

"Wait, hold on," she said, laughing at Robbie's carried-away imagination. "What Indian friend?"

"You know, like the Lone Ranger has. When Grandpa was alive, he told me all kinds of stories about Texas Ranger John Reid and how he was rescued from death by the Indian Tonto, then how he dedicated his life to frontier justice. Tonto called him Kemo Sabe."

"Oh... well, I don't think this man is a Lone Ranger type. He's more of a musician, a pianist. He sings for a living. I don't think the Lone Ranger sings."

Robbie's brows shot up. "He's a singer? Like Michael Jackson? Maybe he's famous. Maybe he *is* Michael Jackson! Maybe you can get an autograph and—"

Amanda placed her fingers lightly to his mouth. "Really?" she droned incredulously. "Did you take a jump to the moon and back without telling me, because you've got some pretty far out ideas bubbling in that head?" She tapped the top of his head for effect, and then leaned closer toward his ear. "Okay, I will confess a little secret. My new patient *is* a little famous. Unfortunately though, I can't reveal his name, at least not right now. I will tell you, however, that it's not Michael Jackson." She inclined her head to view his brief disappointment; it was quickly replaced with curiosity, so she continued with her secret. "I'm a bit embarrassed to say this, but... I don't think I've ever heard of this man before. When his sister offered me the job, I believe I truly surprised her by not jumping at the offer. I think she expected no less than a scream from me."

Robbie sat back in his chair, a frown on his forehead. "I've heard about girls like that. Some girls faint and do stupid things when they get close to famous people. They even try to *kiss* them. Gross! You're not the fainting kind, are you? What if this guy is really handsome?"

Amanda shook her head. "Nope, even if he's handsome, I don't think I would ever faint. You're very, *very* handsome and I've not fainted yet."

Robbie grinned. "Maybe he'll be the one to faint. Wait till he sees he has the prettiest nurse in the whole entire world."

Amanda smiled at his flattery. "Yeah, yeah," she said, patting a finger on his nose, "and the smartest nurse in the whole world, and the funniest nurse in the whole world, and—"

"I'm going to miss you." His eyes were suddenly void of the laughter they held just moments before.

Amanda swallowed the lump in her throat, her own eyes blurring with tears. "We've got all day together," she said.

And though their day was filled with laughter and tender moments, evening closed in much too quickly.

"I wish you didn't have to go," Robbie said, holding her hand tightly. "I wish I could go with you in case you decide not to come back."

His words were startling, so earnest and so bursting with fear that her eyes immediately welled up with tears. She grabbed him up and held him close in her arms. "No one in this world loves you like I do," she whispered in his ear.

It was all she could do to let go and tell him good-bye. As a nurse, she'd said a lot of good-byes, never knowing if she'd ever see her patient again. But she would see Robbie. He was the one person left in her life that she could truly love. Someone who appreciated her love. Someone she could trust to return that love.

"Amanda," he yelled as she headed for her car. She stopped, looked back. Through a haze of tears, she saw the little boy who wanted so much to run to her, but could do no more than clutch the arms of his wheelchair. "I love you, Amanda!"

She fought the urge to run into his arms, hold him, and never let him go. She felt choked up and couldn't speak, so she pressed a kiss to her fingertips and blew it toward him. Then pointed a finger to herself, crossed her heart, and pointed back to him.

Robbie smiled and did the same. "Now and forever," he said, stealing the line she would often say.

She nodded. "Now and forever."

Amanda walked solemnly to her car. She slid into the driver's seat, closed the door, and sat for a long while in the dark. She felt numb, suddenly uncertain about the rash decision she'd made in leaving Robbie, so soon out of the hospital and just when he would need her most.

Or was it that she needed him?

She had a void in her life: a widow for nearly two years, and heartache that had lasted a decade. She'd been vulnerable and gullible for years. But no more, she promised herself. Never would she allow another man to strip her sensibilities, treat her as less than the woman she was.

A brief warning eddied through her body then, a chilling sensation that began across her face and plummeted down into her chest. She struggled with disconcerting thoughts as she traveled home to her apartment. As she lay down to sleep, thoughts of her new patient kept drifting to mind. She didn't see a face. It was just a gnawing feeling—one that kept her wondering just what it was she was getting herself into.

# 3.

# CLOUDBURST

"MINUS SEVENTEEN DEGREES!" Amanda gasped. The pilot's announcement caused her to cleave to her seat long after the plane had landed.

"It's really not so bad," a heavy-set female said, while pulling down some carry-on luggage from an overhead rack. "I thought I'd freeze here, too, but Colorado is so beautiful you won't even think about how cold it is."

Indeed, the weather was the least of Amanda's concerns as she left the plane and made her way to the gate where Melissa stood waiting with an overly exuberant smile on her face. The petite woman waved one hand in the air, the other one holding a very large shopping bag. Before Amanda could say a greeting, Melissa snatched her by the arm, dragging her through the crowded airport, shouting among the bustle, "We've got to hurry and change before Dan sees you! I talked him into waiting at baggage claim."

"Change? Who is Dan?"

Melissa scurried her through the busy terminal, dodging passersby on their way to what Amanda could only assume was the women's restroom. Her arm locked by Melissa's, she desperately hung on to her tote bag, pocketbook, and a small carrying bag, which was nearly yanked from her person as she bumped into a large man who had tried, unsuccessfully, to move out of their way. "Sorry!" she and Melissa shouted in unison—Melissa's apology for Amanda; Amanda's for the poor guy she'd rammed into.

Circling into the restroom entrance, Melissa answered, "Dan's my husband." They stopped in front of a row of sinks and taking a deep breath, Melissa then added, "He's also my brother's best friend and financial manager... the one who is going to be paying you." She blinked a couple of times, a frown of worry wrinkling her brow. "Oh, gosh, but you're more gorgeous than I remembered! It's the hair, I think. You have it down today… that dark, rich brown really brings out your eyes, makes them even sunnier looking. You're simply lovely… and I'm so sorry."

"Excuse me?" Amanda's focus on Melissa was distracted by other women going in and out of the restroom. She moved away from the swarm of traffic, Melissa following her lead.

"I wanted to tell you before you got here. Really, I intended to. I just didn't know how to do it. I was afraid you wouldn't come if I even suggested… that is… I'm a fashion designer, a color artist, you see, so we really don't have a problem!"

The smile on Melissa's face was starting to look a lot like guilt.

"Okay, you're totally confusing me now. Maybe even scaring me a little. Perhaps we could start from the beginning?"

"Actually we don't have time."

Melissa reached inside that large shopping bag she'd been carrying and popped out a mid-length, Gothic-style dress of yellow-beige and pale green with pin-tucked shoulders, a crocheted front inset at the bodice, a high waist, and loose three-quarter sleeves. Amanda couldn't imagine the type of shoes one would wear with it. The style wasn't terribly awful, though a bit pagan and eccentric for her tastes. It was the colors that she abhorred—muted tones that would washout her olive complexion. Amanda's attention shot warily to Melissa's heart-shaped face, aghast to find a plea written all over it.

"Oh, no. Oh, no-no-no-no!"

She shook her head adamantly while Melissa begged, "You have to! Amanda, *please!*"

Kate had warned her of Melissa's somewhat "flighty" and "off the wall" demeanor. She hadn't expected this though. "But a bold adventuress like you," Kate had added. "You'll really like her. You both have a lot in common."

Amanda would admit that she had done some pretty crazy things in her adolescent years. But those days were long gone. These last years with her husband, Paul, had mellowed her mischievous ways quite considerably.

"I wouldn't ask if it wasn't absolutely necessary," Melissa said. "You just don't know what horrors I've been through these past months. I can't afford to make another mistake." Melissa grabbed Amanda by the arms, bumping her against a sink. "If you go to Garry wearing that white blouse and that royal blue skirt—which by the way is his favorite color *and* a color that looks fabulous on you—Daphne will have you out in a New York minute! She's supposedly Garry's girlfriend, but she's really his crutch I'm sorry to say. Insanely jealous and conniving to boot."

Amanda had no idea she'd be contending with a pernicious girlfriend. She'd only been told about the bad patient. Melissa wanted her to go dressed like a pale-looking oddball?

"But more importantly," Melissa said, the light in her eyes dimming, "my reason is Garry." Melissa dropped her hands to her sides, a genuine tear falling down her face. "He's very self-conscious of his physical state right now... an impaired right arm and leg, not to mention other noticeable scars—one from the temporary tracheotomy he had, another on his right cheek. To bring in a pretty woman would only intimidate him, draw him deeper into his shell, the one he's been creating for himself since the accident. He's used to women fawning over him, admiring fans looking up to him, not pitying him. He thinks everyone pities him. Are you getting what I'm saying?"

Amanda didn't want to. She sighed. "Unfortunately, I do. The more stress your brother is under, the harder his healing will be."

"Yes!" Melissa said, her feet clearing the floor. "Just put this on." She dumped the unwanted dress into Amanda's hands. "I'll get out the makeup. Oh, and we'll need to get that hair up too." While Melissa rustled through that humongous shopping bag, Amanda stood by feeling helplessly suckered. "Just a bit of contouring with a few wrong colors on your eyelids and face is all I'm doing," Melissa promised, bringing out a small makeup pouch. "I'll make it as natural as I can, but oh, we have to hurry! Dan will surely get suspicious if your luggage comes out before we do. He's forever thinking I'm up to something."

"I can't imagine why," Amanda said lightly, glancing sideways at an amused woman standing just feet away. The woman's salt and pepper hair and big-boned body reminded Amanda of that T.V. actress—Maude, who starred on *Golden Girls*. Maude wiped her hands on a paper towel and mouthed the words "good luck" just before she exited the room.

Melissa lifted her eyes to Amanda's face, an array of makeup brushes in her hands. "Maybe you should put on the dress before I work on your face," she said.

"I don't know, Melissa. I'm feeling a little uneasy about this. Honesty is an important aspect of a nurse/patient relationship. What if your brother finds out I'm deceiving him?"

Melissa's vacant stare lasted only a second. "Think illusion rather than deceit. Is anything ever as it seems?" She bit down on her lower lip, smiling in the process.

31

"Stop worrying, Amanda. He'll just think you're a plain Jane who wears eccentric clothes. You've a whole bag of them." Amanda frowned. "Okay, well some are hardly plain," Melissa amended, "but they serve the purpose. Lots of earth tones and subdued colors like gold, beige, and orange that winter complexions should avoid. You're definitely a winter. Oh, and talking about winter, I bought you a coat, which Dan has for you. I ran across this stuff at a unique shop in town called 'Fashionistic.' I was inspired in an instant! Had to call Kate to get your shoe size."

Amanda couldn't help but laugh. "Don't tell me you've got shoes in that bag too."

"Of course, and jewelry too!" She reached in and pulled out a small multicolored beaded purse. Opening it, she pulled out a pair of amber crystal earrings with little dangling dragonflies on them. "These will match your dress."

Amanda was amazed at Melissa's last-minute creativity, suddenly intrigued by the adventure being offered. It brought back fun memories of her spunky years. "I love dragonflies!" she said. She took off the pearls she wore on her ears and replaced them with the dangly amber earrings. Then she wound up her hair into a very tight bun.

In one crazy moment, it all seemed okay. One thing she did know for certain: she was supposed to be here in Colorado. She felt it strong in her heart, so deeply intuitively that as she moved behind a stall to slip on the unflattering dress, a gush of tears escaped her eyes and ran warmly down her cheeks. It was as if Robbie was already hers, and her whole life would be changed from this moment on.

So what if she had to appear a little differently for her new patient; what difference could it make? She wasn't here to impress him, but to rehabilitate him, to assist in the healing process, and help him realize that he held the true key to his own healing.

"Hurry, Amanda! I'm excited for you to meet Garry. He's in for a real treat!"

Amanda exited the stall and glanced in the bathroom mirror.

"Or *something*," she said, sighing heavily at her unflattering reflection. "Trick or treat, Mr. Danzlo."

# 4.

# NOT WHAT YOU SEE

DEEP WITHIN A forest of frosty aspens and pines, in a magnificent cedar log home shimmering with icicles, stood Nicolas, anxiously awaiting the three people who were soon to arrive. He stepped out from the doorway into the chilled air, the woodsy smell from the smoke-stacked chimney permeating his nostrils. He loved this new home that was flawlessly crafted inside and out. The front of the house was decked with a wide wraparound porch and hand peeled posts. Giant glass windows flanked each side of a huge stone chimney, which served as a dramatic center gable for the rest of the home. He sighed at the backdrop of snowcapped mountains rising in the distance. To his left, a hundred feet from the house, glimmered a large pond, completely iced over.

Nicolas was thankful for the quiet moment, for his entire morning was spent assisting and fetching and trying to calm his agitated boss down. He couldn't wait to meet "the miracle of miracles" Melissa had been raving about, whom his disgruntled boss had loosely labeled "the witch from Avalon."

Nicolas was ready to accept both—the miracle and some Merlin magic. He'd been living in the *Mists of Danzlo* far too long. Eleven years in his employ had not prepared him to be a round-the-clock nursemaid these past weeks following a lengthy hospital stay. He could only hope this woman was a high priestess in disguise, filled with passion and adventure. She'd surely need these qualities to endure the coming days, particularly with the boss's girlfriend returning sometime next week. Daphne Dimont was notorious for firing grief into a situation. Just a few honest words from her mouth could start a combustion. Her honesty could be downright brutal sometimes, making everyone around her miserable. There was enough grief floating around without her.

Nicolas tried not to be too ecstatic when the Land Rover came into view. He watched as the passengers exited the vehicle.

"Come inside quickly before you freeze!" he said, holding the door open for the three guests. The three paraded in loudly, all stomping snow off their shoes on the large broadloom rug he had conveniently provided for their entrance. Closing the door behind them, he turned to take their winter coats.

"Nicolas, this is Amanda Fields," Melissa introduced. "Garry's new nurse." Melissa winked at him encouragingly and handed him her tweed coat.

"Yeah, Garry's new nurse," Dan spoke behind her, a sparkle in his green eyes and a hint of mirth in his voice. It was seldom Nicolas saw this waggish side to his character. Whenever it showed up though, one could be sure Melissa was around. She had a way of bringing out the best in Dan, both the fun and the fire.

Nicolas observed Amanda with some bewilderment. The girl appeared frail, her rusty-brown coat seeming to swallow her thin frame, her face rather pale. She stood no more than an inch or two taller than Melissa and seemed to lack the impressive and spirited demeanor Melissa had rambled on about yesterday. But perhaps it was the sheepish expression, or a sleepless night from the look of those faded circles under her eyes that gave this impression. He placed Melissa's coat over his left arm, extending his right hand warily. "Pleased to meet you, Ms. Fields."

"Oh, please, call me Amanda," she said with instant buoyancy, her hand grasping Nicolas' in a mighty shake. "We'll be seeing lots of each other in the weeks to come. No need for formality." Amanda's hand was cold in Nicolas', but he found much warmth in her voice.

Amanda released his hand to remove her bulky wool coat, pulling a pair of reddish-brown framed glasses from one of its pockets. "My handy-dandy reading glasses," she said, placing them on her face while Dan took her coat. She thanked Dan and sent Melissa a showy grin. Melissa tilted her head and, oddly, returned that grin with an even bigger one of her own, a look of surprise and pleasure marked on her face. Baffled by the girls' exchange, Nicolas's thoughts became distorted at the sight of Amanda's outlandish dress. She slid those plastic-rimmed glasses up on her head and spoke to him in a pleasing and confident tone. "Melissa has told me much about you, Nicolas. I understand you hold down the fort here. I believe you can be of great help to me, and I'd like us to work together. If that's okay with you?"

"Yes, ma'am," he nodded, trying to keep his eyes off the odd-looking dress. He didn't know what he was drawn to most, her sweet personality or her tasteless state. Her lashes were coated with brown mascara, so unlike the darker shade of her hair, and her cheeks were rouged with... *orange*. But her smile was pretty, her teeth white and perfectly straight. Nicolas saw sincerity in that smile.

Dan helped him hang coats in the foyer closet. Returning, Nicolas watched as Amanda dreamily gazed at the great room, taking in its giant cedar beams, cathedral ceiling, and gorgeous timber loft. All the floors were designed with beautiful shining hardwood, partially covered by fashionable hand-woven rugs of burgundy, gold, green, and tan colors. The fireplace stood magnificently huge along the front wall of the house, its height reaching the ceiling and constructed with the same variation of tawny, gray, and ecru stones outside. Logs crackled and sizzled inside the hearth, radiant flames dancing and circulating the smell of hickory in the room.

"Nicolas, how's Garry?" Melissa asked, interrupting his steady gaze on Amanda. "Is he awake?"

"Awake," Nicolas affirmed, nodding his head. "But his mood foul, I'm afraid."

Amanda's attention moved in his direction, her brows raised with interest; it made him a little nervous.

"It's okay, Nicolas. Amanda's not easily discouraged," Melissa assured. "I'll just take her in to meet Garry." She grabbed Amanda's arm.

"Miss Melissa," he intervened. "Mr. Danzlo didn't shave this morning, refusing his bath yet again. He awoke only an hour ago. He drank brandy for his migraine, says the pills do him no good. And well, the glass, which he threw across his room, is still lying shattered by the fireplace. He wouldn't let me clean it up, mainly because he wants no one in his room. I fear he's definitely in no mood to see a nurse."

"Is he ever?" Melissa paused in dismay. Her gaze moved toward the hall where Garry's room was. "Maybe I should go in and talk with him first."

"No, wait, Melissa. I'll just go in alone," Amanda said. "No need to warn him."

Melissa's head snapped around, an elfish smile growing on her face. Dan stumbled against the sofa at the same time Nicolas let out a cough.

"Hey, I'm a professional," Amanda said. "I meet new faces every day. Meeting the unexpected is part of my job. Believe me. A nurse never knows what she'll find behind a closed door. If my patient is not happy to see me, he'll just have to get over it."

Silence stilled the room momentarily. "Be our guest," "Yeah, sure," "Go ahead," they said in unison, pointing down the hall toward Garry's bedroom.

# 5.

# WHO NEEDS YOU?

AMANDA HAD A courageous smile on her face when she turned and headed for her new patient's bedroom. However, with her three onlookers moving stealthily on her heels, she had to admit she was a tad bit nervous. As she approached the only room with a closed door, she glanced over her shoulder for reassurance that this was Danzlo's room. Three heads nodded.

Amanda raised her knuckles and knocked on the door. No answer. She knocked again. No answer.

"He's not asleep," Nicolas said behind her. "He thinks no one will enter without permission, though if I deem it an emergency, I don't hesitate."

"Oh," she said, hearing the hint in Nicolas' voice. "I don't hesitate in emergencies either." She opened the door and walked into the room.

The door closed behind her, by one of those new friends of hers, no doubt. Her eyes drew immediately to the man on the bed, her gaze locked with two raging blue eyes. It was much like being in the midst of a cloudburst, watching the sky split open upon a treacherous sea, the Persian blue waves heading toward her both intimidating and magnetizing.

For one long moment, she stood with no breath, though her heart beat like the ticks of a thousand clocks; its million vibrations oscillated through her head, warning her this new job would be no easy task. Somehow she'd have to get this man to realize that his inability to walk was all in his head—for she and Melissa had gone over his medical records thoroughly in the car. Except for a lack of exercised muscles and bones, there was no indication otherwise.

Her eyes briefly broke from the storm he delivered, but that's all it took—a brief glance away—and she was suddenly in another world. She stepped back against the door, awestruck at the magnificent room before her. It was four times the size of an average bedroom, its high ceiling a rafter of cedar planks supported by cross beams. A large skylight beamed a lopsided rectangle on an oriental rug of rich medium blues. On the far side of the room stood royal blue drapes, partially drawn open, concealing like a tall cloak and covering a continuous row of framed glass windows. Adjacent to the drapes, to the right, was a spacious master bathroom, its light on, its door ajar, giving her a partial view of a large whirlpool tub and its shining brass fixtures. And opposite the king-sized bed, towered a huge stone fireplace, its big white and earthly-colored stones offsetting cedar wooded walls. The hearth blazed several oak logs, the crackling red and yellow flames toasting the room in perfect warmth. Amanda breathed in its woodsy smell, allowing it to meander through her senses while her focus moved back to the man in the bed.

A stubborn man. She could tell by the square chin and the hard planes of his face. His hair was unruly, a golden wheat-color. It was cropped in layers and a bit overgrown. She took in the strong nose, the high cheekbones, the thin top lip. His shoulders were bare and broad; a body well-formed, lean and very tense.

Though no words had been uttered by either of them, his glare said it all, those intense blue eyes gazing upon her body fiercely. It wasn't the hot and heavy kind of fierce a woman would normally find in a man's bedroom. It was more like the kind of ferocious fierce a mouse would find in a lion's den.

She swallowed hard, for this lion had killing on his mind. She did the first thing a nurse should never do. She panicked. With her eyes squeezed shut, she began to sing—a habit learned from childhood, effective in warding away unpleasant emotions. *"In the jungle, the quiet jungle, the lion sleeps tonight. In the jungle, the quiet—"*

"Enough!"

Her eyes flew open at Garry's hoarse voice. She watched as he painfully tried to prop himself up on his left elbow. Nurse instinct had her sallying forth to help him.

"Stop right there! I don't know who you are, but you had better get the hell out of my room."

Amanda halted, the glasses on the top of her head sliding forward and landing perfectly across her nose. She didn't dare move. As the moment ticked by, she decided it was the stubble on his face and the disheveled hair on his head that made him look so rugged and fierce. Maybe those intense blue eyes weren't as dangerous as they appeared. Maybe what she was really seeing was hurt and pain. She was suddenly drawn to it—his pain. She advanced another step.

"Come any closer and I'll... I'll call the police!"

How strange. His expression seemed to truly hold fear. Who did he think she was? A burglar? Attempting to remove the glasses from her face, his next booming words ceased the action, and she found herself sliding them further up on her nose.

"Just back out of this room and find some other fan club to join!"

Stunned, Amanda blinked a couple times. Didn't he realize she was his new nurse? But then, dressed in this unsightly outfit, why shouldn't he think she was none other than a loony fan, sneaking into his bedroom to have a peek at his famous self. She supposed such things happened to celebrities.

"Mr. Danzlo, you have me all wrong. I'm not who you think I am. I'm no fan of yours, believe me. I-I mean, I'm your nurse!"

Fear on his face transformed to terror. "Like hell you are!" His eyes were large, horrified. His shoulders jerked backward, his head jolting against the headboard. He screamed, "Nicolas!"

"Nicolas won't be coming, sir," she said in a raised voice. "I work for you now. If you want someone, you have me."

His brows shot up. "Lady, I don't want you!"

"Ah, but sometimes we have to deal with things we don't want... to deal with."

A deadly silence overtook the next few seconds. Garry's lips pressed tightly together, his left cheek starting to twitch as the deeper meaning of her words struck a sour chord within him.

Who was this woman? What was she?

His eyes scanned speedily down her preposterous looking body, then back up to her preposterous-looking face. No ancient crone as he'd earlier imagined, but definitely the pale and ghoulish look of a new-age witch. "I want you out of my house. *Now.*"

"Oh, come, Mr. Danzlo, I haven't even introduced myself. Geesch. Your sister was right. You're a real crab. As grouchy as they come."

He was fighting to stay calm, but all he could think about was strangling this woman. If Melissa were in his room, he'd strangle her too. "If you don't get out of here, Miss—"

"Amanda Fields. Ms. Amanda Fields," she filled in. "I'm a widow."

A snide remark about her widowhood was on the tip of his tongue, but then he thought he saw grief cross her features... as if he should care. "Ms. Fields, if you don't get out of this room, I'm going to—"

"Going to what, Mr. Danzlo?" Her eyes twinkled at him from behind her goofy-looking glasses. "Will you jump out of bed and get me?"

Garry stiffened. "If that's supposed be funny, I'm not laughing. I suggest you take your sick humor, *Ms. Fields*, and go elsewhere. You're wasting your time here."

"Only the future can tell whether I'm wasting my time, Mr. Danzlo. If anybody's time is being wasted, I'd say it was yours. Whether you admit that you need me or not—"

"Need you?" Garry laughed hoarsely. "Who would ever need you?"

Amanda paused, looking undaunted. "If *that's* supposed to be funny, *I'm* not laughing. Think we might be even now?"

The woman standing before him was astounding, her arms folded tightly beneath her breasts... generously large breasts, he noted. His focus stuck there for a moment longer than they should have. *Good God! What was he doing looking at this woman's chest?* His gaze shot to her face. She was still wearing that impervious and determined look that said his words didn't bite. Unbelievable!

It was curiosity that had him viewing her long and hard, head to toe, crudely discerning her unseemly and tasteless condition. Her dark hair was pulled severely back. Small, pointed-edged glasses sat low on her nose, for they kept sliding down that slim nose. He watched as she adjusted them quickly. He tried to distinguish the color of her eyes, but the glare on her glasses made it impossible. And her cheeks were... orange.

His gaze captured her mouth.

It didn't quite fit with the rest of her oddities. Somehow those full and glossy, bronze-berry lips had a lurid appeal, disturbingly interesting. The slight quiver of her lower lip had him contemplating her eyes again. No, she wasn't completely undaunted by him, he realized with amusement. This scrutiny of her body was unnerving her. Or dare he think, making her nervous.

His gaze journeyed down her ugly dress and ended at the laced-boot shoes while her fingers drummed her hips and her foot hammered the floor.

"May I ask what you think you're looking at?" Amanda said, her cheeks flushed from his rude perusal.

"To tell you the truth, lady, I haven't figured it out yet."

Amanda blinked. "Mr. Danzlo, if it's hurting you hope to achieve, I suggest you start collecting your sticks and stones. As for your uncouth words—"

"You could be spared if you just turn yourself around and get the hell out. Take the hint, Ms. Fields. You're fired."

"Oh, no, Mr. Danzlo. Keep this under your crude little hat: each time you fire me, your sister rehires me."

"I said," he emphasized the order much louder, "You're fired! I'll take care of my sister."

Amanda laughed, rather hysterically, and then responded in cheerful calm. "Oh, really, Mr. Danzlo. Surely you don't expect me to believe such a story? From what I hear, and see," she said, her eyes inspecting the entire length of him and then, glimpsing a broken glass by the fireplace, "You don't even know how to take care of yourself. You can't possibly make me think you could take care of your sister." She shook her head at the absurdity of such a thought. "No-no, Mr. Danzlo. You'll have to accept the fact that you're undoubtedly stuck with me. As sure as I'm standing here, you'll never have to be alone. Just think, many glorious days are yet to come. I'm getting excited just thinking about them myself. Now, if you'll excuse me," she said, straightening her ugly dress, "I'm really quite tired. The plane trip was long and I wish to freshen up before we start those challenging weeks ahead of us... *together.*"

Smiling, she nodded and left the room.

Amanda slammed the door, nearly tripping over Melissa, Dan, and Nicolas as she stepped into the hall. Eavesdroppers, she noted with disgust as she walked on past them.

Melissa trailed giddily behind her, saying, "She's a star!" while Dan and Nicolas made out like nails, stuck to the floor by Garry's room, their eyes wide, their mouths agape.

"What an act!" Melissa praised, pulling Amanda into the kitchen. She turned her new friend around and hugged her. "You were terrific! I knew you could handle him."

"Melissa... your brother is a rude, pigheaded beast."

"I know. He is, isn't he?" Melissa said consolingly, pulling out a chair for Amanda to sit down. "Let's have some hot tea and rest ourselves a while."

# 6.

# SOME KIND OF FRIEND

GARRY WAS BLAZING in defeat. How would he ever get rid of that indomitable bully of a woman? Wait till he got his hands on Melissa.

A knock sounded on the door. The door opened. Garry bounced upright, underworked muscles bearing pain in the process. *If that was that woman again, he'd—*

Dan leaned a shoulder against the doorframe, a smirk on his face.

"Well, what the hell are you looking at?" Garry asked.

"Actually, I'm not sure. Haven't figured it out yet," Dan teased.

Garry's focus flew behind Dan, making sure no unwanted person was lurking there. "Shut the door," he whispered loudly, a tilt of his head urging his buddy in.

"Sure," Dan said, closing the door. "You know, Garry, you shouldn't talk so impolitely to the opposite sex. You might be sorry one day."

"I'm already sorry. Sorry for laying eyes on—" He coughed and stretched a kink out of his neck. "Did you see her? Please tell me she was just some figment of my imagination. What'd she do? Jump out of an ugly box or something?"

Dan chuckled. "She is rather eccentric looking, isn't she?"

"That's putting it mildly. You're going to help me, right?"

"Help you what?" Dan asked, amused.

"Get rid of her, of course."

Dan angled a brow. "Hold on a sec. I don't interfere with my wife's doings. If I did, life wouldn't be very pleasant at home. And that's another thing… getting back home again. It's been an experience staying with you, but I don't want to live here, especially with you. You're my pal, but you're driving me nuts. It's time Melissa and I departed, leaving the dirty work to someone else. Get my drift?"

"Yeah, I get your drift." He knew he'd been a pain these past months, and he did feel guilty for all the time his family had given him. It had taken days to persuade his mother to return to New York. She did so, finally last week. "Well, friend," he added, "When you and Melissa leave, make sure you take *her* with you."

"Let's not fight over the woman. You keep her. You deserve her more than we do."

Garry snarled. "Some kind of friend you turned out to be."

"Come on, Garry. Other than unappealing looks, the woman has character, a sweet one at that. I can't tell you what a shocker it was to meet her at the airport looking like, well, you know what, yet there's something about her, something that pulls me—"

"Under her spell!" Garry said, his brows to the ceiling.

Dan, usually so analytical, paused to reflect on Garry's serious and rather frightful expression, and then he burst into laughter.

"This is no laughing matter. I need some help here."

"I completely agree," proclaimed Melissa, who came barging into the room to stand beside her husband. "And I've brought you help."

Garry glared at his sister with contempt.

Dan cleared his throat. "I think I'll skip this conversation and leave while I'm still safe."

"Shut the door behind you," Garry instructed, keeping his eyes on Melissa.

The door clicked shut, silence enclosing the two in the room.

"I think you're being unfair," Melissa said matter-of-factly. "Amanda deserves a chance."

"A chance to make my life more miserable?" he said. His jaw was tight and the scar on his right cheek ached. "And what is this unfair bull stuff? Are we playing a game, sis?"

"No, dear brother. We're playing real life—your life."

She blinked back tears, looking like the little girl Garry used to care for, protect while growing up in the gritty streets of Brooklyn. His eyes moved from hers and focused on the dying flames in the large fireplace across the room. He took a calming breath.

"I'm sorry, Melissa. I know you mean well, but, I don't want—"

"I don't care what you want!" His eyes shot back to his sister who stood like a rod, fists at her sides. "I happen to love you and whether you believe or care that I do, well, I really don't give a, a... *fig bar!*"

Her words and stance were suddenly amusing. It wasn't often he saw Melissa so riled up with anger. It was a change to her sometimes too-bubbling personality. "No, considering how you enjoy a good fig bar," he jested. Melissa's taut expression loosened. She wiped a tear. "It's not funny!" she said, choking out the giggle he had successfully retrieved. He offered a hand and she warily took it in her own.

"I happen to love you too," he said sincerely, reaching out for her with his left hand. She accepted his hand reluctantly.

"Well, you have a crazy way of showing it. Why do you have to be so incredibly impossible?"

"That's what brothers are for." He caressed her fingers between his own. "It's your stupidity for bringing—"

"Stupidity?" She slung his hand away and stepped back from the bed. "Are you calling me stupid?"

"Ow! Of course not!" He rubbed his only good arm against the edge of his pillow. "I was referring to the nurse."

"You're calling her stupid?"

"No, I-I just meant it was foolish for you to get—"

"Oh, so now I'm foolish. Well, let me tell you something, brother of mine." Melissa laid her hands on her hips, moving her head in a jive sway. "It seems to me that you're the stupid and foolish one, and the sooner you look in the mirror and realize that, the better off you'll be! As for that nurse out there,"—she pointed sternly to the door—"she's a highly skilled professional who has come all the way from Florida to take care of you. She's good-natured, a sweet person, and you had better start giving her some respect because she's not going anywhere. She's staying here—with you!"

Melissa stormed out of the room without another word, slamming the door behind her.

Garry groaned. If it wasn't his mother, it was Melissa. If not Melissa, Daphne. And now this Amanda Fields. He had a sickening feeling she would probably top them all.

Another rap came on the door. "Good God, who is it now?"

"It's me, Nicolas, sir."

"Well, what are you waiting for? Just walk on in. Everybody else has!"

Nicolas entered the room. "I came to rekindle your fire, sir."

"My fire is rekindled, Nicolas! I'm so hot, I feel like I'm burning in an inferno!" He coughed, his throat raw and sore.

"Are you all right, sir?"

"Just fine, Nicolas. I'm tired."

"Perhaps I should call Miss Amanda to come and check—"

"No! Good heavens, no. Just leave me be, please."

"As you wish, sir. Though I would like to clean up the glass now, if you should so permit me. We wouldn't want our new guest getting cut on her first day at work."

"Speak for yourself, Nicolas. And hurry up about it, I've got to think! And wipe that smile off your face. I tell you... that woman is not staying!"

# 7.

# I MADE IT THROUGH
# THE RAIN

EXHAUSTED FROM THE morning's turmoil and from trying to figure out how to get rid of his afternoon surprise, Garry fell into a deep slumber. He aroused late evening, the aroma of fresh brewed tea and savory smells of roast turkey and potatoes filling his nostrils. He moistened his dry lips with his tongue. Raising his eyelids, he tried focusing on the object before him. He worked his lids fiercely, opening-shutting, opening-shutting, but she wouldn't go away.

"I see you decided to wake up," came the official voice of his new nurse. "Is this how you wile away your time? Sleep away the hours?"

*Oh, God...* the woman was real. He had hoped she was a dream. One bad and horrible dream. "Why the hell are you still here?" he spoke sharply.

Amanda winced, but then calmly smiled. "I suppose fools get lucky like that, Mr. Danzlo. I've come with your dinner tray."

"I'm not hungry," he lied.

Her brow lifted. "Really?" Placing the tray on the bedside table, she raised the silver dome from the platter, swaying it to and fro, the rich tempting smells of roasted meat causing Garry's stomach to growl. Amanda closed her eyes and exaggerated a sigh of pleasure.

"Ahh, but it's so good, sir," she chanted. In the same tender voice, she added, "And you will eat; if you don't, it will be forced down your throat with unkind shoves." She smiled again, placing her attention toward the preparation of his meal. She released the silverware from a napkin and buttered a warm roll.

Prepared to protest, Garry suddenly found humor in Amanda's cheerful display. She had changed her dress, though only to another just as odd-looking—a

45

jumper with an oversized bow and frilly collar. Her hands were slightly shaking, her teeth nibbling on her lower lip as she readied his meal. She was wearing those weird little glasses that kept sliding down her nose. With one trembling finger, she slid them back up. *Hmmm*, he thought, *maybe there is a way to get rid of her.*

She glanced up from the tray then, nearly knocking it over as her gaze locked with his. He had made sure his most alluring smile was plastered on his face while staring into those glassed frames that covered her eyes. He'd been used to girls swooning over him, for whatever reason—something to do with his "sexy smile" and his "bright medium blues" or so he'd been told. He felt victory on his side as she stood at a standstill, looking at him, the corners of her mouth smoothing gently. She swallowed, a light blush rising in her cheeks. But then, it left so quickly he wondered if he had imagined it, for she suddenly returned his smile with an even more alluring one of her own. She no longer the seducee, but the…

His eyes drew immediately to her parting lips—that mouth that was so disturbingly interesting—and for a split second he wondered if those lips would feel as soft, taste as sweet. Good God Almighty. What was he thinking? What was he doing? What was *she* doing! She was slowly untying that gaudy, oversized bow at her neck, edging herself steadily closer, her voice coming low and *sexy?* "Do you need help?" she asked.

"*Help?*" he chirped.

"In the bed." She lowered her glasses on her nose, observing him above the plastic rims.

"Wh-What?" Garry inched away, though no escape was to be had.

"To sit you up in bed… so that you can *eat…* your supper."

"No! I-I can do it myself."

"Can you? I wouldn't want you to *strain* anything. Come, let me help." She grabbed him in a big bear hug, jerking him to a sitting position while he smothered a cry in the midst of her frilled collar. His unexercised muscles were painfully sore.

"Let go of me," he demanded, pushing himself unsuccessfully from her grasp. "Get your hands, get your body off me, Ms. Fields!"

"But, Mr. Danzlo, I thought…" Her gaze roamed over him admiringly.

"Well, you thought wrong!"

"No, Mr. Danzlo, you thought wrong." Her eyes were now ablaze. "If you ever, *ever* play this offensive game again, so help me, I'll—"

"Woman, I wouldn't want you if you were the last female on earth. You got that?"

She flinched for a bare second. "Perfectly."

Going for his tray, she crammed it onto his lap. She stood, breathing hard, arms folded tight beneath her breasts while she waited for him to begin eating.

"I've lost my appetite," he blustered, now humiliated.

"Shall I restore it for you?" she asked.

He wouldn't put it past her to do just that. With a slow, heavy exhale, he tried cooling his nerves. "If I eat, will you leave? I promise to be a good little boy and eat all my vegetables."

"I'll leave you, Mr. Danzlo. But remember this little cliché: We'll meet again."

Scowling, he picked up his fork and began eating, hoping this would get her feet moving. It did. "Close the door on your way out," he said.

The door clicked shut.

"Good. Now I can eat in peace," he muttered in silence, the room feeling strangely bigger, emptier. He had to find a way to get rid of her. "Tomorrow," he said aloud.

AMANDA STOOD OUTSIDE Garry's room, her head leaning against the doorframe. The day had been long and exhausting. She was alone in a strange place with a butler and a troubled man. Melissa and Dan had left for Los Angeles after a long discussion that afternoon, while Garry was asleep. Her only worry was being left with a man who despised her. But Melissa was right that things would be better with them gone so she could work toward her goal. And Garry's goal. Somehow she'd have to convince him he had one.

She went in search of Nicolas and found him at the kitchen sink washing the last of the dishes. "If you don't mind, I think I'd like to turn in for the night," she said wearily. "I feel a little tired from the trip and—"

"By all means, Miss Amanda. I'll check in on Mr. Danzlo later and collect his dinner tray."

"Thank you, Nicolas. Oh and would it be okay if I made a call to Florida? I promised Robbie that I'd—"

"Yes, the little boy you spoke of so fondly. You wouldn't want to disappoint him. Make as many calls as you need to while here. You'll find a phone in your room, equipped with several lines. The first button is Mr. Danzlo's private line, however. You might want to avoid that one."

"Yes, I'll do that. And again, thank you. You're the best."

He nodded. "Miss Amanda," he said in a soothing tone. "Don't be discouraged. He's not himself. It's an act, you know. He really is a fine person."

Amanda smiled. "I'm sure he is. I'm not leaving so fast, no matter what sort of fight he puts up. A good night's rest and I'll be good as new, ready to tackle our patient."

She exited the room, Nicolas staring after her, a curious eye on the swishing dress and the lock of hair that fell silkily across one shoulder as she rounded the corner.

AMANDA'S ROOM WAS across from Garry's. Entering it, she secured the lock, threw off her glasses, fell across the bed and wept. Humiliation and shame raked through her body as she thought about how quickly she had responded to Garry's little play on her emotions. Mentally, he was distraught, she knew, but why had she responded to him the way she did? For one split moment, she had felt a warmth from his smile beyond anything she'd ever felt before, his eyes seeming to touch through her very soul. Yet it was a hoax. Why would her body betray her like that? Normally she was more aware of things like that. With him, all she'd felt was confused.

She was beginning to think it was a mistake—taking on this job, being alone with a man who possessed charismatic qualities. He was admired and respected all over the world, Melissa had said. The very thought seemed absurd after what she'd witnessed of his character today. Yet she, too, had been unfettered by one small look into his eyes. She could only hope he didn't see just how much he'd affected her. He had managed to break through her shield of defense, a silent proclamation that she needed no man, wanted no man, nor would another ever get so close as to make her feel hurt again. Yet this stranger had somehow left her hurting, though somewhat differently.

She had seen beyond his disheveled hair, the scraggly beard, the piercing eyes. His raspy voice was certainly no indication of an attraction, so unlike the mellow singing voice she'd heard about; the temporary tracheotomy performed the night of the accident had altered his vocal chords. However, strange though it was, his voice had an effect on her today. It blew through her like a winter storm—chilling her, filling her, *thrilling her.* It made no sense. He wasn't even a nice man. He had wounded her feelings, tried to manipulate her.

"Well, it won't happen again," she said aloud, pounding a fist against the rose silk coverlet on the bed. She opened her fist and suddenly smoothed the crumpled spread with her fingers. It was lovely—the coverlet, the bed, this room. She fell in love with it the moment Melissa brought her here, announcing the room was all hers for the remainder of her stay.

She lay on the most magnificent brass bed she'd ever seen. All of the other furnishings were made of rosewood—a dresser, two large wardrobe pieces, a corner desk and a rocking chair. The large bay window across from the bed was equipped with a window seat. From the window, she had a captivating view of the front lawn and numerous snow-covered evergreens. A large cedar wishing well, adorned with icicles, stood just beyond the porch. Looking to the right was a patch of sky amid the trees, dark and dotted with more stars than she could count.

Amanda's gaze roamed the room in appreciation, her focus moving from the soft white sheers, outlined by rose drapes and tied with silk tassel ropes, to the bed clothes of the same rose color. Fluffy shammed pillows lay inches from her elbow, trimmed with cream eyelet. *Wonderland,* she thought. The whole house was like a dream come true, the air outside, so fresh and clean. She knew the mountain breezes would somehow make up for the salty breezes she would miss from the Atlantic Ocean. It felt like a home.

*A real home.*

She eased back on a pillow, suddenly feeling numb, the image of her husband lying in his own blood vivid in her mind. She had found him in the middle of their living room floor in that place she once called home. She realized now it had never been a home. Just a place where loneliness lived.

Although there were many suspects in Paul's murder case, including herself, not one was convicted. But she felt guilty—guilty of loving with all of her heart, for believing and trusting, for caring too much for someone who didn't even deserve it. She had experienced his raging jealousies, witnessed spiteful actions so unlike her own caring nature. She had seen his mood swings and put up with it because she thought she had the ability to tame him. Hadn't she married him for better, for worse? Wasn't she a nurturer, a healer?

She stared up at the brass-trimmed ceiling fan, one lone tear sliding down her temple. How she hated her naivety! And to think she'd been a virgin on her wedding night. Had Paul even cared that she had waited for him? Had anything meant anything to him? Except money, power, competing against the world, against his friends… against Eddie. *Always Eddie.*

Amanda squeezed her eyes shut, begging unwanted thoughts away. Her craving to hold someone right now was so intense she felt she might scream. But whose shoulder did she have to cry on? Whose shoulder was ever there to cry on when she needed someone most?

The answer to that question seized the beat of her heart as she lifted her head from the bed, her blurry gaze moving to her purse on the floor. A folded note lay inside, placed there only two days ago, the handwriting clear in her mind as were the words on the paper.

*Don't turn your back on me, Amanda. I can give you everything Paul didn't—companionship, security, love. I know you need money. I can help you. Just ask and I'll give you the world. I love you. I always have. Please call… Eddie.*

"No, Eddie," she cried quietly in the folds of her hands, wishing she could stamp out the one memory that forever taunted her. It was the one time in her life when she forgot who she was, whom she belonged to. Eddie had kissed her like Paul never had, shown her what it was to taste a man's love.

She'd always appreciated Eddie's handsome, native looks and his crooked smile. She had kissed those lips many a time, but only for brief pecks, for they were just friends; they'd been friends since junior high school. It was Eddie who had introduced her to Paul. Eddie who had been best man. And then later, Paul's partner in law.

Something had happened those last couple of years, something that was still a mystery to her. Eddie had left the partnership and didn't come around much anymore.

That day, she'd been vulnerable after her terrible fight with Paul, a few months before his death. So when she opened her front door and saw Eddie, she was so glad to see him. It happened so suddenly, his strong arms around her, his face so close to hers. When he bent down to kiss her, she wanted that kiss. She took it with greed, if only just to feel what she knew she'd never had.

*You're mine, Amanda,* she had barely heard him say as she drank in her thirst for love, welcoming the sweet affection, the blessed warmth of a man's embrace. *Paul was a fool to think he could keep you from me. He's never loved you, but he knew I did, and he married you because of it. You belong to me, Amanda. And he'll see, love… what's mine is mine.*

The fear came then. It was the change in his voice, the strangeness she'd seen in his smoke-gray eyes just before his lips took hers again, less sweetly, more possessively. She could feel his anger by the way his muscles quivered, his breathing deep and tumultuous; it confused her. Reality suddenly crashed through her castle of dreams, snatching her blissful moment, drowning her with naked shame, disgrace, dishonor. It was as though she'd just realized whose lips kissed her… he, who whispered lies. *Oh God, they were lies! They had to be lies. Paul loved her. He did when he married her, he did!*

She tried to fight Eddie then, to escape, but he wouldn't let go. *Eddie, please! No, please!* she had cried. He had smothered her screams with his mouth, hard and so very angry. He threw her upon the bed, his hands moving fiercely, ripping off her clothes in passionate rage. *You're mine, not Paul's. You were never Paul's!* he shouted with bitterness. She was screaming then, trying with all her might to get up as his hands clutched her like an animal with its prey. She felt drained, numb when he finally seemed to hear her and he stopped, cold, his eyes wild, confused. She vaguely felt his lips drinking the wetness from her face, her hair, his voice suddenly tender and loving and caring, "I'm sorry, love. Please don't cry. I'm so sorry…"

Then Paul walked in.

Had Eddie known Paul was coming home? And why didn't Paul do anything? Her own husband just stood there, eyes steady on Eddie while Eddie stood, bringing her to stand with him. Then Paul spoke.

"Did you enjoy my wife, bud? Wait, don't answer the question. Just get the hell out."

"Paul…" she tried to speak, to move toward him, but Eddie held her back, hiding her naked form behind his own.

"You hurt her Fields and I'll kill you," Eddie warned.

Paul only laughed. "She's my wife, remember? I own her. But rest assured, ole buddy, I won't be beating my beautiful wife." Then he spoke to her, his eyes never leaving Eddie. "Amanda, honey, go shower, wash off that filth. I hate leftovers."

*Oh, God, oh God, make the memory go away!*

Amanda sat up on the bed and reached for a pillow. She held it tight against her for a long time, realizing she'd allowed herself to be used and abused over and over for years. It had to stop. Right now, right here.

Wiping her eyes fiercely, she took a deep breath and closed her eyelids. She tried to envision her new patient being kind to her, being pleasant and smiling. Visualization could be a powerful tool in manifesting what you wanted according to all those self-help books she'd been reading since Paul's death. She'd been visualizing herself with Robbie for weeks, seeing them spending time together, having him at home with her, sharing the life they both dreamed of.

She saw an image of the little boy now. Robbie—the one she could trust and love without any doubt of being loved back. He was her peace.

Glancing at the clock on the night table, she realized that he was surely in his pajamas waiting by the nursing station in hopes of her call before his bedtime hour at nine.

She grabbed the phone and dialed the number to the children's home. She'd not waste her time with concerns over the past. It couldn't be changed. Nor would she waste her time worrying about tomorrow when tomorrow wasn't even here yet.

"Robbie? Is that you? Were you waiting by that phone?"

A squeal of laughter rang through the line. Amanda smiled, falling back against the pillows. For the next fifteen minutes, she reveled in her one special moment of the day.

# 8.

# SHE SHOULD'A BEEN MINE

EDDIE CHANDLER STOOD at the large, floor-to-ceiling window in his richly decorated office that overlooked the intracoastal waters of Palm Beach. It was night, the moon's reflection scintillating a billion lights across the water. He was focused on the yachts and ships docked on the other side of the waterway, until a small sailboat came into view. It sailed along the coast peacefully. He could barely make out the man steering the boat, but the woman he saw clearly. She lay back on her elbows, her face upward toward the moon, her dark hair blowing in the gentle breeze.

*Amanda.*

It wasn't her, he knew. He saw her only in his imagination; he was always seeing her.

"You're so beautiful," he whispered. He watched with envy as the man moved toward the woman, placed an affectionate hand on her face. They took each other's hand, locked for a long while. "That should be us," he said. "It should've never been Paul, and the bastard knew it."

The urge to drive his fist through something—anything to ease the pain of his thoughts—had his body quaking. He stiffened it, waiting for the reckless impulse to subside and leave him with some fragment of peace.

A minute passed, and then he walked slowly to his desk. He sat down in the black leather chair behind it. He thought about the many women he could so easily have. But he only wanted one.

*Damn!* What was wrong with him? He had work to do. Files were piled high on his desk. He had to be in court all day tomorrow. He picked up a dome-shaped, gold paperweight he'd had for years, intending to retrieve some papers from beneath it, but he paused, reading the engraving on its underside. *Fields & Chandler, Attorneys at Law.* He half-laughed.

"You deserved what you got, Paul Fields. You hurt Amanda one too many times. I told you, don't fu—"

The phone rang, startling him. He picked it up. "What?" he said. "She's where?"

He slammed the phone down and opened the side drawer of his desk. His hands were trembling as he took out a bottle of vodka and a glass. He poured the clear liquid into the glass, drinking it down in one swallow, his eye twitching, convulsively.

*Amanda... what've you done? How do I protect you now?*

His hand wrapped securely around the empty glass, his fingers squeezing till the glass burst into pieces across his desk. Blood poured from his hand, and for a moment, he just sat there staring unseeingly while his mind tried to grasp what he needed to do now. Amanda needed him; she just didn't know it. Thank God she didn't know. If she knew what he'd done since Paul's death to keep her safe and alive, she'd be terrified—not only of the danger that Paul had left her, but she'd be afraid of *him.* He'd failed to earn her trust, more than once. He'd screwed up, but she'd forgive him. One day she would.

*Damn you, Paul. I'm still making sacrifices, even with you gone.*

He looked down at the blood on his desk, the cut on his hand still oozing red. He tore his shirttail from his waist and wrapped the hand tightly to stop the bleeding. A framed image of Amanda stared back at him from across the desk.

"The world is crazy, Amanda. Full of assholes like Paul. I'll never let you down. I'll protect you. I'm the only one who can."

# 9.

# SWING STREET

THE SCENT OF freshly brewed coffee drifted through the hallway as Amanda made her way to the kitchen bright and early her second day. As she approached the room, Nicolas stood with a smile on his face and two empty cups in his hands. They were early morning strangers, but Nicolas had her feeling like an early morning friend.

A pattering tat-tat-tat sounded across the linoleum floor. From the opposite end of the room came a beagle dog with large chocolate eyes and long floppy ears.

"Oh, he's darling, Nicolas. Or is it a she?"

"A she, and her name is Bagel." Bagel lifted her right paw.

"My, my, quite a smart one you are." Amanda said, reaching out to shake the outstretched paw. "So, Miss Bagel, where were you yesterday?"

The dog barked twice. Laughing, Nicolas explained that he had awakened early to pick Bagel up from a nearby farm. Joe Yancey was the local vet. "It was one of those, er, female operations. Too restless lately."

"Oh," Amanda said, giggling. "So, you got fixed, huh, girl?" Her new hairy friend peppered her with warm, wet licks. "Now, if we could just fix your master." She turned to Nicolas and winked. "Is there a very large hammer around?"

Nicolas bubbled with laughter. "Miss Amanda, it's going to be a pleasure having you around. How about breakfast?"

"Breakfast…" she took a sip of coffee Nicolas had placed before her. "What time is it? Seven-fifteen? You'll be eating with us, right?"

"Oh, no, Miss Amanda. I was going to fix you something and make the usual tray for Mr. Danzlo."

"No. Set the table for two. No tray," she said.

"No tray?"

"Mr. Danzlo will be getting up this morning to eat, but I want him clean and shaved first. We may be awhile. Better move breakfast to eight-thirty. Also, I'd like for you to eat with us each morning if you don't mind. I'd prefer to have at least one person around who likes me. Mr. Danzlo does have a wheelchair, doesn't he?"

"Why yes. Yes, he does."

"I'll probably need help getting him up this morning, but he'll soon be getting up by himself."

"By himself, Miss Amanda?"

"In time. All we have to do is be fearless, keep a positive attitude, and smiles on our faces. We'll fake it with great expertise."

"Right," Nicolas agreed wholeheartedly. "I'm feeling like Tarzan already."

"And I feel like Cheetah," she said, standing up. "Jungle City, look out. I'm heading down Swing Street, ready to surprise that untamed beast. Ahh, and life was so sweet," she sighed. Amanda swiftly turned and walked out of the kitchen, the brown-eyed Bagel tagging along in her wake.

"RISE AND SHINE. Up-Up-Up!"

Amanda flung back the royal blue drapes, great shafts of sunshine blinding Garry, whose eyes sprang wide-open. Bagel, leaping on her master's full bladder, had Garry yelling his discomfort while the dog's tongue licked, her floppy ears tickled, and Amanda's lively voice rang merrily in song.

"O-OH, what a beautiful MORNing. OH, what a beautiful DAY. I'VE got this beautiful FEEL-ling. EV-'ry-thing's GO-ing MY WA-A-AY!"

Garry stared horrified at the woman bowing several times before him. He hauled the covers over his head, and cried in agony, "God, help me, I've died and gone to hell."

"No, no, Mr. Danzlo. You haven't died," Amanda told him. "Though, if you don't change your ways you never know where you might end up. I recommend a happier, cooler place."

It wasn't easy holding back the smile threatening to break his stern face. The woman was a clown. Out from the covers, his eyes pierced hers. Amanda's smile never wavered. He released his slightly, and then remembered the night before. He turned away.

"I suppose I owe you an apology," he said. "I acted a bit lewd and, well, disrespectful yesterday evening."

Her slight head movement, the arched brow and slack jaw indicated that he'd surprised her with his apology, as if he wasn't capable of one. And then she smiled. "Apology accepted," she said graciously. Her attention moved quickly to the dog in his lap, wagging its tail and licking his face.

"Hey, girl, I missed you," Garry said, rubbing Bagel's coat with his left hand.

"So, Mr. Danzlo! I'm ready when you are."

Garry jolted at her voice. "Ready?" he asked, his stomach starting to churn with apprehension. "For what, Ms. Fields?"

"For your bath and shave, of course. And your breakfast and all the other fun stuff I've got planned for you today."

Garry's heart thumped hard in his chest. "Nicolas!" he cried out.

"I thought you learned yesterday that there's no use calling him," she said. "He's preparing our breakfast. I'm here now for your service."

"NICOLAS!"

Amanda giggled. "Come now, Mr. Danzlo. Nicolas is not coming."

"He's coming to bathe and shave me."

"No, Mr. Danzlo."

Garry swallowed hard. "If you think I'm going to let some woman bathe and shave me—especially by the likes of you—you had better prepare yourself for—"

"Especially by the likes of me? Why, Mr. Danzlo, you wound me. You can be such an unkind man at times."

"And you can be such a—"

"Unh-unh-unh!" she crooned, waving a finger in his face. "I'm a lady and wish to be treated as one."

"Oh?" he said. "And I suppose you never say any bad words?"

"Pretty much never. Though concerning you, I have been tempted."

"And concerning you, I've been more than tempted."

"Good, Mr. Danzlo. We've found something we almost have in common. Now, as for your bath, I have no intention of giving you one. You're a big boy. You can do it yourself. I'll go and prepare some water for you and—"

She spotted an object next to the bed on the floor.

"What is that?" she asked, wrinkling her nose.

"You mean you're a nurse and you don't know?" he said.

She stared again at the plastic container with contempt, her brows drawn in and tight. "A urinal. I know what it is. What is it doing there?"

"You're a nurse and you don't know what it's used for?"

Her hands went to her hips. "I suppose there's a bedpan lying around here too."

Garry didn't answer, wondering what in the world she was so hyped up about. His nostrils flared while his face heated with the embarrassment of the conversation.

"Mr. Danzlo…" She was standing with arms akimbo, feet apart. "Your car accident happened four months ago. You are not incontinent, nor are you an invalid. You have legs and arms that move. Your right side might be impaired to a certain degree, but your left side can compensate for your right. You can bathe yourself, you can shave yourself. And from now on, you will get out of this bed even if it takes pushing you out. And you will definitely start using the bathroom for your business."

"Ms. Fields, I'm really getting fed up with your—"

"Right, *you're* getting fed up." She dropped fists at her sides. "Nicolas," she called out loudly. "Please come in here."

Nicolas came quickly to her rescue. "Yes, Miss Amanda," he said, coming to a halt at the door.

"Please take this," she said, holding the urinal away from her body while her head turned from the repulsive object, "and do something with it. Throw it as far away as you can. Better yet, burn it. Whatever. Just get it out, please—"

"Now wait just a blasted minute," Garry said.

"No, you wait a minute." Amanda turned to Nicolas. "That'll be all, Nicolas, thank you." Nicolas left and Amanda averted her attention back to her adversary. "You do have a problem, don't you?"

"I sure as hell do. I'm looking at it. So when are you leaving?"

Amanda released a slow breath. "I'm not leaving, Mr. Danzlo. In other words, you're stuck with this problem. Forever, if that's how long it takes to get you on your feet, and for you to start living your life like a real man."

The next moment met with awkward silence. He felt the color drain from his face; he saw it drain from hers. Horror, bereavement. That's what he witnessed in the lines of her face, just before she swung around, hiding what he knew to be tears.

"I'm sorry," she said. "I shouldn't have said that. So totally uncalled for. I should be supporting you." She turned briefly to meet his gaze, and then turned away just as swiftly. "Please forgive me. I'll go get a basin of water for—"

"Ms. Fields…" Garry was struck numb. Not only by her tears, but for the genuine apology she had clearly portrayed. He had never felt an expression of regret so deeply. He wanted her gone, that was true, like the rest of the nurses and therapists who had come to help him. But he was the one who deserved the misery, not those around him. Not this Amanda Fields, who had displayed great strength and patience. So she yelled, lost her temper a moment ago, proved she was human. It took her two seconds to say, "I'm sorry." That was more than he could say for any other woman he'd ever known. And why was she crying? Not because of *his* harsh words, but because of her own. He hadn't hurt her. She'd hurt him. And it broke her to tears.

She slowly turned, wiping her face. Brown mascara streaked her cheeks. She looked like a child with a dirty face.

"Ms. Fields, you took away my big Dixie cup, and I've gotta go. What do you suggest?"

Sniffling, she giggled, her eyes radiantly lit behind those funny looking glasses. "I-I'll go get Nicolas to help me get you up."

"Yes, you do that," he said seriously. She smiled sweetly when she left and a crazy sensation undulated through his body. It was stranger than strange. It bothered him immensely. She wasn't at all appealing. Yet something drew him to her, within him, taking up space in his mind. Physically, she was making it impossible for him to get her out his mind, for as the day moved on, she was everywhere. Beside him, behind him, in front of him. The trip to and from the bathroom was one matter he wanted to believe never happened—he'd let out more than a few expletives when she'd insisted on staying to help Nicolas steady his standing robed body at the toilet. So what that Nicolas couldn't handle him on his own, proved when they'd both nearly dropped him on the floor.

The bath and shave at his bedside was just as exasperating. He'd sloshed more water on the floor and the bed than he had on himself, she not lifting a hand to help him—until that moment she offered to wash his back. One touch of her icy hands on his skin sent his body rocketing sideways on the bed. "So sorry, Mr. Danzlo," she said, laughing down at him with that musical little laugh she had. "I'm just one of those 'cold hands, warm heart' kind of girls." She laughed some more while he yelped at her chilly hands assisting him back up. As for the shave, he'd nicked himself so many times with the razor that Amanda finally gave in, allowing Nicolas to finish the job, for he'd been adamant that she wasn't touching him with a razor; she might just cut his throat.

Had Garry not received several phone calls during the day—one from his mother, two from Daphne—the day may have been overly intolerable. For once, he didn't try rushing his mother off the phone, glad for the respite from his assiduous nurse. He took full advantage of Miriam's windy conversation.

"You brushing your teeth, son? Don't be lazy like your old Uncle Hershel, letting his teeth rot out of his head. *Oy!* Did I tell you what he did last week?" He'd answered, "No, Ma," knowing full well he'd heard the whole spill about his uncle's drunken adventure during Aunt Anne's birthday party from their last conversation.

Miriam—his hard-core Jewish mother. To her, tradition was everything. He had an ancestry of pure Jewish blood that went back for more than two thousand years, something she'd never let him forget. Particularly after September 22, 1964, the night his mother dragged him hysterically down the street toward the Imperial Theatre in New York for the first presentation of "Fiddler on the Roof"—that unforgettable play about Jewish tradition. His mother had practically begged, borrowed, and stole to get those tickets. He was thirteen at the time, had recently undergone his bar mitzvah—the ceremony marking him as an adult and confirming his commitment to the Jewish people.

She had come out of that play stone-faced, wholly disheartened, for ironically the play had been about accepting that change comes, and how Tevye was unable to stop his daughters from following their hearts. All the way home, she'd cried and reminded him, "We must preserve our heritage at all costs. Remember the Holocaust?" *No ma, I don't. I wasn't there. I'm glad I wasn't there!* he would think, but dared not say. "If we don't act like Jews, then we may as well give Hitler his victory," she'd finish. *Oh, the nightmares from that line!*

Garry, the child, the youth, never told a soul about how it took him years to rid his mind of those horrible dreams of concentration camps, and the terror and filth of it all. Though he hadn't been there to experience it, he'd heard enough stories on the streets, in school, from strangers, neighbors, and relatives in his little Jewish community.

"Garry, you listening to me? What's going on there? Put that new nurse on the phone."

He should've known his mother would grow suspicious, once she'd been allowed to talk on the phone so long. Luckily, Amanda had left the room and he'd somehow convinced her to call later. He knew without a doubt, she'd hung up, only to call his sister to get all the information she needed. By the time Amanda returned, Daphne had called.

"Darling, I miss you," she had said in that sexy, sultry voice of hers. "Are they treating you well? Do you need me home?" Funny how a voice can knock the breath out of a man; it did the first night he'd met her behind stage. From that point on, she had showed up often wherever he was, and he didn't mind. Before he knew it, she'd become his lady, enjoying her beauty immensely, as well as her intellect in business. He'd found her fascinating to talk to, and sinfully proficient in bed. But later, a bit suspicious and jealous at times. He hadn't minded overmuch—it showed she cared for the most part—but he'd be lying if he didn't admit that he enjoyed having time away from her. Today, he missed her. That didn't mean, however, he was ready to relay that Melissa had brought in another nurse.

Between the phone calls for Garry, Amanda had received two from Melissa. Both times he'd been sitting in his wheelchair nearby. This only stirred his ire as the women did more laughing than talking. His interest piqued, however, when the name Robbie was mentioned, something about a call Amanda had made last night, evidently to a young boy inquiring about Colorado and her new patient. Did Amanda have a son? It was his curiosity that had him eavesdropping on her conversation.

*Definitely not cowboy material,* Amanda had said she'd relayed to the boy. *Oh, if only she had a lasso... where was Tonto when she needed him?... No, this Lone Ranger was just a musician who liked to make a lot of noise, mostly with his mouth.*

Amanda laughed; he didn't.

BY LATE EVENING, Garry was finally in bed, spent and fast asleep.

"Oh my," Amanda began as she and Nicolas sat down in two comfortable green plush chairs situated in the great family room, "How did we survive this day?"

"I don't know, Miss Amanda, I'm pooped."

She smiled, taking in the ungainly way Nicolas slouched in his chair, legs sprawled out in front of him. Beside his right foot lay the weary dog, floppy ears drooping on the floor.

"It's hard to believe I've only been here two days," she said, sprawling her legs out in the same ungraceful manner. "It feels like two months."

"Miss Amanda, I've been with Mr. Danzlo for more than a decade. It feels like a century."

Laughing, she asked, "How have you put up with him all these years?"

"At times, not easily," Nicolas confessed. "Other times, it's been a pleasure."

Nicolas's face beamed with earnest pride then, warmth shining in his eyes. Not an easy thing for her to imagine—this amiable Garry, the lamb inside of the lion. However, Amanda did see a flash of his devilishly handsome blue eyes dancing in her mind's eye, the very ones that had tried to seduce her last night. She saw, too, that heart-hammering smile she'd witnessed this morning—aimed at the dog, yet a smile that had generated enough power to propel her heart to her knees.

She straightened in her chair, sending Nicolas a wry smile.

Nicolas smiled back. "I know, it's hard to believe that Mr. Danzlo could be anything but the Grinch in the flesh," he said. "But the truth is, he's a generous man. Compassionate, sincere, appreciative, and totally loyal. An honorable man. I will admit he can be, at times, an irritating, stubborn-headed mule."

Amanda raised her hand. "I'll second that." She sighed, and then shook her head. "He's undoubtedly my worst patient to date. Heavy, too. Did you see his face when we took him to the bathroom and he realized I wasn't leaving? I guess we could've sat him down on the toilet seat, let him steady himself on it. But I wanted him to get the feel of standing. He should've never taken to the bed all these months."

"He was a bit upset that you stayed," Nicolas said, chuckling. "The hilarious part was after five minutes of fighting with him, you came up with the line: 'Mr. Danzlo, if you've seen one, you've seen them all. Will you *just* do your thing.'"

"I think I offended him a little, but he was wearing on my nerves."

"It was more so the shock in knowing you said it. It shut him up though, didn't it?"

"Yes, it did. We make a pretty good team, Nicolas. I bet we're the best pair of sliders, mounters and transferers this side of Colorado!"

"You betcha," Nicolas drawled in a Southern accent.

"Yep. And I bet that once Mr. Danzlo regains his dignity and independence where bathroom privileges are concerned, things will go much smoother for the both of us."

Nicolas upturned a brow, not looking too convinced. After seconds of silence, Amanda reclined her head, the back of her hand resting on her forehead in a dramatic show. "Ah, Nicolas, what yonder paths our lives will weave. With that yonder master, we're sure to grieve."

Nicolas flung back his head in a roar of laughter, his hands clutching his round belly. "Oh, Miss Amanda. Though chains of Danzlo have you bound, you're such a joy to have around."

"Very good," she commended. "And kind of you to say. Thank you. For everything."

A gracious smile formed on Nicolas's lips. "You're most welcome, Miss Amanda."

She sighed. "I'm glad at least one person here doesn't hate me."

"He doesn't hate you," Nicolas said. "He just, well, he might dislike you a little because you're a threat to what he's fighting... and *not* fighting." A shadow crossed Nicolas' face then. He clearly wanted to say something more, yet the words didn't come.

"Tell me Nicolas, what is Danzlo struggling with? It's more than just physical, isn't it? When Melissa hired me, she shared a few words about what happened before the accident. About their father's suicide. She knew very little, but felt it somehow related to Mr. Danzlo's unwillingness to receive help."

An awkward silence passed before Nicolas answered. "I can't say, Miss Amanda. I gave my word, and I'm a man of my word. I'm afraid it's up to you to find out. From him." He then added with an air of concern, "Guilt has a way of ravaging one's very soul, doesn't it?"

Amanda nodded, accepting the small hint. "It can if you let it. Somehow it changes us, warps our mind. It took me a long while to get over the gnawing guilt I felt over my parents' death. I don't think I told you, but they were both killed in a plane crash a few years ago, a smaller private plane I had encouraged them to take so they could start their vacation early. I put them on that plane, and I never saw them again. It hit me hard. It takes time to heal. Time to understand. Wisdom doesn't come easily."

Nicolas reached over and grasped her hand in his. He squeezed it, empathy bright and clear in his eyes. Amanda smiled at him. It was in that moment that Nicolas began to stare, a curious look planted on his face. It immediately caused her to feel for the glasses she'd slid upon her head—a spontaneous gesture that was quickly becoming habit these past couple of days. For the most part, she wore them atop her head around Nicolas, but she realized they were starting to become like a security blanket, particularly around Garry Danzlo.

Somehow, she felt safer hiding behind them around him.

"Miss Amanda, would you like a cup of hot cocoa?" She could see it wasn't the question Nicolas had intended. But then, she'd been a little paranoid today, worrying that Nicolas could see right through her disguise.

"That sounds delicious, Nicolas!"

"Ah, then, hot cocoa it is. For the two of us."

# *10.*

## READ 'EM AND WEEP

"PSSSSSSST. HEY! SLEEPYHEAD," said a loud whispering voice.

Amanda sat in an armless, oak chair next to Garry's bed, her legs folded Indian-style beneath her tie-dyed, crinkle skirt of gold rust and beige brown, topped by an orangey cowl neck sweater. The giant of all smiles curved her mouth.

Garry jerked the pillow from beneath his head, covering his face while he smothered a cry of grief.

"Now, now, Mr. Danzlo," Amanda intoned sympathetically, "there's no need to cover that face of yours. I mean, your face is not all that bad looking, though it could use, well, there's nothing serious I can't overlook."

Sliding the pillow up on his forehead, he peered at her with a malevolent stare. He was ready to say a few things himself about *her* unusual face, but she never gave him the chance.

"Now what is your excuse today? Wait a minute, I know. Your bones are aching. Your muscles are sore. I worked you much too hard yesterday. You have a headache. *I'm* it. And because of all these ill-fated, dreadful things that have happened to you, you need complete rest for the next six months."

"Yes, to all of the above," he answered. "You must be smart. Or maybe you're psychic?"

"I prefer the word intuitive. Though, in this case, I'd say I'm just smart. I'm a nurse. I'm supposed to know things concerning my patients. It's called nurse-wit."

"You mean nit-wit," he said.

Amanda smiled with silly blinks of her eyes. "No, actually that name is given to the patient of the nurse. You see, the nurse-wit helps the nit-wit get brain-wit."

65

A grin threatened to crack Garry's reserve. Somehow, he managed to hold it in check and narrowed his eyes instead. "Has anyone ever told you you're a nut?"

"Why, as a matter of fact they have, Mr. Danzlo. And since you're a singer of music, surely you've heard the song, "Everybody Loves a Nut." I've always hoped those words were true. I would hate to go through life without that comforting knowledge."

Amanda's innocent expression caused Garry to release his grin.

"Aha! *I-see-a-smi-ile*," she chanted, her eyes sparkling behind those ridiculous-looking glasses. Warmth invaded Garry's body as he beheld the silent sweet laughter in her eyes. He tried distinguishing their color, but the glare against the glass of those plastic frames made it impossible. He could only see what looked like sunshine.

"Mr. Danzlo," she said, turning away from his intense gaze, "we have lots to do today. We should get started."

Unfolding her legs from the chair, she stood. It was like waking up from a trance, his gaze shooting from her uncomely outfit down to her uncomely feet. She was wearing strange leather flats laced with fluorescent orange shoestrings.

"Really like those shoes," he said.

"Why thank you," she said. "They'll be much more comfortable than those black boot-shoes I wore yesterday. My feet were killing me by late evening."

"I bet they were," he said. "And these go with your wardrobe so much better. The shoestrings really... *stand out.*" He expected some bit of agitated behavior on her part, but like always, she surprised him with an unpredictable response.

"I think you're right, Mr. Danzlo. I tried lacing brown shoestrings in my shoes this morning, but they didn't give that special 'touch' to my skirt."

Nicolas came through the door carrying breakfast on a heated tray. "Breakfast in bed this morning, sir," he said, placing the tray on the bedside table.

"What's this?" Garry said, feeling victory at hand. "Don't tell me my extraordinary nurse thought a nice boy like me deserved breakfast in bed. Or was I so bad yesterday, she learned a lesson. Does this mean I can enjoy staying in bed today?"

"No," came the abrupt voices from both male and female.

"Oh, I get it," he said. "You've teamed up to destroy my life. Two enemies living in my own home."

"Far from enemies, sir," Nicolas said.

"And far from destroying your life," Amanda added. "The truth be told, Mr.

Danzlo, I have other plans for you this morning. We can't be having breakfast at lunchtime, too much time wasted yesterday, so we're trying something new. So let's hurry. Up-up! Let's get you to the bathroom so we can start this marvelous day."

Garry had a bitter taste in his mouth, a flush of weakness as Amanda and Nicolas helped him make the dreaded trip to the bathroom. After a quick wash at the sink and after donning fresh clothes, they returned him to his room and sat him in the wheelchair to eat his breakfast. Nicolas left, and Amanda stayed to ready his meal. Garry refused to eat until she left as well. "Fifteen minutes tops, Mr. Danzlo, and I'll be returning." Garry growled on her way out.

True to her word, Amanda was back in exactly fifteen minutes with Nicolas. Garry felt exhausted already. "I guess it would be too much to ask for you two to put me back in bed?"

"Not at all, Mr. Danzlo," Amanda said, throwing Nicolas a wink over her shoulder. Garry felt a brush of nausea. *They're going to lay me down*, he realized confused. He watched Nicolas and Amanda suspiciously as they helped him onto the bed. They were up to something.

"You can leave now, Nicolas," Amanda said sweetly.

No, *she* was up to something.

"Mr. Danzlo, I let you get by without much exercise yesterday, except for going to and from the bathroom, and to the kitchen for meals. I'll admit that used a bit of your energy. However, today I have much more planned for you."

"Here? In bed?" He gulped.

"Oh, stop looking like a scared cat. I'm not jumping in bed with you."

"Well, thank God for that," he said.

"Mr. Danzlo, you can thank God for a lot of things. It may do you good to be thankful more often. Shall we begin?"

"I'm so thrilled, I can hardly wait."

"Good. I want you to close your eyes and concentrate on your right side. Put all your energy into that right side, and then roll."

Garry wasn't sure he was hearing right. "You want me to roll. On the bed? Like Rock and roll." He started to chuckle at the thought.

"Yes, but I want you to use your right side as your sole strength."

He stopped chuckling. *She was serious.* "Woman, you're crazy if—"

"Mr. Danzlo, if I have to climb on that bed to make you roll, I will most certainly do it. You've got a king-sized bed, plenty of room, and I expect some action. We can fight about this all day; however, things could go much smoother if

67

you'd just cooperate. I could have a hundred patients today, and I'd be willing to bet you'd be the only one I'd have to verbally and bodily threaten."

"Well, aren't I the lucky one. God bless the other ninety-nine."

Amanda, took a deep breath, and spoke calmly. "Later, when you regain some of your strength and get some blood circulating in that body, we'll try the floor."

"*I'll* try the floor," he said. There would be no "we" about it.

"Well, if you'd rather roll on the floor, be my guest."

"Woman, you're irking me."

"Well then, that makes two irked people here. Concentrate, Mr. Danzlo, then start rolling. With your right side, Mr. Danzlo."

The rolling exercises didn't go well at all. Garry began the deed in anger, wishing that god-awful woman out of his face. But she wouldn't leave, she wouldn't let up. She just kept on encouraging. So he forced himself at the task, hoping he might get her to leave more quickly. But he found the exercise hard, his efforts pushing with frustration. He told her he couldn't do it; she told him he could. And he hated her. *He hated himself.*

Garry was now in his wheelchair, lunch over, and time for another begrudging attempt.

"Mr. Danzlo, I have a surprise for you," Amanda proclaimed, her hands clasped happily in front of her.

"Another surprise? You're leaving permanently?"

Amanda smiled. "Your surprise is in the other room. I'd not disappoint you by leaving."

"Oh, please, disappoint me," he said. "Let freedom ring, honey. You can have the TV, I'll keep the dog. It'll be tough getting over losing you, but I'll mend my broken heart somehow. Anyone can do the heartbreak, Ms. Fields." That last line had Amanda's brow raising quizzically. "It's a title of a song I know," he said.

"Oh." She wheeled him out of the kitchen area and stopped at the doorway leading into the great family room. "Close your eyes, Mr. Danzlo," she said too happily. Perturbed, he closed them. She wheeled him further into the room. "Okay, you can open them now. Ta-daaa!"

Garry stared at the table covered with small objects—a doorknob and latch, a sponge, a rubber ball, a zipper, an old fashioned egg beater, buttons, and other odds and ends.

"What the hell is this?"

"Mr. Danzlo, must you curse?"

"Must you aggravate the living hell out of me?"

Amanda clenched fists at her sides, yet her voice was composed. "If I can tolerate the overly large portion of aggravation you hand out, surely you can tolerate the smaller I give back. Now, what you see before you is called a utility table, Mr. Danzlo."

"You mean a junk table."

"It's made up of nothing more than a collection of simple household items. The reason for these prosaic things is to help improve your muscles and coordination, to relearn simple, yet necessary acts of everyday life and existence. In other words, Mr. Danzlo, these are your toys. You can play."

"You don't have to treat me like a child," he hissed.

"And you don't have to act like one."

Silence and tension threatened to break Garry apart. He realized they were each fighting a different battle... his anger, her tears. He felt those tears somehow, beneath the undying, nurturing strength and patience she personified. It angered him to witness her caring nature and to experience it so wholly. She made him feel confused. Yet, he knew she spoke truth. He was acting like a child. He was a man for God's sake. So why was he fighting? And why were they fighting back? Melissa, his mother, Nicolas, this woman. Everyone. What was the use? What did he care? What did *she* care?

"Mr. Danzlo—"

"So, what am I supposed to do with these things? You don't plan to leave me alone with these small objects, do you? I could swallow one and choke to death. Or maybe that was your plan?" His brow turned upward, a hint of a smile edging on his mouth.

"What a wonderful idea. A quick way to get rid of you since I won't be leaving."

A moment passed in silence.

"So, what are you waiting for, Ms. Fields?" he asked, his voice turning soft, husky. "Why haven't you left the room?"

"Well," she replied, thoughtfully, "a woman has a right to change her mind. I'm not apt to back out on obligation, even when that obligation is most tempting to neglect due to an exceedingly bad patient. I reclaim your case, sir, with open arms and my undying, cautious skill. Rest assured. I shall never leave you alone to choke to death."

Garry closed his eyes and shook his head. "Where did Melissa find you? Why did Melissa find you? I get it. She thinks I'm on the verge of insanity. She's trying to finish the job."

"It's not like that at all," Amanda said, placing a comforting hand on his shoulder. "Your sister cares about you very much. As for me, she probably knows no one else would put up with you."

She smiled down at him. He smiled back.

Removing her hand from his shoulder, she held it between them. "Now, let's get started," she said. "I want you to take hold of my hand and squeeze it as hard as you can."

Garry looked at her outstretched hand, ignoring her request.

"I don't have cooties, Mr. Danzlo. I just want to find out how much strength you have."

*Cooties?* He hadn't heard that expression since grade school. With a mischievous smile, he reached for her hand, squeezing with all of his might.

"*Ow,*" she yelped, jerking her hand free. "I did not say your left hand."

"Nor did you say my right," he said, smirking.

"You know which hand I meant. Y-you have a lot of strength in your left hand." She was still rubbing its soreness. "You could do so much more if you'd only use it."

*Yes. Like wring that little neck of yours,* he thought.

"Now will you please take my hand. With your right hand this time?"

She looked rather amusing standing there begging him to hold her hand, not to mention how funny she looked period. "And if I don't wanna?" he said with a slight lean her way, one blue eye shining while he lifted a brow.

"Ah, but you're gonna, aren't you?" she said.

Garry's gaze became stuck on those eyes. He felt the warmth of them, and the warmth from her voice—soft and almost childlike. He suddenly had the craziest urge to take off those reddish-brown frames she wore and see the true color of her eyes amongst the light rusty and purplish shadows on her lids. But he felt most drawn to her mouth. Her smile played innocently on her lips, and yet her lips were full-bodied and provocative. They tantalized him to touch them with his own. She licked her lips, and he watched in fascination.

*For the love of… What was he doing?* How long had he stared this time? Crazy, crazy notions. His head was filled with them. It was this celibate life he led. He'd had no woman for months. Daphne had handed him a thousand excuses why they shouldn't have sex again just yet. He wasn't even sure he could perform without making a fool out of himself.

But this wasn't about lovemaking. This was about a kiss. He wanted to kiss his nurse. Good God. This ridiculous-looking woman! Angry with himself, he grabbed Amanda's hand.

"Is that the best that you can do?" she asked, concerned.

"Yes, that's the best I can do," he snapped, tearing his hand away.

His change in mood brought a brief moment of perplexity to her face. "You're going to be using these objects on the table to strengthen that right hand," she stated warily. "You'll be surprised how strong your hand can be after some practice. It's like playing the piano. Practice makes perfect."

He winced at her example. He didn't believe he could ever play piano again.

As though she'd heard his thoughts, she added, "Once you practice for a time at this table, then we can practice at your piano."

"Woman, are you out of your mind? I'm ruined. I'll never play again. Can't you see this hand? Look at it. Deformed, just like my right leg. You think this hand can play?"

"Yes," she said simply. She swallowed hard, raising her chin to defend her opinion. "Your body is not deformed, Mr. Danzlo. You may have some scars and weakness, but other than that, I believe you will both play the piano and walk someday."

"Well, your opinion is bullshit!"

"Mr. Danzlo, please. There's no need for vulgarity. I-I only ask that you give me a chance to prove that you can do—"

"I know what I can do and what I can't, Ms. Fields."

"Well, then you have a very low opinion of yourself."

"That's right. I'm a lowly sonofa—"

He stopped. Had he restrained from the vulgar remark for her sake? What should he care what she liked and didn't like? He broke into ironic laughter.

Unexpectedly, her hand reached out and pressed tenderly against the side of his face, her fingers sweeping across the scar on his right cheek and meeting his hair.

His left hand flew to her wrist. He held it tightly while she took in a breath, held it.

"I don't want your pity, woman. If it wasn't for Melissa, believe me, you wouldn't be here. I don't need you, or anyone else."

Amanda closed her eyes, biting down on her lip. "Please," she cried softly, "I understand what you're feeling."

*"Understand?"* He released his grip furiously. "No one understands what I feel."

His left palm shoved against the table's edge; it crashed to the floor on its side, its objects sailing in every direction through the room. "Get out!" he screamed.

He closed his eyes, blotting out her dispirited trembling form. Amanda—the one still waiting with hope. Why wouldn't she go away? And why did it torture him to see her broken in despair? *She was nothing to him!* So why the hell was she affecting him so?

"Ms. Fields," he said again, "I said get out and leave me alone."

He lifted his eyelids and saw Nicolas standing at the kitchen entrance, eyes plagued with vexation. Then, the older man dropped his gaze, and dipped his chin to his chest. And there was Amanda, still standing by like he knew she would be, her posture straight, her expression calm. He had felt her presence, strong and warm. Even when he'd fought against her only seconds ago, she had stood clearly in his mind as though he'd never closed his eyes.

He looked at her now, their gazes locking. They drank in each other's hurt and humiliation—his shame, and her defeat.

Then, Amanda lowered her head. She paused a second, and then walked away.

# *11.*

# SOMETIMES WHEN
# WE TOUCH

AFTER THE UTILITY table episode, Garry had ordered Nicolas to take him to his room. He wanted only Nicolas to tend to his needs, and Amanda had abided his wishes for the time being. However, she felt he'd had enough solitude and letting his emotions simmer. If she allowed him the whole day, he'd be more impossible tomorrow.

The dinner hour approached. Amanda entered his room quietly, spotting him by the bed in his wheelchair, his eyes closed. She softly sat on the bed facing him, trying to think of something witty. Instead, she found herself gazing at his face, regarding it appreciatively, for she didn't see it often in this tranquil state. But then his eyes flew open, his gaze penetrating.

Her breath caught and she nervously began singing Martin Charnin's *Tomorrow* from the 1977 Broadway musical *Annie.*

"If only you were a day away, Ms. Fields. I thought I told Nicolas I didn't want to see your face the rest of this day."

Amanda sighed. "Then don't look at my face, Mr. Danzlo. It's time for dinner."

She got up and wheeled him to the kitchen. She was glad he had avoided her face the rest of the evening, especially during the call he'd taken at supper.

"Hey, beautiful," his voice answered warm and husky on the phone to Daphne. She was checking up on him again. "What? You're coming home early? Possibly the weekend? That would be great, sweetheart." Nicolas and Amanda exchanged glances. Nicolas furrowed his brows. "Oh, you did, huh?" Garry smiled, the laughter on the other line resonating lyrically through the phone. "Hmm, promises, promises. We'll see when you get here. Yeah, me too. Stay safe. Yes, kisses."

It was like an invasion of privacy for Amanda as she listened to Garry speaking endearments to a woman. Garry seemed excited and genuinely taken with Daphne, who didn't seem at all like the crutch Melissa had spoken of. Maybe she could speak with Daphne once she returned from Europe. Amanda would gladly assist in teaching Garry's girlfriend some rehabilitation techniques, especially if it meant getting Garry motivated.

Though "beautiful" and "sweetheart" were the endearments Garry used while talking to Daphne; "sexy" and "hot" were the words he used while talking about her. The latter he did after the call, mostly to himself, for Nicolas and Amanda weren't interested in his graphic details.

THE NEXT MORNING, Amanda dressed and walked over to the brass floor mirror in the corner of her room. She stared at her reflection for a long moment, acutely aware of her Cinderella role, or at least the part she played before the ball: with only wishes in her head and an ugly wardrobe. It bothered her that Garry couldn't see her true beauty. "Sexy" and "hot" were far from how she was looking right now. She was tempted to wear her make-up more natural to her coloring. Would Garry think her pretty and appealing? Would his words be so harsh, his actions so contemptuous?

*Would he feel the same disturbing pull I feel each time we're in the same room together?*

She gasped at her own thoughts. Where in the world had that come from? She closed her eyes.

*No, Amanda. You're just feeling intimidated. The fact that you couldn't stop thinking about the conversation he had with Daphne last night has brought on this crazy notion. That's all. Whatever magnetic pull you think you're having is due only to your emotional need at the present, the need for someone to love you like you want to be loved.*

It didn't help matters that Garry had a handsome smile. He was a little irresistible to look at too, particularly when he had a clean shaven face. She'd always been a sucker for naked faces. When his blue eyes sparkled with mischief, they made his winsome smile even more handsome. Perhaps all those visualizations she'd done last night only worsened her feat ahead. She had imagined him as an innocent little boy, like Robbie. Sweet, adorable, and behaved. She'd used such visualization techniques to heal herself of Paul—imagining him as a child who trusted with his whole heart and believed that those around him would steer him in the right direction. She had needed to see Paul beyond the imperfections that his ego had created when he was alive. She had tried to do the same with Garry, only her imagination had taken her further into his youth, and then into his adult life. He started to look a little too good.

No, she needed to keep her heart tucked safely away for Robbie, not for a man. She'd continue this charade and stay hidden behind the clothes and makeup to insure protection against temptation. Her main goal was to rehabilitate Garry and get him back to his career and herself back to Robbie.

Inhaling slowly, she calmed her frail emotions. She said a small prayer for Garry, for his healing, then another for herself to lift her self-esteem, and her confidence. Taking another slow breath, she began to feel revitalized.

*Okay, Garry Danzlo,* she said to that insolent man who wasn't there. She crossed the room toward the writing desk. *I'm going to write a letter. And this letter is going to be from you. You're going to say sweet words today. No insults, no scornful remarks. By the time I finish, you may even be a likable person!* She pulled out a pad of paper. "But not too likeable," she said aloud, as flashes of his handsome grin passed in her mind.

Twenty minutes later, she was in the kitchen with Nicolas relaying her great plan for Garry on this new day. "Nicolas," she said, "Mr. Danzlo is getting a bath today. A real one!" Moments later, she stormed into Garry's room with a merry wakeup song on her lips:

"The sun is rising out of bed, and in the east the sky is red, so UP and AWAKE you SLEEPY HEAD, so EARly in the MORning…"

Garry's eyes flew open wide, his body flat and tense as Amanda concentrated on her song and moved resolutely toward the royal blue drapes.

"… a shame to sleep the hours away when all the world is bright with day, and nature calls to work or PLA-A-a-ay…"

One pull of the draw rope, the drapes flew open, filling the room with bright light as Amanda finished her song's last line with a buoyant voice. *"SO EARLY IN THE MORNING!"*

Closing his bulging eyes, Garry muttered between clenched teeth, "I'm going to kill her. I'm going to kill her today."

"Oh, look, Mr. Danzlo. The sky is filled with pink. Do you know what that means? Snow, snow, snow. At least, that's what I've been told is a good sign. Have you heard that? Nicolas said that the radio was calling for flurries early afternoon. Just another grand thing to make our day more special! Right, Mr. Danzlo? We have so much to be thankful for. God truly does miraculous things, don't you agree?"

Garry rose up on his left elbow. Too angry to say mere words, he snarled with eyes that were narrowed and vicious.

"My, my, Gran-maw!" she responded, her hands on each side of her face. "What BIG MEAN EYES you have!"

Garry was struck with an urge to smile. He desperately restrained from doing so by pulling down the sides of his mouth from the inside. "Better to see what I plan to kill, my dear," he said.

"And Gran-maw, what a *nose* you have on that mean face, sir. I-I mean, ma'am! And those *teeth*. How ferocious-looking." She took a step back, widening her eyes.

"Better to sniff you out and tear you apart in tiny shreds, my dear."

Amanda stood for a moment, all silent and innocent-like. Putting her hands on her hips, she said, "So, aren't you supposed to jump out of bed now and chase me around the room?"

"Funny, real funny." He sneered, the humor he once felt completely gone. "If I could, believe me, I would."

"But I do believe. I believe you could, and would," she added with a grin. "Your problem, sir, is that you don't believe. You have little faith."

Garry frowned. "Maybe your problem is that you have too much faith."

She tilted her head as if in thought. Then she walked to the side of the bed where he lay. "I'd rather have too much than too little, Mr. Danzlo. But then, what is too much?" Amanda's expression became thoughtfully grave. "Is it too much to desire a thing with all your heart, or to discover a dream you want to believe in? Who needs to dream if there's no hope behind it?" Her eyes were questioning, yet compassionate. "I heard somewhere that a dream is a promise of all you can become. I believe there's a dream inside you, Mr. Danzlo. I can help you with the promise... *if you let me*."

Her last words were no more than a whisper, but he heard them clearly. They touched him. Maybe it was the way she stared down at him with such genuineness as she spoke. He found himself staring back, a little too seriously perhaps, for her feet began to shift on the floor and her face colored a shade of pink. She looked away; her eyes steered toward a log crackling in the fireplace.

"Do I get fed this morning, or will you starve me as punishment for yesterday's bad behavior?"

Amanda heard his teasing tone. She responded with a little tease of her own. "No," she said, spinning around to face him. "I think I'll... *we'll* punish you later, Nicolas and I."

"I'm sure," he said with a wary frown. "So, where is Nicolas?"

"He's in the kitchen cooking and preparing a delicious breakfast and waiting for us."

Garry lifted a brow. "Are you going to attempt to tackle me *alone* today?"

A shuddering breath escaped her lungs. "I think I can handle you alone," she said, straightening her stance. "All you have to do is help me."

"And if I don't?"

"If you don't, I seem to remember a large bucket in one of the bathrooms. It would do nicely filled with lots of cold water. And then I would—"

"You wouldn't!" The muscles in his neck tightened.

"Oh yeah? Do you challenge me? Are you daring me?"

Amanda's spunk was revived. Garry swung back his covers with his left hand and began edging himself inch by inch off the bed.

"I knew you'd see it my way, Mr. Danzlo," she said.

During breakfast, Nicolas and Amanda chatted lightly while Garry listened and observed. He had never known Nicolas to speak so comfortably with a woman in his life. Nor had Garry ever remembered being so moved by one woman himself—one minute disliking her; the next, feeling totally entertained. Amanda knew how to pluck his nerves, then turn around and play them gently.

Lowering his focus to his plate, he listened to her voice beside him. Her soft laughter sung through his senses while a light fragrance of rose drifted to his nostrils. She was smiling. He closed his eyes, saw her lips, moist, alluring... the taste of cherries on his tongue. He groaned with a heady thirst.

The fantasy was crashed when he looked at her goofy semblance and those reddish-brown glasses lying crooked on her nose. But those tantalizing lips moist with pancake syrup snatched his full attention, and the way she licked them aroused him despite himself. He coughed, nearly choking on his saliva. He threw his fork down; it clanged upon his plate. Grabbing a glass of orange juice, he downed it quickly.

"Mr. Danzlo, what's wrong?" Amanda asked, coming instantly out of her chair. Garry, so appalled she might touch him, flung backward and dropped the glass. Next thing he knew, her hands were stroking his face, her fingers on his forehead, on his cheeks, leaving him speechless. She cried out, "Are you choking?

Can you cough again? Try to cough!" But instead of coughing, he was warding off those female hands that roamed and caused his face to flush. His only good arm flailed uselessly except to kilter her off-balance, and then her body suddenly toppled sideways across the wheelchair. On instinct, he grabbed the back of her skirt and a handful of her backside as well, and with a mighty twist of strength unfitting him these past confining days, he flipped her upright, bottom side down and straight into his lap.

Both sat frozen, their faces inches apart—hers frightened, his stunned to near death. He'd caught her in his arms, yet the only thing he was aware of was that her breath smelled of boysenberry syrup. He licked his lips; she licked hers.

Before he could think about what he was doing, he pushed her onto the floor.

"Mr. Danzlo!" Nicolas bellowed, horrified, helping Amanda up. "Have you lost all your scruples, sir? Apologize this minute."

Garry sat stiff in his wheelchair, as shocked as Nicolas. He'd never been that rough with a woman in his life. It wasn't her fault he'd wanted to lick the boysenberry right off her lips. The very thought scared the hell out of him.

"Mr. Danzlo, we're waiting."

Amanda straightened her glasses, her dress. "I'm okay, Nicolas. He doesn't have to—"

"No, he *will* apologize. Won't you, Mr. Danzlo?"

Garry glanced up sheepishly from his wheelchair. It was strange receiving an order from Nicolas, but Nicolas had every right to give him one. What if he'd hurt the woman. Garry looked at Amanda, her expression unreadable, her eyes curious. She didn't appear to be hurt at all. "I'm sorry, Ms. Fields, for pushing you out of my chair. It was uncalled for. Let me assure you, if I could take it back this very moment, I... *I wouldn't.*" He was teasing her, a grin to prove it. "Go on and slap me. Right here," he said, pointing a finger to his cheek. "I deserve it. I can take it."

Then she bent down and kissed that cheek with her sticky lips. His brow lifted. "That was for being honest and for making the effort to apologize. Oh, and to sweeten you up for the big event Nicolas and I have planned for you this morning."

Garry's smile turned upside down, fast.

Moments later, he was screaming and cursing, determined to keep his robe on; they were determined to take it off. Amanda finally just ripped it off while Nicolas held tight to Garry's waist. By the time they had him settled in the bathtub, Nicolas and Amanda were soaked with water, both stomping out of the bathroom and slamming the door behind them, probably thinking with any luck he might drown.

"Nicolas, I've always been a very patient person," Amanda confessed wearily, both of them sitting down in the family room, their feet propped up on ottomans, "but that man tries my patience to the very end. He's like an abominable monster. You just want to push him off a cliff. I can't seem to reach him at all. Maybe it's me. What's wrong with me, Nicolas?"

"Why, Miss Amanda, the only thing wrong with you is seeming too good to be true." Nicolas smiled genuinely.

"Oh, Nicolas, if only he would say words as sweet as you do. But no, not Garry Danzlo. He's probably in the bathroom speaking sour words this very minute."

GARRY ATTEMPTED TO ease backward in the tub using his hands, but his right one disappointed him as usual, his right side giving way to the water. His unbalanced weight flipped him facedown against the porcelain floor. Submerged completely, he splashed and sputtered. He mustered all the strength he had available, and by pushing against the tub's bottom with his stronger left hand, he accomplished the feat of sitting upward in the tub. Once done, his face heated with embarrassment. He turned toward the closed door in fear he had attracted unwanted attention. He stared at the door, suspense thumping through his chest till at last he decided no one was coming. He relaxed.

Closing his eyes, he rested his head on the back of the tub. He tried to conjure a nice picture in his mind—something pleasing, inviting. His thought was to visualize the beautiful Daphne. To his chagrin, a silly face wearing goofy glasses came into view. Teasing, laughing.

His eyes flew open. "A stain in my brain! Must she be everywhere?"

Someone rapped on the door. Garry heard the all too familiar voice. "Did you call? Are you all right?"

"No to both questions, and don't come in here!"

"I had hoped your bath might have cooled your hot temper, Mr. Danzlo. But maybe I'll get that bucket, fill it with ice to cool you a little."

"Woman, you do and I'll pull you in here with me!"

"Really?" she said, amused outside the door. "I'm suddenly out of your wheelchair and into your tub. Interesting. But I wouldn't want to get you too excited. The heat might boil your water, and you're hot enough. I'll just go get Nicolas so he can help you finish your bath."

As she walked away, Garry's laughter burst through the walls. *She? Excite me? That goofy woman?* Her lips were appealing, but that was as far as it went. He tried to imagine making out with her, but the vision that came to mind was himself nude on top of Bozo the Clown; the only "hot" he was getting was from all the ugly cloth she smothered him with.

His laughter grew harder. The woman did have a sense of humor; he'd give her that.

# *12.*

# MANDY

AMANDA STOOD IN the middle of the great family room facing Garry. She decided it was too soon to attempt another try at the utility table. No need to set Garry's temper off just when his mood had lightened from his bath.

"Well," she began, "What would you like to do now, Mr. Danzlo?"

He looked at her as if she'd gone mad, his head tilted, his brows strained inward. "I don't remember doing anything I've wanted to do since the moment you walked into my house."

"Mr. Danzlo, you don't have to be unfriendly. We have weeks ahead of us. It would be nice if we didn't act like foes. I'm not here to fight against you, but for you."

Garry frowned. "And what is this you're fighting for me, Ms. Fields? I can fight my own battles. I don't need someone to do it for me."

Her forehead wrinkled. "If you were successfully fighting the battle you evidently have within you, then no, you wouldn't need an ally. However, you aren't fighting at all, and I stand beside you in hopes that together we gain victory." She stood erect, chin held high for effect.

"So patriotic of you," he said. "I don't deserve such loyalty."

"You don't deserve loyalty?" Amanda backed into a green plush chair next to his wheelchair. "Tell me, what makes you say that?"

A scornful, penetrating gaze was her only answer. She realized Garry wasn't ready to share anything personal with her just yet. Soon, she'd have to get him to open up about those hidden feelings about his father, the suicide, and whatever else related to his despair.

"I know what we can do, Mr. Danzlo! We'll chat. No need for all work and exercise. We'll spend this time getting to know each other." She scooted back in her chair and got comfortable.

Dead silence.

Garry's face was void of expression. Amanda swallowed hard while her fingers massaged the chair arms. "This is a really fine place you have. Real cozy and homey." She glanced around the spacious room as though seeing it for the first time. "And this chair. Real nice and comfortable!"

Thirty seconds ticked by wordlessly.

"So," she said. "You're a singer?" Garry's cheek sagged, a brow lifting with jeer. "I mean, I know you are," she said. "Melissa told me about your music, your love for piano, the many fans you have."

"Don't tell me." His voice spoke with its usual stringency. "My sweet, innocent nurse doesn't know who I am, nor my music and songs."

"I'm sure I've heard your music at some time or other. You know how you listen to a song on the radio, but never catch who's singing?"

"You're serious," he said stunned. "Maybe I'm not so popular after all."

"I enjoy reading," she explained. "Not much of a radio/TV person. Too busy with nursing, my energy work, my holistic studies."

Garry's expression went frigidly awry with the mention of her alternative healing.

"Perhaps at some point we can try—"

"I don't go for that witchery crap."

"Using a natural resource for healing is hardly—"

"Then naturally resource someone else."

Amanda sighed. "What kind of songs do you write?"

He paused at her abrupt change of subject. "I write the songs that make the young girls cry, or so they tell me. Ballads of love and special things that bring hope and…" he didn't finish the line. His eyes lowered. "I write more music than lyrics. Don't you like music?"

"Of course. I've sung to you to brighten your mornings, haven't I?"

His eye slanted. He wasn't amused.

"Actually, my husband didn't like music much, especially the kind I wanted to listen to, so I didn't play it at home. He hated parties, dancing. But I love to dance. A few girls dragged me to a place called *The Copacabana* one night. I had such fun, met a famous musician… though I don't recall his name." She felt foolish. "My favorite is jazz, mostly the old traditional stuff. Do you like jazz?"

Garry didn't respond with words, but Amanda thought she'd seen a spark of interest in his eyes. She decided to spur it. "I just love the sounds of saxophone, piano, and bass together, don't you? Oh, and guitar. Did I mention I play guitar? Nothing professional, but I can play a few tunes. I adore those great musicians like Mundell Lowe, Gerry Mulligan, and those old-time jazz singers like Billie Holiday, Dinah Washington, Louis Armstrong... Sarah Vaughan, too. Oh, and Mel Torme. He's got such a nice, smooth voice. Hey, wouldn't it be neat if you could get with a couple of these guys and make an album? That is, if you like jazz."

"I like jazz," Garry said solemnly.

And he did, he liked jazz a lot.

He'd always dreamed of recording some oldies with the Big Bands. But that's all it was, a dream. Daphne had discouraged any ideas he'd ever brought up about jazz. She hated jazz. Pop music was the rage, what she could market without any doubt of success. *It's not what you want, Garry; it's what your fans want,* she would tell him.

"So why don't you?" Amanda asked. "Maybe you could even sing a duet with Mel Torme. Or even Miss Vaughan. Wait till we start those breathing exercises. Your voice will be good as new." While Amanda's eyes glowed with excitement, Garry's narrowed.

"What are you thinking, Ms. Fields? You want me to make a fool out of myself? I'll never have the voice I once had, or the fingers to play. Your idea is dumb."

"No, my idea is good. Yours is dumb." She crossed her arms, as if daring him to argue. When he didn't, she smiled. "You know what other kind of music I like, Mr. Danzlo? Classical romance. Ahh, intimate music." She sighed, slouching in her seat, her eyes closing, her face lifting heavenward.

Garry gawked at the woman beside him. She looked far from being the romantic type. Unpredictable again, he thought. He found himself smiling at her, and then moved his focus to the big picture window across the room. "I enjoy intimate music," he said softly.

His mind became absorbed in vague images of a woman—the one who stole his dreams in the night. She was his private, intimate music. Bewitching him, haunting him, making him thirst for her touch. Since the accident, she'd appeared in his dreams only once—a taunting nightmare that left him devastated, for he'd lost her in a great maze, hearing only her desperate call for help: *Where are you, Garry? Find me,* she cried, *please find me.*

His failure to find her had him believing that the dream was surely a reminder of his failure to save his father's life. He'd abandoned all hope of his phantom woman ever returning now. Surely gone like his career. And yet, he closed his eyes thinking of her now and a pleasing vibration undulated down his body.

"A penny for your thoughts," Amanda said softly beside him.

He turned at her voice, realizing she must have been watching him the entire time. "My thoughts are worth much more than a penny," he said in a low, hoarse tone.

Her gaze was intense and quizzical. "I play piano, too," she blurted. "Of course, I don't play as well as you. I only had a year and a half of lessons. I do know how to read music, play a few songs. Just simple songs. Mostly children's songs…"

She was saying a mouthful, her words flying out as fast as they'd possibly come.

"… and then there were times I played piano in the recreation room at the hospital in pediatrics where we gathered the children for activity. So how long have you been in music?"

Garry eyed her with a solemn expression. "A long time," he stated flatly. He was suddenly amused, pretending boredom by tapping his fingers on his chair arm, looking away now and then. Her chatty display of words was oddly stimulating. He sensed her nervousness had something to do with him. For some reason, this pleased him. "Ms. Fields…"

"Yes?" Amanda said, perking up in her seat.

Her naive expression and hasty response nearly broke his deception. "Never mind."

Silence fell, though not for long.

"You know, you don't have to call me Ms. Fields. It makes me feel older than I am. I'm only thirty-one. I'd much prefer Amanda. No reason we can't be on a first name basis." Garry frowned. "Of course, if you don't want me calling you Garry…" her voice trailed off. "I just thought, well, no one I know calls me Ms. Fields. Always Amanda."

Garry didn't say anything.

"But then, I never wanted to be called Amanda," she mused aloud, sitting back in her chair. "When I was a little girl, I wanted people to call me Mandy, but no one ever did. No one ever listened. I was stuck with Amanda."

As she talked she constantly pushed up those pointed-edged glasses that slid down her slim nose. When she wasn't using her fingers for that, they drummed in a quiet rat-a-tat-tat on the chair arm.

"I really liked the name Mandy. But, Daddy would never call me *Mandy, my sweet candy*. He called me *Amanda, my Panda Bear*. I lived my whole childhood in a room overcrowded with stuffed panda bears. Sounds precious now that I'm older, but when I was younger, it wasn't cute. I was pretty animated as a kid. I would stomp around the house and scream my frustrations to the walls: *Amanda Panda is no bear. Amanda Panda has long hair. Amanda Panda doesn't care to be called that name anymore, for Amanda Panda is a BORE.*"

Garry hid his grin by yawning. She brought to mind his childhood memories. Melissa too, in her frustration, would stomp around the house protesting her feelings to the world. Amanda's little pouts and staunch manner summoned up the past as if it were only yesterday.

"I believe Daddy called me 'Amanda Panda' just to provoke me," she said. "Now Mom, she was the quiet one with a beautiful voice." Amanda's eyes lit up. "'Sing me a Linda Song,' I'd say. Linda—that was her name. A pretty one, I thought, and since she sang pretty songs, it was only natural that her songs became Linda Songs to me. My favorite one was about scarlet ribbons. Have you heard it? You know, the little girl who prays while her mother listens?" Before Garry could respond, she was singing a line from Jack Segal's *Scarlet Ribbons (For Her Hair)*, music written in 1949 by Evelyn Danzig.

She sang with a nice dulcet tone, unlike the boisterous one she used when she sang her little morning ditties. He would've enjoyed listening to her sing the rest of the song, but she was too busy telling her little story.

"And then," she said, her eyes widening, "the next morning, miraculously, those ribbons showed up, her mother never knowing where they came from. Anyway, ever since childhood, on every birthday when I blow out my candles, I wish for scarlet ribbons. I guess it's the kid inside that still keeps me wishing." Amanda tilted her head and sighed. "I've kept that a secret all these years," she said "I guess that's why I never got them." She made a goofy, over-the-top frown that Garry sensed was real.

"Ah, a sentimental journey these wishes of mine," she said dramatically, leaning back in her chair. "But you never know when they might pop up and hit you on the nose." Amanda glanced at him mischievously. "They would hardly miss yours, huh?"

Her nose joke was so unexpected, he nearly burst out laughing, but he knew that's exactly what she was trying to get him to do. He sent her an evil eye instead, which only prompted a smile in hers. "Just kidding," she said, giving him a light shove on the shoulder. Garry just stared blankly.

"You don't talk much, do you?" she said, her brows furrowing.

"I doubt I'd get a word in edgewise the way you babble," he said.

She sat straight up in her chair. "I don't babble. I gave you plenty of chances to cut in on the conversation. But did you? No."

"I understand. Really. You're a motor mouth."

"Ooooh! If I were mean, I'd hit you!" Amanda pounded a fist on the chair arm.

"Now, now, Melissa, temper, temper." Garry finally exploded with laughter.

Amanda sulked. "You can stop laughing anytime now, and my name's not Melissa."

Garry shuddered with mirth. "But you act just like her."

She folded her arms in front of her. And then with a curious brow, she asked, "Is that good or bad?"

Garry paused. "Actually, it's rather terrifying."

"Really?" she said, her face brightening, an index finger now resting against the jut of her chin as her head leaned sideways. Her lips wore a satisfied curl. "This may hold some nice advantages."

Garry didn't like the tone of her voice. He could smell misfortune brewing. He wasn't particularly fond of these taunting ways of hers, but he'd be lying if he said he didn't enjoy her zany personality.

"Lunch is served if you two are ready to join the table."

Nicolas stood in the threshold of the kitchen, his voice causing Garry and Amanda to jump in surprise. *Had they been flirtatiously playing?*

Nicolas smiled.

THE REMAINDER OF the day went by surprisingly smooth. Amanda was able to talk Garry into doing some simple range-of-motion exercises. By mid-afternoon, it began to snow. Amanda grew preposterously excited with each snowflake that fell. Excitedly, she pranced and sang to the dog; she sang to Nicolas; she sang to Garry while it snowed, snowed and snowed.

Garry humored himself that evening watching her merriment, thinking her the biggest flake of all. Once, he'd even found himself singing with her, an event that initially started out as a threat to throw her out into the cold. She had responded with melody, her "but" reply moving pleadingly into Frank Loesser's *Baby's It's Cold Outside.*

While Garry's lyrical version kept insisting how she needed to go, Amanda's lyrical version entailed all the reasons why she needed to stay.

And so it went for most of the evening, a cheerful kind of mood that even Garry had to admit was unusual. The snow continued to fall as night came upon them. Amanda's excitement calmed, though the enchantment of the white drops falling from heaven still had her dancing from window to window, Garry drawn to regard her. By late evening, he began to notice with agitation just how much Nicolas had been smiling. Ever since Amanda Fields had come into their lives.

"Even Bagel likes her," he muttered under his breath, watching Amanda play with his dog. She had worked her magic on all of them. Had softened him today, coerced him into exercise, made him laugh. She was affecting something inside him that he couldn't figure out. It scared him so much, he didn't want to know what it was.

She was the enemy, he reminded himself. With her bewitching power, he could be brittle to her every command in a matter of days.

"I'd like to go to bed now," he said.

Amanda, confused by the severe tone and quick change in mood, glanced over at Nicolas. Nicolas looked just as puzzled.

"I think we can arrange that," she replied, turning to Garry with her usual cheer. Her good spirit was more than he wanted to tolerate for the evening.

"Now," he demanded.

Amanda's voice stayed soft and compliant. "Okay," she said, and started toward him.

"Nicolas will put me to bed."

"No, I will put you to bed," she assured him. "Nicolas has other duties to perform. Unfortunately, I have the intricate duty of taking care of your physical needs."

"Woman, I assure you, that is one thing you don't take care of, nor are you capable."

His crude remark paralyzed her for a moment, and then she marched toward his wheelchair, her eyes ablaze. She grabbed hold of the chair handles and pushed him speedily down the hall. Inside his room, she jerked the chair to a stop. "Start stripping, Mr. Danzlo, unless you want me to tear off your clothes." Stomping across the room toward the hanging drapes, she pulled on the draw rope to close them securely. Inhaling and exhaling deeply, she returned to stand by his wheelchair while he cursed under his breath and ripped at his shirt. He couldn't get the blasted thing off.

Amanda didn't move to help. He finally looked up with glaring eyes. "You could offer some assistance," he said, once he realized he didn't have the ability to do it alone, cramped in the wheelchair as he was.

"Yes, I could, couldn't I? But I'm not sure my help would be sufficient or that I'd be *capable* of performing your needs. Of course, I could try my very most best, attempt to be somewhat satisfactory in what *capabilities* I might have acquired as a nurse."

"Satisfactory will do. Or I'll be content to go to bed fully clothed if you'd rather not—"

"Rather not what?"

His eyes narrowed, blurring with moisture. The words finally dragged painfully from his mouth. "Help me."

She was beside him in a second. She helped him stand, his hard lean body against her soft pliant one, both of them working silently together to discard his clothes.

It felt strange having this woman touching him. Stranger still were the warm-hearted sensations she delivered while doing so and how harmonious and natural it all felt. Amanda Fields, an eccentric-looking lady whose hands touched him tenderly and carefully, whose shorter body supported his taller one, keeping it from falling to the floor.

He felt like half a man, yet this woman made him feel whole—the one element that was always missing whenever he was alone with a woman. He'd always yearned for it, never knew how much until now.

"There," she said, tucking him in bed. "Was that satisfactory?"

He looked at her face to see if malice was present. Her lips were smiling. He should've known. The woman never stayed mad for long.

"More so. Thank you."

She swallowed. "You're welcome."

Picking up his clothes from off the floor, Amanda folded them neatly, the room too quiet for comfort. "You know, you never did tell me much about yourself today while we talked, my *motor mouth* never giving you much chance, I guess." She smiled, waiting for his response, but she didn't receive one. "Perhaps you'll share more at some other time."

"Perhaps," he said, solemnly. He watched her turn and place his folded clothes on a nearby chair. When she turned back, he caught her gaze.

Seconds later she was clasping her hands in front her, saying, "Well, I'll leave you to rest, now. Good night, Ga—"

She bit down on her lip, as she nearly slipped by calling him by his first name.

Restraining a smile, he nodded. "Goodnight, Ms. Fields."

# *13.*

# I WANNA BE
# SOMEBODY'S BABY

PEACE RESIDED IN the house when Garry awoke the next morning. No loud wakeup songs to pierce his ears. No funny face teasing or pestering. The floor length drapes were closed, leaving the room dark. The clock on the bedside table read nine o'clock.

*Where is everybody?*

The phone rang next to the bed, startling him. It was his private line. He picked it up.

"Darling, I'm home in L.A.. The trip in Rome was a bore. I just had to come back for you. I want to see you. I want to kiss you."

"Daphne." Garry slid up against the headboard, the sheet riding sensually across his groin. "I thought you were coming on Friday."

"Yes, darling, I know we discussed the weekend, but I just couldn't wait another three days. My hope was to take the first flight in from L.A., once I do a little repacking for cooler weather. Only, the flights are delayed due to snow. If I'm lucky I may possibly get an evening flight. I just don't understand why you bought that place. You know I despise cold weather. Especially the snow."

"I bought the place for me. I don't mind cold weather, and I like snow."

Silence.

"Well, of course, darling. I hardly have to worry about being cold once I'm there. You'll keep me warm."

"And who will keep me warm?"

More silence. Then Daphne sighed heavily on the line. "Oh, darling, you sounded so much happier the other day, more like your old self. Let's not argue. You know I'll keep you warm. We'll keep each other warm."

"Oh? You think you might be able to touch certain parts of me now? Or were you thinking more on the line of bringing an electric blanket with you?"

"Garry, how cruel! I'm trying hard to adjust," she said, sobbing. "You make things so difficult." Garry heard her sniff on the other line, yet he couldn't say anything. There was silence, and then she spoke again. "But I still love you. I love you, darling."

He closed his eyes, his left hand clenching the receiver. He felt like an ass. He'd made her cry, made her feel used. She had sacrificed much for him these past months. What else did he expect? He was a damned cripple.

"I'm sorry, Daph. I'm glad you're back. I am. I shouldn't complain."

"You have every right to, darling. You've been through so much. I'll see you tonight. Or early morning, whatever flight I can get."

"I'll be waiting," he responded, a hint of desperation in his voice.

DAPHNE HUNG UP the phone, a wily smile on her lips while her chauffeur fondled her from behind, one hand beneath her silky blouse, the other within her pants. A tongue slid behind her ear just before strong warm hands ripped her blouse open, her bare breasts dangling free.

"Oh, Max," she breathed, her partner grasping one of her nipples, kneading it while taking the other into his mouth. "A girl does need to satisfy her appetites, don't you agree?" Max hummed an affirmative as she held his head. "It's not like I don't miss Garry. I do, but… *the scars*, Max, on his leg, his hip, his hand. They give me the creeps."

Max raised his mouth to her lips. "Your lovely skin deserves better," he spoke softly against them.

"This is only temporary, Max. It has to be," she said between his brief kisses. "Somehow I'll get past this aversion concerning his injuries. And I'll get him to marry me."

Max throated a chuckle as his mouth wandered aimlessly down her neck. "Why? Because he has money and I don't? Or because he can put you in the spotlight?"

Daphne's body stilled in his hands.

"Bingo," he said, his face lifting to hers, a smirk on his thin lips. "Who else but your credulous champion would keep you around *and* provide the public recognition you crave."

Daphne pushed herself from Max's arms, the corners of her mouth pinched, her eyes narrowed. "I deserve it, Max!" she said, moisture forming in her eyes. "This is the closest I've ever been to any dream I've had for myself. Garry's given me chances no one else ever would. And I want more out of life than the shit I've been handed through the years." Daphne's breath labored as a memory festered in her mind. "I saw my first penis at the age of seven, Max. Did I ever tell you that? It came with the package of having an alcoholic mother I had to watch drink herself to death. I didn't ask for every man she brought into the house to take advantage of me. But in the process, I've learned some things, Max. I take care of myself; because you can bet no one else will. I'm so sick of men taking advantage of me, and making promises they can't keep."

Max rubbed his chin. "Married men do tend to have that habit. How many marriages have you wrecked so far? At least that last one paid you a pretty penny to get you out of his life."

Daphne's cheeks fired with rage; she came at Max with the heel of her palms, sending him backward on his feet. "David loved me, Max! Men *are* capable of loving me. There were just… complications," she stuttered as she tried to convince herself that what she was saying was true.

Max stepped toward her. "Hey," he said softly, raising a comforting hand on her cheek; it grew rigid beneath his touch. "Of course you're capable of being loved. You've just made mistakes. Everyone makes mistakes."

She nodded, wiping a tear from her face. "I can't make one with Garry, Max. He's not like the others. He's made of something good. He's loyal. I've seen it. He doesn't break promises. This accident… it's just messing with his mind right now. Soon, things will be back to normal. He's not married, Max. This time I'll be blameless." She tapped a fist on his shoulder and sent him a half smile—a silent reminder and half-apology for hitting him earlier.

Max's eyes sweltered with lust. "You're a sexy bitch when you get riled up." He jerked her hard against him, pumping his rigidness against her pelvis. Daphne responded with an intake of breath. She needed his touch right now. Anyone's touch.

"Life isn't fair, Max," she said against his shoulder, reveling in his lewd affections. "You take what you want, anyway you can. Garry does owe me. He owes me a lot, right?"

Max rammed his fingers up the cove between her legs. She gasped. "Oh yes, Max. Darling, more, more."

GARRY LAY BACK on his pillow. He tried to be excited about Daphne's upcoming visit, but the thought wasn't very moving. Once he had hung up the phone, her sexy voice gone, the sensuality she impressed upon him left like it always did. He closed his eyes, wishing to feel more. He felt nothing. The room was quiet. The whole house was quiet.

He rose up on his left elbow, listening for sounds coming from other parts of the house. None came. Something wasn't right. "Why would Amanda let me sleep this late?" he said aloud. Did last night's behavior get her bags packing? No, Amanda Fields wouldn't give him the satisfaction. But her leaving did cross his mind, and for a brief moment, disappointment swallowed him.

Then Nicolas came into the room. "I see you're awake, sir. I came in earlier, but you were still asleep." Heading toward the drapes, Nicolas opened them, Garry glad for the forewarning to shield his eyes. "A wonderful morning," Nicolas commented. "The snow has finally stopped falling. A near twelve inches on the ground."

Pushing the wheelchair close to the bed and locking its wheels, he helped Garry swivel his feet to the floor. He slid his arms beneath Garry's like Amanda had showed him, and began lifting for the transfer from bed to chair.

Though Amanda was on his mind, Garry stubbornly held back the question that gnawed at him. He didn't want Nicolas getting the wrong idea.

"Breakfast is waiting in the kitchen, sir. We'll take a quick run to the bathroom and—"

"Where is Ama... Ms. Fields?" Garry blustered, the suspense killing him. Not to sound too interested, he added snidely, "She's normally in this room by now, plunging a sword through my soul with her ridiculous harassment."

Nicolas grinned. "She had some things to do. Have no fear, you'll see her."

"Fear?" Garry feigned a laugh. "Fear because I will be seeing her." *God, I sound like a petulant teenager!*

Nicolas kept his mouth shut while he continued to help him to the bathroom. Once Garry was dressed, Nicolas wheeled him down the hall toward the kitchen.

"You know, Nic, I could get an electronic wheelchair. You wouldn't have to push me."

Nicolas raised a brow, his gray eyes gleaming. "Ah, but Miss Amanda has other plans for you. She says pushing buttons won't do. Exercise is essential. She also says you'll eventually wheel yourself. And furthermore, that you'll be—"

"Forget it, Nicolas. Pretend I never asked."

Garry drank his morning coffee and ate a few bites of his breakfast. He pushed his plate away. *Where the heck is she?* "Take me in the other room, Nicolas. Please."

Nicolas placed Garry in view of the huge window overlooking the front lawn. As he drew open the luxurious oyster sheers, Garry wasn't interested in looking out, his eyes too busy searching elsewhere.

"So where is she, Nicolas? What was more important than nursing me this morning?"

Nicolas waved his hand with a slight bow toward the window. "She's outside, sir, building a snowman." His gray eyes were twinkling as he exited the room.

Garry jerked his head toward the window, staring in disbelief. Amanda reared up from the corner, rolling a large snowball. An even larger ball sat nearby.

*A nut!* It was below freezing outside.

With each huff of chilled air Amanda breathed, a puff of foggy vapor came from her mouth and nostrils. Her cheeks and nose were apple red. Bagel was with her dressed in a green sweater, out in that freezing snow, drowning in the stuff. Amanda wore an oversized coat with large brown buttons down the front. Her big-legged britches were tucked inside men's boots. His boots!

Thick green mittens covered her hands, her head adorned with a brown woolen cap and topped with a fluffy orange ball. Her cap kept sliding down her eyes.

What a sight. And not an unpleasant one. She was absurdly cute in a bizarre kind of way. A few chuckles sprang from Garry's throat as Amanda tried hefting up that giant ball she'd made to place on top of the other large ball of snow. Huffing and puffing, the globe wasn't budging. She kicked a furious foot at the large creation, and falling to her knees, she sloughed off snow until it was small enough to make one good upward heave. Once done, she rolled a quick snow head, collected two long sticks, crunching them into the snowman for arms. Two black pieces of coal made the eyes, a carrot for a nose, rocks for a mouth and then her finishing touch—a black and yellow-checkered scarf around the snow-body's neck.

Amanda stood back with gloved hands on hips, smiling at her masterpiece. Garry broke into laughter when the dog began to run in circles around Amanda, the canine tangling between her big booted feet, making her lose her balance. She fell flat on her back in the snow. Before she could raise herself, Bagel jumped on her, licking her face and the snow off her glasses, which were haphazardly atop her head.

Sometime between the escape from the snow-bogged beagle, Amanda must have spied her observer sitting by the window, for within seconds, a snowball torpedoed toward Garry, splotching itself hard against the glass pane. Recoiling, he glared, half-perturbed, half-humored at the woman outside rolling in the snow in a fit of laughter.

He watched Amanda and his dog disappear behind the house. He smiled when he heard Amanda's breathless voice and Nicolas chuckling when the two snow bunnies hopped in through the back door. Between the dog's barking, Amanda's excited cackling, and Nicolas' jolly welcoming, the house vibrated in noisy chaos.

Garry felt suddenly alone as he sat in his wheelchair listening from the great room. Then Amanda's joyous voice echoed through the walls with the story of how she scared the big bad wolf with her swifty snowball missile.

"I heard that," Garry said loudly.

A moment of silence passed before a burst of laughter rang out from the kitchen.

With boots, coat, sweater, sweatshirt, mittens, hat, and scarf off, Amanda stood on the threshold leading to the great room dressed in baggy corduroy pants and a flannel shirt. Garry had anticipated her entrance, his eyes catching sight of her first. Their eyes met.

Her hair was a mess, those dark tresses falling down every which way from its pinned-up state. She was something to smile about all the way down to those hilarious-looking woolen socks of alternate colors. Garry thought her adorable.

The sight Amanda saw was much different.

Garry wore a captivating smile that radiated warmth through her cold, wet body. "Good morning," she said with a sigh and a buoyant smile.

"Good morning," he said, his tone genuine. Amanda had to catch her breath. His blue eyes never left her golden brown ones, and for a moment, she feared she wasn't wearing her glasses. She quickly felt for them. They were there.

"Did my nurse have fun playing in the cold snow so bright and early?"

She batted her eyes, and then with both hands on her hips, said, "Oh, definitely. But I should've had my patient with me. You would've made a great target for snowball practice, or a skeleton for my ingenious snowman."

"A snowman in a wheelchair? Now, that would be different."

She searched his face for some mark of hurt or contempt, but his brilliant smile never faltered. To hope Garry's mood could last forever was unthinkable, but it was wonderful to see him this way.

His eyes sparkled blue. Crow's feet crinkled the outer corners of his eyes, accentuating his smile. He was wearing a pale blue shirt open at the collar. Though his tracheotomy had left a tiny scar, the column of his throat and the bare skin at its base brought her eyes to a delectable standstill.

She immediately closed them hoping to shut out loose thoughts. Her body was responding on its own, sensuality blasting through her like a windstorm.

"Woman, what are you doing?"

Startled, she opened her eyes. "I was imagining you as a snowman," she said.

He quirked a brow. "You had no smile on your face. You didn't like what you saw?"

She had liked what she saw too much! "No. I mean, yes! You'd make a fine snowman. Please excuse me."

She was gone before Garry had a chance to respond.

In her room, Amanda stared into the mirror. Her hair was a dark stringy mess, and her eyes were smeared with brown mascara. She had forgotten she had the rubbish on when wiping her eyes with her wet mittens. Her cheeks were still red from the cold outside, mixed with orange from the rouge. Surveying her wide-legged corduroy pants and her plaid flannel shirt of pumpkin orange, pickle green and burnt purple, more tears fell. She looked like a hobo! Tears trickled down her cheeks as she realized Garry had seen her like this.

Disgusted, she ripped off her clothes, not bothering to unbutton the shirt. Buttons flew in all directions. All she wanted was to jump into the shower, scrub her face, wash her hair, and cleanse her body until it squeaked from being clean. Her dismay was soon remedied as hot water splashed against her skin, steam from her shower filming the bathroom mirror.

Washing and scrubbing, she decided she had to get her act together. She wasn't here to impress Garry Danzlo. She was here to nurse him back to health. She had to stay in control of her mind, her body, and ignore these romantic yearnings. They were starting to get out of hand. Garry would never be attracted to a waif look-alike who'd been jumping at the woodside junk yard, the place she evidently acquired her wardrobe. It was hard enough inspiring him to consider her as a friend.

It was so unfair. She'd spent years loving and caring for a husband, receiving little love and affection in return.

"I want to be somebody's baby," she muffled a cry within the folds of her drying towel. "I want someone who will make me feel beautiful things. *Like Garry does.*"

IF ANYTHING WAS bothering Amanda, Garry certainly wouldn't have guessed it. Her jaunty nature was in full swing when she returned to start her day with him. She bribed him with her delicious Florida key lime pie if he would sit down at the utility table and accept thirty minutes of therapy. He said he'd do it if he could eat the pie first. It was a deal, though not before she promised to make a banana cream pie next, his all-time favorite.

He was sorry he ever sat down for therapy; he huffed and growled when he was unable to pick up a button with his right hand.

"It is a little button, Mr. Danzlo," she consoled. "Sometimes, that's even a problem for me." Garry scowled, but he didn't flip the table over. Later, Amanda had him perform exercises in his chair. During his late afternoon bath, while she sat on the floor outside the bathroom door, she discussed exercises he might perform in bed. She believed if he'd allow himself to try, he could raise himself up and down from his chair and even transfer to and from the bed all by himself. When it came time for bed, she challenged him to do it.

"Not tonight," he told her.

"But I know you can do it," she urged. "If you'd just—"

"Don't," he said.

Amanda was silent, then she sighed. "Of course. Maybe tomorrow." She left his room with disappointment in her eyes.

He felt a tug at his heartstrings. *Was he afraid of finding out he couldn't do it, or finding out that he could?* He was uncertain about a lot of things.

He lay in bed awake for a long time, his thoughts on Amanda. Somehow he had found comfort in her touch, peace in her voice. She had a way of making him smile when he least felt like smiling. And when he fought, a lot of times she'd win, and it felt good. He realized his headaches had lessened considerably. He was actually starting to find joy in his day.

*Then here comes the night,* he mused, *bringing in the loneliness, the nightmares.*

He was afraid to go to sleep tonight. Afraid of dreaming. He suddenly remembered Daphne, her flight likely delayed till morning. He had completely forgotten to mention to Nicolas she was coming. But his whole day had been busy, Amanda filling every moment of it.

Lying alone, he realized he wanted a woman this hour. He wanted a soft body next to his own. Someone he could hold and touch, kiss and make love to.

He tossed and turned for a long while. Then, sleep finally came.

He stood in darkness, in the same dream, the same alley. He looked to his left, to his right, in back of him, in front. He saw nothing, no one. He was alone. He was always alone.

He fell to his knees, burying his face in his hands. He wanted to die.

Then she touched him—the woman, his intimate muse. And his heart stilled. He closed his eyes and drank in her warmth. *Oh, my lady,* he cried, then took her hand from his shoulder and brought her slender fingers to his lips. He caressed them, tasted them, slowly nourishing his hunger. He tried to rise from his knees that he might take her into his arms, but the force in his dream seemed to have nailed him to the ground. The urge threatened to take his sanity as he struggled against an overwhelming need, quaking within his loins.

But she was touching him, and suddenly, it was all that mattered.

He pulled her around in front of him while standing firm on his knees. His hands took hold of her possessively, lovingly, one arm around the back of her thighs, another around the curve of her hips. His face nuzzled against the softness of her abdomen. He reveled in the magic of her fingers running gently through his hair, radiating warmth to his trembling limbs. He held her tightly, afraid she'd be snatched away. As she began to sing sweet music, filling him with the love he craved, she disappeared. He opened his eyes, his body cold, his arms empty. Yet he wasn't alone. The black caped figure stood before him, framed in the dark. He waited for the maniacal laughter to mock him like it had so many times in the night, but no laughter came. Then the caped figure stepped forward from the shadows, revealing himself for the first time.

*Papa.*

Fire began to consume the old man—blood, sweat, and tears pouring down his aged face as the flames rose higher. He was screaming in pain.

Horrified, Garry screamed with him.

"Wake up. Shhh. It's okay. Just a dream."

Amanda's voice came softly through his sleep, bringing him out from his torment. Garry awoke with fright, springing forward into her arms. "Lie back down. You were dreaming," he heard her say in the dark. The only light in the room shone in from the bed lamp from across the hall where Amanda had been sleeping. For a brief second, he thought she was the woman from his dream, for no glasses were on her nose, her hair dark across her shoulders, and her face just a shadow in the dim lit room. Amanda's fingers tenderly brushed against his forehead, traveled to his temples, her thumbs sweeping across wetness on his skin.

Reality set in.

"That's right, Ms. Fields!" he said harshly, pushing her hands away. "It is okay. You can leave my room now."

A sharp pain pierced his temple, and he grabbed hold of his head with both hands. Amanda reached out and rested a hand atop his. "A migraine?"

"Yes," he said, his voice deeply hoarse, shaky. He was very aware of her hand on his. Then both her hands slid beneath his two, her palms lying warm against his temples, her fingers lightly meshed in his hair. He clutched those soft hands beneath his, meaning to jerk them away, yet something kept them there.

"Shhh, say no more. Relax," she soothed. "Close your eyes and allow yourself to feel the healing energy flowing from my hands. It's okay. Completely natural, I promise you."

Was this the "channeled" energy he had heard Amanda speak of to Nicolas at the supper table the other night? Garry had refused to speak to her that night, avoiding her face. He'd made no comment aloud, though silently he had sworn that she'd never practice that quack magic stuff on him, yet already his hands were loosening their hold on hers. They finally let go and fell limply to the bed. He had wanted to refuse those hands, but the strange heat emanating from her palms felt so calming on his skin, relaxing, her touch so tender and compassionate.

AMANDA LISTENED AS Garry's respirations became more even and less labored. He was resting peacefully now, a light snore to his breathing. She attempted to move off the bed, stood, but his hand reached for hers. "Stay," she heard him whisper in the dark. Her heart leaped, and then beat rapidly in her throat. She couldn't see his face. Was he awake or just dreaming? She moved closer toward the head of the bed, allowing scant light from the hall to cross his features. He looked to be asleep, yet his hand lightly tugged hers, urging her toward him. She realized she was scared, shaking, while some force within took her quietly to his bed where she sat down and leaned her back against the headboard. She stared down at his sleeping face beside her legs. She barely breathed. Yes, he was asleep. So why was she still sitting there?

Her gaze was drawn to his lips. She watched in fascination as they moved slightly with each breath he took. She began to imagine what they might feel like against her own—surely warm, tender, and deliciously sweet. So absorbed in her reverie, she reached out and placed a finger gently on them. He kissed it in his sleep. She had planned to pull back, but his mouth opened and captured her finger between his teeth. She didn't breathe, didn't move while he gnawed on it. She felt his tongue suddenly sucking, tasting. He captured her hand. Her finger slid from his mouth, his lips brushing the side of her hand, the back of her hand, just before his tongue slid slowly and sensually, in and out between her fingers.

Her senses cried out in pleasure, and in fear. She struggled with both, fear gaining victory fast that he'd wake up. He'd realize she had shamelessly let him make love to her hand, while he slept. Without her glasses and makeup on, he'd surely see her naked guilt.

*Guilty, guilty, guilty.*

She carefully slipped her fingers from Garry's hand, but in the process, he plopped over and nestled his head into her lap. He had pinned her down, his left arm draping off the bed. Her head fell back against the headboard, her eyes closed, her heart banged in her chest while her mind pleaded for it to calm down.

Hours had passed when Amanda awoke from slumber, an uncomfortable ache in her back, a strange heaviness on her legs. Her fingers stirred, sifting through soft strands of hair.

Something moved on her legs. Her eyes flew open.

She focused on Garry's head still lying in her lap, his left hand cupping her right thigh. A bare thigh. Her robe had come undone, her knee-length flannel gown raised to accommodate his hold. She panicked as she glanced at the clock on the night table. 5:25 a.m. Nicolas was sure to be up soon. She had to go, and now.

As she tried to speculate just how she'd be maneuvering her body from Garry's, her gaze took an ambling walk along the whole length of his frame. From those sandy locks on his head, down to the curve of his neck, and across those broad shoulders that expanded beyond the width of both her legs, her prying eyes took stock of that solid arm clasping her leg and that smooth, firm skin along his back. Wending on past the waistband of his thin boxer shorts, it was there that her point of concentration dropped like an anchor—the light filtering across the bed giving her a radiant, well-defined view of his buttocks.

Her eyes squeezed shut. *I've got to get out of here!*

Easing his hand into hers, she tried lifting her leg in hopes of sliding out his hand and moving it safely away. Garry groaned, his nose nuzzling deeper into her lap, his lips brushing and teasing her bare inner thigh. Lusciously wild sensations went up-up-up, down-down-down, her love-neglected body. Heat prickled her skin as his face found a more comfortable spot higher upon her lap. His right hand slid up her thigh, his left cupping just below her butt.

Amanda was swinging on stars. She'd fall any second now, she just knew. The process of eliminating his body from hers called for a lot of patience, slow cautious moves, and prayer.

Somehow, within seconds, she was out of Garry's arms and off the bed. Reaching gently for the covers bundled at his feet, she covered Garry's near naked form. Amanda rushed to her room, shut the door, locked it and fell across the bed in exhausted relief. *Good grief!* She couldn't believe how lucky she was. If Garry had awakened, she'd have big explaining to do. She'd spent days trying to teach him to trust her. If he discovered what he didn't know, it would blow every bit of that trust out the door. And she'd be flying out alongside it.

The disguise was for Garry's wellbeing, she reminded herself. A precautionary measure to ensure less trouble from Daphne. Less trouble? Just how much should she expect from this girlfriend of Garry's?

"Oh, how do I get myself into these things!" she scolded, her fists beating a tattoo on the bed.

DAPHNE DIMONT EMERGED from the shadows, murder playing havoc in her mind as she moved stealthily across the floor of Garry's bedroom. She stopped at the doorway and glared at the door across the hall, her mind steaming with vague images of the woman who'd just removed herself from Garry's arms.

Only moments before, Daphne had been ready to tear the throat out of the woman she'd found in Garry's bed. So angry, she had hissed, causing the other woman to stir from sleep. That's when she'd quickly stepped back from the light shining in from the hall, deciding to wait and watch before making any rash decision. She'd made many mistakes in the past by acting too hastily in delicate situations. She'd not make one this time.

Her suspicions had begun as she'd passed the rose-colored room on her way in—the empty bed, the ruffled bedcovers, the glasses on the table next to the bed lamp. She was now glad she'd hid in the shadows in Garry's room, holding back her temper to watch.

So this was the new nurse, the one who had shortened her trip. Daphne knew Melissa would find another nurse. She just didn't think it would be this soon. That bitch sister of Garry's was always spoiling things for her. She'd received a call from a dear friend yesterday. Garry had a new addition to his house. Melissa and Dan had moved back to L.A. Daphne knew Melissa would not have left Garry without solely trusting someone to care for him.

Who was this nurse? What kind of relationship was she having with Garry? He must be getting along with her, or else she wouldn't still be here.

Well, Daphne had gotten rid of one nurse. She could get rid of another, if this one posed to be a threat. But she would have to play this one by ear. The scene she'd come upon appeared innocent, evident by the surprise on the woman's face upon awakening—the panic, the cautious moves made to disengage herself from Garry. But Daphne had also noticed the way she had gazed upon his body. She was possibly pretty, though it was hard to tell with the scant light available in the room.

Anger started to build, Daphne's mood already foul after taking a midnight flight to this place she despised. Upon arriving, her luggage had mistakenly gotten on another plane, the airline promising to deliver it personally to her by the noon hour. She'd wasted hours at the airport, and another hour to get to this godforsaken hole in the woods, not to mention the snow and ice she had tracked through once the limo dropped her off. By that time, she was ready to bang on the door, but luckily she remembered the extra key beneath the ceramic pot on the porch. She had spied Nicolas placing it there the last time she'd visited while he was clearing the porch of snow and ice.

The rivulet of light beneath the nurse's door quickly flicked off.

Daphne stepped back, turned and faced Garry's bed. She could barely make out his face, but she heard his restful breathing. Closing his door, she quietly approached him, discarding her hose and panties. Raising the hem of her dress to her waist, she sat down on the bed, her back against the headboard as the other woman had sat. She reached for Garry's left hand—the unscarred one—and gently placed it midway between her bare legs. Garry groaned in his sleep, repositioning his head against her. She guided his hand higher between her thighs until his thumb was snug and warm against her wet crotch.

Daphne laid her head against the wall, closed her eyes and smiled.

# 14.

# WHO'S BEEN SLEEPING
# IN MY BED?

GARRY WAS DREAMING, his mind half-conscious of the body next to his own—a woman, her fingers kneading his shoulder while his own weeded through her spongy curls, her womanhood warm and wet in the palm of his hand. Somewhere in the midst of his dream, amongst the smell of expensive perfume, he breathed a lighter fragrance. Tasted it on his lips. *Soft rose.*

Consciousness jerked him from sleep, his hand and torso leaping back from the flesh he'd been touching. He fell flat on his back, confused, his eyes wide as he stared at the woman beside him.

"Daphne," he said, his voice raspy, his heart pounding while his mind spoke a different name.

"Yes, darling, it's me," she said, reaching for his left hand. She brought it to her lips, inhaling her own scent. Her tongue licked his dampened palm. "Did I startle you? You look surprised to see me. If I didn't know better, I'd think you expected to see another woman." She took his left hand and cupped her breast with it. "Tell me you missed me, Garry."

He gazed at the nipple growing taut against her silk blouse. She guided his thumb across it. "I missed you," he said huskily, caught in the spell of her beauty.

"That pleases me, darling. For that, you can have me for many days to come."

Garry's brow lifted. "You're staying? Longer than a couple of days?" She neglected to mention that bit of news on the phone yesterday. He'd have to prepare Nicolas. And the one across the hall. "Amanda," he whispered unconsciously, his gaze darting to the door.

"Did you say something, darling?"

"No," he said, returning his attention. "I was thinking… what a surprise to wake up to."

But his thoughts were far from Daphne. Last night whirled in his head. The nightmare. Amanda. When had she left his room? She had come, hadn't she? He couldn't seem to remember. Pieces of a dream came crashing through his head, confusing reality with fiction. *The faceless woman.* She touched him in the night, her fingers combing through his hair while he held her body in his arms and her skin against his face.

"Garry, come kiss me," Daphne commanded. "I'm starving for attention."

He focused on those blue sultry eyes of hers, and then those glistening lips she'd just licked. He swallowed hard. She was sexy. Very sexy. "You've got my attention," he said. "Come get the kiss."

"Garry," she pouted, "you can meet me halfway." She bent toward him with parted lips, the open collar of her silk blouse revealing a pleasant view of décolletage. Garry's body fired with an ache. It wasn't long before his lonely heart gave in.

NICOLAS' FEET BURNED holes in the kitchen floor, his furious pacing making the dog antsy and whiny. Peeking around the entrance door for the hundredth time, Nicolas couldn't understand why Amanda wasn't up yet. He'd give her five more minutes and if she didn't come walking out that bedroom, he'd go knocking on her door. It was eight o'clock. She never slept this late. There were plans to make. Desperate plans.

Daphne couldn't have come at a worst time. And just when things were starting to look up. If it hadn't been for the dog growling beside his bed sometime before daybreak, Nicolas wouldn't have awakened and realized Daphne was in the house. Bagel had rules when it came to Daphne. She knew to stay away, forbidden to attack her. Anyone else who wasn't supposed to come through the front door would've met with a fight and a howling bark loud enough to wake the entire household.

If Nicolas didn't know better, he'd think Garry Danzlo neglected to inform him of Daphne's early visit on purpose, just to get things off track. But no, Mr.

Danzlo probably forgot. Yesterday had been busy, too fun, the man's mind solely on Amanda. Nicolas had to make sure things stayed that way.

AMANDA FLUNG OFF her covers and jumped out of bed. How could she have overslept? She was doing a lot of dumb things lately. She should've gone to bed as soon as Garry was asleep. But she wanted to stay. Just a little longer, she kept telling herself. *Dumb, real dumb.* She ended up spending the night with the man.

After a quick shower, she donned a blouse of yellow-beige, topping it with a tent dress of muted browns and greens; it was lightly screen printed with a druidic oak tree holding intertwining Celtic knots. Soft leather flats with Celtic knots for buckles completed her outfit.

She stepped out of her room, determined she would not think about the happenings of last night, how it felt to have her fingers in Garry's mouth and the warm, erotic sensations he brought to her body with his lips and tongue. She'd not remember his hand beneath her naked thigh, or his face upon her nearly naked lap.

Her heart pounded as she faced Garry's door. She should check on him, she convinced herself. Unfortunately, she didn't hear Nicolas calling from down the hall, warning her not to go in. She opened the door.

"E-Excuse me, so sorry," she stuttered as the woman in Garry's arms tore from the kiss he was earnestly giving her. Amanda was stunned enough to find a woman in Garry's bed, but the real stunner was Daphne's exceptional beauty—her face creamy and flawless, her cheekbones faintly glowing and sculpted, winged eyebrows, plenty of lashes, and lips that were glossed with shocking pink. Daphne wore a silk blouse of the same color, and clearly no brassiere. But it was the eyes, a clear azure-like blue, that transfixed Amanda most; they were almost haunting to her way of thinking. She found Daphne's iridescent shimmer both glamorous and chic, and very intimidating. "I-I didn't know. I'll just leave—"

"Garry, who is this person?" Daphne stared at her with bewilderment, her brow arching.

"I didn't mean to disturb you," Amanda quickly said, flushed with embarrassment. "Please forgive me." She started out the door.

"Ms. Fields, wait."

She turned to Garry's attentive face. His gaze captured hers appreciatively.

When she looked at him, she relived the night, the tantalizing warmth of him. *Please don't make me stay*, she pleaded silently.

"I want you to meet Daphne. Daphne, this is Ms. Fields, my nurse."

"Ms. Fields?" Daphne said, as though the use of her surname was pleasing to her tongue. One side of her shiny lips curved upward. The odd gleam in her eye was patronizing.

Amanda looked away, looked at Garry. He was watching her with affection—or at least it appeared that way for his blues were sparkling with interest, somehow questioning, his expression soft, yet grave. Amanda felt her breath being sucked from her lungs, his gaze so intense and magnetizing. Was he remembering last night? Did he know she...?

"Darling, how rude, you're staring at the girl." Garry's face reddened.

"Mr. Danzlo had a dream last night," Amanda quickly said. "A nightmare and—"

"Well, of course. I should know. I was right here. I came in the nick of time to soothe him back to sleep."

Amanda, so dumbstruck at hearing the blatant lie was speechless.

"That was you last night, Daph? In this room?" He looked confused.

"Darling, I was here in this bed comforting you all night! Surely you don't think it—"

"Was me?" Amanda found nerve to say. She was angry with Daphne for lying, mad at Garry for not remembering she'd been with him the first part of the night. She didn't care about the rest of the night. She didn't want him to remember that half.

Daphne squealed with laughter and ruffled Garry's hair with her shiny, painted nails. "Darling, your nurse has such a sense of humor. Where ever did Melissa find her?" Her gaze shimmered upon Amanda with amusement. "Dear, girl, I would be terribly jealous if my Garry did even half the things to you as he did to me last night. Particularly, those things he was doing just moments ago." Her slender fingers caressed the curve of one breast causing one nipple to protrude hard against her slinky, silk blouse.

Embarrassment burned Amanda's cheeks. "Excuse me," she managed to say before running out the room. The door clicked shut.

"Daphne, you didn't have to be so..." Garry's focus was on the closed door.

"What, darling? I was just being honest. Something you value greatly in all people. And I must say, honestly, she's quite an ugly little chit, don't you agree?"

"She's different." For the life of him, he couldn't think of a better word. Remorse played heavily on his senses at the moment, guilt crushing his chest for all of his past degradations. "You embarrassed her."

"You think?" She laughed lightly. "Come, darling, it's anatomy. Nurses know it well. But you might be right. Sex might be one of her least knowledgeable subjects. I can't imagine any man who would want—"

"She was married once," he said abruptly. "Her husband died."

Daphne paused. "You sound like you're defending her, darling. Perhaps, you know something I don't." Uncomfortable fear was markedly on her face. Or was her hard angled brow and pursed lips signaling accusation?

"You think I slept with her while you were gone? Think I'm such a horny bastard that I'd go to bed with any woman as long as she provides a good screw? I don't want that kind of sex. I don't think she would either. Like I said, she's different. She's the type to want love first. You know anything about it?"

"Now, darling, you're being cruel. You know I love you."

His expression became serious. "Then show me, Daph. Make love to me now. Let me experience what real love feels like."

Daphne stiffened. "Garry, what's gotten into you? What's happened since I've been gone? You've never talked like this before." She got up from the bed and crossed the room to the draperies.

"That's right, walk away. You always do."

She turned on him. "I didn't walk away last night."

"Good God," he yelled, his mind befuddled with images—the woman in his dreams, Amanda, the black-caped figure, his father, Amanda, Daphne, Amanda. He looked at Daphne as though he'd gone mad, his mind torn between what he thought was real and what wasn't. "I don't remember last night. I thought I did, at least part of it, until I was told differently. I thought my nurse had... Damn, these dreams! They're driving me insane. I can't tell what's real anymore."

He stared hard at Daphne, fighting back tears he felt stinging his eyes. She stared back for a moment, and then slowly moved toward him.

"I'm real," she said softly, climbing back on the bed. She laid her hand against his left cheek. "I'm going to be here for you. Every day. Every night. I promise we'll make love again. I just need a little more time." Her eyes lowered, and so did her hand. She swallowed hard. "Your accident was such a shock, the injuries, and now seeing you like this, confined to the bed, miserable and unable to make your beautiful music. It's weighed on me heavily, Garry." She sighed with a tremor.

Garry's face softened. He lifted her chin and gazed into her tear-filled eyes. "I'm a fool, Daphne," he said. "And I'm sorry. I shouldn't expect—"

She kissed him hard on the lips, causing Garry to groan in pleasure. Then she raised on her knees and brought his head down against her chest, laying her head upon his. "Thank you, Garry. You're the only one who's ever believed in me. Who's ever given me a fair chance to prove what I can do. And who accepts me for what I can't do."

Garry squeezed her waist gently with his left arm, ignoring the discomfort in the rest of his body while holding his position. And then Daphne spoke again, her body tightening as she said each word.

"She's changing you, Garry. That nurse. I saw the way she looked at you, the way you looked at her." Garry froze against her. "You've been alone with her for days," she said. "She's playing on your vulnerability." Garry attempted to release himself from her embrace, but Daphne held him more securely. Was it love and concern he was feeling in those constricting arms? Or fear and jealousy? He wondered.

"She knows you're a man with physical needs, Garry," Daphne said with a soft warning. "She'll use it to obtain what she wants, something she never gets. She can't be trusted."

Daphne was touching his skin affectionately, the pad of her fingers brushing lightly down his bare back, then back up with a gentle rake of her nails. He couldn't remember when he'd ever experienced such tenderhearted affection from her. He gave into it easily, feeling cared for, cherished. "No. No one's changing me," he spoke against the buttons of her blouse. "You've got Ms. Fields all wrong. She's nothing to me. I'm nothing to her." His scarred right hand lay flaccid at his side. Daphne preferred it that way. He'd not touch her beautiful skin with his ugly, maimed hand.

# 15.

# EVERYTHING'S GONNA
# BE ALL RIGHT

NICOLAS STOOD QUIETLY in the kitchen, listening for Amanda to come out from her room. After visiting Garry, she had run inside it and locked herself in. Nicolas had fought the impulse to knock on her door, but realized she needed some time alone.

Her door opened, footsteps sounding from the hallway. Expecting her to stop at the first entrance into the kitchen, she continued on into the great family room to its far end. She entered the entrance, which led into the formal dining room. There she stopped before the large oval framed window. She stared out toward a cold, crystalline forest draped with icicles and snow.

"Miss Amanda," he whispered, now a short distance behind her. She turned, sending him a smile he knew must be forced. Her eyes were reddened, swollen. He sighed with compassion. "I know Miss Daphne upset you. I couldn't hear everything, but I'm sorry I was too late to warn you."

"No need for an apology," she said, stepping closer to him. She paused, her features strained with emotion. "She's very beautiful."

Nicolas studied her heavy features. He wanted to lift that sagging corner of her mouth, and convert her hopeless stare to the radiant one he'd come to admire. "Miss Daphne may be beautiful on the outside," he said, "but she's not always so on the inside. She has her moments of kindness, yes, but, well, I've seen things." He lowered his head. "It's not my place to gossip—"

"No, of course not," she said compassionately. "I wouldn't want you to—"

"Just know that Mr. Danzlo isn't always aware." He lifted his eyes. "He's known to be quite gullible sometimes, I'm afraid. Too trusting, particularly when it comes to a pretty woman." He offered a weak smile as he gazed into Amanda's face. He noted that she was wearing less makeup around her eyes, less pronounced on her cheeks. He wanted to say something to her, to ask. He opened his mouth to do so, but the words didn't come. He didn't know just how to begin.

Amanda turned back to the window. "Daphne doesn't really seem to be his type," she said, her voice cracking. "I mean, I really thought Melissa had exaggerated when she'd told me that Daphne could be so…"

"Insensitive, conniving?"

Amanda nodded. Her eyes were glassy as she faced him again. "We were getting so close to our goal, Nicolas. We were accomplishing good things, and now we'll be losing touch. The past week's work will be lost."

Amanda was suddenly in his arms, squeezing him, weeping upon his shoulder.

"Please don't cry," he said heavily, his hands gently patting her back. "We still have time, days ahead of us. We'll think of something together."

Amanda moved from his compassionate arms, wiping her tears. She attempted a smile. "I love you, Nicolas. You've become such a wonderful friend since my arrival. I usually have more control over my emotions. I don't know what's wrong with me. I guess I didn't sleep so well last night, or something."

Nicolas wanted to ask her about that something, for he sensed there was a story to tell, but another question was on his mind.

"Come, Miss Amanda. Let's have a cup of coffee. I'll fix you something to eat."

They walked into the kitchen area, sitting at the table with two cups of coffee, fresh and hot. They gave in to the blues, minutes passing quietly by.

"You could take her legs," Nicolas said at last, "and I, her arms. We'll throw her out into the blistering snow and lock the door behind her."

Amanda giggled. "I don't think so, Nicolas. She'd probably sue us for messing up her hair."

Nicolas' laughter bounced off the walls. He had to hold on to his seat to keep from falling off. Calming, he took a sip of coffee, his mind on the situation at hand. "I'm thinking Miss Daphne won't endure staying here very long. She hates rustic living, meaning this house, and Colorado. She's not fond of the dog either. If we play our cards right, we could make things quite miserable for her. She may be here for Mr. Danzlo, but he doesn't always give her the attention she craves. I give her no more than a week at the most."

Amanda's brows knitted in horror. "A whole week? Nicolas, we can't sit around and do nothing till then! Mr. Danzlo can't stay in bed for days. We'll have to fight back. Make a plan. Yes, we'll plot a doozy!"

"Now you're talking!" Nicolas said with enthusiasm. "I knew you'd come through. I'm truly thankful you came into Mr. Danzlo's life. You're a blessing in disguise."

Amanda choked on her coffee, sputtering and coughing while Nicolas was quick to provide a napkin and some hearty pats on her back. So it was true! He was finally going to say what he'd been wanting to for days. "Miss Amanda—"

"Nicolas," she said, jumping from her chair, crossing the room. Her nervousness showed with every step she took. "Now, let's see. There's got to be some way to—"

"Tell me why," Nicolas said smoothly.

"Why? What?"

Nicolas smiled. "Why you're hiding behind those unusual clothes you wear, the make-up, and those phony glasses you've got up on your head and wear only when you're around the boss."

"Pardon?" she asked, her hands now at her sides, balling and crinkling her dress. "They're reading glasses. They really are. I just keep them handy."

"Miss Amanda, you don't have to explain or pretend anymore. I was completely baffled at first, but I'm beginning to understand. Anyone can tell you have a pretty face."

"Oh, Nicolas, that's awful! Am I that transparent? I wanted to tell you, but Melissa was afraid it would get back to Dan. She knew he wouldn't approve. I told Melissa—"

"I knew it. Melissa was the only logical explanation I could imagine. Miss Daphne would be one matter, but also to avoid Mr. Danzlo from a big setback. I'm sure Melissa told you how embarrassment, humiliation, and intimidation played parts during one of her hires."

"Oh, Nicolas, if you saw through me, surely Mr. Danzlo—"

"No, he hasn't. Believe me, I can read him like a book. If he was even a bit suspicious, I'd know." Nicolas smiled.

However, now that the truth was out, he began to weigh the true consequences of the situation. While Melissa, with all good intentions, tried to play her cards more safely this time around, it was possible she'd made the biggest mistake she could ever have made in her brother's life.

But she wouldn't know this. Melissa knew nothing about her father's deceit—

that Jonathan Danzlo was none other than that same old man—Jake Fayman—whom Garry Danzlo had befriended two weeks prior to the suicide. It had crossed his mind more than once to reveal the secret to Amanda, for what if it was the key to helping him? He realized he could never share that secret with her now. How upsetting for her to know she was reenacting the same incognito, the very act of betrayal that sent Danzlo to his doom four months ago?

"Don't worry yourself," he consoled, placing a comforting hand on Amanda's shoulder. "The most the boss will do is eventually realize you have a pretty face. I think he already knows you have a pretty heart."

"Oh Nicolas, you say the dearest things. I so appreciate that. Now that I've gotten myself into this, I see no way out. If I told Mr. Danzlo now, just when he's starting to trust me, he'd never forgive me. I suppose I could simply start dressing differently, tell him I'm giving myself a makeover, but now there's Daphne to contend with…" Amanda laid a hand against her chest, a wrinkle furrowing her forehead. "She hates me, Nicolas. I felt it the moment she gazed at me with those haunting blue eyes of hers. She's proven how much trouble she can make. I'm stuck like this, Nicolas. At least until she's gone. And that's only if she decides to leave. God help me if she ever discovers I'm hiding behind this ruse. She'd make sure that Mr. Danzlo never trusted me, and he'd hate me too."

Nicolas sighed with empathy. "Keep faith. Things will work out." Pausing, he said, "Miss Melissa called this morning while you were still in bed… *oversleeping*."

Amanda wiggled at the emphasis on the word. She took a sip of coffee avoiding his face. Something had happened last night, Nicolas realized. Danzlo's restless sleep and moaning in the night had awakened him. Intending to get up, he'd heard Amanda and changed his mind. One wall separated his and Danzlo's room. It wasn't quite sound proof. He'd heard Danzlo demanding she leave, but Nicolas didn't think she did, for then came a whisper, and all was quiet. So quiet, Nicolas had fallen back to sleep. Had she gone back to bed? Where was she when Daphne came? He'd heard two doors shut before daybreak, one that creaked—Amanda's, and later, the quiet one—Danzlo's.

"Nicolas. Yoo-hoo." Amanda waved her hand in front of his face. "You said Melissa called. Did she ask for me?"

"Oh, yes, but I didn't want to wake you. So upset about Miss Daphne's unwelcomed visit, I blurted out the terrible news to her. I think it was a mistake. I believe we'll be having another visitor soon."

"Melissa's coming back? Oh, Nicolas, with the three of us, we can't lose."

Nicolas opened his mouth and then shut it. He wouldn't tell Amanda that Melissa's visit could mean bigger trouble.

"Everything is going to be all right. And you know what the best part is? My burden is lessened just knowing I don't have to pretend with you anymore. Maybe someday I won't have to pretend with Garry either. Maybe by some miracle, he'll understand, too."

She smiled and hugged her own shoulders, not realizing she'd spoken Danzlo's first name aloud, but Nicolas noticed.

"Let's start making plans right now, Nicolas. Get this show on the road."

"Just what I was thinking. Mr. Danzlo, after today, watch out. Here comes big fun."

Amanda stood up from her chair. "And we're ready for it, honey," she added, dancing her feet to a rhythmical beat.

# 16.

# BREAK DOWN THE DOOR

A LOUD SHRIEK vibrated the house. Then Garry heard a mournful cry, followed by a long, drawn out scream. Garry bounced up in bed. "Daphne!" he bellowed, "God help. What's going on?" *Where is Nicolas? Amanda?* He attempted to move off the bed, but his weak right side made the task too difficult. He cursed himself for being lame, cursed his inability to provide a rescue.

The screaming stopped. The house became morbidly quiet. Then great stomping sounded as though an angry Godzilla was treading through his home. The unknown assailant was heading straight for his bedroom. Garry's heart pounded like a sledgehammer, knocking the breath from his lungs. They were doomed. *They were all doomed!*

The door slammed open. Godzilla stood at the threshold.

"THOSE TWO… LOW-DOWN… PEA-BRAINED BARBARIANS! They should be shot! My beautiful luggage, my beautiful clothes. All ruined!"

Garry stared, stupefied.

"They did it on purpose, I tell you! Left this house knowing my luggage was due to arrive. It's a blizzard outside and your so-called servants are gallivanting around in that bulldozer you call a truck while my luggage sits on the porch stacked up like stiff snowmen. It'll take days for those suitcases to thaw. Oh, what shall I do? I'll have to lug those frozen things in myself. I'll ruin my nails. I'll sue that airline. I'll kill those two culprits when they come back. Oh, I hate them, I hate them, I *hate* them!"

Daphne turned, storming down the hallway, unleashing a string of curses.

Garry lay back on his pillow. He should've awakened Daphne when he'd heard the knock on the front door. But she'd been up all night, needing sleep, desperately, she had said. Besides, he was sure Nicolas had taken care of the matter once the knocking had stopped. He knew they were outside—Nicolas *and* Amanda. He had dozed off sometime after Daphne had fallen asleep, awakened by her loud snores. The hacking of an ax and its echo resounding off the forest trees outdoors had him sleepless thereafter. He had imagined his two employees cutting and stacking wood, apparently having a fun time doing it from all the chatter and laughter that went on outside his window. Their voices had affected him. *She* was affecting him. Ms. Fields. *Amanda.*

Why did he keep seeing her in his mind, feeling as though she had... *She had what?* Touched him last night? That he had touched her? But Daphne had laid with him in the night, and Amanda didn't deny this. So why had he felt disappointed? What if Daphne was right? What if his little Ms. Fields wasn't so sweet and innocent after all? The woman had certainly proved her intelligence, shown her crafty skills in the short week he had known her.

A week? Not even a week. He'd known her only four days. He felt he'd known her a lifetime. How could one person affect another so strongly so fast? He realized he missed her. He missed her funny face and cute personality. But that was all. That had to be all. She didn't have anything else to miss.

*She knows she's unattractive, darling. She knows you're a man with physical needs. I fear she's trying to take you away from me.*

Laughter burst from Garry's mouth, the memory of Daphne's words suddenly hilarious. He lay on his pillow gazing up at the cedar planked ceiling, his mind thinking *Bozo*, his nurse clown, smothering him with yards of ugly cloth. "Ridiculous!" he said aloud.

But even as he spoke the word, he felt heat grow in his groin, his male organ doing a shimmy beneath the sheet.

NICOLAS AND AMANDA spent a wonderful afternoon together. They hadn't stuck around to find out what actually happened to Daphne's luggage. They dared not look on the front porch, just in case it sat there when they fired up the Land Rover and rounded the front of the log home. Buckled up tight, they bounded out into a snowy field, four-wheeling. Nicolas driving boldly, Amanda laughing at this adventurous side to Nicolas she'd never seen. Afterward came a trip into town, lunch at the *Down To Earth Cafe*, a visit to the post office to check the box for mail, and then on for a serious shopping spree. They got home in plenty of time to prepare the dinner meal.

Now late evening, Amanda sat musing at the writing desk in her room, her elbows atop it, her chin in her hands. Nicolas and she had expected a rip-roaring fight from Daphne once they had returned that late afternoon, but Daphne hadn't acted the littlest bit peeved. Had Garry talked with her, calmed her down? Did he have that much of an effect on her? And why wasn't he mad? A half-dozen suitcases lay sprawled open all over the great room, thawing out when they had gotten home. Amanda, feeling guilty, offered to take Daphne's clothes to the cleaners the next day.

"How marvelous, you dear girl," Daphne had said when Nicolas and she delivered dinner to Garry's room. "Garry will take the expense from yours and Nicolas' wages. Naughty deeds must be paid for."

Whether it was the fact that Daphne had succeeded in humiliating them both in front of Garry, or that she was reminded of Daphne's underhandedness that morning, Amanda was unable to hold her tongue. "Yes, naughty deeds often backfire, too. Even for those who manipulate the truth for their own personal gain."

Her shrewd remark sent hot pink streaking across Daphne's cheeks. Amanda had ignored it while placing a tray on Garry's lap. Her fingers brushed briefly against his and she suddenly found herself captured by his stare, one marked with curiosity and confusion. She wasn't too sure he'd actually heard what she'd said, a distant gleam shining strangely in his eye. But Daphne had certainly heard. An eruption of sneezes had her escaping to the bathroom. Amanda had decided to take her leave too. She was almost to the door when Garry called after her. She turned and smiled at him. "Sweet Dreams, Mr. Danzlo." And then she walked out the door.

She wondered what he must be thinking now, and too, what other lie Daphne had conjured up to cover her guilt. The loud muffling voices from across the hall lasted only ten minutes. All she knew for sure was that Garry had wasted a whole entire day in bed. "Well, he's getting up tomorrow," Amanda said aloud, slamming her hand on her desk. She gazed down at the letters she had slapped—one from Robbie, and the other from the Medical Director of Good Samaritan Hospital— Doc Conyers, a respected colleague and friend. She reopened his letter, rereading the postscript: *Your friend Eddie Chandler came by the hospital, said he'd been trying to reach you. I told him you were up north visiting a relative and you'd be back in a couple of months.*

Amanda picked up a pen, trying to ignore the uneasiness she felt concerning Eddie. Eddie knew she had no living relative up north. Her aunt had passed away years ago. Doc had lied and Eddie was sure to know. But it was best to keep her whereabouts a secret—not only for her own sake and privacy, but for Garry's as well.

Living with a celebrity had a way of stirring a slew of enquiring minds. Reporters were always ready to provide their avid readers with the juiciest of entertainment. Thus far, her presence in the Danzlo home was unknown; Melissa had taken great precaution to ensure that. However, that didn't stop one persistent photographer today in town. He knew exactly who Nicolas was. Thank goodness she'd been bundled up warmly—scarf, woolen hat, her bulky coat. And with her glasses on, she'd looked no more than a timid youth.

"Please, a little privacy with my niece today," Nicolas had pleaded, a protective arm around her shoulder as she'd snuggled her face against his coat. She'd called him Uncle Nick the rest of the day.

Luckily, Amanda had some experience with dodging photographers and reporters. Her recent past surrounding Paul's death was nothing to be proud of. Who knew what trashy stories might develop in print if her name ever went public again? There had been a lot of scandalous articles in the Palm Beach Post last year, relating Paul's association with organized crime in Miami, Fort Lauderdale and the Margate areas. He owed much money. She'd lost everything then, even the recently acquired private practice she'd worked so hard to obtain—her dream of beginning a healing arts center ruined. Paul had ridiculed her new interests in the healing arts. He'd called her a *visionary crackpot* while she educated herself those last years of his life. The only support she had had was Eddie.

After Paul's death, Eddie had offered the funds she needed to keep her practice open. But she had refused him. He was also the one who had managed to keep reporters at bay where she was concerned. He had provided her the legal help during that trying time. She hadn't wanted his help, but Eddie had begged for the chance to prove he was sorry for that one day he'd lost control, to show her he was the same caring guy she'd known since junior high school. A popular and brilliant defense lawyer in Palm Beach, she had accepted his help, realizing that she had no one else to turn to.

She didn't want to need anyone. And she certainly didn't want to be dependent on Eddie for help, for money, or anything else. Why couldn't he accept that? She was surviving without him.

With pen in hand, Amanda responded to Doc's letter, briefly describing her adventures in Colorado and the bit of trouble she was running into with Garry's girlfriend. She avoided any response concerning Eddie, writing about the weather and Nicolas instead. Closing her letter, she signed her name, already formulating a creative idea for Robbie's storybook letter.

She tapped her pen lightly on the desk's surface, her left hand resting in the lap of her icy pink robe. Nicolas had argued with her for ten minutes in front of the store window today where the elegant gown and robe had hung on display. He informed her it was a "must get" item and if she didn't get it, he was going to buy it for her as a "cheer" gift—the perfect thing to make her feel beautiful. He dared her, and she finally stopped arguing, went in and bought the thing. She was such a sucker when it came to a challenge.

Finally, she began Robbie's imaginative letter. A rap sounded on the door. "It's me, Miss Amanda. If you've gone to bed, I won't disturb you."

"Nicolas, come in." Walking across the room, Amanda unlocked the door. Holding onto the creative thought in her head, she quickly returned to her desk. Nicolas closed the door behind him, Amanda busily writing. "I'll be right with you," she said without looking up. "Let me finish writing this one thing." When she finished, she laid the pen down with a smile. Robbie would definitely be laughing at those lines. Standing, she swung around, her face without glasses or deceiving makeup.

Nicolas stood speechless.

"Is something wrong?" she asked. "Is Mr. Danzlo all right?"

"No. Yes. Miss Amanda…" Nicolas said mesmerized. "I've never seen a lovelier woman."

Amanda glanced down making sure her robe was securely fastened. It was. "Thank you, Nicolas," she said graciously. "In these days of hideous confinement, it's nice to hear a compliment. I'd forgotten you hadn't seen me without—"

"If Mr. Danzlo could see you now, I assure you Miss Daphne would not be in this house."

Nicolas' words sent a tingle of excitement racing through her body. Her face felt hot. She sat down before she fell down. Nicolas mistook her reaction.

"Miss Amanda," he spoke hurriedly, "be assured the boss would not take advantage of you. I didn't mean to sound as if, well, *if he only knew!*" A gale of laughter suddenly exploded, Nicolas unable to retain his laughter. Amanda didn't see the humor. "I'm sorry," he said, trying to stifle himself, "but Mr. Danzlo would not be the patient he is if—"

Laugher exploded again.

"Nicolas, what's so funny?" She started to laugh, too.

"I can just see that first scene in the bathroom all over again," he said between hard chuckles. "Mr. Danzlo thought he was embarrassed then! If he knew he had a pretty nurse standing beside him at the toilet, I don't think he—"

Amanda bubbled over. Their loud laughter rang throughout the house.

Garry's voice suddenly roared through the walls, "There are people in this house who would like to sleep!"

Nicolas locked the door, their laughter growing harder after Garry's loud reprimand. Within seconds, Daphne was in the hall, one hand banging on Amanda's door, another trying the knob. "Nicolas! What are you doing locked in there with that woman. Come out here this instant."

Silence.

Nicolas and Amanda exchanged glances, their mouths open in outrageous surprise. Shrills of laughter blasted out spontaneously. Moments later, they heard Daphne's steps retreat, the door across the hall slamming so hard the house shook. Amanda released a held breath, and then whispered, "Nicolas, no telling what they suspect we're doing in here. What do you say, you and I discuss tomorrow's adventure?"

"Just what I came in for! I say let's get on with it."

"Okay, this is what we'll do…"

GARRY HEFTED HIMSELF against the headboard of the bed, his shoulder jolting against cold wood as Daphne slammed the door. She approached him, halting at the bed.

"What did I tell you, darling? That nurse is trouble. She's corrupting your poor Nicolas. I finally gave into you when you defended her about the ordeal concerning my luggage, but what about this evening? She deliberately tried to stir things up between us—flipping words around in that clever little head of hers. Somehow her humiliation became my own. If that's not manipulative, than what is? How can you trust someone like that?"

Garry was lost for words; his mind had been reeling in circles for the past two hours. He kept reliving flashes of the dream he had dreamed the night before, brought on by one brief touch he'd shared with Amanda. Why couldn't he recall what she'd said before Daphne had gone into a sneezing fit—a habit he'd witnessed only once before, triggered by emotional upset too overwhelming for Daphne to handle. Whatever Daphne *thought* she had heard Amanda say triggered the sneezes; however, he couldn't believe that Amanda would ever intentionally hurt anyone. And certainly not to the extent Daphne was suggesting.

"I understand you want to trust her, Garry. She's actually made some progress with your rehabilitation, and for that I am grateful. But something just isn't right here. What about the luggage? Does that little evil deed sound like something your loyal and obedient butler would do? Nicolas is in her room, right now, with the door locked. You know what they're doing."

Garry blinked, pushing back anger. "They're laughing, Daphne. They're just friends."

"Laughing?" she said, raising her ear to the peaceful quiet that now filled the house. Garry swallowed his discomfiture. A second passed and the creaking of Amanda's bed sounded as though two people had sat upon it. "Cozy little friends, aren't they?"

Garry wasn't sure if his rising ire derived from Daphne's accusations about Amanda Fields or the fact that his butler was locked in the other room with his nurse. But of course they weren't doing anything behind closed doors. Just like he wasn't doing anything behind closed doors with Daphne. He suddenly wished the two across the hall knew that.

"We're all innocent, Daphne," he said.

Daphne observed him questionably. "Now, what's that supposed to mean? I haven't accused you of any offense, particularly a sexual one. Why, you probably can't even—"

Daphne's face grew pink, her last words an obvious slip of the tongue.

"Probably can't what?" Garry's voice deepened.

"Darling, I didn't mean—"

He moved away from the touch she attempted. "Tell the truth. You don't think I'm capable of getting it up. No wait, that can't be it. I've managed to get it up several times for you, you just weren't interested. So it must be you think I can't keep it up. I'm not man enough to get the entire job done. I'd be unable to fulfill the duty like a *real* man without being sloppy about it? I mean, after all, I am a cripple."

"Garry, you're being ugly. I just meant… well, I know it would be hard for you to…"

"Perform," he finished for her. "Let's keep it nice and clean."

Daphne's brow rose. "She's really changed you, hasn't she? No more bad words? She's worked her little powers on you good this past week. No cursing. My, my."

"Jealous? Or just changing the subject?" Silence fell. "Must be changing the subject."

Daphne stared at him a moment, then lowered her eyes. "Garry, let's not argue," she said. Raising her eyelids slowly, a tear slid down one cheek. "It's not like us to be so harsh with each other. I know you've had a lot on your mind, and yes, I am jealous. Another woman has been taking up your time, time I should have with you. Time I want with you."

She eased herself onto the bed, Garry watching, warily, waiting for her next move.

She placed her fingers on his face. His eyes closed, his body fighting a tender storm as her soft fingers moved down the side of his neck, across his bare chest. He wanted to stop her, for the moment wouldn't last. It never lasted, for she always walked away, never finishing what she started. Yet he sat still against the headboard.

"I want to move you like she moves you," he heard her say. Her fingers brushed across his abdomen, back and forth, then lower. Garry groaned. "She has a professional skill I don't have." Daphne softly stroked him. "Intelligence from working with a variety of men in need. I'm sure she's even worked with those in psychiatric wards. Melissa would be sure to choose the perfect nurse for her dear brother, considering she thinks you've got some problem of the mind."

Garry's eyelids flew open, sobering quickly from his lusts. He snatched her wrist from his skin. "Just what are you getting at? You think I've got mental problems?"

"Oh, darling, no," she soothed, raising his hand to her lips. She kissed it softly. "I think nothing of the sort. It's Melissa who made the comment to me before she took that trip to Florida. I was only making a point."

"What kind of point?" He reclaimed his hand from her grasp, lowering it to the bed.

"Oh, come, darling, you're not getting mad, are you? We were having fun a little while ago." She smiled, wetting her lips while she reached out and flicked his nipple with the pad of her thumb. He shook with the delicate touch, unable to hold in his smile as she teased him.

Daphne smiled. "I was only trying to defend my uncertainties concerning your nurse," she explained. "Like I said, she has a professional skill. Where I have only beauty, she has the brains. And if she can move the mind, she can easily wrap you around her little finger, even though she's unattractive to the eye." She sighed, grazing her nails lightly across his chest. "Beauty's not everything you know, and that's why I'm so worried." Her mouth formed a soft pout. "The woman even has experience in working with the physically handicapped—she's probably even gone to bed with a few. It's her job to know how to make things work, you see. And I'm so new at this. I don't want to make you feel inadequate, frustrate you, just in case you couldn't... follow through."

She swallowed. Garry stared blankly, not saying anything.

"Well, it could hurt your ego, darling. I don't want that." She sighed sadly. "If only I was less pretty, more intelligent like your nurse." She began to slowly unbutton her blouse. "If I was more medically knowledgeable, I could deal with your physical condition better. I could forget the ugly scars that maim your body, stop remembering the lovemaking we once knew that surely won't be the same now. No, darling. All I have is this pretty face." She opened her shirt to reveal two bare breasts. "And these little things." She brushed her fingers across her taut nipples, her mouth pouting.

Laughter burst from Garry. "You're a hell of a tease, Daphne."

"Mmm, darling, a slightly bad word. Maybe I can move you yet. I like to hear real dirty words, remember?" She raised his arm and snuggled against him, her breasts against his chest.

Garry thought about the wild sex they used to have. How she would beg for the foulest of words. Oh yes, he remembered. But those days were long gone. Things were different now. He doubted she'd ever touch him completely again. For even now, as she lay next to him, stroking him affectionately, she lay on his left side. Touching only his left side.

"I want to marry you, Garry. I know you're the only one I want for the rest of my life. Time and patience will heal this physical problem we have between us. Besides, sex isn't everything in a marriage, is it? We'll still have each other. And we won't have to be lonely anymore. It's such a lonely world when you don't have someone. Darling, are you listening?"

"I'm listening."

"Well, I think we should get married."

Garry stared into space. *Marriage.* His music was dead, the accident taking care of that part of his life. All he had now were the nightmares that haunted him, the ghost of his father who tore into his dreams, driving his mind insane with guilt. He felt so undeserving of anything. He had ruined another's life. If he were to marry, would he not be ruining yet one more? What woman deserved a deformed man as a bedmate and partner?

Amanda's face popped into his head. *You are not deformed, Mr. Danzlo! You may have a few scars and some weakness, but I believe you will both play piano and walk someday.*

"Well, your opinion is bullshit!" he spoke aloud, reliving the exasperating scene with his nurse.

Daphne flung from his side, anger flaring sparks in her eyes. "What did you say to me?"

"I-I'm sorry!" he apologized. "I was thinking aloud. Not about you or marriage," he said quickly. "I was thinking about... I was talking to... Ms. Fields." Garry sat without breathing, while Daphne turned a raging red.

"Ms. Fields," she began, her respirations deep and rapid, "is not in this room!" She jerked her blouse together, fumbling with the buttons for closure as she continued to shout. "I'm laying practically naked next to you, talking about marriage, and you're thinking of Ms. Fields. How dare you even compare me to that slut!"

Garry frowned. "I was doing no such thing, and the woman is not a slut."

"Isn't she? But then, how would you know? You've been so busy defending her all day, you can't see what the truth really is. She's got you stuck up her ass so far, you can't see anything."

His face heated, his jaw clenched. "That's enough, Daphne."

"Oh, I don't think so, darling." She tilted her head. "I think you're not going to be satisfied until you've had some of that stuff she gave Nicolas tonight. Here, let me go get her for you." She walked to the door.

Garry jerked straight up. "Get back here! What is wrong with you?"

Daphne paused, then turned with tears in her eyes. "I told you," she said, sniffling, "she's what's wrong with me. You don't know what she's really like Garry. Outside this room, she... she's not the same person you see. She wants me out of this house. Did I not go into sporadic sneezing just hours ago? That should be proof enough that she says ugly things to me."

Garry leaned his back against the headboard, observing her thoughtfully. "It proves only that you were upset about something you thought you had heard." He rubbed his chin. "In fact I suddenly recall an element of fear instigating that last episode you experienced, something you'd gotten yourself into and couldn't get out of... until I was there to rescue you."

Daphne eyes flittered. "I know you're not insinuating... that was an entirely different situation! Why not just tell me you don't believe me? Oh Garry, what has she done to you?" Daphne rubbed one temple, finding a seat in a nearby chair. "She's already begun to ruin us. Making you believe she's a sweet person who does no wrong. But it's all a plan to manipulate you. Ask her, Garry. I bet she majored in psychology, trained to manipulate one's mind."

He frowned. "Now I know you're being ridiculous, your jealousy way over the top. Whatever she has said to you, I'm sure you misinterpreted. She's only here to help me. Were you not surprised this morning when I took that trip to the bathroom? You couldn't believe I could accomplish such a task. You can thank Ms. Fields for that. Or do you not want me to get well?" His brow raised.

"Of course I want you to. I want us to get married," she said, her hand on her chest. "I'm not getting any younger. I want a child by the time I turn thirty. I've two years left. So your rehabilitation is important to me, to us."

Garry paused, his expression grave. "Why would you want to burden your life with a lame man? You know I can never be the same."

Daphne rose slowly from her chair. "Because I love you, Garry. I can't see myself with anyone else. And I don't want anybody taking you from me. Can't you hire another nurse? You could fire this one and—"

"She stays," Garry said harshly, startling himself as well as Daphne. Days ago he had wanted the woman to leave.

"And me?" Daphne asked, stumbling against the chair she rose from. He didn't answer, his mind churning with the fear he'd felt in letting Amanda go. Daphne turned from his face, looking toward the bathroom entrance where another room adjoined it. "I'm sleeping in the guest room tonight."

His brows raised. "You've always slept in the guest room, Daphne. Ever since my accident. Why should tonight be different?"

Her face fell, her eyes filling with tears. It made him feel shame in his words. She did sleep in his bed today. On the left side.

She started to walk away. "Daphne," he called to her softly. She glanced back, her face pale with distress. "I'm sorry," he said. "I know you're trying. It's not been easy for either one of us. I do ask that you tame down the jealousy, okay?" He paused. "I'll think about what you said. Marrying you, that is." She gazed at him quiet and unmoving. And then a slow smile formed on her lips. "You're an enticing wonder of beauty," he said with sincerity. "I just want you to know I appreciate that. I appreciate you."

Daphne nodded, a tear falling down her cheek, her smile still in check.

"I think you're going to find yourself wrong about Ms. Fields," he told her softly. "She's a good nurse."

Daphne's smile faded. "We'll see," she said, then left the room.

# *17.*

# MY EYES ADORED YOU

GARRY GLANCED AT the clock beside his bed the next morning. 5:44 a.m. He watched the clock flip to 5:45, waiting and listening for Nicolas's alarm. Nicolas always got up at 5:45 sharp each day and was out of his room by 6:00. But 5:46 came, 5:47, and Garry heard nothing. Suspicion began creeping into his head. He didn't want it to, but Daphne's accusation that his butler was sleeping with his nurse gnawed at his brain. His heart began to pound so loudly, he was afraid he'd miss sounds outside his room.

They're just friends, he kept telling himself while Daphne's words screamed in his head—"*You know what they're doing.*"

The clock flipped to 5:55. The alarm sounded in the next room and was quickly shut off. He listened as Nicolas stirred from the bed. Nicolas's own bed, not Amanda's. "You're a fool, Danzlo!" he told himself. He shut his eyes, hating himself as he listened to the pulse in his ears subside. Nicolas had probably allowed himself some extra minutes of sleep after a late night. How foolish to think his own butler would be sleeping anywhere except in his own bed.

The door across the hall creaked open. His heart stopped, anticipating his own door to open any second. The creaking door was Amanda's, he knew. She'd check up on him, even if just to see if he was sleeping comfortably. He waited, yet she didn't come. Then he heard a knock, the click of another door, whispering voices, a giggle. It faded down the hall.

They've gone into the kitchen, he thought. She didn't bother to check on me. His eyes moved to the bathroom door where the adjoining guest room was. Daphne was snoring again. He remembered the look on Amanda's face when she came into his room the other morning, finding him kissing Daphne. He had seen her face transform, from ghostly pale to crimson. No, she'd never chance another encounter like that.

Garry rose on his left elbow, his ears stretching to hear any commotion in the kitchen. Was that a chair screeching across the floor, a bump against a hard surface? He envisioned a scene—his nurse passionately thrown against the table, his butler pouncing on her, ripping through fabric while Amanda enfolded the butler's nearly-bald head with her hands, kissing Nicolas's forehead, his eyes, his cheeks and mouth with those luscious lips of hers.

Garry fell back on his pillow, his mind exhausted, his body pumping an overload of adrenaline. He blinked a couple of times, his mouth salivating for the taste of cherries. He smacked his lips and swallowed.

"You're sick, Danzlo," he said, throwing a pillow over his face. "You're really sick."

SUNRISE SHONE BRILLIANTLY over the snow-topped mountains, morning dew glittering upon frosty firs and pines as sunlight scintillated across acres of white earth. The day promised to be a good one.

Nicolas and Amanda tiptoed down the hall toward Garry's bedroom, Nicolas in the lead.

"Are you sure she's not in there?" Amanda whispered over his shoulder.

"I'm sure," Nicolas said, halting in his tracks. Amanda slammed into his back. Both grunted.

"Shhhhh!" they hushed each other simultaneously.

Garry heard shuffling outside his room. He glanced at the door, the knob turning. He straightened his head on his pillow, closed his eyes and feigned sleep.

Two entered slowly. "Is he asleep?" Amanda whispered as they made their way in, Amanda clinging to Nicolas' shoulder.

"Yes, he's asleep," Nicolas said, his gaze drawn to the mess in the room. He abruptly stopped. Amanda collided into his back with a klunk.

"Look at this dump!" he said too loudly, anger rising at the sight of empty brandy and sherry glasses sitting about the room, leftover cheese and cracker crumbs on the bed table, crumbs on the bed, and chocolate candy wrappers strewn on the floor.

"You're going to wake him," Amanda scolded softly. Then she surveyed the room, her focus lingering uncomfortably on Daphne's mink coat hanging haphazardly across a chair, a pair of leather shoes scattered by the bed, sheer stockings draping off the headboard, a silk scarf intermingling with the bed sheet, and a half-empty box of imported gourmet chocolates lying open beside it. Taking a step, her shoe crunched on a cracker. She cried out in disgust. "A pigsty."

"Shhhh!"

Garry tried his best to keep a calm sleeping face. It wasn't easy with these two carrying on like Ollie and Stanley. He peered through narrowed lids, observing the two cleaning his room, especially Amanda, who grabbed the shoes off the floor, the stockings and scarf from the bed, then paused a moment before the box of chocolates. Choosing one, she popped a chocolate into her mouth, grabbed up the box and placed it among the goods in her arms. Snatching up the mink coat with one hand, she threw it on the floor, dropped an armload upon it, wrapped it in mink, and then heaved her ball into the adjoining room.

"Tsk, tsk," he heard her say. "Someone should take better care of their expensive wear."

Nicolas stood nearby wearing a giant smile on his face, his eyes on Amanda. "So true," he said. He collected the glasses and a plate of leftover cheese, cleaning up crumbs the best he could. "I'll be back in a minute," he whispered, heading out the door, his arms fully laden.

Garry was alone with Amanda. Seeing her turn toward him, he closed his eyes. She was staring at him. He could feel it. Seconds went by, his heart ticking strangely away in his ears. What was she doing? Had she eased nearer to the bed? Then the sheet lifted from his waist. *No, she wouldn't...* and slid against his chest and across one shoulder. *No, of course she wouldn't, dummy.* Then her presence was gone.

Slowly, he opened his lids. He spied her at the fireplace. She was shoveling out the old ashes and soot, placing them in the tin bucket on the hearth. She rubbed at an itch, smearing black cinder across her nose. *Cinderella,* he thought. Now, if only her fairy godmother would come create some miracles, he might consider taking her to the ball.

Nicolas entered the room bringing in a pail and a folded-up newspaper held strangely away from his body. Tagging at his heels was Bagel, trotting at an even pace, her jingling collar playing melodically with the faint tinkling of water that sloshed against the side of the tin container Nicolas carried. They headed straight for the bathroom. What was Nicolas up to? The door to the adjoining guest room clicked shut, the pattering of the dog's feet prancing on the bathroom floor. Then Nicolas came out of the bathroom minutes later, empty handed and the dog nowhere in sight. "I'm through, Miss Amanda," he said softly. "I'll go get breakfast started. You wake up Mr. Danzlo. Need any help with him?"

Amanda stood by the fireplace, Nicolas about to exit. "No, that's okay, I can do it," she said. "If he gives me any lip, I'll just clobber him one, then tie him up if I have to."

Garry's eyelids popped opened. Nicolas looked directly his way and then his focus shot to Amanda. "I think I'll go start breakfast now. Good luck, Miss Amanda."

Garry closed his lids.

Amanda paused a moment, gazing on the closed door. She was alone with Garry.

Turning, she slowly made her way toward the bed, nervousness and excitement jittering in her stomach. She sat down on the bed's edge, staring down at her sleeping patient. He looked so male, so irresistibly tempting, she shot off the bed. She moved to the oak chair nearby, placing it parallel to the bed frame. Sitting in it sideways, she rested an arm against the chair's back and used it to pillow her head. Then she began to sing.

"Are you sleeping, are you sleeping, Mr. Danz-LO?... Mr. Danz-LO?... Morning bells are ringing, morning bells are ringing, Ding Din DONG!... Ding Din DONG!"

With each "dong", Garry winced. He never opened his eyes. Suddenly it wasn't Amanda's voice singing, but Garry's, low and husky.

"No, I'm not sleeping, for you are creeping, in my head, beside my bed... now I'm going to kill you, take my axe and thrill you, all day LONG! While I sing this SONG!"

Amanda held back an explosion of giggles. "My, my, Mr. Danzlo. You are a man of talent. Your voice is still a bit rusty, but I have a feeling after we start a few breathing exercises and work with those throat muscles, you won't sound half bad. Melissa told me how you could write a song in a whiz. You did very well. Hmmm, I'm hungry, aren't you?"

Garry peered at her. "I might be hungry. Are you going to feed me?"

"No!" Amanda jumped up from the chair, fists at her sides. "I'm not Daphne."

"I'll vouch for that," Garry teased with a grin.

"You're getting up, Mr. Danzlo, so we can eat breakfast in the kitchen. I suggest you start moving or I'll... I'll..."

"What, Ms. Fields? Clobber me one, and then tie me up?"

She paused, realizing he'd been awake ever since Nicolas was in the room. "Ohhhh!"

She jerked the pillow from beneath his head and began attacking him violently with its downy fluff. Garry roared with laughter, which only made Amanda wallop him harder. Sometime between the savage assaults from her flailing arms, Garry managed to grab hold of her waist with his good arm and drag her down onto the bed with him. She fought with a vengeance, struggling in his hold, and then found her body crushed beneath his.

"Get off me you brute, you scoundrel, you beast! You... you twerp!"

"What did you call me?" he said, his eyes wide with make-believe fury, his face much too close for comfort.

"I said you were a brute, a scoundrel, a beast, and a twerp."

His brow raised. "Call me a brute, scoundrel or a beast, but I won't stand for being called a twerp. Is that understood?"

"Yes," she whispered, wetting her dry lips.

His gaze aimed suddenly on her lips. Amanda lay motionless, hot waves pulsing in every direction of her being while her chocolate breath blew against his face. A volcano of emotion erupted inside her, lava shooting up her legs and crashing hot against her breasts. If he didn't get his nude body off her, she'd drown in that fiery wave that was sure to gush over any second.

"Mr. Danzlo..." she said softly, her bottom lip quivering.

"Ms. Fields..." he said tenderly.

His voice vibrated against her chin as his gaze lifted to her eyes. She realized she must've lost her glasses in the struggle for he was staring as he'd never stared before. She could sense his emotion, feel it in the palms of her hands; the beating of his heart thumped wildly against them as he looked into her eyes as though viewing through a glass window, mesmerized by the wonder of what he'd never seen before. "Golden brown hues of sunshine," he whispered against her lips, "I feel their warmth."

Amanda didn't breathe, afraid if she did, the moment would pass away. Or else she'd wake up from this dream. Her eyelids flittered as his nose suddenly grazed hers lightly. His gaze became so intense, she felt seized by an overwhelming urge to cry, for in his eyes stood passion, as bright as shining topaz and she wanted it so badly she could taste it.

He must have read into that want, for his lips lowered to her great surprise, and brushed the corner of her mouth. She whimpered, her lips feeling dry, her tongue instinctively rushing to wet them. Garry instantly snatched her tongue with his own, groaning as he savored it with his own.

Garry's mind was on cherries.

*Oh God, she truly tasted like cherries!* He imbibed the sweetness of her mouth, his mind drunk with it, unknown to all else. Her chocolate flavor and that distinct taste of cherry drove him into delicious insanity. He immersed himself into the kiss; he couldn't get enough. His left hand cupped behind her neck, urging her closer, his mouth sucking the very breath from her while his tongue plunged for the treasure within that candied orifice. She succumbed to his onslaught most heartedly—her swaddling tongue like a feverish, reckless whirlpool driving him deeper and deeper into the recesses of her mouth. There was something poignant in the way her soft hand pressed against the side of his face, her other one trapped and tight against his rib cage, next to his pummeling heart. This only spurred him more the wilder, for her passion was so sweetly devoting and so damned good and hot. As his hunger grew, so did hers likewise, and she moved her hips beneath him, first sensually, then quite vigorously. He ground his groin against her skirts.

Then it was all over but the crying, for he'd spilled his seed within the tangled sheets that wrapped him, his long hard shaft throbbing like a wild thing against her clothed body.

He sprung from her and she fell backward, her feet landing off the bed and haphazardly on the floor. He grabbed frantically for the blanket, she, frantically for the glasses upon the carpet, their worn mouths breathing laboriously.

"Leave," he shouted, humiliation and embarrassment engulfing him. She was nimbly fixing her disheveled appearance—smoothing down her dress, fingering her hair in place. Glancing up as he spoke, their eyes locked just before a scream sounded from the bathroom. Then came a loud clank against tiled floor, metal scraping amid more screams, and the dog barking ferociously. The bedroom door slammed open, and Nicolas flew in. From the bathroom came Daphne—hair and shoulders dripping water, the hem of her silk negligee covered with muddy dog tracks, and her right foot ensconced in a tin pail.

Garry's jaw dropped, just before he hollered.

"Out! Both of you, out." he ordered. "And that goes for you too, Bagel," he added, glancing over to his guilty-looking dog.

The frightened animal flew on all fours, practically tripping Nicolas and Amanda as she raced ahead of them out the door.

The three culprits gone, Garry focused his attention on Daphne. He could feel the bitter wrath fuming from the woman standing rod-still upon the threshold of his bathroom.

"I demand you fire them both now," she squealed. "Or I leave!"

He was angry, though he couldn't decide if it came from the prank played on Daphne, or her command to fire the two. His mind was too fixed on the quake in his lower body from sexual release, his lips weathered and still tingling from the kiss he'd stolen.

"You don't demand anything of me. If you want to leave, you know where the door is."

Daphne stood with fists at her side. "Is that how you treat the woman you love? I gave up a lot to come to this rat hole in the woods. Worst of all, I've had to put up with looking at that conniving, ugly chit you call a nurse."

"Enough."

"What's the matter? Can't take me talking about your precious nurse? She's such an ugly nothing you deserve her, Garry. But then, you're so stupid you're probably in love with her."

"Get out, Daphne, before I—"

"What will you do, darling? You can't do anything. You're an invalid. No better than your father was. How lucky he was that you killed him so he'd no longer have to suffer his worthlessness."

A nerve jerked in his temple. His cheeks burned, and then just as suddenly, his entire body drained cold. Daphne had made him feel more humiliated than he'd felt minutes ago with Amanda. He was always playing a fool. Worthless, just like Daphne said. He'd driven his father to his grave. And if he hadn't scared his nurse to the point of packing her bags, he knew now he had no choice but to tell her to go.

Daphne stood at the bathroom threshold, her face red with fury one moment, and completely pale the next as she watched his face transform.

"Oh, Garry… darling…" She sobbed. "How could I be so cruel, so wretched to have said those awful things? But I was so angry. I'm sorry, I'm sorry!" She started toward him, but forgot her foot was embedded in a pail. She stumbled sideways against the doorframe, water dribbling off her head, onto her nose, into her mouth. She spit and sputtered, kicking her bucketed foot against the tile floor. "Ew!" she spat. "The water's been sweetened. They put sugar in the water, Garry." Her body shook with repulsion as she swiped at her face, stickiness spreading across her delicate skin. A string of sneezes soon led into some choking coughs.

Garry's eyes widened—at first, for at her near fall, then with shock at the extent of the prank played on her, and finally, concerning her coughing spell. "Daphne, are you all right?"

Her sticky hands and muddy body huddled against the doorframe. "Yes, darling," she coughed, crying, "yes! You do care for me. You know I didn't mean those ugly words, don't you? Your life is priceless to me. Never worthless." She sniffed back her tears. "I was so furious. I'm not a patient person, you know, one of the things we have in common. It's one of my many faults." She wiped at her tears, trying to push back the tendrils of blonde hair that fell across her face, but only to have her sticky fingers adhering to her hair. She tried pulling them lose, taking a few hairs along with it. She bit her lip to keep from screaming again. "Oh, Garry, how much more shall I take? They're out to get me. Both of them. Have they not proved themselves now? But I can only tell you this, for you have to see for yourself. I love you, Garry. Please don't hate me now. Please, don't."

Garry was quiet for a long moment. Almost too quiet.

He studied the plea in her eyes—a near fear that somewhat concerned him, yet the empathy that roared more strongly inside him took precedence over what doubts he felt in their present relationship. They'd been through a lot together in such a short time. She'd gotten him through some tough times, and he'd done the same for her. They'd been good for each other, up until this point. And why all the trouble now? Because of a certain zany nurse who had turned his emotions upside down? He gazed at Daphne standing so enticingly wet in her negligee, so naturally seductive, sensual, her sultry eyes anxiously awaiting his response. *What had possessed him to even want to touch another woman?* Especially this Ms. Fields… a witch to be sure, for only a spell would cast him into her arms so intimately. He thought about the trouble she had caused since her brief stay. She'd somehow wooed him out of the bed, as well as in the bed. And Nicolas wasn't even the same person. Nicolas would never pull a stunt like this on his own.

Something had to be done. He gazed at Daphne with new respect. "I don't hate you, Daphne. It's my fault your visit has been so intolerable. I plan to change that. I'm telling Ms. Fields she has to go. She's caused enough trouble."

Daphne's eyes lit like blue diamonds, and for a brief second, Garry felt something odd in her response. The gleam in one eye, and the way her mouth pinched on one side. It appeared almost triumphant. He must have imagined it, for all he saw now was gratitude. "Oh, darling, I think you're making a wise choice. And I'll have you to myself once again. I'll go clean up so we can be together."

She attempted to turn, but her hand stuck to the doorframe. She pulled it free. She grabbed hold of the doorknob behind her, her foot and pail clanking against the bathroom floor as she struggled to move around to close the door. She nearly knocked herself down while closing it with her hand still intact on the outside knob. Garry watched, trying not to laugh at her pitiful predicament. She smiled for him, yanked her hand free, and slammed the door shut.

Garry fell back on the bed, his laughter about to burst until he felt the wet sheet slide against his belly, his mind recounting Amanda's eyes that he'd gazed into. And her lips that he'd kissed. He felt himself harden. A knock sounded on the door from the hallway. His gaze jerked to the door, his heart thumping double time.

"It's me, sir, Nicolas. Can I come in?"

Garry grabbed the sheet, balling it up against himself. "Just a second!" His left hand did fast work while his right uncomfortably reached for the blanket nearby. "Okay," he said.

"Is everything all right, sir?" Nicolas asked, regarding him curiously.

"Of course it is," Garry blustered, and then realized he'd forgotten the incident concerning Daphne. "I mean, no, Nicolas, it's not."

"Sir, I hope you don't think Miss Ama—"

"I want you to fire her, Nicolas."

Nicolas' eyes widened, his face aghast. "She had nothing to do with it, sir. I swear it. The bathroom ordeal was completely my idea. She tried to talk me out of it."

"I don't believe you, Nic. Only she could come up with something as crazy as—"

"But it's true, sir! I thought to use molasses… thicker, you know. I figured more sticky, but she insisted on plain sugar once she realized I wasn't backing down on *my* idea."

"Good gosh, Nicolas. What possessed you to use either one?"

"We thought to make her sweeter?" A short silence followed.

"Fire her, Nicolas. That's an order."

Nicolas stepped back, his short frame stern. "I refuse that order, sir."

Garry was taken aback. He'd never known his loyal butler to downright refuse an order. He tried again. "She won't listen to me, Nic, so you've got to do it for me."

"Then I guess she doesn't get fired, sir." Nicolas started out the room.

"Nic, wait! I'll fire her. Come back." Nicolas turned. Garry cleared his throat. "I need clean sheets."

"But sir, I just changed the linens yesterday morning. Why would—"

"Don't ask, questions, Nicolas, just do it! One top sheet will do. And hurry it up."

Nicolas left, hurrying back with a clean top sheet. It lay neatly folded across his arm. "Shall I take the one you've got balled up under the blanket, sir?" he asked too formally.

Garry frowned. "Here, take it," he said, passing the bundle of cloth while grabbing the clean sheet from Nicolas' arm. A small tube dropped to the floor from the balled-up sheet, landing at Nicolas' feet. Nicolas bent to retrieve it, looking up to his boss with an inquiring brow. "Yours, sir?" he asked, offering it to him.

Hesitating, Garry reached for the small object. He took it in his hand, staring down at it, speaking only one word. "Cherry."

"Miss Amanda's favorite flavor, sir."

Garry glanced up feverishly. "Is it?"

"Shall I take it to her, sir?" When Garry didn't answer, Nicolas added, "I'm sure she's got another. Go ahead and keep it."

"No," Garry said quickly. "I mean, I don't want it, Nicolas." He held out the flavored Chapstick for Nicolas to take.

"Then you give it to her," Nicolas said, pivoting on his feet to make his exit, "when you fire her, sir." He shut the door behind him.

Garry glowered at the door, yet only a second, the object in his hand taking hold of his senses. *That's why she tasted like cherries,* he realized. He had devoured the taste on her lips, the taste in her mouth. Like candy. He closed his eyes and pictured her as she told him one of her silly stories.

*But no. Daddy never called me "Mandy, my sweet candy." He had to call me "Amanda, my panda bear."*

He looked toward the bedroom door, wondering where she was, wondering what she thought of him now. *The cad!* Or had the kiss been as good for her as it had been for him? She had whimpered beneath his deepened kiss, yet had given to him completely. She had given, hadn't she? Or had he just taken.

Unconsciously, he snapped off the cap from the Chapstick tube, the smell of cherry drifting to his nostrils. The taste of chocolate was sweet on his tongue. *Mandy… sweet as candy*, his mind spoke.

He lay back on the pillow, his heart pumping fiercely, his mouth suddenly dry. Her eyes had possessed him then, but the addictive drink from her lips held the curse—for he realized now he wanted more. He wanted it badly.

Daphne's words echoed in his head. *She's such an ugly nothing you deserve her… but then, you're so stupid you're probably in love with her!*

He bounced up, sliding his back against the headboard. "No," he swallowed hard. "That's not what it is. That's not what it is at all! I'm in love with Daphne… beautiful Daphne."

*No, you're not, Danzlo*, his subconscious said.

"Yes, I am!"

*Then why haven't you ever told Daphne you love her?*

"I have!"

*No, you haven't.*

"Of course I have."

Silence.

"Okay, I haven't. I'll tell her today. And I'll fire Ms. Fields today… or tomorrow."

# 18.

# I'M YOUR MAN

"HE WANTS TO see me *now?*"

Amanda blinked several times, the anxiety and fear she'd felt for the past twenty-four hours now at a whopping peak. She tried to appear calm in front of Nicolas, but she could tell he knew better. Something had happened between her and Garry, and she'd denied her friend the facts.

But she hadn't seduced the boss. Not on purpose. The only thing she was guilty of was allowing his passion to run wild and free while she lay beneath him in total bliss. All right, so she took in every smidgen of that vivacious kiss, sampling him back with as much intensity. And maybe she did take advantage of that delicious heat he'd filled her with from head to toe. But how was she to know her body would betray her by moving against his rock hard erection? She had become wanton in a matter of seconds... *a frisky little minx!* Surely that's what he thought of her now.

"Now," Nicolas affirmed. "He wants to see you while Daphne still sleeps."

Amanda swallowed the knot in her throat.

"Miss Amanda?"

She looked up, her vision a blur as she tried smiling for Nicolas. He stared back with worried eyes. "He needs you, no matter what he tells you. Remember that."

The huge knot found its way into her stomach, somehow cutting off the air to her lungs. Was this it? *Slam, bam, no thank you, ma'am?* Good-bye? Of course she could argue with Garry, tell him she was staying and that was that! No need to let him know she was falling in love with him. Or how she wanted to be where he was.

Or how much she enjoyed knowing he was in the other room and not a couple of thousand miles away... like Robbie was.

*Robbie.* What chance would she have of ever adopting him if she lost this job? And nothing really meant more than Robbie. Her home was with him, not with a man who didn't love her back, for surely that was the truth of it. Paul hadn't loved her. Why should it be any different with Garry? She'd seen his face yesterday, horror plainly etched into his features. He'd commanded her to leave. She found herself facing his door, somehow finding the guts to knock.

GARRY'S HEART LEAPED in his throat when Amanda opened the door. He'd been up half the night thinking, trying to convince himself that Amanda Fields had to leave his home, and his life. She meant nothing to him, only trouble. She'd been so heavy on his mind, what little sleep he had managed to get in the night was filled with a dream about her—a goofy-looking witch who'd thrown off her pointed black hat. She had lowered her glasses, peeked over the frames with seductive eyes while she flung off dark clothes, one by one, backing him into a corner, gluing him against the wall. She'd suddenly turned into an enchanting sorceress, forcing him to drink from a cup she offered—cherry juice—her hands playing black magic all over his body. He awakened in a sweat, his male organ throbbing for release.

She stood in the doorway now, facing him. He tried to remember she was the troublemaker, the enemy, yet the only thing he could recall was the color of her eyes when he'd kissed her candied lips. She wore her eye shadow differently today, less severe, those golden orbs taking him on a sensuous trip. They were smiling at him now, checking him out carefully. He was fully dressed today, assisted by Nicolas bright and early. He wasn't taking any chances. No more sleeping nude as long as she was in the house. He supposed it was the shoes that brought the smile to her lips. He did look a little ridiculous lying on the bed with shoes on, not to mention he had ungodly big feet.

"Hi," she said, her fingers crinkling the sides of her dress. Her glasses slid down her nose. She bit down on her lip as she pushed them back up and walked closer to the bed. She looked at him gravely. "I understand you called for me. Do I get whipped now or later? I'm hoping later, for I'd like to be prepared for this kind of thing. You know, like getting the pots and pans rigged up under my skirts and all."

Her statement was so unexpected, yet so like her, Garry found himself grinning. It was that innocent play he most enjoyed about her. For a long moment, they just smiled at each other Slowly, their smiles fell and they grew uncomfortable in their own skin. They looked away at the same time.

"I want to apologize for yesterday," Garry said to the wall opposite him. His heart labored like a pounding machine, threatening to beat him to death if he should see one ounce of emotion on her face. "Somehow I, ah, lost control of myself," he glanced up on impulse saying, "kissing you and…" his eyes caught hers, then locked on her freshly wet lips. They were quivering, as though pleading for his own to kiss them again. He jerked his gaze back to the wall. "And everything," he finished curtly, knowing full well her lips weren't pleading for him. His were pleading for her.

"I shouldn't have hit you with the pillow, sir. It was my fault."

He glanced back as she took full blame. "I shouldn't have grabbed you. My fault."

A moment of awkward silence passed between them.

"No, and let's not forget," she began lightly, "how you threw me on the bed like some hungry starved animal. Must've been the twerp in you."

Amusement took hold of his senses. "Twas no twerp that ravished you with a macho kiss."

"No, only a scoundrel could've given such a kiss!"

"Ah, so you admit it was macho."

"Hmmm," she mused, hands on hips, her head tilted, "was pretty close to that."

His brow rose. "You know it was close to that."

His words had come too seriously, he realized, their playfulness ceasing. "It was lust," he said abruptly, "nothing more." Whether his words were to convince her, or to convince himself, he knew only that he regretted them, for hurt crossed her features. "I didn't mean—"

"Oh, come on, Mr. Danzlo," she said, changing emotion before his eyes. "You know you adore me. You can't resist me. It's my clothes, isn't it? No, wait, it's my shoes. I've seen the way you look at them. And my face. I have a cute face. How could anyone not love it?" She blinked repeatedly. Garry laughed. Then she stood up on a chair, her height way above his head. "Oh, but sir, I must disappoint you for I have a slew of men in line just waiting for my irresistible charms at my Floridian doorstep. Yes, this very moment," she announced, towering over him with arms open wide. "A bunch of impatient scoundrels, those ones. Ah, but Mr. Danzlo, you're the sweetest scoundrel of all scoundrels." Then she began to chant a 1964 song by the Motown songwriting team Holland-Dozier-Holland, *How Sweet It Is (To Be Loved by You)*. Amanda's shoe tapped as she sung a few lyrics.

Garry laughed so hard, his head hit the headboard of the bed. Then the bathroom door slammed open against an adjoining wall. All gaiety ceased.

"Just what is going on in here?"

Daphne stood at the threshold, her eyes viciously on Amanda. Amanda hopped down from the chair. Garry straightened. "Well? I'm waiting!" she demanded.

"We were having a discussion," Garry said quickly.

"About airplanes," Amanda added, making up a quick excuse for standing in the chair. "I was telling Mr. Danzlo how I've had introductory lessons in flying. I was showing him how I landed this one plane."

"A very interesting maneuver," Garry said, his gut about to burst from restrained laughter. He knew Daphne didn't believe them in the least.

"Such light conversation, darling, after you've fired the poor girl. What a good sport she is."

Garry wanted to crawl under the bed. His focus went immediately to Amanda. She was looking at him, as though he truly were a scoundrel.

"Oh, dear," Daphne sliced through, "did you not tell her yet, darling?" Her gaze was on Amanda only. "You'll have to excuse him. He's never been much good at that sort of thing, firing employees he's especially enjoyed working with." She smiled. "But with marriage in the near future…"

"Marriage?" Amanda blinked.

"Yes, didn't Garry tell you? We're getting married. That's why we won't need you any longer. I'll be taking care of him."

A rise of heat scorched Garry's brows; Daphne ignored the daggers he threw her way.

"Darling, you really must be more informative when it comes to your employees. The poor dear might think you're dismissing her because of a lack of skill."

"We've only *discussed* marriage, Daphne," he said.

"Well of course, darling. We discuss it at least once a day."

"Excuse me," Amanda cut in, her attention on Daphne. "Funny how things just fall into place for everyone," she said. "Mr. Danzlo doesn't have to worry about dismissing me. I came in this morning to let him know I've already begun packing." She glanced at him, and then back at Daphne. "You see, I'm needed back home. Business that can't wait."

"How marvelous! I mean, that things have worked out for us all. Isn't it, darling?" Daphne climbed upon the bed beside Garry.

Amanda didn't wait for the reply. "I've got to finish packing." She exited the room, shutting the door on her way out.

"Of all the—"

"Darling, don't be mad. I did it for you."

"Me?" Garry fumed, pushing her hand away. "You did it for you. It's always for you."

"That's not true, and you know it. You couldn't fire her, so I fired her for you." She got up from the bed.

"God help me. I don't even remember why I planned to fire her in the first place. I'm going crazy, I swear I am." He ran his hand through his hair, bowed his head. Then, with a slow, shaky voice, he said, "Maybe I don't want her to go. Maybe deep down inside I know she can help me, yet the very thought scares me." He paused, unable to lift his eyes to Daphne, afraid he wouldn't see the compassion he needed right now. He just stared at his lap. "I've lived these past months like an undeserving nobody, yet she tells me I don't have a worthless bone in my body. And strangely, when I'm with her, I believe her. Then, the moment she walks out the door, I see nothing but an incompetent man, incapable of being anything but."

The room was deathly silent. Garry gathered enough nerve to raise his eyes at Daphne. He wasn't at all surprised at seeing her pale face and inert eyes. He quickly moved his focus to the flames in the fireplace, words he'd been holding inside spilling out. "If it weren't for me," he said, "an old man might still be living today. So what that he was a bastardly father, a man I hated because he ruined my life as a child. Did that give me the right to destroy his life?"

Garry didn't expect a reply from Daphne. Nor that she could understand. She didn't have it in her. There was no forgetting or forgiving to her way of thinking.

"Garry, let's go home to California," she finally said. "We'll get you the best doctors, and a good nurse."

"I have a good nurse," he shouted up at her. "At least I had one a moment ago. She's packing now."

Daphne stood back, aghast, watching in horror as Garry's expression went forlorn, his eyes gloomily on the door.

*My God! He really is in love with her, and he doesn't even know it!* How did it happen? How *could* it happen? Amanda Fields was an ugly duckling.

Yet the visage she saw that early dark morning was totally different than the one revealed the next meeting. Amanda's unfashionable wardrobe denounced her true beauty. But it wasn't her looks that attracted Garry. He adored her personality, the woman's sweet and innocent character. Amanda had a soft heart. *Yes, like his own*, she thought, a keen idea taking birth.

She burst into tears, startling Garry. She dropped her face into her hands, convulsing her shoulders, her blond hair fanning out before him.

"Oh, Garry, I can't keep it a secret any longer. I know you've got so much on your mind right now, and I shouldn't add to your problems. But I'm scared." She came to him, grabbed hold of his left hand, kissed his palm, gazed into his concerned eyes. "I can't lose you. I'd just as soon end life now. You don't understand, because I... I..."

Garry's brows drew together. "You what?"

Daphne sighed. "Five months ago, I was carrying your baby, our little baby. But your accident came and I lost it. I became too emotionally upset, I guess." She burst into tears again.

Garry could only stare, stupefied by her confession.

Daphne sniffed. "I didn't want to tell you I was pregnant at the time, for you hadn't asked me to marry you, yet I thought you would. I didn't want you to feel obligated. I wanted you to marry me because you loved me." She let out a shuddered breath, and swallowed. "When I lost the baby, I lost a part of you. That's why I couldn't come see you in the hospital for so long. I thought you were dying, and I'd already experienced a part of you dying inside me. But you got better," she said, squeezing his hand, "and I was so thankful you were alive. It's because of my miscarriage that I've neglected to give into you sexually, not so much your physical state. For you see, I was physically hurt too."

Garry sat speechless, his mind and body stilling against the windstorm that beat and berated him inside. All the time, he'd accused her of thinking him too maimed to make love to, yet here lay the real problem. She had carried his child, lost it, and then almost lost him. He wanted to believe her, for it certainly would answer a lot of questions concerning her behavior toward him these past months, relieve his doubts. Surely she was telling the truth. He raised his hand, and cupped her face.

"I'm sorry," he said. "I'm sorry you had to go through that alone." He wrapped his arm about her shoulder and brought her head against him, holding her in his arm for a long moment.

"I want to marry you, Garry," she spoke against his skin. "I want back what was taken from me. No other man could ever replace you." Garry kissed her on her head. "We both have physical needs, darling. We'll both get help, once we're married." A long silence passed, and then he spoke softly against her hair.

"Okay, Daphne. I'll marry you. You won't have to hurt anymore."

Daphne sprung to his face, kissing his cheeks, his mouth. "Oh, darling, I'll be the best wife."

Garry smiled through her kisses, happy to see her happy. She cuddled against his neck, her lips teasing against his collar. This was the perfect time to say, "I love you," but he didn't say it. He just held her close, wondering why he didn't want to.

# 19.

# BLACK AND BLUE

THE LOS ANGELES INTERNATIONAL Airport bustled with people. Melissa scurried through the crowd, dodging bodies as she made her way to the departure gate where her flight to Colorado was due to leave.

"Last call for Flight 74 leaving for Denver," the loud speaker echoed through the terminal. Within seconds, Melissa was at the service desk, gasping for breath, slamming her ticket down before the clerk. "First class seating," Melissa puffed out as the man behind the desk quickly looked over her papers. Handing her a boarding pass he told her to have a nice trip, motioning her toward the gate where a female attendant patiently waited. Melissa rushed toward the attendant with her pass in hand. She stopped short as a familiar scent careened her nostrils. *Polo*—the same male fragrance that had taunted her senses earlier that morning when she and Dan had stopped for coffee. The eerie premonition she'd had then was now in double measure. *She was being followed.*

Melissa whirled around, her eyes searching the crowd for the man she knew she would see, her gaze briefly fusing with another's just before her onlooker disappeared into the dense crowd, so quickly Melissa thought she'd imagined him.

"Excuse me, Ma'am, the plane's ready to leave. Your boarding pass?"

Melissa turned to the voice behind her, her face feeling drained of blood, her hand shaking as she handed the flight attendant her ticket. A skycap reached for the heavy tote Melissa carried, "allow me," she vaguely heard him say. She unconsciously took his outstretched arm, letting him guide her through the jetway to the forward cabin where she was soon seated. He placed her tote in the overhead rack. "Thank you," she said absently, turning her attention beyond the window beside her, expecting to see him somewhere out there—the tall one with the dark features and smoke gray eyes. Amanda's friend and foe. *Eddie.*

Melissa knew little about Eddie Chandler, only what Amanda had shared prior to Melissa hiring her. Amanda had wanted to make sure Melissa knew of her recent past—her husband's murder, her involvement in the court trials, and about Eddie. There had been scandalous articles due to her long and close friendship with Eddie. She'd made mistakes. But Eddie had gotten them through it, his brilliance in the courtroom outstanding.

"He's in love with you, isn't he?" Melissa had said boldly after hearing the edge in Amanda's voice. There'd been moisture in Amanda's eyes, her smile too tense. A nod assured Melissa her hunch was true. "But you don't love him. That is, you're not *in love* with him?"

Amanda hesitated before responding. "At times I thought I could be. I didn't want to be. When Paul and Eddie severed their partnership a couple of years ago, Eddie had stayed away for a while. The next I saw him, he seemed different. His behavior was wild and untamed. Even during the court trials, there were times I felt I didn't know him. He would say things so out of the ordinary, do things that were unlike his nature. One moment he'd be secretive and withdrawn, then next, laughing and teasing like his old self. Sometimes he scares me, Melissa."

Their conversation had been held at the hospital where Amanda worked; Melissa and she had been sitting at a secluded table in the cafeteria. It was the whiff of Polo cologne that had caused Amanda's focus to jerk to the tall man passing them, heading toward a snack machine. Amanda had sat back in her seat with a sigh of relief on her lips.

"So he wears Polo cologne, huh?" Melissa had said with the interest of a detective. She always did love mysteries. "Is he tall? Strong?"

Amanda smiled. "Macho strong. And yes, tall, dark, and extremely handsome. His mother was a full-blooded Apache. She died of a fever when Eddie was twelve. He didn't know his father till then. His uncle had taken him from his Arizona home, moved him to Florida to spend the rest of his childhood with his father and stepmother. Both are dead now, and Eddie was left with a great inheritance. He's a very wealthy man. He wants to help me financially, but I won't let him."

Melissa nodded her understanding. "And he respects your wishes. Will you be telling him about your new job in Colorado?"

Amanda shook her head. "He doesn't need to know where I am. I don't want him to know."

The sound of another late passenger boarding the plane disturbed Melissa from her reverie. Her gaze instantly shot to the entranceway. She almost expected to see the tall, dark one enter the cabin, but instead it was another man of medium height, with reddish hair and mustache. A face she had seen just an hour ago. Her focus followed him to the seat only two down and across from hers. She turned forward, facing the cockpit like a white knuckler who'd never flown in a plane. The stewardess spoke to her, smiling. "We'll be up flying and landing in no time. It's not so bad, you'll see."

Melissa only nodded, her mind far from the introductory safety instructions the stewardess began teaching the passengers. Her mind was on the man sitting a couple of seats behind her. She could almost swear he was the driver of the big black sedan that followed close behind them that morning. She had pulled down the sun visor, looking into the mirror while putting on lipstick, the car behind them visible in the mirror. The man behind the wheel had seemed to be staring straight at her, the reason why she remembered him. Medium red hair, the reddish eyebrows, the fair skin, the mustache. But the real giveaway was the black patch he wore over one eye. It had to be the same man!

So who was he? A hired hand of Eddie Chandler's? He looked creepy, dangerous.

Melissa looked out the window, the plane ascending into the murky clouds. She suddenly wanted to be in Colorado beside her brother's nurse. *I believe he's found you, Amanda.*

She twisted in her seat, looking back over her shoulder between the high-back chairs. *One-Eyed Jack,* Melissa quickly named him, was looking right at her. She turned back, a stewardess standing next to the empty chair beside her. "May I get you something? A drink, juice, peanuts?" the stewardess asked.

Melissa looked down at her watch. It was after eleven o'clock. She pulled down her tray table from the seatback in front of her. "A bloody Mary, please, with a twist of lemon," she said, blinking up to the stewardess. "Could you make that a double?"

NICOLAS WAS WEARING a hole in the kitchen floor—from the sink to the hallway entrance, back to the sink to the hallway entrance. He was fighting the urge to go to

Amanda, fall on his knees and beg her to stay. Appeal to the fact that Mr. Danzlo was temporarily insane.

The woman was packing. How had it come to this? He thought he'd heard laughter, yet when Amanda came from Danzlo's room, tears were brimming in her eyes. Nicolas had been standing at the end of the hall when she'd exited the room. She had come toward him like a walking corpse, speaking as she stopped before his face. "I have to leave, I have to go," she spoke gravely, her eyes distant. "Don't stop me. They don't want me. It's over." She blinked a couple of times. "They're getting married, Nicolas." He started to say something, but his words were hushed with the touch of her trembling fingers against his lips. "Don't," she pleaded. "I have packing to do." She walked away and hid behind closed doors. Nicolas, speechless, could only stare at the empty hallway.

Hours had passed since then, Nicolas having more than enough time to gather the information he needed to put some sense to the situation. He'd gotten two private sides to the story, one from Miss Daphne, another from Mr. Danzlo, the latter story giving the most insight to the matter. Nicolas had all but gotten on his knees as he prayed for an answer. His answer came walking through the front door that afternoon.

MELISSA EXPECTED TO be greeted by both Amanda and Nicolas as the door opened for her entrance. The last thing she expected was Nicolas' short arms to be thrown about her in a big bear hug the moment she crossed the threshold. He'd never done such a thing in his life. He was laughing, and between the laughter he exalted her, "Praise and hallelujah. It's you!"

"Nicolas," Melissa said, half-laughing through her breathlessness, her arms pinioned at her sides while Nicolas held on tightly. Then quite suddenly he released her, his expression serious as he looked into her face. "He doesn't know what he's doing. It's a trick, I'm sure of it. That woman was never pregnant. He's too blind to see fact, letting the best thing that ever happened to him slip away. She's packing while he thinks to marry another, but he's in love with her. He can deny it all he wants, be as stubborn and stupid as he likes, but the wet sheet proves that a fire burns hot between heaven and hell."

Melissa stood like a dumbbell heavy on the floor, her mind trying to comprehend Nicolas' words. She should never have had that second Bloody Mary.

Before she knew what was happening, Nicolas was dragging her body, coat, suitcase and all, across the floor into the kitchen. "Have a seat, rest your feet," Nicolas said, plopping her into a chair. "I'll make coffee, you start planning."

AMANDA WAS STARTLED from sleep, her head aching, her eyes sore from the many tears she'd wept. At first she thought she was home in her West Palm Beach apartment, for she had awakened with the same nightmares in her head about Paul. Yet this dream included Daphne. Daphne lay in Paul's arms. They were kissing, touching each other, while she, the wife, sat hunched over in the corner of the bedroom, holding her bruised face, the one he had slapped. She could hear the masculine voice speaking upon the bed, but in her dream the voice wasn't Paul's. It was Garry's. He spoke tender words to the woman on the bed. Soft, endearing. They whispered loudly in her ears, taunting her. She squeezed her eyes shut from the agonizing pain they caused. Yet her closed lids only provided a different kind of pain. Now she felt his voice against her lips, her breasts, her belly, with warmth and sweetness beyond reason. The fiery heat was consuming. Within the passionate flames, came her name, spoken clearly, lovingly from his lips. She cried out, whimpering his name, over and over.

Amanda lifted her head from the rose silk coverlet, a hot tear falling as she glanced over at the clock by her bed. The morning was gone, the whole afternoon spent. She had fallen asleep, unable to bring herself to start packing or to make the call to the airlines for a flight to Florida. She was too tired and emotionally exhausted. Just yesterday Garry had kissed her and last night when she couldn't sleep, her thoughts and feelings had driven her mad. Even now, whether from yesterday's tender moment, or from the dream that still lingered fresh in her mind, her body was pink with desire.

*It was lust, nothing more*, Garry's voice came quickly to her head. His words had hurt deeply. *Lust?* Was that all he felt as he kissed her intensely, ravishing her as he drank her senseless?

She eased from the bed, combing back her tangled hair, which had come undone from its pinned-up state. She stumbled across the room, grabbed the suitcase and placed it on the bed. Opening it, she began putting things into it, one by one. She decided she would go into town, stay at a motel, then leave in the morning.

A knock sounded on the door. She paused a moment, then continued on packing. A second knock sounded. "Amanda, it's me. Melissa."

Amanda twisted around, and for one brief second, she felt happiness well up inside her. Her need for a female companion was overwhelming, someone to talk to who would understand what she was feeling. She felt very close to Nicolas, and she had shared many things with him, but not her feelings about Garry.

"Amanda, open up. We need to talk." Melissa's voice was urgent.

Amanda wiped her eyes and dried her hands on her wrinkled skirt. She opened the door, barely glancing at Melissa, afraid of crying some more, so she turned and continued on with her packing. She went to the redwood dresser to retrieve her flannel gowns; Melissa went to the suitcase to retrieve a half dozen socks and a stack of lacy underwear.

"Long time, no see," Melissa said cheerfully unpacking Amanda's things. She headed for the dresser as Amanda headed for the suitcase. "Don't suppose you missed me, huh?"

They swept past each other, neither bothering to look at the other. Amanda swallowed the lump in her throat, thinking of the many times Melissa had called on the phone to see how things were going, two and three times a day. She thought of the laughter they'd shared with their silly phone talk, the quick friendship she'd been blessed with. She didn't have many women friends she felt really comfortable with. And never one like Melissa.

"I missed you," she said hoarsely, placing three neatly folded flannel gowns into the suitcase. She started back toward the dresser, Melissa passing in the opposite direction.

"Well, now you won't have to miss me!" Melissa said blithely, approaching the suitcase on the bed. "I'm staying here for the week."

"And I'm going home to Florida."

Melissa paused only a second, then with both arms, scooped up the entire contents of packed goods in the suitcase and headed toward the open dresser drawers. Amanda, deeply concentrating on her task, walked to the bed carrying the half dozen socks and stack of lacy underwear she'd previously placed into the suitcase. She stared down, dumbfounded at her empty suitcase. Turning toward Melissa, she frowned.

"Garry doesn't want you to go," Melissa said gravely.

Amanda's breath caught, her heart beating pitter-patter in her chest. "He said that?"

"I, uh, haven't seen him yet," she said. "But I know it's true."

Amanda's frown returned, her feet grinding the carpet as she made her way back toward the dresser. She snatched the giant load from Melissa's arms, stomping back to the bed where she dropped it like a bomb into the suitcase. Slamming the piece of luggage shut, she twisted the latches, not caring that the strap of a bra and some flannel fabric hung out at the seam. Nor did she care that there were other things to pack. She headed for the door.

"You're in love with him, aren't you?"

Amanda stopped. She stared at the door, her hand tight on the suitcase handle. Slowly, she put the luggage down, turned and faced Melissa.

"I didn't want it to happen," she said in defense, as though some horrible crime had been committed. "I don't understand how something like this could've happen so fast. I tried to fight it, to ignore the feelings that kept bothering me, and perhaps I could've won the fight if he hadn't kissed me yesterday. But he did and—"

"What?" Melissa said incredulously. She rushed forward, placing her hands on Amanda's upper arms. "He kissed you? Looking like... *like that?*" Her eyes ran over Amanda's distasteful state.

Amanda nodded. Swallowing nervously, she added, "Lasted a near two minutes, I think. Wiped me out. Left me breathless. Left him breathless. And excited, if you know what I mean."

"Under the sheet," Melissa said.

"The sheet?" She hadn't mentioned that Garry wore only a sheet. But then, she remembered Melissa was good at guessing mysteries. She smiled at Melissa's keen insight. "Yeah, under the sheet."

"And..." Melissa urged, anticipation in her eyes.

"And then he sprang from me so fast you'd think I had cooties! Told me to leave. Then Daphne—"

"No wait, the sheet! You can't leave out the best part—the climax." Melissa giggled.

Why was Melissa hung up about the sheet? "The sheet," she explained, "he balled up in front of him, hiding you know what. A throbbing thing, I'm sure. Do you think men feel a lot of pain when, you know, when they can't finish the job? I'm a nurse, but I don't specialize in that sort of thing. I never left Paul destitute."

Melissa appeared disappointed. Instead of answering her question, she grabbed the handle of the suitcase, saying, "You can't leave," and hauled it into the closet.

Amanda attempted to snatch it back, but she couldn't get past Melissa.

"Melissa, get out of my way. I have to leave. They're getting married."

"Over my dead body they are. I had better be dead if Daphne ever becomes my sister-in-law. I want you for a sister-in-law."

Her gaze fused with Melissa's. "I've got to go." She made another attempt to get the suitcase.

"You don't get it do you, Amanda? Surely you've wondered what it is between you two. It's really quite simple. Garry's your destiny. Your soul mate, or perhaps even your soul flame. That's stronger than a soul mate, I've heard."

"And you've been reading too many novels lately," Amanda said, shoving her way into the closet. "A romantic fantasy this week? I think you should stick to your mystery novels."

"Are you denying that he kissed you? That he *wanted* to kiss you?"

Amanda blinked back a dam of tears. Melissa was confusing her. "I really must go now." She attempted one last time to get at her suitcase. Melissa moved aside, strangely allowing the gesture. Amanda grabbed the handle and retrieved it out of the closet.

"I saw Eddie. He was at the airport in L.A."

Amanda paused, and then sat her suitcase back on the floor.

"And One-Eyed Jack. He followed me on the plane."

Amanda grew stiff. "One-Eyed Jack?"

Melissa abruptly dragged her to the bed where she explained what she'd seen. Upon landing, One-Eyed Jack was nowhere to be seen. However, after reaching the arrival gate, she was approached by an airport attendant who handed her an envelope. Melissa reached across the bed, lifted her pocketbook from off the floor, and pulled out a white sealed envelope. "It's addressed to you."

Hesitant, Amanda took the envelope, noting the familiar handwriting on the front of it. "Eddie," she whispered.

"Eddie? How could he… oh wait, One-eyed Jack—"

Amanda raised a halting hand. She shook her head, too numb to speak. Nervously, she opened the envelope, and then stared blankly at the note in her hand. "I'm so sorry, Melissa. I see now I shouldn't have come here. I may have placed us all in danger."

"What are you talking about? What does the note say? Is Eddie threatening you?"

"No, Melissa. Not Eddie."

Melissa reached for her hand. "Is he warning you? Handling the situation?"

Amanda gazed up, unable to conceal her worry. "I don't know what Eddie's capable of, Melissa. Inside, I think I know... and that's what scares me."

"So, this guy on the plane, who was he? He's not with Eddie?"

Amanda wet her lips and swallowed. "One-Eyed Jack, as you call him, works for a man named J.D. Bowers, a loan shark from Miami, someone Paul had owed money to. Eddie said he was ruthless. We had thought he was possibly Paul's assailant, but Bowers swore he wasn't lucky enough to get his hands on Paul first."

"So why harass you? It's not you who owed him money."

"I don't think he cares, so long as he gets his money. I believe Eddie knows more, but he won't tell me. He just keeps reminding me that I'm always safe." She glanced down at the note in her hands. "Somehow, we have to trust Eddie and believe he's keeping any danger at bay, at least for now, because there's another big problem we need to contend with." She sighed shakily. "We've got to convince Garry to let me stay." She handed the note to Melissa.

Taking it, Melissa read the only two words on the page: *Stay put.*

A line slowly curved on Melissa's mouth. "I knew the angels would find a way to keep you here."

Amanda fell back on the bed, her mind swimming in turmoil. If this was the work of angels, it must surely be Judgment Day.

"Now, don't worry about a thing. I'll talk to Garry. I got you here, didn't I? I can keep you here. I just need some creative juice." Melissa began tapping her head. "Creativity, come in please."

*Oh yeah,* Amanda thought, watching Melissa. *It must be Judgment Day.*

# 20.

# I DON'T WANNA KNOW

MELISSA STOOD OUTSIDE Garry's door, trying to gather enough nerve to enter his bedroom. She wasn't about to go in and tell Garry the real truth—that Amanda was in danger of being abducted by a notorious criminal her deceased husband had been involved with. Melissa realized that even if she could get Garry to believe such an incredulous story, he'd blame her completely for hiring a nurse from hell.

Melissa sighed. Secrets seemed to be piling up all around them. It was bad enough she'd made a dishonest woman out of Amanda—having her parade in illusive clothes—but now she was about to, well, she wasn't sure what she was about to do.

Turning the doorknob, she entered Garry's bedroom. He sprung up on his elbow.

"Melissa?"

"Is that delight or disappointment I see on your face, bubba?"

Garry paused. "Neither. What are you doing here?"

"That's what I was going to ask you. I've never seen you in bed so fully clothed. Shouldn't you be in the other room? Were you not planning to say good-bye to Amanda?"

Amanda's name brought his eyes alert. "I thought you were her coming through the door. She, uh, hasn't left yet?" Melissa shook her head. "Oh, good," he said, "I didn't think she'd leave without good-bye."

"Would it matter?"

Garry lowered his eyes. "No, should it?" He eased himself up against the headboard.

Melissa didn't speak for a long moment. She waited for Garry to look up. When he did, she said, "I want you to ask her to stay."

"She doesn't want to stay. She's got business to—"

"No, she doesn't. She only said that because she didn't want to come between you and Daphne. The truth of the matter is she needs to stay, for several reasons."

"Oh? Let me guess. She needs money. All women need money." He paused, and then frowned with disappointment. "I see. I hit it on the nose."

"She wants to adopt a little boy, Garry. He's wheelchair-bound and has no family. She's a widow, you know. Her husband left her nothing, only debt. She needs this job."

A quiet moment passed, and then he smiled. "I'm a nice kind of guy. I'll just overpay her when she comes in to say good-bye. I'm sure I'm paying a ridiculous price for a nurse anyway. What's a few more thousand?"

Melissa frowned. She wanted to tell him he was a jerk. A few thousand didn't come close to the tens of thousands she'd promised Amanda. Not near the amount she really needed. *All right, calm down*, she told herself. *No time to get hysterical.* Amanda wasn't going anywhere. *Think! Think quick!*

All of a sudden, Melissa rushed toward her brother, grabbed his shirtfront and began shaking him. "You can't let her go!" she cried. "She'll… she'll marry him." A reckless idea zooming forth. "She'll marry Jack. Yeah, Jack," the red-haired devil soaring through her head, a tale larger than life developing upon her lips. "And Jack is huge! I'm talking sloppy, fat huge—undeserving, no personality, no respect for people or animals, not a care for anything except food and himself. A real jerk. Warner, that's his last name. Jack Warner sits in a corner, eating whatever he wants, whenever he wants, shares with no one, selfish as they come!"

"Blast it." Garry sputtered, fighting to free his shirt from her grasp. "Let go of me. Talk sense."

"If you send Amanda back to Florida," Melissa said, "she'll marry sloppy huge and selfish Jack. *Bald* Jack. I've seen him Garry. A real slob, a big blob! And mean, too." She started pacing the floor. "But he's got money, lots of it. Made Amanda a proposition. He knows she's desperate, knows she'd do anything if it meant getting Robbie. She could have Robbie as long as she agreed to be his bed partner for life."

Garry's face creased at Melissa's story, yet this news showed heavy in his eyes.

"He wants her body, Garry."

That lifted his ears, a smirk slowly curving his mouth. Garry apparently thought her statement outrageous, yet Melissa knew that he was attracted to

Amanda, even if only a little. She was determined to uncover that magnetic force with a fine toothcomb.

"You'd think she wouldn't have much under all that fabric she wears," she began, "but clothes can be deceiving. I should know. Beneath all that cloth is what men dream about. I helped her unpack her first day here. We yakked while she changed into fresh clothes. You'd never think a woman with her severe modesty would be wearing nothing but a strap of lace beneath those skirts, would you?"

Garry cleared his throat, "No," he croaked out. He began yanking on his collar.

"Frilly little under things. One needs the perfect hips for that sort of wear. You can be sure Amanda hasn't anything to worry about. Her hips enhance long, tanned legs, not to mention what God has blessed her with up top. I wouldn't have normally taken notice of such a thing, but how could I not when she wore that low-cut French bra? Daphne would die for ha-bongers like that! That's what Dan calls them—*ha-bongers.*" Melissa paused, attempting a straight face while she stared into Garry's pink one.

"Melissa..." Garry said, looking as if he was swallowing a log in his throat, "you don't have to—"

"What's the matter, Garry? Surely I'm not embarrassing you about ha-bongers and all." She stood with her arms akimbo. "Good grief, you're the one who taught me about the birds and the bees. You were so worried I'd go and get pregnant as soon as I started dating. Said I had the looks to knock the socks off a guy."

She smiled, dropped her hands from her hips and moved closer toward him. Leaning in just a bit, she lowered her voice beside him. "I think you'd say the same thing about Amanda. If ever you saw her naked, that is. Of course you never will, but I'm just making a point. The point being, I can't imagine Amanda having sex with Sloppy Jack." Melissa's eyes widened as she stepped back. "His bed is probably loaded down with candy wrappers and piecrust, held up with cinderblocks and cement. He'd probably squish her flat the moment he laid on her. Of course, she could always take the dominant position," Melissa said casually, fiddling with a ballpoint pen lying on the night table. "Amanda was known to do that quite often when she was married." Garry's brow raised, and Melissa leaned toward his face again. "She dared to share that bit of info with me when I dared to share some private things with her. You wouldn't believe what wild things she's done with a bowl of Cool Whip. I thought I knew it all."

Garry snatched the bed linen that lay next to his too-flushed body, a fistful of concealing sheet strewn across his mid-section. "Cool Whip?" he gasped.

"Yeah," she said, straightening, "gave me some new and fun ideas to tease Dan with. So you see, that's why Amanda needs to stay. She deserves someone better than Jack Warner. His short, blubbery fingers couldn't come close to pleasing her. Why it would take no less than both of those greasy, beefy hands to cover one of her breasts. She deserves a hand like... like," she seized Garry's left one, "like this, with long talented fingers that can tease and please her, touch her completely." Garry snatched his hand back. That's when Melissa spied the tube of cherry Chapstick lying in the half open drawer by the bed. Amanda had bought it at the airport the day of her arrival. Nicolas had relayed how it had fallen from the tangled sheet. Garry had kept it. "You wouldn't want some selfish slob kissing her lovely lips, would you, Garry? He'd probably devour her like a chicken leg."

Anger rose in Garry's face, his hands balling the sheet in front of him.

"Yep! While Amanda gags on raw liver, Jack'll be ravishing cherries and whip cre—"

"Like hell he will!" Garry roared, springing forward, Melissa catching him before he fell off the bed. She pushed him back against the headboard and looked into his bereft face. "I-I mean, that would be like hell," he added, "for her to live like that. She can stay."

Melissa flung her arms around his neck. "Oh Garry, you won't regret this! You're a hero. I thank you and Amanda thanks you. I'll go tell her the good news."

Garry sat on the bed amid the crumpled covers, watching his sister fly out the door. The moment she was gone, he kicked at the sheet and blanket while he ripped open his shirt and unbuttoned his pants. Air, he needed air.

He lay back on the bed, his eyes staring glazed at a cracked beam in the ceiling. I'm doomed, he realized with chagrin, his left hand swiping up sweat from his chest and belly.

And to think the trouble was nearly over. *Fool!* He'd brought it back twofold.

# 21.

# I LET MYSELF BELIEVE

THE MORNING WAS blistery cold. Eddie Chandler halted at the edge of the woods, his warm breath a silent haze in the frosty climate that enclosed his stalwart body. His boots sunk deep in fresh snow as he stood warrior-like, his ears keen to approaching danger. His smoke gray eyes focused steadily on the great log home glittering white beneath the dawning sun. The front bay window, left of the long framed porch, was Amanda's room. He'd seen her there, looking out, her near presence causing his blood to warm.

*I'm going mad*, he thought, his mind fighting back the involuntary quiver of his right eye. He had barely remembered chartering a jet, arriving in Denver just before Melissa Rosten had exited her plane. His main concern at the time was to eliminate J.D.'s man before the thug had a chance to follow Melissa. He'd done so with little trouble, and then shipped him back to Florida in a crate. Maybe J.D. Bowers will think twice before sending another man.

When Eddie had arrived at the Danzlo estate, it was late night. He had parked his rented car several miles from the house, and then traveled the rest of his journey by foot. He'd been fully prepared with warm gear; however, he'd been standing watch for many hours now. His body felt numb with cold, his mind somehow not feeling his own.

He gazed down at his gloved hands, watching his fingers open and close as he willed them to. He realized his will was growing weak these days, and he'd had a couple of blackouts that had awakened him in places he ought not be. He *must* be in control. He had to foster it with all of his strength if he expected to keep Amanda from danger.

It had come as no surprise finding J.D.'s man in California tailing Melissa. He expected no less of the bloodthirsty shark from Miami to send his barracuda on a malicious game. Leaving the state had been a bad move on Amanda's part. If Eddie had known she was leaving, he could've warned her. But Amanda shared nothing with him. Not anymore. Their relationship had begun with Paul, had died with Paul. But by God, she should've been his from the beginning. He'd been a fool to allow the marriage, but Amanda was so happy at the time, wanting the marriage, asking for his blessing. He couldn't deny her. Had never been able to. *Until now.*

Amanda had thought to run from him. But she was afraid, that's all. He'd foolishly caused her to fear him. He had to prove to her she had nothing to be afraid of. He'd protect her with his life, and she would soon realize she belonged with him. His eyes burned as he focused on the window, begging her forth. *Amanda. Amanda.*

A shadow appeared behind sheer curtains; the curtains danced aside. Eddie stepped back.

AMANDA GAZED OUT her bedroom window, her eyes centered on the cedar wishing well just beyond the alpine fir. The icicles along its ridge were a blur of glittery stars as she tried focusing through tears that were fast forming. She should be happy about staying. Yesterday she'd cried knowing she was leaving and that her chance to rehabilitate Garry would be lost. His health was the important thing—his full recovery. She would help him regain his strength, get back his life and career. Meanwhile, Eddie would take care of those external matters. She had to believe that, so she could leave and be with Robbie, and Garry could be with Daphne.

Amanda clutched her heart as though to get it back, her mind pleading to the wishing well: *I don't want to love Garry. I don't want to leave, yet I don't want to stay.*

She glanced over her left shoulder at the closed door of the adjoining bathroom, listening to Melissa's melodic voice humming through the sprinkling of water that ran in the shower. Melissa had been thrilled, so proud of herself for accomplishing the great feat in getting Garry to allow Amanda to stay. Amanda still wasn't sure just how Melissa had managed to change Garry's mind so quickly. Melissa had assured her that Robbie was the reason behind Garry's change of heart. He'd been touched by her wish to adopt the boy. She suddenly wanted to tell Garry all about Robbie, and share with him more about her life as well.

*If only I could get some private time with him.*

She turned and walked across the room toward the door. Just maybe, by some mere chance, Daphne wasn't with him right now. A moment later, she'd gotten the nerve to knock on Garry's door, a mixture of emotions reeling through her body—hope, apprehension, excitement, dread. She had waited till morning to approach him, giving him the night to break the news to Daphne. She entered the room when his voice ushered her in. The first thing she saw was the tall blonde, standing just feet away, accusation in her eyes.

Amanda forced a smile. "Good morning."

"Would've been. Missed your plane? Or was there something here you wanted and couldn't leave behind? *Something that isn't yours?"*

"Daphne!"

Amanda's focus swerved on Garry. His skin was taut across his cheeks.

Daphne's melodious laughter cut the silence. "I was just kidding, darling," she said over her shoulder at Garry. "Can't anyone in this house take a joke?"

Garry's reproving stare was unwavering.

"Hmmm, darling, I do believe Nicolas was right. You need to get out of this stuffy old room. He's such a dear to send in your *rehired* nurse so you could eat breakfast in the kitchen this morning." Daphne smiled sweetly, turning her attention back to Amanda. "Do take care of my future husband, Ms. Fields. Don't drop him or anything." She turned on her heel and left the room. Amanda's gaze met Garry's.

"I'm sorry," he said, "for Daphne's sick humor."

Amanda returned his apology with a smile. "Oh, is that what that was?" Her head tilted against her right index finger. "Funny how humor can be so dynamic. *"*

Garry laughed. Then his expression became serious. "She's not all bad."

"But of course. You plan to marry her, right?"

Garry paused, swallowed. "Right."

"Well, then, she must have some good to her, or else you wouldn't marry her. I, for one, believe you can't judge a book by its cover."

He smiled. "No, Ms. Fields, you can't."

He gazed at her with new respect, thinking how he'd first judged her and how different she seemed now. So she dressed a little funny, had eccentric tastes, could be bossy at times. But he'd learned that beneath that exterior was an incredible woman who had a sweet and witty personality. She was caring and kind. He could easily visualize Amanda as the perfect mother for the little boy Melissa spoke of yesterday. Daphne would never think of adopting a lamed child, would never even consider it. "Daphne is jealous of you," he said, not intending to speak his thought aloud.

"Of *me?*" Her tongue slid across her lips then, the gesture throwing Garry's mind amuck, the room growing hot.

"Which is absolutely crazy," he assured hastily, lifting his eyes from her moistened lips.

"Absolutely," she concurred. "Mr. Danzlo…"

His name sounded like an endearment on her lips, the dulcet tone in her voice catching his full attention. His gaze claimed her mouth once again; her lips were wet, glistening… *alluring*. She started to fiddle with her dress, her hands smoothing down the sides of her jumper, ironing out the wrinkles as she pulled on the material in an act to straighten her wear. Garry's focus instantly lowered to her bosom now taut against gold-brown fabric, his mind filling with French-cut bras and straps of lace. His gaze lowered even further, his imagination taking him far beyond the call of reason. His eyes shot back to her face.

"These last days have been difficult for us both," she was saying. "I just want you to know—"

"Our relationship is strictly business, Ms. Fields, from this day forward. I mean, it's always been that way. Always will be. We're business collaborators, not friends. I'm getting married."

Amanda's lashes flickered. Whether hurt or anger he glimpsed behind those glass frames, he couldn't quite tell. But he couldn't let it bother him.

"I wanted you to know that, Ms. Fields. I allowed you to stay because, I know your situation and—"

"And you felt pity for me," she finished for him. He started to correct her, but she wouldn't let him. "So sorry to inform you, sir," her voice formal, her stance erect, "but you didn't allow me to stay. I allowed myself to stay. You're the one who needs help, not me." She went for the wheelchair across the room.

It took a thoughtful moment for Garry to respond.

"The hell, you say. I can fire you!"

"Has that ever stopped me before, Mr. Danzlo? I think not." She ripped the covers off him. He was fully clothed. She took hold of his legs and pulled them over the bedside, flipping him left and face down in the process. He gagged on sheet.

"Oh, so sorry, Mr. Danzlo. So terrible of me to forget how weak you are." She flipped him back over. "But that's what a few days break will do for you, and that's why we'll be having no more breaks. Work, work, work for you!"

She ignored Garry's moans and groans while she continued with her chore.

"Yep, gotta get that business collaboration on the roll," she said. "No time for friendship." With unusual strength, she bounced him up on his good leg and plopped him down into the wheelchair. "Yes-sir-ree, no more stealing kisses. Strictly business for us. Gotta get you ready for that future marriage of yours. Get that body in good working order. *Whoops*, look at the time!" She was behind him now, jerking the wheelchair into forward gear. "Don't wanna keep that future wife of yours waiting. She might think we're doing hanky-panky. Of course, we're not. Never have, never will, right, Mr. Danzlo? Gotta save that for your sweetie." She patted him on the shoulder and pushed him down the hall.

By the time they reached the kitchen, Garry was holding back a grin, his anger lost somewhere between "no more stealing kisses" and "doing hanky-panky."

One thing was for sure, his day would not be dull.

# 22.

# IF YOU REMEMBER ME

THE DAY HAD been more than dull and intolerable for Daphne. She was bored and uninterested in Garry's rehabilitation and highly annoyed by the company she had to keep—namely, that chit nurse who kept touching and assisting Garry by the hour. It was bad enough putting up with Melissa, the bitch sister with all her wisecracks and deliberate attempts to keep Garry's attention on Amanda. By sunrise the next morning, Daphne decided to bless the entire household with her departure, the front door closing as Melissa and Amanda were making their way toward the kitchen for coffee. Daphne's personal chauffeur had arrived to take her away.

"I can't believe it!" Melissa cheered. "The bat has taken flight."

Nicolas chuckled. "Yes, but unfortunately she plans to return by afternoon. She's making a trip into town only."

"Ah, shucks," Melissa said. The three burst into laughter in the kitchen. Then Bagel the beagle trotted weakly into the room, her unsteady body barely making it through the doorway. She stood only a second, and then fell over, as though dead.

The three were suddenly beside the dog. Amanda assessed a pulse. Bagel had one, but barely palpable, her breath shallow and almost unobservable. "She's still alive. Nic, call—"

But Nicolas was donning his coat, wasting no time on calls. "Yancey, the neighbor, has a small practice at his ranch. He tends horses, cattle and such. We'll take Bagel there." Nicolas scooped the dog into his arms. Melissa snatched her coat from the utility room where she'd left it last night after a walk in the snow with Amanda. Amanda grabbed the Land Rover's keys from a hook near the refrigerator and threw them to Melissa who caught them as she barreled out the back door.

163

"Amanda, stay with Garry," she yelled, "and listen out for the phone." She hopped into the truck, and in seconds, tires were crunching across the snow-packed drive.

The house fell strangely quiet. Amanda realized that for the first time since her arrival, she was truly alone with Garry. Should she tell him about the dog? If Bagel didn't survive for some reason, then Garry might blame her for not being truthful. Honesty was always the best policy.

*Honesty*—the very word brought tears to her eyes. She hadn't been truthful with Garry since the day she'd laid eyes on him. Haunted by that knowledge, she had told Melissa early that morning that they needed to confess their wrong doings, and soon. But Melissa was adamant that this was not the right time for confessions, at least not while Daphne was in the house.

Well, Daphne wasn't in the house. Perhaps this was her chance. Garry might very well forgive her if she confessed it all right now, explained why it was so important for her disguise. She'd tell him she wanted to be totally honest with him so he could trust her.

With that thought in mind, she pivoted to the stove to prepare a surprise. First, she would need to butter him up.

GARRY LEANED UNCOMFORTABLY against the cool headboard of the bed. He'd grown immune to discomfort, at least the physical kind. The emotional kind that lay deep in his gut was a different story. Last night's sleep had been filled with more nightmares, waking him to cold and bitter memories of his father, and unwanted feelings of hatred. Had it not been for the alias Jake Fayman, who walked into his life one day, his reaction to the death of the old man could've simply been nothing. Yet instead, he felt betrayed by two men, though the two were one and the same.

He closed his eyes. He was kidding himself if he thought to find peace, for she came, his imaginary Eve. She was no longer a comfort, but a disturbance to his crazed senses. It was as though he was experiencing her tears while she cried out his name. *Garry, Garry*, her voice sauntered through him with desperation. She seemed to have lost him. "I'm here," he whispered wretchedly while her despondent voice kneaded and twisted his heart, killing him softly. "Baby, I'm here."

A light feminine fragrance meandered around him suddenly. He inhaled; the taste of rose settled on his lips.

Garry bounded off the headboard, his eyes opening as panic moved through his bones, causing him to scan the room, the door, the bed, his lap. It was like *déjà vu*—the way he felt the morning he awoke to find Daphne in his bed. He thought he'd lain with another woman… *with Amanda Fields*. But it wasn't true. Yet the feeling was there, was always there.

*The dream.* He'd dreamed of his Eve that night. He felt her fingers warm against his lips, pliant in his mouth. His Eve could feel so real sometimes.

He leaned back against the bed, Amanda's lips suddenly before his eyes, moist, inviting. The image was so real, saliva came gushing through the pores in his mouth. He shook his head to erase the vision, swallowing a river while flinging the covers off his near naked body. He wore only boxer shorts, which Nicolas, very early this morning, helped him don before assisting him with an early trip to the bathroom. The thin fabric of the shorts was no relief to his too warm body, his back sweating, sliding against the wood surface of the headboard.

He tried maneuvering his body forward, toward the side of the bed so he could dangle his legs. His weak right side kept pulling him downward each time he attempted to straighten himself. *Pitiful!* he thought. He put forth the effort to sit upright like a normal person, manually adjusting his right leg upon the bed to stable himself.

A string of curses threatened to spew, but he held them inside. He was determined to get both his feet steady on the floor. When he accomplished the feat, he relaxed and found himself whispering, *thank you. Thank you, Amanda.*

He closed his eyes, allowing the warmth of her name to billow upward to his ears. Such a compassionate giver, who saw everything positively and with hope. She was the friend everyone should have. The friend he desperately needed.

"Knock, knock," said a feminine voice outside his room, followed by a rap against the door.

Garry's thoughts went berserk. Amanda *the friend* was at his door. She'd see him near naked on the bed. "Who's there?" he said, frantically looking for the sheet and blanket. He'd flung them off with such vigor moments before, that they both lay across the room in a heap on the floor.

His robe then. He spied it lying over the chair next to the door he didn't want opened. His breath ceased.

"Close," Amanda answered cheerfully.

"Clothes?" Garry screeched. "Clothes, who?"

"Close your eyes, I have a surprise."

Garry was not ready for the end of this knock-knock joke. He'd made a vow to never be without clothes in Amanda's presence again. Not after what happened last time. Where was Nicolas? Why hadn't he come back like he'd promised?

"I don't like surprises," he said. "Go away."

Laughter rang on the other side of the door. "Oh, Mr. Danzlo, you're so funny. Everybody likes surprises. So close your eyes, I'm coming in anyway."

Hearing the door knob jingle, Garry twisted, shock sending him off balance, his upper body tilting to the right, his left hand clutching a fistful of fitted bottom sheet in hopes of saving himself from a deadly fall. Amanda came in just in time to see the elastic of the fitted sheet *pop* from its bed corners. Like a ball in a slingshot, Garry went zooming forward, sheet and all.

Amanda didn't have time to think. The food tray in her hands whizzed through the air like a giant Frisbee, whirling a near twenty feet from her hands to land not-so-smoothly on the mattress while Garry, the ball, made a not-so-smooth landing on top of her. He knocked Amanda silly with a *slam, bam, thud* on the floor.

"Aaaugh!" "Hmph!" "Ungh!" moaned the two on the floor.

"Good grief, Mr. Danzlo, are you alright?" Garry squirmed in her arms and made low gruffly noises as though he were smothering from that sheet that fit like a glove over his various body parts. "*Ow, ouch*, stop hitting, stop wiggling and let me help you!" she said after he elbowed her in the rib, his knee jabbing her right thigh. "Please tell me if you're hurt!"

"No," he shouted, the sheet lid springing off his head, his face rebounding, then plastering against her ample chest. A few seconds passed in stunned silence. The smell of rose musk up his nose and against his mouth spurred his chin upward. He stared into a bereaved face he mistook for pain. "Are you alright, Ms. Fields?" he asked. His left hand free, reached up to straighten her glasses. Amanda lay breathless as he fixed them much too slowly, his blue eyes gazing into her brown ones with a spark of amusement. His lips suddenly curved into a smile.

"Just what did you think you were doing, Mr. Danzlo?" she scolded. "You could've been hurt badly. Didn't I tell you not to get up without assistance?"

Garry's smile vanished. "You tell me to do a lot of things, Ms. Fields, but that doesn't mean I have to listen to you." He tried to twist himself out of the sheet, rolling off her in the process. He only tangled himself more, getting more frustrated by the second. "Woman, get me out of this thing!"

Rising on her knees, Amanda bent over her mummy-wrapped patient. His head and left arm and hand were the only body parts sticking out from the sheet. "You tell me to do a lot of things, Mr. Danzlo, but that doesn't mean I have to listen to you." She started to stand and walk away, but he grabbed the hem of her skirt with his strong free hand, jerking her back down upon the floor. She screamed, clutching the glasses on her face with one hand and holding her dress down with the other. Flat on her back, she was bombarded by his sheeted body. She looked up into Garry's looming face.

"Thought you were smart, didn't you? But I'm smarter," he said with a triumphant gleam in his eye.

"Ha, you won't think you're so smart if Daphne walks in and finds us like this," she said with some seriousness. Her lips pressed in a fine line. "You know how jealous she is. Aren't you concerned?"

He hesitated, studying the curiosity in her eyes. "Daphne's not here," he finally said. "She's gone into town. But perhaps you know that?" He didn't mean for his line to sound so accusing, as though she'd taken full advantage of Daphne's absence. If anything, it was the other way around. "If you hurry and unloosen me from this sheet, Ms. Fields, we may escape the gaping faces of Nicolas and Melissa. I'm surprised they haven't come in with all the raucous we've been making."

Amanda cleared her throat. "Well, they're not here either."

Garry's face drooped heavily.

"You see, the dog was sick and they had to take—

Garry was off her in a second, panic on the rise. He rocked frantically in the sheet on the floor, striving for freedom. He had to get out of this sheet, and into some clothes. He didn't trust himself, nor his body, with Amanda.

Amanda consoled Garry about the dog as she helped untangle him from the king-sized sheet. "As soon as the vet discovers the problem," she said, taking one corner of the fabric in both hands and gripping it well, "I'm sure Bagel will be fine." She stood with feet apart and with one tremendous jerk, Garry went spiraling across the floor, sheet-free, his body landing brutally upside a desk. Garry gawked with disbelief, and then sent Amanda an offensive eye across the room. Her mouth displayed an askew smile, worry lines wrinkling her forehead. "Sorry," she gulped.

He lay haphazardly against the desk naked, except for his boxer shorts, staring over at a face full of purity and concern. Then his lungs exploded with a gut full of laughter. "You're one dangerous woman, Amanda Fields! Any man would be lucky to be alive after your delicate nursing care." He roared even louder.

To hear him actually say her first name put her into a stupor for a couple of seconds, then she stomped across the floor to the chair by the door, grabbed his robe and flung it in his laughing face. "Cover yourself, Garry Danzlo. Only despicable patients like you are lucky to be alive." She turned toward the bed where her large tray, beholding a special breakfast for two, was in a shamble. A juice glass lay over on its side, an orange creek running between the silverware and plates. The white thermal decanter filled with coffee was tipped across a silver domed platter. And who knew what mess lay under the dome. Amanda pouted. "Your surprise is ruined."

Garry raised himself upright with the support of his left arm, his legs sprawled in front of him. His laughter stopped once he saw Amanda's frown. His eyes followed hers to the breakfast tray on the bed. "Food, for the almost dead patient! She *does* care. Sit it right here, nurse," he said, slapping his hand on the floor beside him. He attempted with some difficulty to don his blue velour robe. Amanda came immediately to his side. "Always to the rescue, aren't you, Ms. Fields?"

Amanda half-smiled. "I'll make you another tray." She paused. "Actually, I cooked enough for two. I thought maybe we might…"

Garry's brow upturned. "Two? Like in, you and me? You were going to eat with this despicable patient?" Amanda's smile grew. "Well, honey, what are you waiting for? Bring it on as is! You eat the first bite though, since you cooked it. Wouldn't want you to die second."

"Funny," she said, and then retrieved the tray from the bed and placed it on the floor between them. She stared down at the white carnation in a puddle of orange juice. He picked it up, orange juice dribbling down his hand as he held it out to her. "To you… for bringing me this nice surprise." Juice pattered on the silver dome like orange rain on a tin roof. Amanda giggled. She picked up a sopping wet napkin, slapping it across the back of his raised hand. Taking the flower from his wet fingers, she said, "For you… to dry yourself."

Garry's smile slackened. "Are you trying to make trouble?"

"I *am* trouble, Mr. Danzlo. It's my middle name."

They both laughed. An awkward silence settled between them—Garry thinking, I knew you were trouble the moment I met you, but especially the moment I kissed you. I should've never kissed you.

"Mr. Danzlo—"

"Ms. Fields—"

They spoke in unison, laughing again as they realized both had something they wanted to say. "You first," Garry said.

Amanda wet her lips. Garry looked away toward the domed plate. As he lifted the dome from its platter, he vaguely heard her say, "We need to talk. Seriously."

Garry grinned down at a disheveled stack of pancakes, the one on top grinning back at him. From what he could tell, each pancake wore a different expression. Amanda had made them with little candies one puts on cupcakes. With a fork, he flipped through the many happy faces, some with little noses, fat ones, dinky eyes, overly large eyes, smiles of all shapes and sizes, but the bottom pancake had the funniest expression of all. Totally squished by too-heavy pancakes. "Oh look, a Mandy-Pandy!" he laughed appreciatively. "The very expression you wore when you caught me on the floor."

Amanda blinked. "Mr. Danzlo, did you hear what I said?"

"Yes, I heard you," he said, eyes raising with a smile. "And I think you're absolutely right. I've been so pigheaded up to this point, holding things in. And you... you never gave up on me. Just kept edging me on, hoping, waiting until I was ready to talk. I think I'm ready now, thanks to you."

"What?"

"You bring out the good in me. I wouldn't dare admit that at first. That male ego, you know? But it's time I tell you how much I appreciate the smiles you put on my face, the laughter you've brought back into my life. After the accident I wanted to give up, felt I didn't deserve to live. I think I'm still fighting that. Sometimes I think I'm really worthless."

Amanda shook her head, rendered speechless by his openness. *His* confession.

"I know," he smiled. "You think I'm worth something. And that's what makes you special, even though you dress a little weird." He teased, grinning. "But hey, who am I to tell you how to dress? Personally, I think you'd look much better without the makeup—"

"How 'bout a pancake!" she nearly shouted, slapping one onto a damp plate. "Think I'll have one, too. I'll fix both our plates, how 'bout it? I just love pancakes, don't you?"

"Ms. Fields, I didn't mean to upset you, offend you."

"Upset me? Not on your life!" Her eyes were like saucers, round, wide.

"Can I ask you a personal question?"

She looked up, gulping a gallon-tank of air. "Sure, fire away," she squeaked like a balloon, snatching up a bottle of syrup.

Garry cleared his throat. "Do you think I'm capable of having sex with a woman?" Amanda dropped the syrup bottle into a bowl of strawberries and cantaloupe. Garry snatched it up before it spilled over the fruit. "What I'm trying to say is," he said, handing the bottle back into her shaking hands, "I'm afraid. Afraid of not performing effectively. Daphne wants us to wait and try after we're married. What if I disappoint her? What if I can't, you know. Or what if I'm unable to… control myself."

There was a mutual uncomfortable moment before she answered.

"Mr. Danzlo, anything's possible. You just have to want it, believe in it. I think you need to work toward rehabilitating yourself first and regain the strength you've lost. Fight for it. Pray for it. Here, take this."

He chuckled at the pile of pancakes and fruit on his plate. She'd served him twice the portion she'd served herself. "I bet you were a great wife," he said genuinely. "You probably spoiled your husband rotten."

Amanda smiled wryly.

"What's it like to be married, Mandy? You don't mind if call you that, do you? Friends, right?" He held out his left hand for her to shake, and then decided to use his right. It took some effort to raise it properly, his jaw tightening as he worked his muscles to do so.

Tears formed in Amanda's eyes. She swallowed hard and reached out for his hand, whispering, "Friends" and then, "Garry" as if they were sacred words. After a short pause, she added, "Garry, there's something I've got to—"

"You know what I like about you most, Mandy?" He looked gravely into her eyes. "Your honesty and your goodness. I know I can trust you. Sometimes that's hard for me to do. I've been betrayed many times in my life. Thank you, for being different."

Amanda sat speechless; a hesitant nod her only response. He could tell he'd made her uncomfortable, so he glanced away and placed a strawberry in his mouth.

"So, Mandy, tell me about marriage? What was it like?"

She wiggled beside him. "I bet those pancakes are frostbitten by now. I should go reheat them."

Had he broached a subject too painful to handle? Her husband had died. He'd never asked her why or how. That part didn't seem important. Only that she'd lost the man she'd chosen to spend her life with. Garry decided to change the subject for now, put a smile back on her face. He glanced down at his plate overly stacked with pancakes and said, "I think you're trying to make me fat."

His words took a moment to sink in, but the corners of her mouth finally turned upward, a glint of a twinkle shining behind her orange-brown frames. "You're right. I want you layered well, so you might someday say I have the most favorable face."

He raised an inquiring brow. "Mine, less favorable than yours? Come here, Mandy." He leaned forward, waiting for her to make the same move. He saw her uncertainty and encouraged her with, "I promise I won't bite." Reluctantly she drew closer, till only inches separated their faces. He reached up and removed her glasses with his left hand, his gaze long-studying her eyes, then her nose, her mouth. "I hate to tell you this," he said, his focus moving back up to her sunny eyes. "Your face is already much more favorable than mine."

His words breathed upon her body. She nervously raised two fingers to his lips, whispering, "Shhhh, don't tell anyone."

The tender touch of her fingers against his mouth triggered something inside him, and he captured her hand, grasping her fingers against his lips while he stared at her with recognition. An abrupt change appeared in her eyes, fear perhaps? She tried to remove her hand, but he wouldn't let her, his grasp tightening around her fingers. Her fingers slipped across his lips as they tried to escape. His mouth opened to the taste of her, his eyes closing, warmth radiating down his throat. An eternity passed before he opened his eyes. Tears stood in her eyes and slithered down her face. He felt them as though they were spilling down his own.

"It *was* you," he said hoarsely. "You were with me that night."

She swallowed, and took in a ragged breath. "Yes. Yes it was, Garry."

He could barely breathe. "Why didn't you tell me? Why did you allow me to—"

"Because she's not the sweet girl you think she is, you fool!" Daphne stood in the doorway, enraged at finding the two on the floor together. "I can't leave one minute and she's trying to get into your pants."

Amanda, mortified, tried to stand, but Garry was clutching her hand. She glanced at his face—a face full of hurt, disbelief, and then anger as he looked up at Daphne. "You lied to me."

"No, I lied *for* you," Daphne corrected, "and for that slut you're holding hands with."

Garry's face hardened. "Call her that again," he dared.

Daphne knew her limits, Garry's murderous stare keeping her silent.

"Perhaps I should leave and come back later," Amanda said, attempting to rise again.

"You need to stay," he commanded. "I want answers."

Laughter reverberated from the doorway. "And you think she's going to tell you the truth? I hardly think so, darling, after all the other lies she's told you. She's not even who you think she is. The real Amanda Fields is hiding behind—"

"Garry!" Amanda jumped up, breaking free from his grasp, alarm, apprehension clear on her face. "I never meant to hurt you, only help you. It's true, I've been hiding behind—"

"A lot of guilt," Daphne intervened, never meaning for Garry to find out that beneath all that garb, was a comely woman. She knew it to be true now, Amanda's panicky behavior saying it all. She'd lose Garry for sure! She'd only wanted to put a scare into the girl. "She's been trying to seduce you, darling!" Daphne feigned tears. "Ever since she got here. She tried to that night I caught her in your bed. She was taking advantage of you while you slept."

"No... *no!*" Amanda cried, taking in Garry's face. "It's not true!"

"I saved you and Garry from humiliation. But you kept on. You couldn't keep your hands off him. It had to end this way. Go ahead, tell him what you did that night."

Tears of disgrace had Amanda crying defense in blindness. "I didn't do anything, I…"

"She touched you, Garry. Tried to arouse you by laying her hand on your—"

"That's enough, Daphne!" Garry cried. His gaze clouded as he tried calming the whir of emotions in his perplexed body. Unknown to Daphne, her vengeful words were having quite an opposite affect than she'd intended, filling him with sheer sensuality. He was sweating like a hog, but he didn't dare take off his velour robe. He'd die in the flames of hell first.

"No, I want her to tell you," Daphne insisted, thinking her little game brilliant. She never saw Amanda touch him, but Garry didn't know that. Never would. "Tell him, Nurse Fields, how you laid your hand upon his belly and made your way down—"

"She's lying," Amanda pleaded into Garry's rounded eyes. "I'd never do such a thing. I only touched… I only touched your…" Amanda, hard pressed at getting her words out, had Garry watching her avidly, waiting for some dark confession he was afraid to know.

Daphne wasn't saying anything either. She was shocked to hear that her lie wasn't quite a lie.

"Ms. Fields…" Garry said hoarsely. He urged her to continue with a nod of his head.

The use of her last name jolted Amanda, disappointed her. "I touched your lips with the tips my fingers. I had no intention of doing more."

"His *lips?*" Daphne said, aghast at such ludicrousness. "Come now, Ms. Fields, you can do better than that. Your intentions went further."

"Good God, Daphne, just stop it!" Garry shouted, so loud, both women jolted. "I don't want to hear anymore!" Flashes of taking feminine fingers into his mouth, suckling them, licking them like candy kept spiraling through his brain. *Had he seduced his nurse?* Dear God, let that part be a dream. It was his Eve, not Mandy… *sweet as candy.* The very thought was erotic, somehow obscene, yet rapturous at the same time. But shame vanquished that bliss within seconds, burning his face and ears. "Daphne, step outside. I want a few words with Ms. Fields." Daphne's face grew taut, her eyes wild with protest, but Garry raised a hand, halting her actions. "I promise, I'll be only a moment," he said, "and then you can return."

Daphne released an angry breath, her next breath filling her lungs with relief and satisfaction. The harsh lines in Garry's face proved he'd been hurt by Amanda Fields. She smiled smugly. "Of course, darling. I'll be waiting in the other room."

Leaving and closing the door behind her, she nearly waylaid Nicolas and Melissa in the hall, for they'd been standing close to the door when she came out, narrowed eyes of accusation branded on their faces. She passed them with a giant smile planted on her beautiful face.

Inside the bedroom, a deadened silence pervaded for several moments.

"Bring me the wheelchair. Please," Garry finally said, his focus not on Amanda, but on the tray laden with the surprise pancakes. He put the dome over their happy faces, closing his eyes, trying to forget the joy he'd felt at being served them, of laughing with the one who made them.

Amanda retrieved the wheelchair from across the room, parked it beside him and locked its wheels. She started to help him up, but his voice halted her. "No, I'll try to do it myself." His gaze never left the floor. He pushed up on his left leg, his back scraping against the desk as his body rose unsteadily. He grabbed the wheelchair for support, but his weight on the chair was one-sided and it nearly toppled over him. Amanda quickly threw her weight on the opposite end of the chair, her hand stretching toward him. "Take my hand with your right," she urged. He hesitated, and then did what she asked, yet his balance was still forsaking him. Amanda caught him around the waist; he caught hers likewise. They stood, their gazes fusing for a long moment. Then he let go of her and backed into the wheelchair, speaking as he sat down.

"How long will it take to rehabilitate me? Get me on my feet, do things for myself?"

Amanda blinked, his question unexpected. "That's totally up to you. It's always been up to you. If you work hard to strengthen those muscles you've let go unexercised, you could probably master crutches within a week. Your left side is strong. You just need some balance, some ambition, patience. You could master a cane within a few weeks, maybe sooner. I'm sure of it."

"Two weeks. You have two weeks, Ms. Fields."

"Are we on a last name basis, again? If you'd let me explain about that night, I—"

"I've heard more than enough. I know all I need to know. Please leave my room now."

Amanda glared at him, anger quickly taking precedence. "No, you wouldn't want to know my side!" she shouted, now hysterical, her voice holding such contempt, Garry's gaze lifted to see if *the* Amanda Fields was actually talking. "Why mess up a perfectly good lie with the truth," she said, spitting fire. "It might mess up your excuse to get rid of me since all you want to do is jump into your bottle, see through a glass darkly, believe what you want to believe, see what you want to see. One-sided is best for you. Then you can avoid situations, pretend they don't happen, forget they ever happened."

Garry's face hardened. "That night needs to be forgotten! I suggest you forget it, too. You're here for one purpose and one purpose alo—"

"You haven't forgotten. Why should I?" She took a step toward him, her nearness causing his pulse to jump. Her eyes gleamed with more than just anger and tears. They suddenly softened. "I touched you while you were sleeping, it's true," she said softly. "I touched your lips. I did it because I wanted to. Because I felt like it. Isn't that why you kissed me the other morning? Because you wanted to, because you felt like it?"

She waited for Garry to say something, but his only response was a crimson face.

"Oh yes, let's forget about that morning, too. Why remember something as insignificant as a passionate kiss, or the suckling of fingers." Her lashes flittered as her fingers crinkled the sides of her dress. "Excuse me, but I never pried my fingers into your mouth that night. You invited them in, *took* them in fact. If I wasn't such a

Godly woman, and so afraid of you waking up, I'd have given you my other hand. I confess. I have uncontrollable desires just like everybody else. When something feels good, you just naturally want more. I should've been shot for falling asleep against the headboard of your bed and waking to find you nearly naked, all laid out before me to admire. Forgive me for being human, for being stupid, for being stupid and more stupid!" She started for the door.

"Mandy!"

She halted, closing her eyes, experiencing the thrill of her name on his lips.

He paused only briefly. "You're not stupid," he said. "I'm the stupid one."

She turned to him, her cheeks a blend of brown mascara and tears. "No, you're wrong about that, but right about one thing—I'm here for one purpose, and I disappointed you. Guess I wasn't kidding earlier. I *am* trouble. It's best you find another nurse." She started to walk away, but his voice halted her again.

"You walk out that door, you best be back! Unless you really want to disappoint me."

Amanda hesitated, then turned, her eyes fusing with his. He continued with grave words.

"I have a dream. You promised me that if I believed in my dream, fought for it, you'd be a part of it if only I'd let you. Well, I'm letting you, Mandy. Prove your words."

Trembling, she nodded. She pivoted to leave, her hand on the door.

"One hour," he told her. "Work begins in one hour."

She left, closing the door behind her, a fresh river of tears falling down her face.

# 23.

## SOMETHING'S COMIN' UP

"AMANDA, LET ME in. Unlock the door."

Melissa stood outside Amanda's bedroom, tapping the floor with her foot. She and Nicolas had thought to give her some time alone, but thirty minutes had gone by.

"Guess you don't care about the dog. Poor Bagel."

The door flew open, Amanda clutching the doorknob with one hand, clutching her stomach in remorse with the other. "She's dead?" she cried while Melissa pushed her way in.

"No, she's fine, but I can see you're not."

Amanda glowered. "You tricked me!"

Melissa closed the door and locked it. Turning, she said, "Daphne is tricking us all! The dog is going to be all right, but we can only thank God for that. Bagel was poisoned, and I betcha I know who did it!"

"What? Who?"

"Who else? Daphne! Guess what Yancey found when he pumped the dog's stomach? That piece of peanut butter toast you didn't eat last night." Melissa's finger pointed to the empty saucer by the bed. "Wasn't Daphne in the kitchen when you made it? One turn of your back was all she would need to sprinkle a bit of rat poison on your toast. Not only is Daphne trying to put Garry against you, she's trying to kill you!"

"Melissa, she may be evil, but—"

"We've got to do something before she destroys Garry and you. As for the rat poison, Garry would never believe us, so we're not going to tell him. Okay, I admit

Daphne may have just wanted to make you a little ill, for the amount of poison was miniscule, but that's hardly enough to excuse what she did." Melissa started pacing. "Somehow, we've got to woo Garry away from her. Completely. The only way to do that is…" she halted, looking Amanda dead in the eye.

"Oh, no. I'm not falling prey to another one of your crazy schemes. Whatever it is, you can just—"

"Do you want Garry to marry Daphne?"

"Well, no! She doesn't deserve him."

"But you do, Amanda. It's time to fight for that right and take advantage of how deeply he cares for you. He kissed you… *passionately!* He has somehow seen beyond the looks and found love within your soul. How much more love would he feel if he could experience all of you… see you for who you really are? But you won't admit this power you have over him. Wet your lips and he's yours. Give him more than that, and he's yours for life."

"Melissa, please." Amanda backed up to sit on the bed, her head feeling dazed. "I didn't come here for love. I came to free myself from trouble, not make more for myself."

"So you found love on the way. Think about it. Your love for Robbie brought you here. It was all meant to be. You can fight for Garry, too."

Amanda stood, the memory of the past hour with Garry vivid in her mind. "He shared wonderful things with me this morning, Melissa." She sighed with joy, her hand going to her chest as though she held the memory there. "He made me laugh; he made me cry. He told me how much he appreciated me. I wanted so much to confess everything then—the deceit, the lies—and I really think the truth would've come out if Daphne had not walked in when she did."

"Yeah, and I bet that little trip back to the house was planned," Melissa said, with an angled brow. "Said she forgot something. *Right.* She was spying. She doesn't trust Garry with you. I don't think Garry trusts himself with you either, which only proves my point." Melissa placed her hand on Amanda's shoulder. "If he's attracted to you now, just think how more attracted he'll be when he sees you in something pretty. No more gag clothes, no camouflage makeup from now on." Melissa glanced down at Amanda's wear and shook her head. "This clownish appearance keeps interfering with his mind waves," she said, lifting her eyes. "The time is now. Well, not now, but in a few hours. Tonight maybe. Daphne will be gone by then."

"Gone? She's going somewhere?"

Melissa grinned. "I told you, a lot happened in the last thirty minutes. Garry had a talk with her after you left his room. She exited Garry's bedroom mad as a hornet. Apparently, Garry has sent her on a two-week trip! Told her if she loves him and wants to marry him, she needs to give him this time to rehabilitate. They'd set a date for marriage when she returns. I think that was the ticket that made her agree to go. So you see, while the cat's away, the nurse can play." Melissa was all smiles, but Amanda wasn't smiling.

"I don't know, Melissa. If he's told Daphne…"

"He doesn't love Daphne. His mind is really screwed up right now. We have to unscrew it. If he says he's in love with you and not Daphne, are you going to deny him?"

"Well, no."

Melissa held out her hand. "Bet me. Within two weeks, he'll say the words."

Amanda's knees knocked at the thought. "And if he doesn't say them?"

"Then you'll be trying on a new dress while you watch me eat pig's feet."

"Ew, yuck! You're on," Amanda said, shaking Melissa's hand. "I thought being Jewish you weren't allowed to eat such things?"

"I'm not. But I don't plan to lose. Ma would have my hide. She's pretty orthodox, you know."

"No, I really don't know, Melissa. I felt really awkward talking with her on the phone yesterday, afraid she'd ask questions I didn't know how to answer. You told her my maiden name was Lowenstein? Good grief. Another lie to add to the countless others. Is it that important to her for Garry to have a Jewish nurse? Surely those other medical professionals you hired weren't all Jewish."

"Well, of course not. But they didn't have marriage potential."

An ill silence pervaded the room.

"What are you talking about? *Melissa?*"

Her friend didn't answer. Amanda's stomach turned over. "Oh my stars. What have you not told me now?"

The little brunette squirmed, a wry smile half-curving her lips. "Just a stupid little vow Mom and Garry made years ago. Hardly binding. So what that she made him prick his finger and seal the pledge with blood. That doesn't mean the promise can't be broken."

The memory of Nicolas' words began banging on her head. Was Melissa talking about the honorable Garry who never broke a promise? "The pledge? Cough it up, Melissa?"

"Our Jewish lineage goes way back, didn't I tell you?" She gabbled quickly.

Amanda shook her head. "Yep, way, WAY back. My grandparents emigrated here from Russia—Yiddish, that was their native language—and they brought with them an ancient book of family records, you see."

Oh yeah, she saw alright. She could barely breathe, let alone get out her next words. "Does Garry know I'm not Jewish?"

Melissa cleared her throat. "Well…" she intoned with guilty tempo, one side of her face askew, "pretty fat chance of that considering I handed the phone to Garry afterwards."

"Melissa!" Amanda stomped her foot, then heavily sighed. "Another confession to make to Garry. The odds are starting to look so *not* in my favor."

"Amanda, I'm sure it's the farthest thing from his mind. Do I think it would bother him to dishonor what mother calls her 'dying wish'? Probably. But love has a way of healing things, changing things. Your mere presence in this house has proven that, hasn't it?"

She couldn't answer.

"Now stop worrying. We've enough on our plates. And talking about plates, I think I'll go check on Nicolas and lunch."

Melissa was gone in an instant, not bothering to close the bedroom door on her way out. Amanda, intending to do so, stopped in its threshold and laid her head against the doorframe. She stared across the hall at Garry's door feeling miserable and uncertain.

"Well, well," came the pompous voice only inches from her door. "Are we daydreaming, Ms. Fields?"

Amanda flexed back, her hand ready on the door knob. Daphne stepped inside.

"You can shut it now if you like."

Amanda glowered. "I wouldn't like."

"No," Daphne tittered, "I guess you wouldn't. But if I was Garry, you'd like, right?"

"I think you should leave."

"I think differently." Daphne stepped closer. She was much taller, her beautiful face bent offensively in Amanda's. "I think someone's going to get hurt if they don't watch themselves, especially if they don't stop fooling around with men who don't belong to them."

"If you're trying to scare me, you're not."

"Oh, but I will, for you see, you've managed to sway Garry into getting rid of me."

"I never swayed him to do anything, except maybe believe in himself and accept help."

"Now that part is true. He's determined more than ever to regain what he lost, at least his physical strength. As for his career, he believes that's lost forever. What do you think?"

Her question took Amanda aback. "You're asking for my opinion?"

Daphne nodded.

"I believe he has a great chance of regaining his career, as a singer and as a pianist."

"Well, that would be wonderful. And much more beneficial. For myself, and certainly for Garry as well."

Amanda didn't like the smugness in her tone or the baneful gleam in her eye. She opened her mouth to say something, but Daphne spoke before she could. "I noticed you called my future husband Garry. No more 'Mr. Danzlo'? If you think I'm going to sit back and watch you steal him, you're wrong." Advancing, Daphne jagged a fingernail into Amanda's chest, backing her up abruptly. "So listen up, bitch!" Daphne bumped her against a wall. "Don't get any funny ideas while I'm gone. Start pumping him and you're dead."

"You're horrid and sickening," Amanda said, pushing her away forcefully, clearing a path to the door. Before she could fly past, Daphne grabbed a handful of blouse from Amanda's shoulder, shiny plum nails ripping it clear off her chest. The remains dangled off one shoulder. Amanda's mouth dropped; she immediately attempted to cover herself with the shredded material, but it was useless. She glanced at the open door, Garry's closed door in full view.

Forgetting all modesty, she ran and shut her door, falling back against it when it closed. She would've been a sumptuous sight for any man to behold, her bosom heaving voluptuously above a low-cut laced bra.

Daphne was speechless, as well as intimidated with her smaller and less firm bosom. Who would know under all that hideous garb Amanda wore that she could be so beautifully endowed. Garry's eyes would particularly be captivated if he were in the room, as he was known to admire women with large breasts. Max was always sorely reminding her of that.

Jealousy, hatred, and envy tore through Daphne's head.

"You deceiving little wench," Daphne said with venom. "I should've gotten rid of you that first morning after finding you in Garry's bed. Where's your real wardrobe, Ms. Fields?" Daphne charged in closer to Amanda, who still leaned against the door, her pulse rattling through her body when Daphne stopped just bare inches from her face smiling nastily. "How like Melissa to come up with such a cunning idea to make you 'not pretty' for my sake," she said. "But for your sake, heed my words: You had better keep the 'real you' a secret from Garry, else that little boy you so adore,"—she tilted her head with a sarcastic grin—"what's his name? Robbie? I'll make sure you never get him. You can kiss any adoption papers good-bye."

Amanda reacted without a second thought, the palms of her hands ramming forcefully against Daphne's chest, toppling her backward and sideways on the bed. "You dare to bring him into this when your mouth isn't even fit to speak his name. It's one thing to threaten me, but to threaten a little boy's happiness makes you nothing but a vile and heartless creature. As long as I breathe, you best stay away from anything that pertains to him!" Amanda warned.

Daphne caught her breath, rubbing her sternum, her eyes round with surprise. Then she broke into maniacal laughter that sent chills down Amanda's spine. "A little feisty when you're angry, Amanda, but they're just words. You don't have it in you to really harm anyone. It's not in your nature." Daphne rose from the bed, sweeping the wrinkles from her Christian Dior dress. "No, darling girl. Your best bet is to hurry and rehabilitate my Garry, and get the hell out of his life. Blow your cover, and you will wish you were dead. That's a promise."

With that, Daphne started for the door. But then she turned, pulling a small red notepad from her brassiere. She waved it in the air. "Just to let you know, I'm ahead of the game."

Then she was gone, the door closing behind her. Amanda rushed to the redwood desk. She jerked the drawer open, her fingers fumbling nervously through its contents. Robbie's letter was gone. Doc's letter and the small notebook with all the contacts of her creditors, the large balances she owed, addresses. Daphne had stolen it all!

The door flew open and Amanda jumped, circling to a stunned Melissa gaping at her torn blouse and exposed chest. "Oh my God!" Melissa screeched. "Did Daphne do that?" Then Nicolas was at the threshold, Melissa slamming the door in his face. "Sorry Nicolas," she yelled through the door. "Amanda's not properly dressed."

"Is everything okay?" Nicolas asked anxiously.

"Everything's…" Melissa swallowed, her eyes on Amanda who kept shaking her head. "Go finish lunch, Nicolas. Nothing to worry about."

Melissa hurried across the floor to her friend. She placed her hands on Amanda's bare shoulders; they were alarmingly cold.

Glassy-eyed and barely breathing, Amanda stuttered helplessly. "She's got my whole life in her hands, Melissa. She knows about the sham, that I'm deceiving Garry. And she has enough ammunition to make sure I never get Robbie. *Robbie…* she knows where he is!"

Melissa nodded, half comprehending. "Okay, just stay calm," she coaxed while her own hands trembled on Amanda's shoulders. "Eddie. You could call Eddie."

Yes, Amanda realized, and for one split second, the very thought brought her hope. But then, just as quickly, another unexplained feeling pushed its way within her gut declaring warning.

She needed time to think, to clear her head. Too many lives depended on it.

MAX SAT PATIENTLY in the limousine outside Garry's home, perusing a Playboy magazine with avid interest. Daphne banged on the driver's window, angry for having to track through snow to get his attention. The window rolled down. "You called?" he said with a smirk.

"Put that book down you horny bastard and go get my luggage. I want out of this place before Amanda comes out of that room."

Max slid from his seat and opened the back passenger door for her. Daphne, wearing a waist-length white fur mink, took one step forward and slipped on a patch of ice. Max caught her with ease from the back, his hands fully enveloping her hips, her shapely buttocks cushioning nicely against his hard erection. He groaned in her ear, slightly pumping his hips. "Max, not here, you oaf! And damn this snow and ice. I don't know how Melissa and Amanda can stand taking daily walks in it. If they're not in the woods, they're by that frigging pond on the pier, laughing and carrying on like two hyenas. If only they'd slip and fall in. Max, you've got to stop."

Max had slid one hand upon her breast, the nipple instantly hardening. He smiled. "I can arrange it," he said, nibbling on her ear.

Daphne glanced to the door and windows to assure no one could see them. All were closed from view. She relaxed. "Arrange what, Max darling?" She bent her head so his lips could travel her neck. He accommodated her, saying, "The fall. They'll both fall in."

She swiveled in his arms so quick, Max almost fell off balance. Surely he wasn't serious? But what a delightful thought. "Max, you're such a tease. Amanda and Melissa both, how fortunate would that be?"

Max grinned. "There's no guarantee it would happen, but I can make the chance available. See that bag of salt by the ceramic pot?" Daphne looked over her shoulder. "It's enough there to soften a good edge of the pond. You've just got to tell me where their favorite spot is. The pier, you said, right? Ninety percent chance of snow tonight, doll face. Salted ice beneath fresh snow could make things a bit deadly, especially on a pier or pond."

"Max…" Daphne said uncomfortably. She was unable to distinguish what she felt most—excitement, or fear of being involved in such a malicious act. Threatening, scaring, and making someone's life miserable was one thing, but he was talking possibly murder. She wasn't a murderer. "What a card, you are!" she said, quickly laughing it off. "Always tricks up your sleeve. You do entertain me, Max, to the max." She averted her eyes. She hadn't been able to control the nervous jitter in her voice. Her mouth dry, she licked her lips.

Max grasped her chin and slanted an eye. "Beyond your comfort zone, doll? Like the rat poison?" he sorely rubbed in.

She slapped his hand away. "A rash decision, and a grave mistake," she said. "I'd only been thinking about doing it, but then the toast was just there on the counter, a few granules on my finger. I did it, spontaneously, wanting only to put Amanda out of commission for a couple of days. I didn't expect the dog would eat it. Garry would've been devastated had Bagel died. Oh, Max. I don't want to think about it anymore. Please go get my luggage." She eased herself into the limo, avoiding any more eye contact with him.

Max leaned into the limo and touched her gently on the shoulder. "I never said that you would be doing the evil deed." He smiled a devilish grin, stepped back and closed her door. He left her sneezing and reaching for the box of tissues on the seat.

AMANDA WAS ABOUT to open Garry's door when Max was on his last trip inside the house to retrieve Daphne's things. He came up the hall from the foyer, and headed straight for her. Amanda stopped with her hand on the doorknob. She'd never seen the young man before. *Was he a friend of Garry's?*

Though still plagued from her encounter with Daphne, she had recovered enough to tend to the work that was most important now—Garry's rehabilitation. The sooner she could get him on his feet, the sooner she could get back to Robbie. She'd made a call to Eddie, deciding the safety within the household was too important to just sit back and do nothing. She needed assurance that Melissa wasn't followed, and she really had no choice but to relay that Daphne had some serious contact info that could not only put them all in danger, but throw Daphne in peril as well. Only, Eddie didn't answer his phone. That, in itself, worried Amanda. All she could do was try to leave a sane message without giving away her fear and anxiety. No need to stir his emotions more. She needed him to focus. She'd try calling him again later.

When Max approached Amanda, he wore a wide grin on his mouth. She smiled back, until the stranger deliberately stepped beyond her personal space, his taller frame halting mere inches from her. She recoiled against the doorframe, her hand releasing Garry's doorknob. He had an attractive face, young and almost baby smooth, his hair a sunny blond and very straight. His eyes were an unusual turquoise color that shone almost pernicious the way they beamed down at her. His Casanova smile was a little frightening, too. "You must be the incredible Amanda Fields," he said in a hushed tone, a slight accent in his speech. His eyes rudely perused the length of her body. "Daphne's told me much about you. You hide your treasures well." He lifted his eyes to Amanda's disconcerted ones, touching her arm delicately. Amanda shivered, shook it off. He spoke again. "I know a good bed partner when I see one. Maybe when you're finished with Danzlo, you—"

She slapped him across the face. The door swung open, banging loudly against the adjacent wall. Garry was suddenly in the doorway glaring from his wheelchair, his eyes murderous on Max. "Get out!" Garry demanded. "Show your face again, and you won't have one to admire in the mirror."

Max stepped back with little change in his expression. "Daphne's right," he said with a smirk, an eye slanted at Amanda. "He does protect you. At least, *tries* to."

Garry lunged forward, nearly falling forward out of his wheelchair. Amanda held him back.

"I'm leaving," Max said, raising his hands in the air. "Just one piece of luggage left." He picked up the luggage by the guest room door and walked away.

Garry waited tensely until Max was out of sight. When he heard the click of the front door closing, his muscles relaxed, and his gaze centered on Amanda. She'd been kneeling over him. She started to stand, but he tugged her back down, took hold of her neck with his left hand. His thumb lifted her chin drawing her eyes upon him. "Are you okay?"

"Yes," she barely got out, a tear falling beside her mouth, forming a puddle against his thumb. Garry watched it slide downward across his knuckle. His chest tightened.

"Max is a punk and a jerk. Always was. He was one of my stage helpers I'd planned to let go, but Daphne suggested she could use him for her transportation needs. She *will* get rid of him if she plans to be my wife." Amanda was trembling. Garry brushed his thumb across her cheek tenderly. "He deserved the slap you gave him."

She nodded with a shuddering breath.

He wanted to cheer her, make her smile. "I'd better watch my Ps and Qs, huh? I was right when I said you were a dangerous woman." But his words only caused another tear to fall. He suspected that the morning's incidences were just too much for her. The humiliating experience in his bedroom an hour ago was enough to handle for one day. He was still trying to handle it himself.

"Mandy, don't cry. I won't let him hurt you again, I promise." He raised his right hand laboriously to wipe the tears from the left side of her face, his jaw clenching with the effort. She caught it mid-air, her expression reeking of... *fear?* No. Surely repulsion. He lowered his right arm, removing his other hand from her neck as well.

"I'm sorry," he said, his eyes downcast, a mixture of remorse and anger grinding his insides. "I had no right to touch your face with my maimed hand. You'd think I'd learn after Daphne's constant reminders of how offensive it is." He stared down at the hand in his lap, repulsed himself by the distorted red and white lines jutting outward from the middle of his hand toward the three fingers he'd nearly lost. He closed his eyes.

She grabbed his right hand and held it tenderly against her face. He tried to jerk it back, but she wouldn't let him. "The makeup, I didn't want you to smear it! Silly, I know, but..."

His eyes stared with anguish, lines of doubt crinkled on his forehead. "Don't lie to me," he said. "I've heard enough lies today. Why don't you just admit that it repulses you, even just a little. Just say it, *damnit.*"

"I'm not Daphne," she said instead. And as if to prove it, she slid his jagged skin across her jaw and glided it sensually down the side of her neck. The experience was both physically erotic and emotionally soul-stirring for Garry. It was the emotional stir that possessed him most, and he found it unbearable not to kiss those lips that were suddenly quivering under his gaze. He reached for her, on impulse, both of his hands bringing her toward him, his mouth barely touching hers when she pleaded against him, "No, Garry," and began to shove his arms away anxiously. "Remember who you're promised to," she finished. She stood then, an intake of breath now blowing out slowly through her mouth. Her cheeks were heightened with color.

He felt his breath had been ripped right out of him. He sat back in his wheelchair, at first stunned by her near frantic behavior, and then embarrassment took him completely. To think she might have wanted him to kiss her; that she might possibly be falling in love with him, for he'd gone over and over in his head everything she had confessed to him this morning about touching him. And wanting to. And in one moment he realized he wanted to touch her, too; to feel *both* of his hands on her. She'd given him a first experience at an intimate touch using his right hand. No, she wasn't Daphne. Daphne only wanted a part of him. And now he knew it wasn't enough.

"Garry, talk to me," Amanda urged while he sat unmoving, unseeing. "I didn't mean for it to sound like a scold. It was only—"

"The truth," he said, lowering his head. He stared down at that disfigured hand on his lap, sighing at his bleak future. "I know the next line: You made your bed, now lie in it."

"Garry, I'm sorry," she said softly. "I see now it was a mistake to have held your hand against my—"

"Don't!" he said, his head lifting to her merciful eyes. "Don't ruin what you so passionately did with an apology. The only mistake made was mine. I was wrong to think this would work. Wrong in letting you stay."

Nicolas and Melissa suddenly appeared, rearing up behind Amanda. Nicolas bolted forward, "You don't mean that, sir," and then Melissa spoke more calmly, "Garry, maybe you should rest today. You're still upset from this morning. You and Amanda can begin your—"

"*Me* and Amanda aren't doing anything. Today, or tomorrow. It's best for everyone if she just leaves now. Wheel me back into my room, Nicolas." He avoided Amanda's disheartened face, his gaze pleading only to his butler.

Reluctantly, Nicolas did his bidding, leaving the two women in the hall, the door closing between them. Melissa turned to Amanda. "He didn't mean it."

"Melissa, what am I to do? It's too awkward between us. And now I have that horrible fear of Daphne finding out! I panicked because he was going to kiss me."

Melissa grabbed Amanda's shoulders, squeezing them. "Don't you see what's happening? He's realizing that he's in love with you and he doesn't know how to handle it. He's fighting it the only way he knows how. He probably even allowed Daphne to talk him into marriage because he's afraid. Afraid to love you. Afraid he already knows."

"Stop, Melissa!" Amanda jerked away, clasping her ears with her hands. "This is way too complicated. With Daphne… and Eddie, I'm so mad at him because he's yet to return my call. He always calls me within five minutes after leaving him a message." She squeezed her eyes shut, forcing back the scream she so wanted to scream. She opened her eyes, beseechingly. "I don't want Garry to love me. Robbie is my life's priority. I'm going back home where I belong as soon as I help Garry get on his feet. I *will* get him on his feet."

"That a girl! Bring back that bold spirit of yours. Tomorrow morning, things will be just fine. Both of you just need some time to think. A lot has happened today." Melissa took her hand in hers. "Okay?"

"Okay," she said, nodding. "I can do this. I'm calm, I'm relaxed. I am in control."

# 24.

# IF YOU WERE HERE
# WITH ME TONIGHT

A *BOOM* SOUNDED from Garry's room that evening. Nicolas rushed down the hall, tore open the door, and stopped at the sight of Garry lying flat on his back in the middle of the floor. One leg was curved under the other. His right hand lay flaccid on his chest, and his left outstretched in a puddle of blood and glass. Garry's eyes flickered open.

Then Melissa flew into his room, shouting, "Oh my God! Speak to us, Garry. Are you alright?"

He smiled lopsidedly, his left hand lifting from the broken glass. "I'm in need of more brandy. The decanter is empty. And broken," he added forlornly.

"Why, he's drunk," she said, wrinkling her forehead toward Nicolas, who was rushing from the bathroom with a towel, immediately putting pressure on the bleeding site.

"If only I could be so lucky," Garry said, scowling toward Nicolas who was responsible for maintaining a low supply of liquor in his container, and then keeping it far from reach.

"Is he badly cut?" Melissa asked.

Nicolas sighed. "You'd better get Miss Amanda in here."

"That intriguing little witch still here?" Garry said loudly, attempting to get up on his left elbow, his forearm smashing glass as he did so. "Distracting is what she is."

"Mr. Danzlo, lie back down and be still until Miss Amanda comes."

"What happened, Nic? She lose her lovely broomstick? Couldn't get home? Just tell her to wiggle her nose... like this." He tried raising his left hand to wiggle his own, but Nicolas wasn't letting up with the towel.

Meanwhile Melissa stormed to the other bedroom's bathroom across the hall, her voice shouting over the hair dryer. Amanda, bent at the waist, wore nothing but a rose-colored towel, her hair blowing upside down with the dryer's breeze. She was suddenly jerked from place, the dryer cord snapping out of its socket. While one hand held the blow dryer, the other was trying to keep her modesty with the loosened towel. "Garry's bleeding to death, come quick!" Melissa shouted.

"*What?*" Amanda screamed, flinging the hair dryer on the bed. She rushed to the door before she realized she had nothing on but a towel. Melissa flung her rust-colored robe against her neck, across her shoulders, muttering, "Arms, arms!" while assisting Amanda in it.

"My glasses!" Amanda said, as Melissa pushed her into the hall. Within seconds, Melissa was slapping the red-brown frames in her hand, shoving her into Garry's room. Amanda fixed them on her face, her hair wild, uncombed from drying. She tightened her robe's belt, halting before the bleeding patient.

"Watch the glass, Miss Amanda," Nicolas said.

Amanda stepped back, Garry's focus instantly zooming in on her bare feet and ankles. He swallowed a mouth full of saliva as his focus moved up two shapely, smooth shaven calves. They smelled of coconut oil, its tropical fragrance spiraling around him. His nostrils flared as he inhaled the sultry scent. Then his heaven was slaughtered at the knees, rust-colored fabric despoiling his view. His gaze shot upward, the monstrous ogress staring down at him behind pointed framed glasses, her dark hair down in wicked disarray.

"Oh great Oz! The witch ain't dead!"

The smell of brandy permeated the air. Amanda bent down and took position in holding pressure on Garry's arm while Melissa and Nicolas carefully discarded broken glass. Garry lay pleasantly intoxicated—not by the small amount of brandy he'd drank—but by the fresh clean scent of Amanda rising up his nose. The honey dew of her shampooed hair, so close to his face, teased him recklessly with pointless yearnings. He pulled his arm from her grasp. "I thought I asked you to go home." His towel bandage slipped off as Garry attempted to get up on his own.

"Stop acting foolish, Garry. You're bleeding." Amanda picked up the towel, pushing him back on the floor.

"Yes, foolish. I've been a fool from the start, yet my nurse keeps hanging around. You'd think she'd let me bleed to death so she could go home." He stared up into her eyes, battling with his wits. For all that was good and mighty, she sure looked fetching tonight. That bit of liquor he drank before spilling the rest in the floor must be doing a number on his senses. Something was different about her, but his mind just couldn't grasp what it was.

"I'll go get some sterile dressings and the first aid kit," Nicolas said, heading out of the room. Melissa exited the bathroom with a wet washcloth in hand, her eyes riveted on Garry. "Get used to her being here," Melissa told him. "And since you've proven too dangerous to be alone, Amanda will be staying with you tonight."

"*In here?*" the two cried in unison. Melissa nodded. Amanda wore a stunned, open-eyed expression on her face; Garry's was ashen, his legs tightening against the floor.

Nicolas came through the door moments later, laden with medical supplies in one arm, and carrying a cup of coffee in the other hand. Melissa inquired seriously, "Nicolas, don't you think it's imperative Amanda stay with Garry tonight?"

Nicolas, taken off guard, eyed Melissa, then the two on the floor. "Oh, imperative, Miss Melissa."

Amanda blinked nervously, taking the wet cloth Melissa handed her. She cleaned Garry's wound, the cut above his wrist superficial, but a good two inches long and still slightly bleeding. She held more pressure on it. She didn't dare look up from his arm.

Nicolas cleaned the blood off the carpet while Melissa bent down behind him with a clean towel to sop up the dampness.

"Here, sir," Nicolas said, bending down on a knee with a full cup of coffee in hand. Melissa knelt behind Garry, lifting his shoulders. Garry furrowed his brows, eyeballing the flexible straw Nicolas had provided in the cup. "It's nice and strong, not too hot," Nicolas told him, ignoring Garry's scowl. "It'll clear your senses."

Amanda lifted her head, Garry glimpsing over at her the same moment. She sent him an encouraging nod, her lips glistening from the innocent lick she'd just given them. Clear his senses, hell! Not while she was in the room. He frowned, and then lurched his head toward the cup, enveloping the straw with a tight-lipped mouth. He finished the contents with a loud slurp of the straw.

"Is everybody satisfied now?" he said a bit sarcastically. No one responded. The next he knew, Nicolas and Melissa were making their excuses to leave, Amanda wrapping Garry's arm with the last sliver of the gauze. Amanda and Garry fixed their eyes on the two at the door, aghast.

"You're not going to help her get me up?" Garry asked, Amanda barely breathing as she hurried to put the tape on his bandage. She rose quickly and grasped her robe lapels together. She secured her belt. "Melissa?"

"You're Garry's nurse," Melissa declared as though Amanda didn't know.

"You can handle him, we trust you," Nicolas said.

The door closed. Amanda ran to it. It was locked, or were they holding it from the other side? She turned slowly, Garry's expression transforming before her eyes. His mouth slowly curved into a lopsided grin, his left elbow supporting his half naked torso, his white shirt rolled up at the sleeves and unbuttoned down the front. He didn't look at all like the frightened man from moments ago.

"They trust you, Mandy," he said, his eyes shining blue mischief. "The question is… do you trust me?"

# 25.

# SOMEWHERE IN THE NIGHT

AMANDA NEVER FELT such a tremendous urge to cry as she did this moment—so much was at stake being alone in this room with Garry. She was much too vulnerable to take the risk. Though in truth, he wasn't safe by himself. It wasn't because he was befuddled with drink; he seemed reasonably sedate actually, his words quite articulate. He had, however, imbibed enough to precipitate a bit of audacious behavior. But something much deeper was tugging at him mentally, on a personal level and possibly socially, too. It couldn't be easy living in such solitude after being used to a throng of fans and fellow musicians always at your side, his life lacking the attention he'd gotten used to. Daphne wasn't providing the attention he needed, and certainly not the love.

Amanda knew Melissa and Nicolas were only trying to help when they tricked her into staying with Garry tonight. She was sure they were watching for any trouble that might arise on the outside. It was the inside she was worried about and that imp-like grin on Garry's face, which proved he was feeling a little loose and adventurous. She quickly felt heat rise in her cheeks from her blazing knees, flames teasing her loins and striding to the center of her womanhood. She was close to wobbling when courage finally took her the couple of steps to where he lay.

She had to get a hold of herself, and help him off the floor.

Bending down she straightened his right leg, laid it parallel with the left, and then came to assist him up. Her gaze fused with his.

"Easier to touch when it's covered up, huh?" Garry said. He wore slacks, pleated at the waist, no belt.

She'd started to say she would've touched his bare leg, but thought better of it.

She moved to place herself beneath his shoulder. "Bend your left leg, Garry, and take my—"

His face buried in her hair. "Hmmm," he whispered, his nose breathing in the honey-scent. "You're smelling good tonight, Ms. Fields."

She fought back delirium as he used her surname facetiously. "Sorry, but I'm not on the menu tonight. Now, please," she said, tending to his right side, "do as I say and help me get you off this floor."

He did so, though quite clumsily, a left-waved smile on his face. "So what is on the menu tonight, Mandy?" They were standing by the bed, a sportive light in his eye.

Amanda observed him with a cock of her head. "Playing the bold and happy rogue tonight, are you? Let me assure you that the only thing on my menu this night is putting you to bed. Period," she added with emphasis. She blinked up at him, expecting no less than humor or some snide remark. His only response was a shift of his weight as he tried to shake off his shirt, the left sleeve sliding off first. Amanda sidestepped to keep her balance and his, assisting him with the other sleeve. "I will say, I do appreciate the lack of cruel lines you were so fond of in the past," she said.

He grinned down at her. "I'm not really a cruel man, you see," his shirt off now, "not all of me. Only half is cruel—the bad, bad right side."

Amanda stilled, her gaze serious and attentive. "Garry…"

But Garry wasn't ready for any grave words from Amanda. His too warm body so close to hers was making him hot and thirsty. Spying a glass near empty of brandy on the bedside table, Garry made a cartwheel swing with his left arm, attempting to reach past Amanda to retrieve it. The only way she could prevent a fall was to push him backward upon the bed, falling along with him while he held on. On first bounce, she slid off him, her feet hitting the floor with a thump. He rubbed his groin saying, "Oo-oo, Mandy, you could hurt a man like that." Her face took on brief concern, the usual look of innocence that bespoke an "uh-oh" blunder. He burst out laughing.

"You're disgusting tonight," she said, fists on hips.

"Sweetheart, I'm disgusting every night." He lay on his back, legs dangling from the bed as he tried to unzip his pants, his hazy mind thinking *bedtime*. "Disgusting to be with, and particularly, disgusting to touch. Ain't it a shame?"

Amanda's face fell. "Garry, don't say that ever." She came forward, bent at the waist, and began unbuttoning his pants while he continued to jerk the zipper that wasn't cooperating. She took hold of him under his arms and bounced him straight on the floor. His left foot barely balanced on its own when his pants dropped to his ankles. Then came the snap; he'd undone his boxer shorts as well. They fell second, atop the slacks.

Garry realized his mistake too late, so used to sleeping in the nude for years. The booze must have dimmed his mind, yet he sure remembered every moment from the time Amanda had walked into his room—from the sight of those tanned slender legs sweltering his senses with their tropical musk, to that attentive, humble, and meek expression she wore on her face now.

He fell back on the bed like nothing had happened, grasping hold of the sheet in the process. Covering his mid-section in a swift second, he lay back on a pillow and closed his eyes. He half-expected to feel a spinning sensation, but dizziness didn't come—though his senses were whirling, pooling his mind and body with the essence of the lady near him. The light, clean fragrance of her careened into his nostrils, teasing his flesh, the honey scent of her hair harassing his taste buds. It made him thirst for some honey-sweet drink that only she could provide. The very thought of her smooth silken legs against his own plagued him, his loins craving for just one touch of them.

No, he wasn't even near drunk.

"Hand me that glass, will ya?" his left arm crossing his chest to stretch for it. His eyes opened when he realized Amanda wasn't helping.

"You don't need more brandy, Garry."

His eyes narrowed. "How do you know what I need? What I need is sleep. Yet for some reason, the brandy's not doing its thing tonight."

"Is that truly why you're drinking? For sleep?"

His brow arched in frustration and anger. "Think I'm in need of something else?"

Without warning, his left hand seized the sleeve of her robe, and she went flying across him, turbulently landing on his left side. He was on his elbow in an instant, staring down into her widening eyes. "You're so smart, why don't you tell me what I need."

Amanda gasped, trying to catch her breath. Her heart was pounding thunderously through a pulsing vibration in her throat. She sprung to escape, but his right leg slid across her thighs, capturing her legs in a weak vise, his left hand grasping her hair. Not tightly, though enough to keep her head down where he wanted it. "What's the matter, princess? Don't you trust me? No? I wouldn't trust me either if I were you. Daphne's out of the house for less than a day, and Mr. Honorable turns jerk, gets wild and free. Shameless, isn't he?"

He watched as her eyelids flittered, his coffee-brandied breath against her face, though she didn't seem repulsed by it. Nor did she show any evidence that his right leg over her thighs abhorred her. She in fact, had both her hands atop that leg, each hand parallel to the other, tensely holding that leg while the rest of her lay stiffly. Her expression was full of uncertainty, fear, and some other emotion he couldn't discern. As he studied her, he was bewildered by her makeup-less face. It appeared flawlessly smooth, radiant, and healthy. Her cheeks were flushed a natural pink, her lips glistening their usual ardor. He stared at those lips that started to quiver. He lifted his gaze.

"Afraid I'm going to kiss you?" he whispered. "Your lips do tempt me, Mandy, yet I'm promised to another. Can't figure it, can you? Guess I'm just a bad boy." He paused, thinking she might speak, but she didn't. "I disappoint you, don't I? Don't feel alone, I disappoint myself."

Behind those ugly frames she wore, tears welled in her eyes. He crumpled dark strands of her hair in his left hand, rolling the soft tresses between his fingers. He'd never seen her with her hair down before. It excited him. As did those eyes, so golden and beautiful. He suddenly wanted her glasses off. He wanted them off now.

He removed them, unthinkingly with his right hand, she, sucking in breath as his elbow innocently brushed across one covered breast. The loosened robe opened wide at the neck as he retrieved his arm back, now finished with his task. "Sorry. Not very skillful yet with this right hand. Hope I didn't touch your skin." He'd been referring to her face, but as he said the words, he saw he'd accidentally opened her robe, revealing the upper section of one creamy breast and a bare shoulder. He wet his lips just before his gaze shot to hers, his head seeming to spin now with the wonder of all he was seeing of her. "You must've flown to my rescue directly from your bath, Ms. Fields. Could it be you're entirely naked beneath this robe?"

She moved quickly to escape. Her hands pushed at his chest, but he captured them both with his left hand. In one swift movement, he covered her entire body with his own, manacling her hands above her head.

"Garry, let me up," she pleaded. "Melissa and Nicolas might—"

"No, they won't come. They trust you. They know you'll help me. Will you, Mandy?"

Her breathing slowed, her body acting on his plea. She relaxed, his hold loosening above her head. He grasped her fingers, entwining them with his own—a gesture that feathered sizzling sensation down her arms till it filled her breasts with the warmth of him. "I'm not sure what I can do to help you," she said with trembling lips.

"Ah, but I think you do, sweet girl." He paused, smiling down into her eyes. "Let's play a game of pretend. How 'bout it? You with me?"

She swallowed with difficulty, then nodded in assent, her gaze never leaving his. "Good. Let's say, we're a couple, alone. That should be easy enough to imagine, right? But here comes the hard part. You have to pretend you're crazy about me, while at the same time, I'm crazy about you." He hesitated, gazing at her gravely. "You're in love with me, Mandy. You love the way I touch you, the way I—"

Her lashes flittered.

"What's the matter, you don't like the game? Afraid I might touch you with the wrong hand?" A wave of disappointment gushed over him, his little pretend game seeming a foolish one. He attempted to roll off her, but her fingers quickly embraced his left hand, keeping it above her head while her left, now free, clasped his right wrist.

"Touch me," she commanded softly. She released his wrist, his right hand suspended above her chest. He froze, a tear burning one of his eyes. And in her eyes, a silent plea, as if she needed to be touched by him as much as he needed to touch her. "Touch me, Garry," she whimpered, this time bringing his hand against the mound of her breast, the tips of his fingers pressed against her neck and bare shoulder.

He barely breathed as he stared down at his scarred hand lying upon her breast. His gaze was mesmerized as her heart thumped rapidly against his palm. He began to move his fingers lightly upon her skin. They climbed the valley to the mountain, not quite reaching the peak. He was afraid.

His focus lifted, sweet passion profound in his body when he saw it likewise on her face. His hand moved there, her eyes closing when his fingers brushed across her lids, down across her nose, upon her mouth. She groaned as they strummed her lips. She kissed the tips of his fingers.

"Mmmm, Mandy, you could drive a man insane. You're truly beyond anything I could ever dream. Be my bride this night," he softly said, caught up in this world of pretense, loving the realness of it, the feel of it inside him. "I want to hold you from this day forward, to keep you safe and warm. I promise to honor you with my whole heart, keep you from weeping. Let me whisper my love to you, make you the blessing of my household… for with you in it, home will surely be my peace."

He took her left hand, kissed it, and pretended to place a ring there. Holding it on her finger, he recited in Hebrew, *"Harei at mekudeshet li, betaba'at zo kedat Mosheh veyisrael."* He smiled into her tear-filled eyes, reading her love, intoxicated by it. "Yes, sweet Mandy, you're consecrated unto me now." He bent down, kissed her gently on the lips. He wanted to be sensitive to her sexual needs, not to arouse her too passionately until her mood was ready. He wanted to gladden her heart first, make her feel at ease with him before he took his bride to their wedding bed. But she was arching toward him now, desire glowing in her eyes, his own desire suddenly uncontrolled.

"Ah, Mandy, what wicked things you do to me. *Yichud* will have to be longer than a few moments, this private time we share together after our wedding. Our guests will just have to wait outside, for I can't bear another moment without having you." He wiped her tears and began to sing, soft and close to her lips.

*Oh Mandy... could this be our magic at last? At last...*

His mouth descended upon hers, her lips meeting his with all the yearning and love he could possibly want from a woman. His mouth devoured hers as he embraced her body and soul, his right hand cradling her head, his left tearing away the robe from her right arm as she rolled atop him. She drank him senselessly with her honeydew mouth and surrendered her flesh to his hands. He took it in love, in hunger, and in greed while her spirit seemed to move inside him like a whirling cyclone. In seconds, he was atop her again, his lips moving across her cheek, along her jaw, her neck, her breasts, his tongue finally enveloping the protruding bud he so ached to taste. It was suddenly in his mouth, rolling in his mouth, and he nurtured it with warmth and moisture. Then he captured the other bud that waited invitingly, firmly. He plundered and savored it, exploring the peak till she gave a cry. His gaze lifted to her face and he groaned at the intensity of passion he saw in her eyes, her desire enhancing his own twofold. "Oh *God...*" he cried, so overwhelmed by the moment, the feeling she was giving him. She softly spoke his name over and over, *"Garry... Garry..."* it slithered across his lips, like a potent spell that enchanted him, body and soul. "My Mandy, *sweet as candy*," he whispered, just before his mouth seized hers in a kiss that took both their breaths away. His hands were all over her, teasing her, pleasing her, her own playing sweet melodies upon his body. "I want you, Mandy," he cried against her ear. "I want you so much it hurts."

He needn't say another word for her legs parted then, and he came into her, their bodies becoming one—in flesh and in spirit. His mouth smothered her name, praying he not spill his seed in her too soon. Yet the moist, soft flesh of her wrapped so deliciously about him, he thought he'd go mad. He came with a violence they both tried to calm by clinging to each other, their bodies drenching with sweat while the storm seemed to go on forever. "I'm sorry," he said disheartened, staring down into her face. "I failed you—"

Her fingers hushed his lips, her head shaking "no" as she moved beneath him, nudging him over until she was on top. He held on to her, groaning as she pressed against him. Her lips were moist and hot against his chin, his neck, his chest. He felt himself harden again, throbbing deep inside her. And his heart welled with joy that she could love him so much, make him feel so much. They moved together in rhythm. He whispered against her ear, against her mouth. He whispered sweet promises as he discovered her, sought more, the exploration becoming an endless, sentimental journey where she was his song, his beautiful song, and he played her over and over again.

"Ah, Mandy," he breathed when their bodies were sated, her head upon his chest, his arms enfolding her gently. "Thank you. Thank you, baby." He felt drunk with her, his body relaxed, his mind at peace. "Now I know what love's supposed to be."

Time passed silently for a long while, until slowly Garry fell into a peaceful sleep. Amanda listened to his light breathing, reveling in what surely seemed to be the sweetest of dreams. But it wasn't a dream. Garry's body was real, and he was holding her body, as though she were someone to cherish—a gift worth treasuring. He'd been everything she'd ever wished for and more. She savored the moment just a while longer, and then finally removed herself with fragile ease, as not to awaken him. Retrieving her robe from off the floor, she donned it and headed to the bathroom. She flicked off the switch to the bedroom, on in the adjoining bathroom, entering the room with one last glance over her shoulder. Seeing Garry's sleeping form shadowed on the bed had her reliving his touch, remembering his warm, fondling hands against her skin.

She quietly shut the door behind her and leaned against it. She allowed her robe to fall open, the soft terry cloth riding sensually across her nipples. They still tingled from Garry's mouth. Her eyelids closed, and she whimpered his name. She slid the robe from her shoulders, inviting the affection of air against her skin, pleased at the tease it gave her flesh as the fabric fell in layers about her feet. She stood completely nude against the cool door, imagining his hands still playing their gentle strum against her, his moist lips journeying her body with passionate fervor. Her own fingers shamelessly caressed her bare skin, touching places he had touched.

It aroused a throb between her legs she couldn't calm down. She wanted him again. And she knew now that she would in the days to come. His moisture slid down her inner thigh then, awakening the memory of his hard shaft inside her. How beautiful to conceive a child from rhapsody such as that. She would carry Garry's child, if it were possible. But she had carried Paul's and had failed. There would be no more babies for her.

She began to cry, her tears coming faster than she could wipe them. They pattered upon the tiled floor as she made her way to the sink and turned on the water. She grabbed a clean washcloth from off the counter and stared down through blurry eyes at the warm water splashing over her hands. God help her, but she didn't want to wipe the semen from her body. It somehow felt holy and very beautiful. She remembered things he had whispered in her ear, asking how he'd come to be so blessed to find one such as she in this cruel world, so good-natured and kind. *Oh, Eve of my life*, he had murmured once. He'd made the night seem both innocent and sacred.

Amanda struggled with what she'd always thought to be right from wrong. She had given herself to Garry knowing he had promised himself to another. Yet, all she felt was blessed.

*Will the guilt come to us somewhere in the night, sometime in the early morning hours?* she wondered. *If so, God help us. Give us strength to face tomorrow.*

# 26.

# HANGIN' ON A NAIL

SIX IN THE morning, Garry rolled over, his face against another pillow. "Mandy...
*baby.*"

His eyelids flew open. He shot up in bed.

A dream. He'd dreamt the most beautiful dream. He lay back down, closing his
eyes with a smile of satisfaction. An image of a firm breast stood clear behind his
eyes. They shot back open. "Just a dream," he told himself, until feminine words
sounded in his head. *Touch me.*

He jolted up again and banged on the wall behind his bed, yelling, "Nicolas.
Nicolas, get in here!"

Nicolas was there in a moment. He scuttled into the room, stopping a couple
of feet from the bed. "You called, sir?"

Panic had Garry searching beyond the doorway, the thought of Amanda
passing by throwing his mind in a tizzy. His entire body felt flushed. He scooted
against the headboard of the bed, struggled to grab the sheet with his right hand,
and wiped the sweat off his forehead with his left. Then his eyes focused on the
bandage around his wrist. Amanda had put it there, the remembrance of her clean,
bathed scent so close to him, sending him down memory lane.

"I was with Amanda last night."

Nicolas viewed him gravely, waiting for him to say more, but for the life of
him, Garry was unable to say another thing. He could only see images of Amanda
beside him, beneath him, on him; it was like rain on hot pavement, his brain
steaming with passionate visions.

"Are you just stating fact, sir, or are you trying to tell me something else?"

Garry paused. "Where is she? Have you seen her?"

"If you're asking if she's still in the house, I heard her in the kitchen about four o'clock this morning. I went to see about her, found her standing at the dining room window with a cup of hot tea. She'd been crying. I held her for a while, but then she wanted to be alone."

*I promise to honor you with my whole heart, keep you from weeping.*

Garry felt like a heel. He'd used her. Yet in reality, there was no one in this world he appreciated more. She played the game for his sake, gave herself totally to prove himself a man, prove love existed. He knew she was full of it—love and compassion—possibly built up from a marriage she'd lost. He had witnessed the yearning in her eyes; he'd taken advantage of it. Advantage of her.

"I said some things I shouldn't have… did things I shouldn't have done. Did she tell you?"

"No, sir."

"Then you must've heard."

"I felt it best to spend the better part of the night in the family room, sir. I sat up late, watching T.V."

Garry let out an exasperated breath. "In other words, you wanted me alone with the woman. It was a mistake, Nicolas!"

"Was it, sir?"

"Must I spell it out to you? I made love to her, Nic, while engaged to another."

Nicolas asked, "And did you realize which one you're in love with?"

Garry froze, his mind paralyzed at the thought of being in love with Amanda, of making love to her again, and again. Receiving her sweet kisses for the rest of his life.

He shook his head.

"How could you even think there's a choice! I-I love Daphne."

"And I love little baby ducks and old pick-up trucks like Tom T. Hall, sir, but I adore a woman who can bring out the best in me, who can touch me inside and out, who can make me laugh and cry at the same time… who gives without taking because she cares about me. But I love her most because she makes me feel more than any other woman ever could."

Garry, unblinking, struggled to uphold his dignity, his honor, and at the same time, hide his fear in knowing Amanda was all these things to him and that Daphne missed the mark by a long shot. To succumb to Nicolas was to admit he was wrong, and like always, Nicolas could read him better than he could himself. It meant telling the one he'd promised to marry that he couldn't marry her because he was in love with another woman.

What it all boiled down to was that he was a coward like his father. *Like father, like son.* He'd grabbed at the only solution he felt available to him. He didn't have the guts to tell Amanda she was driving him physically insane. Then she would've left. He was always afraid she'd leave. Afraid she'd stay.

"If you're through with your speech, Nicolas, you can help me out of this bed."

Disappointment shone in the butler's eyes. "Yes, sir," he said, turning to get the wheelchair.

AMANDA GAZED AT the falling white flakes through the back door window. It had snowed most of the night, heavy at first, slowing as the morning sun rose. She'd never gone to bed.

The dog stood beside her, looking much more spirited than she did last evening when Nicolas brought her home from the Yancey ranch. She recovered nicely from her poisonous meal, her tail wagging against Amanda's leg. She barked up at Amanda twice.

Amanda looked down and smiled at Bagel who sat on her hind legs, her front paws dangling before her chest. "Oh, you want up, huh? Wanna see the snow?" Amanda picked up the dog, wiped the chill from the window with one front paw, and looked out toward the winter wonderland. "Looks inviting to me, but perhaps you should stay in this morning. You're still recovering." The dog barked, pranced in her arms, licked her face. "Okay, so you're feeling better. Maybe just a little while."

Amanda put the dog down, picked up a pair of boots by the door, and sat on a bench by the washer machine in the utility room. A voice startled her from the adjoining kitchen doorway.

"Morning," Melissa said cheerfully. "Those are my boots you're putting on." Amanda glanced up. "I'm only saying that because you're used to Garry's boots now and I'm not. They'd swallow me and I plan to go outside with you. I got dressed for the occasion."

Amanda inspected Melissa's coat, hat, and scarf attire. She threw off the one boot she'd put on and bent to retrieve Garry's boots. Melissa assisted her.

"Thanks," Amanda said curtly.

"I'm sorry the boots were the one thing I forgot to put in your wardrobe," Melissa said. "As soon as we can go into town, we'll get you some. I must've been dead tired because I didn't even hear you come into the room to get a change of clothes."

Silence.

Melissa sighed. "I guess you're kind of mad at me for last night… holding the door shut and all, so you couldn't leave Garry's bedroom."

More silence.

Melissa tilted her head, sighing once more. "I guess being with Garry last night was intolerable, huh?"

Amanda stood with boots on and walked to the back door. She opened it, welcoming the white flakes pattering cold against her warm face. She looked over her shoulder at Melissa, her feet on the threshold. "It wasn't at all intolerable. That's the problem." She walked out onto the snowy deck and down the steps toward the pond, the dog following behind. Melissa kicked on her boots and headed after them, making fresh tracks in the snow.

"THAT RIGHT LEG is getting stronger," Nicolas praised. "Won't be long and you'll be up and walking."

Garry, dressed in blue jeans and a flannel shirt, sat down in his wheelchair with little help from Nicolas. "I do feel stronger this morning, Nic. You'd think the bath would've tired me out."

"Must have been that good workout last night."

Garry cast a furled brow at Nicolas who went about his business straightening the room. He knew Nicolas would keep quiet about his private life. Melissa was the one who couldn't keep quiet, letting things slip out, even when she didn't mean for them to. She'd fired up big trouble for him in his youth. He remembered the day Melissa had slipped the news to his mother that he'd climbed out the window one late night, had a bit of fun with a couple of his good buddies. They were the dangerous days. He'd found courage then.

But the car accident changed him. He'd been ready to call everything quits, his career, his life.

Then Mandy came.

Never in his life had he spoken such tender words to a woman as he did last night. And why? Because sexual relations between a man and his wife was seen as something holy in Jewish tradition? He'd never elicited an attitude of reverence for God before. He couldn't even imagine such a thing with Daphne, wedding night or no. She'd laugh in his face, her Jewish morals forgotten, shoved aside.

The wild barking of the dog outside shook Garry from his thoughts, his gaze moving outside the window as Nicolas flung open the drapes. Distant screams echoed terror through the wintry sky. "God help!" Nicolas shouted, racing out of the room.

Garry froze in his wheelchair, his focus glazed as he caught the end sight of Amanda crashing forward into the ice-covered pond, its bleakness swallowing her up whole. Melissa fell second as she tried to reach out and save her friend. Garry reacted by grasping the arms of the wheelchair and lifting himself up. But his good arm placed too much weight on the left side of the chair, causing it to tilt over. Garry plunged to the floor, the chair lurching toward him and digging into his ribs. Enraged, he hurled the chair across the floor with his left hand, slamming it against the bed rail. In madness, he crawled to the window, his heart hammering the floor, his lungs barely retaining breath.

The dog was howling.

As Garry reached the window, he cursed himself for being handicapped, for allowing stupidity to weaken his ambition to make himself stronger. "Damn this body to hell!" he cried, grabbing hold of the window ledge. He raised himself on his left knee, his eyes searching frantically out the window. He saw Nicolas and Melissa crouched in the snow. But where was Amanda? *Dear God, where is she?*

# 27.

## LUCK BE A LADY

MELISSA STOOD ILL-BALANCED on two numb feet, her boots brimming with icy water while her knees knocked violently together. She was vaguely aware of Nicolas running up from behind her. He stopped and gaped in awe beside her.

One moment, Melissa had gotten Amanda to smile and the next she was attempting to save her from a dreadful fall. Only she had slipped as well into the frigid pond, blindly grasping for Amanda when a mighty hand began to pull her own body out of the water. Into big, strong arms Melissa went. She barely had time to gawk at the dark handsome face that had saved her, for after he placed her on safe ground the tall one ran swiftly back to the pier where she and Amanda had fallen, the brawny man shedding his outer clothes just before diving head first into the freezing water.

He soon came up with Amanda, laid her aground, his mouth upon hers, attempting to breathe life into her lungs. Amanda coughed, the residual water spewing from her mouth. The man then swept her into his arms and carried her into the house.

Melissa's knees gave way to the cold then, her legs buckling into snow. Nicolas crouched behind her and lifted her frozen body into his arms, though not as swiftly and skillfully as Amanda's shining knight. "He's half-Apache," Melissa whispered, teeth chattering to the stunned-faced Nicolas as they followed the two who were already at the back door of the house. She had taken one look at the prominent cheekbones and jet-black hair and knew immediately who their savior was. Amanda had given a good description of Eddie, the man who was once her closest friend. The stern expression on Eddie Chandler's face as he carried Amanda away bore token of his drive for truth and justice, as if this very incident had reason for such, and not just a mere accident.

EDDIE ENTERED THE house, guessing his way through to the back hall leading to the bedrooms. He approached the only room where the door stood ajar. Amanda hung limply in his arms as he neared a king-sized bed. His steps faltered as he caught sight of Garry huddled against the wall by the window, a face plagued with suffering. A wheelchair lay on its side, wedged against the bed frame at the end of the bed.

"Is she...?" Garry spoke first, too choked up to finish the sentence as he stared at Amanda's lifeless body in this stranger's arms. Blood glazed her face, skin cut by shards of ice.

"She's okay," Eddie answered, placing her upon the freshly made bed.

"The bedspread—wrap her in it until we can remove her wet clothes," Garry said, worming himself across the floor. He pulled himself up against the bed and leaned across it, his eyes searching for proof of Amanda's breath.

Eddie paused but a second, taking in Garry's deep concern for Amanda, and then took hold of the spread. He wrapped Amanda warmly in it. Melissa appeared at the door, shivering and wet. Eddie saw her, speaking the same moment Garry did, "You okay?"

Melissa could only nod and cry as she saw Amanda on the bed, unconscious.

"Take a warm shower, sis. Get into some dry clothes. We'll take care of Amanda," Garry said.

Melissa glanced at Eddie. He was looking at Garry, a strange expression on his face she couldn't read. If Garry knew who this stranger was in his house—especially his relationship to Amanda and her mixed feelings for Eddie—she doubted Garry would be the polite host he was.

Nicolas came up beside Melissa, his focus on Amanda's form wrapped securely in the bedspread. His weary eyes met Garry's.

"Nicolas, call—"

"It's taken care of, sir. The paramedics are on their way." Nicolas moved to help him from the floor, but Garry halted him.

"Blankets, Nic. More linens. A warm gown. I'm last on your list."

Nicolas nodded, turned to leave and caught the silvery appreciation in Eddie's eyes. He paused before the dark-tanned stranger. "We thank you for saving Miss Amanda's life. She means the world to us."

Eddie glanced over at the one shivering in the doorway, and then the one on the floor by the bed. "Yes, I can see that. It is good," he said oddly, turning to Amanda who now lay trembling beneath the spread, semiconscious. Melissa and Nicolas exchanged quizzical glances at Eddie's offbeat response. Garry's sole focus was on Amanda.

After Nicolas and Melissa left, Garry edged his way closer to the head of the bed. He used the headboard for support as he hoisted himself up on his left leg. Amanda coughed, Eddie talking down into her face. "Amanda, sweetheart, can you hear me?"

Eddie's low voice, the intimacy it held, and the unexpected endearment caused Garry to lose his balance, his grip on the headboard slipping, his left heel whipping the floor. He fell backward upon the bed and rolled like a doughnut. Eddie tried breaking the inevitable crash by snatching Amanda out of the way, but to his dismay, became part of the collision. Both men grunted. Amanda moaned.

Nicolas came through the door, his sight on the two men smothering the poor woman. His hands flew up, blankets, linens, and a gown raining through the air as he rushed to save her. He shoved the two men aside to find Amanda's face covered by the bedspread. He tore it off. "Miss Amanda, are you all right? Can you speak?"

Amanda moaned again, her eyes fluttering open as she tried to focus on Nicolas. She asked, "Where am I?"

"You're in a room with bad company," he told her, glaring at the two men on either side of her.

"Garry?" Amanda's eyes closed, too weak to keep them open.

Eddie chuckled. "Well, at least she knows who the bad company is."

"She didn't mean that," Garry said. He frowned.

Amanda stirred. Her movements spoke desperation. "Eddie," she called out, trying to force her eyelids open. Her arms reached out for him while she cried out his name again.

"I'm here, love," Eddie said, "No one will harm you. You're safe."

"No, Eddie, she's going to hurt him! Must keep him safe. Promise me, promise me."

"What is she talking about?" Garry asked. His gaze fixed on Amanda's arms clinging around the other man's neck. *She knows this man.* Jealousy, fear, and confusion played a trio in his mind.

"Shhh, it's okay. All is well. Lie back down," Eddie said. He grasped her arms, released them from around his neck, and pushed her gently back on the bed. "Nothing to worry about." His words calmed her and her lids shut, though her body shivered beneath the spread.

Eddie rose to stand. "She's delirious," he said. He stared down at Amanda's injured face for several seconds, and Garry watched as an involuntary twitch pulled at his right eye. Eddie tried blinking it away, just before he turned his attention on Garry. "When she's well enough, she needs to go home."

Eddie's gaze sent a cold chill up Garry's spine—a disturbing fixed stare that held mystery, and yet spoke a thousand words. In one short moment, Garry had witnessed an indescribable anguish in the stranger's smoky eyes, and a depth of love for a woman that ran very deep. Amanda and Eddie had a history together.

"I trust you to take care of her," Eddie said, starting to leave. "I've things to tend to." He circled the floor.

"And if she doesn't choose to go home?" Garry called out, a hint of defiance in his voice.

Eddie looked back over his shoulder, sending Garry an all-knowing look. He smiled, a gleam of promise shining in his smoke-gray eyes. "She'll be coming home, Danzlo."

He was gone in a flash, leaving Garry with a disquieted heart and mind. But Garry had little time to ponder.

"Quick, Nicolas, let's get her out of these wet clothes," he said, uncovering her body. He attempted to unbutton her coat, buttons popping off, material ripping as he freed her from the icy clothing that threatened to give her frostbite and hypothermia. Nicolas was at her feet, pulling off the one boot that was still on, her socks, the heavy corduroy pants sopping with water. He came to assist with the upper garments, but Garry had managed to strip her nearly naked and now held her upper body against his warm chest. Her head cradled in his arm while he stared down at her neck. He couldn't breathe, his face suddenly pallid and cold. His focus blurred on the delicate necklace—a silver cross. It shone like a portent staring back at him, come to destroy his life.

"Mr. Danzlo…" Nicolas murmured empathetically, knowing full well what his boss was thinking. *Amanda was taboo.* "We must hurry and get her dry."

Garry lifted his gaze, letting out a gasp of air.

"Everything's going to be fine, sir."

Garry hesitated only a second more, and then quickly worked with Nicolas to remove the remaining wet items from Amanda's body.

GARRY WAS WRAPPING Amanda warmly in a gray cashmere blanket when Nicolas, his arms fully laden with wet linens and the spread, left the room promising to return soon to help with her gown. Meanwhile, Garry pulled her more securely into his lap and lent her the extra warmth of his body. In the process of straightening her, the soft blanket slithered off one bare shoulder and breast, his gaze captive to it. The memory of last's night's sexual venture brought a tingling sensation to his lips. He could almost feel his mouth on that tender shoulder, on the full roundness of that breast. Her nipple was teasing him, its lofty bulb spurring heat into his loins, encouraging his fingers to touch her.

The sound of a throat being cleared at the door interrupted him. "Is that our patient?" a paramedic asked.

Like a naughty boy caught holding a cookie jar, Garry snatched the blanket, slamming the lid on his treasure chest… rather, her chest. He blinked up at the three paramedics, two male, one female. They stood just inside the room, their eyes lit with speculation of the worst kind—Garry, guilty as charged. He wanted to die, and to add to the embarrassment, Amanda was starting to squirm, calling out his name as she'd done last night during their throes of passion. *Garry… oh Garry.*

Publicly, the name Garry Danzlo had not disappeared off the face of the earth, though that's what it seemed the famous singer/musician had done after his traumatic car accident back in October. Unknown to Garry, the three paramedics had seen an article in this morning's paper, an interview with a Miss Daphne Dimont announcing her engagement to the mending musician who was presently recuperating in his Colorado home. The wedding date was not specific, yet she hinted at a mere two weeks, the marriage to take place as soon as Daphne returned from a two week trip Danzlo had generously gifted to her so he could work diligently to regain his strength before he tied the knot. Yes, it was believed Garry Danzlo would be back on his feet soon. A miracle and blessing for those millions of fans who have adored him and still do. A model-like photo of

Daphne was plastered above the headlines, BEAUTY TO MARRY AMERICAN HEARTTHROB.

The three medics approached the king-sized bed where Garry sat with the nearly naked woman who was surely not the one they'd seen in the papers. The dark hair and olive complexion was a far cry from the blonde and porcelain-skinned woman in the photograph on the front page of the Denver newspaper.

"She's my nurse," Garry quickly said, nodding to the body in his arms. "Fell through the ice in my pond. I was just warming her until you arrived."

"Uh-huh," said the first male tech. "May we?" The paramedic reached for Amanda, whom Garry held like a safety deposit box in his arms. Garry tried to hand her over, but Amanda blindly held on to him, crying, moaning as though she were drowning again. She clutched his shirt for dear life. The paramedics had to pry her hands from him, attempting to calm her with words, assuring that she was in no danger; they were medical professionals here to help her. Her eyelids flickered open. She suddenly leaned toward them, crying, "Melissa! Where is she? Is she okay?" The three looked to Garry for an answer, for they knew only of one in need.

"Melissa's fine, Mandy. Lie back down and let these people tend you." He tugged the blanket up and around her shoulders to save her modesty, pushing her gently back down upon the bed. She looked at him, her gaze searching, somewhat apprehensively, though with intimacy, clear to anyone watching

"Ah-hum," said one male paramedic, eyeing his fellow attendants before turning to the patient at hand. "Airway, breathing, and circulation… there doesn't seem to be a major problem here. We do need to take your vitals, Miss—"

"Fields," Garry said. "Are you in pain, Mandy?" One paramedic took her blood pressure; another placed a thermometer in her mouth and took a radial pulse. The third had antiseptic and gauze, cleansing her face, finding the main source of blood—a cut about an inch long on her forehead, not quite deep enough for stitches. Amanda's hand went to her head.

"Your head hurt?" Garry asked, and she nodded.

"We'll give her something for pain," said the female attendant placing steri-strips vertically across the cut on her forehead. She covered it with a sterile bandage. One of the males reassured, "Vitals are fine, pulse a little low, temperature down a bit, but that's to be expected. You have a strong, steady heartbeat, Miss Fields. I don't think an EKG will be necessary." One male checked her body and limbs for scratches, bruising, tender spots, while the other asked Amanda questions about her medical health and history. Amanda humored the three medics with a few lines about Garry's big feet and the stupid boots that caused her near death. She had them all laughing, except Garry who'd been waiting for one certain handsome paramedic to finish his too-thorough examination of her body. Then Amanda's pain shot was ready to be administered.

"Wait, somebody hold my hand!" Amanda screamed, her eyes squeezing shut, her hand shooting out for someone to take. Garry took it. Her eyes opened to his touch. Garry's expression was no longer tense, but amused. She frowned up into his face. "Go ahead, tell them I'm a bad patient," she dared, "and I'll tell them just how bad of a patient you are." He smiled then, she turning toward him to deliver her derriere to the medical attendant behind her. She barely made a face when the shot was administered; however, immediately afterwards, she flopped on her back, sighed, and closed her eyes.

When the young, male paramedic suggested they take her to the hospital for a precautionary twenty-three hour observation, Garry spoke up. "She's not going anywhere. If she requires observation, she'll have it here. I'll hire a professional if you think she—"

"That won't be necessary, Mr. Danzlo," assured the other male. "She certainly indicates no signs of altered mental status—no loss of memory, nausea, vomiting, or other signs that give clues to a concussion. Keep her warm, check her temperature every couple of hours. Try to keep her awake for a while. If any changes occur, give us a call."

Amanda giggled then. The pain shot was having an immediate and delightful effect on her. "That's right, you guys. Don't call us, we'll call you." She giggled again, her face suddenly looking very flushed. "Whew. Is it getting hot in here or what?" She threw off her cover, unmindful of her nudity. Garry threw himself upon her while snatching up the ends of the blanket. "Oh, no you don't, Garry Danzlo," she warned, pushing him off her. "Best you keep your distance. You're hotter than any ole blanket I know."

The three medics stood wide-eyed, their faces filled with amusement as Garry reddened with embarrassment. "She doesn't know what she's saying."

Amanda began giggling again, but this time without stop. This was not the normal Mandy. "What drug did you give her?" Garry demanded. Amanda was about to say something through her giggles, but he threw the blanket over her face.

"Stadol," a female attendant answered. "Appears she has a low tolerance for medication."

"Yep!" Amanda puffed against the blanket against her mouth. "Low, high, somethin' like that. Forgot to tell ya, guys."

"What does that mean?" Garry said horrified. "What are you going to do about it?"

"Actually, there's not much we can do, except let it wear off. The effect is much like alcohol."

"Yeah, Garry-berry." Amanda muffled against her blanket. "Like brandy for Mandy. Ooo, it rhymes, what a crime."

Everyone laughed except Garry. "Any pain, Miss Fields?" the paramedic chuckled.

"Pain?" she blew, the blanket burping up and down with each breath she took. "Pain, pain, gone away. Good ole Stadol saved my day." Garry removed the covers from her face. Her eyes, largely round, gleamed up at him. "You sure are a handsome devil, Mr. Danzlo."

The med team began packing up their stuff, grinning all the while. "I think we can leave now," said one. "Looks like she's in good hands to me," said another.

"Wait," cried Amanda, reaching out to grab the female tech by the pants leg. "Don't cha want his autograph? He's a famous singer, ya know. Sung to me last night, he did."

Garry's right hand clamped over her mouth. "The woman talks too much," he explained. "My singing days are over."

Amanda shook her head, mumbling something beneath his palm, and then she bit him. He jerked his hand with an "ouch"—her opportunity to blab about how well he could sing, and how he was going to sing for everybody soon... and how he was going to play piano for her tomorrow so he could get those fingers ready for the big performances coming in the near future... and how he'd be walking on crutches in just a couple of days because he proved to be a pretty strong, flexible man last night... and how his fans are going to love it when he showed his handsome face again... and though Garry refused to believe all these things, they were true, and if he didn't *start* believing, she was going to stop being so sweet to him.

To shut her up and get those paramedics out, Garry started autographing pieces of paper handed him... EKG strips torn off the cardiac machine. "My girlfriend will die when I give her this," said the youngest male, "and when she does, I'll be ready for some of that mouth to mouth re-love-itation. Yep, a hot night tonight! Make sure you write 'to Mary' okay?"

"To Mary, with love," added Amanda, her head against a pillow. "Make it good and swee—"

Garry drowned out her words by using her face for a desk, being careful not to get too close to the bandage on her forehead. After he'd signed autographs for Pam and another for Rick and Cousin Dolores, he dismissed the medical team, hoping they were true to their word about not spreading any gossip concerning their visit to his house. In particular, his relationship with his live-in nurse.

He looked down at her giggling face when they were finally alone.

"Didn't that feel good, signing autographs again?" she asked. "You write well with your left hand."

He smiled. "That's because I'm left-handed."

Amanda rose up on her elbows, her brow squished upward against her bandage. "You are? You mean I've been complimenting your left-sided abilities, thinking you worked hard to strengthen the side that I thought to be the weaker?" Garry nodded with a grin. "You pig!" She rose up on her knees to attack him but he was fast to catch those flailing arms, laughing, all the while until the blanket slipped down past her waist revealing two beautiful, firm breasts and then some for his eyes to feast upon. How he was standing on his own two knees, he'd never know. All he knew was that his body was reacting instantaneously, last night's love scene replaying in his head. It vividly pictured every delectable movement she made against him, on and beneath him. He felt himself tremble as his gaze engulfed all of her, down to the dark curly hairs of her womanhood, back up to those golden eyes he adored. He saw her, too, staring at him, yet not at his face. Her focus was on the bulge in his pants. To see her looking at it so intensely was like a double dose of seduction, and it grew larger, harder. His eyes moved and fixed on the silver light glittering on her neck... *the cross.* She must have donned it this morning for she wasn't wearing it last night. It was like a spear piercing his heart, stabbing him recklessly while his mind fought reality—his relationship with this woman... taboo.

Amanda's gown was out of his reach, but he suddenly remembered Nicolas hooking his blue velour robe on the post at the foot of the bed this morning. He bent backward, leaned and grabbed it, swinging back so forcefully, he almost knocked Amanda off the bed for trying to cover her with it. He couldn't get it on her fast enough, so she obliged him by trying to put it on herself. She fought his hands, pushing at him angrily as she tied the belt, her eyes filling with tears as she tried to leave the bed. He took hold of the velour material, forcing her to stay upon the bed. She fell across it, twisting, fighting to get back up, but he wouldn't let her.

She hit and scratched him, pushed him as hard as she could. Garry could tell it wasn't her usual strength, the injection she'd received diminished her power of resistance. Her struggle was sloppy and overcome quickly by tears of helplessness.

"I hate you, I hate you!" she cried, banging her hands lamely on his shoulders as he leaned over her trying to embrace and comfort her. "You're ashamed of me. Ashamed of last night. I was a fool to come here. A fool to care."

"Mandy, stop it. Look at me. Look at me and listen." He took her face in his hands, forcing her eyes to open. Their golden hue appeared glassy, drugged, hurt. "If anyone's a fool, I'm a fool. I could never be ashamed of you. What happened last night was special. But it was also a mistake. It should never have happened. It's not your fault, it's mine. Yes, blame me, for I took advantage of you. I knew what I could get from you because you're always so giving and loving, never taking, always thinking of someone else and not yourself. I coerced you into playing a game of pretend, knowing full well you'd play along and give in to my selfish male needs. I knew you'd share with me everything you could bestow on a man. And I took it with greed, as well as longing. So go ahead and hate me, Mandy. I deserve it. Even now, *I want you.* God help me, but I do. I found out you're as beautiful on the outside as you are on the inside."

Amanda stared up at him, her drugged and dazed mind trying to analyze everything he was saying. Considering the sincere expression on his face and the intimacy in his eyes, she could tell he wasn't exactly telling the whole truth. Just as she hadn't told the truth when in a fit of anger and disappointment, she said she had hated him. He'd said their moment together was very special, and that even now, he wanted her. That was enough to make her believe she had a chance with him. No matter what he said.

"You've got to get last night out of your mind," he told her, as though reading her thoughts. "What we shared won't happen again. It can't happen again. When Daphne returns, I'm going to marry her. I'll be living in California with my wife while you'll be living in Florida. There you'll meet some lucky man who will sweep you off your feet, love you like you deserve."

Amanda didn't like what Garry was saying. If he as little as hinted a "thank you" for teaching him how to have a more fulfilling love life with Daphne, she'd kill him. If he wanted another woman for a wife, let him think she wanted another man.

"Hmm," she said. "Maybe Eddie." The near drowning ran through her mind like a blurry dream. Eddie had saved her life, came to her rescue as he'd done so many times in the past. To realize he was near was strangely comforting.

"Eddie?" Garry's gaze hardened. He leaned forward against her. "The man who carried you from the pond? Called you 'sweetheart'?"

"He called me sweetheart?" she said incredulously, as if she didn't know. "He rescues me often. Says he's my Gabriel angel."

"Well, good ole Gabe." Garry rolled away from her and scooted his back against the headboard. "Remind me to congratulate him on the one thing I could never do... rescue you."

Amanda had upset him, differently than she had intended. "You only say that because you don't believe in yourself, Garry. Yet, last night you proved a feat you once thought was impossible. I assure you, your ability to 'do' and 'give' to a woman is more than I could ever hope to witness or receive. What does it matter that you didn't rescue me from the pond or carry me to the bed in your arms? Whose arms held me as I laid here? Whose blanket was wrapped securely around me when the cold threatened to consume me? Was that not a rescue?"

Garry was focusing on the flames in the fireplace across the room. They seemed to flicker through his soul at her words, warming him with tender praise. *Blast it!* She always knew what to say, forever praising him for the little things. His attention moved to her face, drawn to her wet and glistening lips, parting, waiting for his response. He wanted to kiss them, to show her how much he appreciated her words, but he fought the urge. He fought her reasoning. He was no hero. "You know what I meant."

"And you know what I meant," she said.

His eyes held hers for a moment before it centered back on the flames within the fireplace. "This Eddie guy... he has deep feelings for you. I'm starting to realize just how little I know about you, about your life before coming here. I should question why this man just happened to be on my property at the time of the accident, yet I'm glad he was. If you had drowned, I don't think I would've been able to live with myself. Because, Mandy, I care for you. I care so much it scares me." Garry swallowed hard, the confession causing his vision to blur as he continued to stare at the blaze in the hearth. "I want you to have a good life when you leave here. If you think you can find happiness with this man, I think you should go for it. You apparently have some feelings for him by the enthusiastic way you spoke of him earlier. Perhaps you're even in love with him, a-and didn't tell me?"

He forced himself to look her way, and there she lay on his pillow, snuggled in his blue velour robe with her eyes closed. Her legs were curled beneath the velvety fabric, her bare feet peeking beneath the hem.

"Mandy? You awake?"

She didn't stir. At first she seemed too still, and Garry leaned over to assure himself she was breathing. As he moved upon the bed, her lips parted, and he saw the slight quivering motion of her bottom lip as air brushed across it, in and out. He sighed, realizing that the drug had sedated her. He covered her more securely in the blanket. Reclining back, he rested his head against the oak headboard. He closed his eyes, listening to the racing of his heart in his ears. *She hadn't heard a word he'd said.*

He realized it was better that way. That she not know how much he cared. There were so many unanswered questions.

His stomach twisted in a heavy knot as he thought of the handsome, brawny man affectionately ministering to her, whispering against her hair, assuring her safety, calling her *Sweetheart.* Calling her *Love.*

Bile erupted in his throat and he swallowed it back, the sour taste burning like a harsh astringent. It was killing him to think she could possibly want another, to imagine her giving even half of what she'd gifted him with last night. Such passion beyond anything he'd ever known. Had he taken advantage of her vulnerability? Or was it really love he witnessed in her eyes, that which he felt radiating now, deep down in his own chest.

His eyes burned with the truth, his eyelids stinging. *He loved her.* And there wasn't a damn thing he could do about it. He thought of his mother, about the lifelong promise he'd made, and how against all odds his relationship with Amanda seemed. All he knew was that he was helplessly under the spell of this beguiling, lovable, and wacky woman.

As his focus moved over Amanda's placid body beside him, he took in those enticing curves and the natural complexion of her lovely face. His mind was quickly becoming befuddled. Little Miss Muffet was looking a lot like Sleeping Beauty. He'd thought the brandy last night had altered his brain waves, allowing him a better picture of the alluring clown. But this was the same lovely visage he'd made love to last night. No makeup. No glasses. No ugly clothes.

A light began to burn in Garry's head. Little by little, things were starting to make sense. For one thing, Daphne's jealousy. To Daphne, looks were everything. Without it, one didn't have a chance against her. But it didn't take Amanda's looks to win him. He'd been strangely attracted to her before last night. Had Daphne known of her hidden beauty? And what about the man who rescued Amanda? Garry couldn't imagine Mr. *Tall, dark, and handsome* picking a mate from the cabbage patch when he could choose any woman from Playboy magazine.

But Amanda was not just any woman. She wasn't even close to the common woman. She was a Jack-Of-All-Trades. She'd played many a role since the day she walked into his house. She was Little Red Riding Hood and Cinderella wrapped up into one, the incredible Wonder Woman who came flying down from Never-Never land to rescue the feeble-minded musician who stupidly wanted to give up on life. And then, her latest and greatest performance played last night as Lady Godiva—riding naked on Garry Danzlo's bed to win him relief from a burdensome sexless life.

Garry was far from being calm as he sat on the bed beside the sleeping Amanda. His brain flipped between scenes of real women and those that were make-believe. From Joan of Arc to Bo Peep, his nurse played every role, while he, the patient, played the sucker.

Nicolas had better return soon, else Amanda was sure to be disturbed from sleep when he tried to strangle her to death. He had to keep reminding himself she'd nearly drowned in a freezing pond and needed rest. His patience for answers was waning more than fast, however. If Nicolas didn't hurry, he had no doubt Beauty would be meeting the Beast in mere seconds, the union guaranteed to be more than frightful.

# 28.

# THIS CAN'T BE REAL

"I WANT AN explanation!" Garry said gruffly.

Melissa winced, her frostbitten body now sweating with the heat of confession—or what Nicolas and she believed to be all of the confession Garry was able to handle. His feelings toward Amanda were too young and fresh to risk destroying what had not yet had a chance to be wholly realized. If it was truly love being awakened in him, that emotion needed to develop and grow, thus making it less likely that he'd send her away. Not only did the budding romance need to ripen, but there were still the issues surrounding the accident and suicide—an unresolved matter too important to dismiss. Without Amanda to lead the way, all would be lost and Garry would go back into a horrid, dark shell. It was apparent now that Garry deserved to hear the whole truth, though not from Melissa's lips, but rather Amanda's. Things had gotten too serious between them and if she was ever to receive Garry's full respect, she'd have to come clean personally. Of course with Daphne's threat hanging over Amanda's head, a confession was near impossible, if not a bit dangerous, at the moment. Daphne had no inkling of the extent of trouble she, herself, could stir, nor the danger she could create for a number of people now that she had that list of creditors.

"I'm waiting!" Garry said impatiently.

"Okay, calm down, Garry. You're taking things way out of proportion." Melissa stood in the middle of the kitchen floor, Nicolas standing beside her, too frightened to speak. "You'll wake Amanda."

"I'm going to do more than wake that woman," Garry said, clutching the wheels of his wheelchair, ready to embark terror on the one sleeping in the other room. His left hand swiveled a wheel in that direction.

Melissa seized the chair handles. "You'll do no such thing. Now listen to me." Melissa stepped around and faced him, grasping both arms of the wheelchair while Garry gripped the wheels tightly. "Okay, so she's been impersonating a bit beyond her true self, because she's not Jewish—never has been, never had any thoughts of converting either. Her maiden name is not Lowenstein, but McKinney." Garry grimaced at the lie he'd been told, or at least led to believe. "But it wasn't Amanda who was behind that fib," Melissa said. "It was me, totally me. Mom was asking too many questions, suspecting things between you and your nurse, just *knowing* things. You know how she is! I thought it best she think Amanda Jewish so it wouldn't cause a big ruckus. The truth is, Amanda is innocent. She's just… kept some things back is all."

Garry eyed Melissa suspiciously, that little twitch at the corner of her mouth giving her away. "There's more you're not telling me, Sis. Spit it out. I want to know all about Sleeping Beauty and that knight who came from out of nowhere to rescue her."

Melissa swallowed hard. "Okay, let's start with her first. I confess that I asked her—begged her actually—to overdo her makeup for the sake of Daphne. I knew Daphne would have her out the door if she ever discovered Amanda was competition. I knew Amanda Fields was a looker beneath all those eccentric clothes she wears. I'm a fashion designer, I just know these things. You'd think a woman with her looks would realize her own beauty and go for a softer look." Melissa half-laughed while half-lying. "She's so unpredictable, isn't she? So varied in tastes, in color. She can somehow be zany and fetching at the same time. You know what I mean?" Garry didn't say anything; he just blinked and shifted in his seat. "Of course, it's what's inside her that makes the real woman, so it wasn't hard to steal the heart of a man, her husband. Paul, that was his name. And Eddie, he was a friend of theirs from way back. Had actually introduced the two of them. Eddie's always been a little protective of Amanda though. Known her since junior high school. Why he was here this morning is only a miracle. Just be glad that he was, or she and I could be at the bottom of your icy pond right now. The only real important thing you need to know is that I found you the perfect nurse. I knew Amanda was the answer to our prayers the moment I met her."

Garry grimaced for the second time. "Prayers?" he scoffed. "Are we talking about Jewish prayer or Christian? Crimony, sis! You could've at least told me she wasn't Jewish before I got myself so deeply involved with her. Instead, I received what I thought was the shock of my life when I undressed her and found the cross on her neck. But now you add to my misery by telling me she's been…" He choked on the word to come, his eyes welling with the sting of tears, "*deceiving* me since the day I met her?" He swallowed the painful truth, his body trembling with the certainty that crushed his heart. "I trusted her," he said, staring down into his lap, slumped forward, "and she betrayed me. I would've never imagined it. Not from her."

"Are we talking about a little extra makeup?" Melissa shouted. She stomped her foot. "Had you been interested enough to begin a real conversation with her, had bothered to ask her anything, she would've told you everything you wanted to know. Only, you've been too busy with your obnoxious self. Try to help you, you'd say no. She'd say stop, you'd say go. She'd encourage, you discouraged. If she thought to leave, you'd say ple-ee-ease do! No wonder she keeps those kooky reading glasses on her face while you're around, because you're so intimidating." Melissa, too riled up and too late to take back any words, realized she'd uncovered another secret Amanda had—the glasses. Garry's flustered face was evidence he'd been playing the foolish patient, but it was the hurt that streaked across his cheeks and transformed to anger that had Melissa and Nicolas exchanging panic-filled glances. Garry's eyes thickened at what he now knew.

Nicolas couldn't watch any longer. He stepped forward. "Sir, if I should speak for a mo—"

"Speak?" Garry cocked his head back. "I think you've done enough damage, my dear and trustworthy friend. Thanks for pushing a woman on me you knew I couldn't have. Blast all, Nicolas! What if I've gotten her pregnant? What should I do, ole buddy? Take her in as my concubine? Daphne would love that."

Melissa paid no mind to her brother's sarcasm, too busy trying to comprehend what he'd just said to Nicolas. *Was it true?* He and Amanda had made love? No wonder Amanda was so emotional this morning. Melissa's attention swerved to Nicolas, the man who clearly knew all.

"Sir, I don't think the possibility of pregnancy is a concern. Miss Amanda lost an unborn child some years back, carried it almost full term. She went into early labor, but there were complications. According to the doctors, her chance of having another child is slim to none. I think it's one of the reasons she has her heart set on adopting that little boy in Florida, the one she writes to."

Melissa's eyes widened. This was like watching a soap opera on television, Melissa tuned in on an all new episode of *The Days of Amanda's Life*. Why hadn't

Amanda ever told her about the baby she'd lost? Melissa zoomed in on Garry.

The curve of Garry's jaw twitched, his left eyelid flickering in same manner. He could deny all he wanted, but Melissa could tell Nicolas's story had affected her brother.

"If you're trying to alter my opinion about her, Nicolas, it won't work. It doesn't change the fact that she deceived me. I could never trust her again. Nor can I trust either of you." Garry seized on Melissa with harsh eyes. "When she awakes, sis, you're both to leave this house. I don't want to see her face anywhere near me… *ever!*" He shoved her hand from the chair arm, grasping the wheels, his right hand struggling to keep pace with his left as he tried exiting the room on his own.

"I'm afraid that's not possible," Nicolas said, halting Garry's departure, "unless you truly don't care that both women face danger if they leave this house. Their very lives would be at stake, and very possibly, the boy Robbie's as well."

With one backward push of the left wheel, Garry circled, his eyes fixed on Nicolas. A brow upturned dubiously.

Melissa waited with apprehension. She wasn't too sure that telling Garry everything was such a bright idea. Garry would never believe Daphne had blackmailed Amanda. She could already tell he was ready to hear a farce of a tale.

"It's true, sir. To make a long story short, Miss Amanda owes a great amount of money, debt her disloyal gambler husband left upon his death. Her husband was stabbed to death, possibly by the same murdering loan shark that's now after Miss Amanda for reasons we're not really sure of. Of course, this is only part of the danger," he related, "for yet another villain is in the picture, one who has blackmailed Miss Amanda into staying here and hiding her identity, else she stands the chance of Robbie getting harmed. Miss Amanda would've confessed her… well, these *secrets*… long before now had these obstacles not arose so soon after her arrival."

Garry stared irritably, a twitch active in his jaw once again. He didn't know whether to laugh at such a preposterous story or to cut Nicolas out of his will. "Now let me get this straight," he said, pretending to play along in this ridiculous ruse. "Amanda was married to a murdering gambler who was butchered by a knife, leaving her to inherit a mountain of debt, probably summing up to more thousands than I'm paying her."

"A gambler, yes," Melissa said. "A murderer, we're not sure, though possible since he was involved with criminals. You'd think a lawyer would have better sense."

"Oh, he was a lawyer? A gambler lawyer husband who had criminals for friends. This story gets better by the minute. Gee, I thought Amanda would have better taste in men than that."

"She had a terrible marriage, sir," Nicolas said, his face drawn heavily. Garry was beginning to wonder if the story could possibly be true. "That poor girl knew all about lies and deceit. Better than you, I dare say. From what I understand, the man that saved her from the pond today was her only support through those horrible years."

*No*, Garry thought. *These two are not going to sucker me into believing such craziness.* The memory of Amanda talking about her husband flittered through his mind. Grief for a loved one, wasn't it? Or was it sadness due to a loveless marriage? But the whole story was ludicrous. "So what about the blackmail?" he said. "You say the boy Robbie is in danger if Amanda leaves here from hiding? Who threatens her?"

Melissa and Nicolas exchanged glances. Garry had misinterpreted Nicolas's statement about Amanda's blackmailer forcing her in "staying here and keeping her identity" as Amanda needing to stay hidden in his home. How lucky could they get? Danzlo wouldn't send her away now if danger existed if she left. "Who threatens her?" he asked.

"Who else but a jealous female, sir," Nicolas blustered. "You see, there's this man who's in love with Miss Amanda. Unfortunately, he's involved with a very jealous woman. She would probably do anything to keep this man. He's quite popular with the ladies... handsome, talented. But his heart belongs to the lovely Miss Amanda. As long as she stays 'undercover' so to speak, the threat of the two coming together is lessened considerably. Unfortunately, the treacherous woman knows about the boy, that he's Miss Amanda's pride and joy. It is her means to blackmail."

Garry shifted uncomfortably in his seat, the questions concerning Amanda's mysterious Eddie now being answered. Everything was starting to make sense— Eddie's concern for Amanda's safety, her plea for him to save Robbie, and lastly, the intimacy witnessed between the two. "Amanda loves him?" he asked gravely.

Nicolas and Melissa exchanged glances. "She does, *very much*," Melissa said.

Garry felt the color drain from his face, his stomach lurching. "I see. And Eddie... he knows this?"

"Eddie?" Nicolas and Melissa responded incredulously.

"Did you think I wouldn't guess?" he said painfully. "I saw the two together. He's her hero. I was crazy to think she could love a lame musician when all along she had a shining knight. And to think I thought of marrying the wrong one. Daphne is the right one. And she's Jewish. Mom can celebrate."

Melissa and Nicolas stood aghast.

"You can't possibly still be thinking to marry Daphne." Melissa screamed. "What do you think last night was for Amanda? Her night for *whoopee*? She's made of better stuff than that, and you know it."

"Your sister's right, sir. Miss Amanda's feelings grow deep. If you love her, sir—"

"I don't want to love her, Nicolas."

His eyes closed as a great turbulence tore through his flesh. It was as if Amanda's very spirit blew a fierce windstorm inside him, mocking him for his remark.

And then everything grew morbidly still. The only sound was the tick-tock of the pendulum in the mahogany-cased clock in the next room.

"I know she has feelings for me," he said, his eyes lowering. "I have them too. Beyond my control. But I'm not the best man for her." He raised his face. "Some things just aren't meant to be. Some good things never last."

"Garry, you have a chance with Amanda. Just take it," Melissa said. "She's where your real happiness lies. Is this really about Eddie, or are you just scared of Mom?"

He eyed Melissa, his stare softening. "Not scared, sis. Mindful. Cautious. I know what kind of trouble she can stir up, and so do you."

"Mr. Danzlo, can I say something?" Nicolas shifted on his feet. "I'm sure once your mother met Miss Amanda, she'd fall in love with her, as we all have. Surely she'd pick Miss Amanda over Miss Daphne."

Garry frowned. "I'm getting a little tired of everyone dismissing Daphne. She's a beautiful woman with faults like everybody else. So she's a little vain; I'm a little arrogant. So she has a temper; I have one too. In fact, we have a lot in common. We'll make a good couple."

The dog trotted into the kitchen, the morning newspaper in her mouth. Bending forward, Nicolas retrieved it. Nicolas was about to place the folded paper on the table when Garry glimpsed a familiar photo at the corner bottom of the front page. He jerked the paper from Nicolas's hands, shook it open and began reading his own engagement in print. According to the news column, he was getting married in a couple of weeks, as soon as his beautiful bride-to-be returned from the pre-wedding gift vacation he so generously paid for.

Garry's hands began to tremble on the newspaper. He tried to calm them, a sudden volcano in his mind making the task difficult. No way would he show his anger now, not when he'd just finished defending Daphne. The fact that she'd done something like this behind his back was... *forgivable*, he commanded himself. A sea of madness and anxiety swam down his throat, pooling to his stomach in one mighty gush. It left his voice hoarse and dry.

"See? The marriage is final. Amanda Fields will soon be history." He accomplished a smile as he handed the paper to a reluctant Melissa. But inside, a colossal weight burdened his heart.

# 29.

# IT'S ALL IN THE GAME

"This is it, Max. Pull in."

Max veered the rented limousine into the parking lot of the Delray Home for Disabled Children, parking in the shade of an old hickory tree. Shutting off the engine, he watched Daphne's reflection in the rearview mirror as she powdered her nose and lined her thin lips with a lip pencil. She filled her lips in with shiny fuchsia.

"Planning to turn on some little boys?" Max asked, raising a sardonic brow.

Daphne shifted her gaze from the compact mirror in her hand to the yard where the handicapped children played, the sound of their voices and laughter muffled behind the closed windows of the limousine. "Your mind is demented, Max. I do men, not boys." She clicked her compact shut.

"Not all men. Let's not forget the invalid you're going to marry," Max said, grinning.

Daphne's eyes darkened. "Shut up, Max! You're trying your limit. I know I left you hot and heaving for more after the phone rang this morning, but that doesn't give reason for this little game of spite you're playing." She reached for her purse, opened it, and inserted her compact. "All those contacts on that paper was a gold mine of information on Amanda. So many hopes have been ruined because of some bastard. If I find out it was Garry who paid off those debts for Amanda, I'll kill him!"

"Look who's being spiteful?" Max said, turning in his seat to view and enjoy the fire flaming in her cheeks. "It wasn't as if your scheme was foolproof. Your lies about Amanda plotting against her creditors to avoid paying her debts was not a guarantee. As for Danzlo being her benefactor, I think you're accusing the wrong

225

man. I'd bet on that criminal defense lawyer Eddie Chandler. I told you he inherited a billion from his old man. Just think, two men in love with the same woman and it's not you. But, Sugar Love, I still want you."

"You'd want a dog if that's all you had available to screw. All I want is this Eddie Chandler found and taken care of! If he's in love with Amanda like we've been told, perhaps he'll bargain to get her back." She placed her Gucci purse beneath her arm. "While I'm in seeing the boy, you stay here, Max, make some more phone calls. Somebody must know where Eddie Chandler is. Oh, and call your contact person. See if he can get any information on that J.D. Bowers person. It was the only one we didn't have a number for."

"You sure you want to touch ground with that one? I'm not getting good vibes on him."

"If your brain didn't work so much on feeling, you'd get something done other than sex. Now just do what I say! I don't pay you for nothing. I've got other things to think about right now, like what to do about the boy. I'm thinking to put a little scare in him for the time being, make sure Amanda knows I've paid a little visit to her precious Robbie. He'll beg Amanda to come back, and Amanda will be too scared not to."

"Unless of course she's at the bottom of your fiancé's pond." Max smirked.

Daphne stilled; her eyes wide and locking with his.

He chuckled. "I told you I was going to do it." He rubbed the cheek Amanda had assaulted, the bitter remembrance hidden well in his voice. "While you were sleeping in Denver, crafty ole Max went sneaking into the night." He slapped his palms together in a cross-like manner, accentuating a job well done.

Daphne was utterly speechless for a moment. Inside she battled an involuntary smile that erupted inside her. Playing impassive about the whole ordeal, she said with a steady voice, "I will have to call Garry tonight and find out what's happening in his neck of the woods." She grabbed her purse off the seat. "Now, ta-ta, darling, while I meet this little retard Amanda adores."

She eased from the limousine, one shapely leg following the other, elegance within every step she took as she headed toward the flamingo colored building. Approaching the big irongate, her right high heel slipped into a crack in the cement, her once graceful body making a clumsy fall toward the ground. Instantly, two powerful hands circled her waist, her soft pliant body shoved against what felt like steel while her fingers clasped on to gloriously firm muscled upper arms. She looked up into the most impressionable face she'd ever seen—enigmatic, confident, and sexually stimulating. His touch had her paralyzed, leaning, and then melting against him while his smoke-gray eyes beamed down like silver skylights, sucking every bit of fluid she had in her body.

"Are you hurt?" he asked with his voice so low it rumbled down to her feet.

"Uh... m-my foot, my ankle," she swallowed uncomfortably, the heat of him burning in her cheeks. But that was no comparison to the heat blazing through the rest of her body when his strong hands slid down and across her hips boldly, brushing the sides of her legs, where on bended knee he took her left ankle in both hands.

"This one?" he asked, lifting those brilliantly polished eyes that senselessly blinded her.

"The other one," she corrected, vaguely realizing he was playing a seductive game. Any other man, she'd be kicking him hard in the groin for daring to touch her without permission. But this man... he was terribly irresistible. No man had ever affected her like this. It was simply not of her making. "I think it'll be fine. Silly me. I'm usually more careful where I walk."

The tall one stood. *Tall, yes.* He had to be at least six foot three or four. Men taller than her own six foot were rare to find, and usually married. His left hand grasped hers, her eyes lowering to the signet ring on his pinkie. No wedding band.

"I hope you don't think me crude," he began, "but I couldn't help but notice you as you left your vehicle. I confess, I couldn't take my eyes off you. Such a beautiful woman."

Daphne did everything in her power to stand on two feet and not fall flat on her face. "Crude? Of course not. I'm flattered." Who was this man? The god of Thunder? "I didn't catch your name."

"I didn't give it." He gazed down at her, an amused curve to his lips. "You first."

Her focus was skeptical, taking in the dark hair that swept his shoulders, the dark tanned skin, the strong jaw line, the distinguished cheekbones. She didn't normally go for the dark type, the savage-like look this man portrayed. "Daphne Dimont," she informed. "And you?"

He smiled. "Eddie Chandler at your service." He clicked his heels and half-bowed.

Daphne stumbled forward, fainting for the first time in her life. Eddie sidestepped, and watched her fall.

# 30.

# THIS GUY'S IN LOVE
# WITH YOU

SOMETHING STRANGE WAS going on at the Danzlo house. Something Amanda suspected her friends were keeping from her. No one was acting quite the same, particularly Garry. He seemed to think he was invincible; suddenly all work, no play, and striving like a mad man to get into shape. According to her two loyal friends, Amanda had nothing to worry about. Garry had confessed his love. It didn't matter how she painted her face, or what clothes she wore. Nor the fact that she wasn't Jewish. Nothing could change his deep feelings for her. And Daphne was history. He planned to marry Amanda, but he was having trouble confessing his real feelings, that's all. He had to prove first that he was worth having. That's why he would be doing a lot of exercise in the upcoming days. He was going to be a new man.

Amanda began to doubt her friends by the third day. She did not like this new man Garry was becoming. He didn't act like a man in love at all. She'd admit his motivation to heal his body was a miraculous change. His determination a marvelous wonder. And, he'd allowed her to do some energy work. Though skeptical that first session, he'd been amazed at the soothing heat flowing from her hands, and at times the feel of undulating waves combing gently through his body. The afterward result left him so stimulated and vitalized, he said she could charge his sparkplug anytime.

His greatest improvement was balance. Somehow he'd conquered it in a matter of days. It was as though he was proving to her he could do anything and everything he once believed he couldn't do. Even the breathing exercises had him speaking with a clearer voice. He was apparently practicing on his own.

She was convinced now that his ambition to succeed had nothing to do with love, but rather on hurrying her back to Florida! He never hinted this verbally—he barely talked to her, except when he had something impersonal to say. The only personal attention she received was his thoughtfulness in ensuring she was well after the accident. The day following the pond incident, he'd ordered her to stay in bed the whole morning and afternoon. He had allowed her up only after a shipment of exercise machines was delivered to the house that evening. Assured she was completely free from any ailments, his attention centered on getting into shape and doing the exercises she instructed him to do. He asked her questions about position, about breathing, and what foods were best for him to eat. He was all business, no play.

What bothered her most was how he ignored her presence. He avoided looking at her when at all possible. She knew she'd never make the front cover of Vogue magazine—her cheeks swollen from the accident, one eyelid purple and blue, the cut bearing the steri-strips looking like someone had branded a tic-tac-toe board on her forehead.

This morning, she'd penned some Xs and Os between the steri-strips on her forehead. She'd waited the entire morning with no response from Garry, not even a smile. Thoroughly disgusted by lunchtime, she plopped down at the table beside him with a paper bag on her head, decorated with black beady eyes, a warty nose and a severe ogre's frown that fit her present mood to a tee.

She wanted a club to knock over Garry's head when he'd asked her to pass the salt. She passed it obligingly, scowling beneath her bag. She reached across the table, felt for the bowl of potato salad and slapped some on her plate. Freshly baked rolls sat beside her, their aroma wafting up her bag as she reached for the basket. Steam drifted upward as she pushed away the linen cloth that covered them, her enclosed environment a little more than stuffy. But she was determined to hold out until Garry said something.

"Could you pass the rolls, please?"

"Would you like just one roll?" she said, flinging one his way. "Or would you like two?" She flung another. "Why not three? Let's put some meat on those bones." She threw the third, hoping at least one found his face.

Nicolas and Melissa were rolling with laughter, but Garry was silent for a moment. Suddenly his voice came through, vibrating against her bag. "Missed me. Three strikes you're out. You'd make a terrible ball player, Mandy."

"Ooooh, just give me a bat!"

"Gee, I was going to compliment your looks today, but I see the bag makes you feisty. Better take it off."

She took it off all right. Then crammed it over his head, watching his head pop through so he could wear it as a neck brace. She walked away, leaving his laughter trailing in the distance.

"YOU LIED TO me, Melissa. He doesn't love me. He can't even stand to look at me."

It was some thirty minutes later. Amanda sat cross-legged on the window seat in her bedroom, cooling her nerves.

Melissa edged toward her from the doorway. "I didn't lie. Not about him loving you. Okay, so it took him awhile to realize you had a bag on your head."

"Like how long?" Amanda asked with concern.

Melissa hesitated. "Like when you threw the first roll. And you did hit him. He lied."

"The first roll?" She swiveled her feet to the carpet. "See, I told you. He can't stand to look at my face. That's not love. He regrets ever going to bed with me, doesn't he? I should've never believed you or Nicolas."

"Would it help if I told you the next two rolls made good hits? One upside his head, the other across his nose. He thought he was dodging them, but you threw some crazy curved balls. You should've seen his expression—full of disbelief and amazed by your expert pitching."

"Good. He deserved a few rolls in his face. But that doesn't change the fact that he hates to look at me, not to mention that he talks to me as little as possible. And now you're talking about leaving this evening when Dan gets here, leaving me with that... that... serious, no-talking *twerp!*"

Melissa smiled. "Yeah, that same twerp you adore and would go to bed with again if he asked you to."

"Quit it, Melissa, this is no joking matter."

"Was I joking?" Melissa pivoted to an invisible person behind her. "Was I joking?"

Amanda gazed at her warily. "That can't happen again. Not with Daphne prowling who knows where. And I've not heard a word from Eddie. Are you sure it's safe for you to leave?"

"Amanda, come on. I told you Eddie said he took care of One-Eyed Jack. Said he was taking care of everything. He saved you from the pond, didn't he? Over two thousand miles from your Florida home, and he was here. He'll keep Robbie from harm, too." She paused, and then frowned. "Can't you see I miss my husband terribly? We'll be back in a few days. Besides, Garry asked me to pick up something for you while I'm gone. Three things to be exact."

"Like what? Curly, Larry and Moe? He probably thinks I'd make a better partner for them."

Melissa giggled. "Amanda, I know it's a little hard to believe that he loves you right now, but there're matters he's trying to deal with. And then our mother called this morning, inviting herself down for a visit. I really need to try and get back before she gets here, but if I don't, try to act Jewish. At least for the time being."

"Why? So I can uphold the name of Lowenstein until you figure out a way for Garry to marry me? Melissa, that's not the way it works. It's Garry who needs to make that decision. And frankly, I don't want him to have to make that decision."

Deep creases lined Melissa's forehead. "But you love him. He loves you."

Amanda sighed heavily. "That hardly guarantees us a lifetime together. Sure, we could just live together, make it work without a sacred contract to keep your mother happy, but would we really be happy?" Amanda stood and looked out the window toward the wishing well. "Garry's a celebrity. I know so little about his world. I think I'm starting to understand Garry's avoidance." She turned and faced Melissa who was now sitting on the bed. "It stems from his inability to deal with our uncertain relationship, and just like always, he's hiding behind that curtain. His fear, his emotions, and his doubt. And here I am, no better—a hider too—setting a great example by wearing clothes and makeup that isn't at all like me." Her eyes widened. "He thinks I naturally dress like this. Wear my makeup like this. Is that crazy or what?"

Melissa became strangely quiet. She stood up and began straightening the bedspread, her fingers delicately smoothing down the edges. Amanda watched as Melissa mashed down some rumpled lump that wasn't there.

"Oh my stars!" Amanda felt a little dizzy: "Does he suspect? Or worse, does he *know*? If so, I have to confess everything now."

"Whatever you think. He's waiting for you in the music room, ready to exercise his fingers." Melissa grabbed Amanda by the arm, dragged her ahead toward her bedroom door, saying, "It's a marvelous thing seeing him at the piano. He wouldn't have done it without you." Melissa pushed her out into the hall.

"But I'm not through talking to you," Amanda said, pivoting to Melissa. "Is he waiting for my confession? Should I —" the door slammed in her face. "Melissa." She banged on the wood.

Her hand stopped in mid-air when she heard Garry's voice calling from nearby. She turned slowly to the right to see him wheeling his chair from the music room. He stopped in front of her. "Is there a problem I can help you with?"

His expression was solemn, the topaz of his eyes shining in her face, warming her with memories so sensual it took her breath away. It was as though his lips were everywhere, tasting and licking her. She couldn't speak, let alone breathe while he waited expectantly.

"I guess not," he said sharply, turning his chair around and heading back toward the music room. He stopped just before the door, "You coming?" he asked, without a backward glance. He continued into the room.

Amanda sighed, realizing she'd angered him. If he hadn't elicited those sexual memories with his lustrous blue eyes, she wouldn't have been so tongue-tied! And she would've realized he was waiting for a confession. *The confession.* Did he really know everything? Considering the fact that she was still here and had somehow bypassed Garry's wrath made it more than likely that Melissa had only *patched* any suspicions he may have had. This wasn't good. All she knew for sure was that Garry was angry. He proved that when he turned away with disgust.

She stepped into the music room and found him bent at the piano. The fingers of his right hand played softly on the black and ivory keys. But they were moving on them clumsily, consecutive notes clashing when he didn't want them to. He joined his left fingers upon the keyboard, his growing ire evident by the rising volume sounding from the piano. The notes clanked and roared until she thought Garry's lashing volcanic fingers and the piano would explode.

"Stop it, stop it," she screamed, running up beside him.

His fists crashed violently upon the piano keys at her voice, his face constricted in pain. His eyes were misty, foreign. She reacted the only way she knew how—in desperation, and in love.

Throwing her glasses to the floor, she cuddled him with her hands, touching his face, his hair, his shoulders, while her lips covered his face with tender kisses. They rained upon his eyes, nose, mouth, and cheeks. Garry's fingers lay lifeless on the ivory and ebony keys as his mind became awakened from misery, his shaking body easing from its timbre. His face was drenched with her tears, and she drank them from his face. She grabbed his hands from the piano keys and embraced them, hugging them against her face, loving them with sweet affection. "These are beautiful hands," he heard her say while she calmed his raging storm. She went down on bended knees beside him and he watched her with wonder as she kissed each finger, one by one. "They can play beautiful music," she whispered softly. "They did once, and they will again. They just need patience, that's all."

Garry slipped one of his hands from her grasp and gently cupped her chin. He stared down into her upturned face. Anger had possessed him in the hall. He'd heard her talking to Melissa. He'd given her a chance to confide some truth, but she didn't take it. Perhaps it was stupid to make Nicolas and Melissa promise they'd not tell her what he already knew—how she was hiding behind exaggerated makeup and glasses she didn't need, and keeping secrets about her past... about the man named Eddie. Somehow it was important to him that Amanda tell him. He wanted to see how long it would take her, though this reason seemed selfish. And so was this design to kiss her as he held her chin in his hand. His face slowly lowered, closer and closer to hers. *Kiss her for the comfort she gave you*, he told himself. *Kiss her because she cares. But don't kiss her because you need to, because you want to.* He closed his eyes a bare inch from her face, his mind fighting the voice in his head that told him it was useless to do this, *for you're only going to hurt her*, it was saying. *You're going to marry Daphne. Eddie's the better man. He saved her and you couldn't. You're just an ex-musician who might make it again one day... or maybe not. Let her go...*

"Thank you," he said, and straightened in his wheelchair, unable to look at those quivering lips he'd left unsatisfied. The dissatisfaction he felt on his own lips was enough to bear. "I'll begin again." He placed his fingers back on the keys, pressing one note at a time as he played the scale, his right trying to keep up with his left, but not doing a good job of it. "You talked to Robbie this morning?" he asked, trying to break the tension. He knew she had talked to him, for he had planned the call. He'd spoken with the boy every day since the pond accident. Amanda would worry until Robbie was safely beside her, so it was Garry's intent to see that he was. The boy was excited about coming to Colorado. He was even more excited that Amanda didn't know anything about it. He'd be a big surprise. *She'll like that*, Robbie said proudly. *Amanda loves me, you know.* Already, Garry was feeling a special bond with the boy, and he hadn't even met him. In a couple of days, Robbie would be on a plane with Dan and Melissa, soon to make Amanda the happiest woman alive.

"Yes, I spoke to him and he's doing fine," she said. Garry felt every sparkle that shined in her eyes. He smiled, for he knew she'd forgotten all about the plastic framed glasses still lying on the floor by his chair. If he could get to them, he'd step on them, her eyes too pretty to cover up. "You're doing fine, too," she suddenly said. "Besides the scale, do you know Chopsticks? That would be a good practice song for your right hand."

"Woman, you wound me. You think *I*, the great musician, would not know Chopsticks?" He began to play, though badly, for his right hand wasn't coordinated enough to bring out the perfect blend of notes. "Okay, so I used to know it. And I played it well, too."

He was teasing her, and he could tell she was enjoying it. As long as he didn't look at her too much or too long, he was fine and he could live without kissing her.

He glanced at her smiling face, his fingers clanging the wrong notes on the piano. He turned his attention back to the piano keys.

"Did you say something?"

"No," he said, not looking at her.

Yeah, that was the ticket. No matter what, don't look into those starry brown eyes with the gold highlights. And never mind that perfect-sized nose, or those luscious full lips that tasted of chocolate and cherries the first time he'd savored them, and each time thereafter—praline, butterscotch, taffy, or peppermint. She smelled of peppermint right now.

He shifted uncomfortably in his chair.

And no more sneaking peeks when she wasn't looking. Even if it meant missing things like the tic-tac-toe game she drew on her forehead, enjoying all her huffing and puffing.

At the moment, her arms were around his neck, squeezing the stuffing out of him. He'd just played a simple round of Chopsticks without a mistake with his right hand.

*Just pretend she's not there, Danzlo. Just pretend she's not there.*

# 31.

# I DON'T WANT TO WALK WITHOUT YOU

"MELISSA, WILL YOU sit down and stop hopping from one window to the next. Dan will be here when he gets here. Come and watch this movie with me. Garry and Nicolas are going through some stuff in the music room, and here I sit all alone." Amanda sighed. "I guess nobody loves me."

Melissa released the sheer drape from her fingers. She smiled over her shoulder at Amanda who sat on the sofa, bent legged, elbows on knees, chin in her hands. She wore a pathetic hang dog expression on her face. "Amanda, you're so melodramatic. Put on a happy face and I'll come sit beside you." Amanda put on the biggest smile she could. Tickled, Melissa joined her on the sofa. "Hey, Bing and Bob! *The Road to Morocco*, right? I love this old movie. Those two are so funny together. Bing Crosby and Bob Hope—kinda like the Amanda Fields and Melissa Rosten team, huh?" She punched Amanda on the shoulder, trying to cheer her up.

"I'll miss you, Melissa."

"I'll miss you, too, but hey, a couple of days, I'll be back."

"No, Melissa, I'm talking about when I'm gone."

"You're not going anywhere, Amanda."

"I am, Melissa. I'll be leaving Garry. Somehow I feel it. I think Garry feels it, too. He just won't tell me. I hope Dan remembers to bring the crutches."

Amanda sighed at Bing kissing Dorothy Lamour on the TV set. They'd just sung *Moonlight Becomes You*.

"Love will conquer in the end, you'll see, Amanda." Melissa took her hand, thinking about her husband. "Do you think Dan is missing me as much as I'm missing him?"

Amanda smiled, scooting back in her seat. She squeezed Melissa's hand.

"I'M GOING TO kill that woman as soon as I see her!"

Dan drove down the winding road, his hands tight around the steering wheel of the car he'd rented from the airport. He didn't want Melissa chancing some of the road conditions by picking him up. The snow and ice were clear for the most part, but the back roads to Garry's log home were pretty treacherous. He didn't want her to risk death on the road. She'd risk it when he saw her at the house!

Garry had given him an earful on the phone. That mischievous little wife had stirred up a heap of trouble. She had told him that all things were good and well. Good and well, his ass! Not only did she neglect to tell him about the near drowning from three days ago—which he was stricken to find out—he received the startling news that his precious wife had pulled a ploy to deceive her brother. Of course it involved corrupting that innocent nurse, whom Garry now claimed has his balls in an uproar. But she was off limits, Garry said. Not Jewish, as Melissa had led everyone to believe. And there's another man, the one who fished the girls from the pond and came out of nowhere to save them—Amanda's hero, and protector.

Had it not been for canceling an important meeting twice already, and then Garry requesting that he make some calls, see a lawyer, and get some legal papers started, Dan would've hopped on a plane right then and there.

When he drove up to the porch, he stormed out of the car and stomped into the house, screaming her name. "Melissa!" She was coming from the kitchen with a giant bowl of popcorn in her hands. Seeing him, she tossed the bowl to Amanda on the sofa and ran with joyous delight to her husband. She didn't see that half of the popcorn had spilled into Amanda's lap, nor that Dan was anything but happy to see her. She was too busy with her face squeezed against his, her body moving like an arousing locomotive against his own.

"Ah, hell," he said, and grabbed her up, swinging her in his arms while he kissed the temptress senseless.

Garry and Nicolas were now in the room watching the sweet reunion, Garry's wheelchair parked beside the sofa near Amanda. His gaze moved on her as she watched the couple with warm envy. A sparkle was in Amanda's eye, but something besides that bespoke that her heart was heavy. "A bit of a pig with the popcorn, aren't you?" he teased, causing her to look his way. His gaze moved to her popcorn-covered lap.

"What's it to ya? Ya want some?" Playfully, she flicked a few popped kernels into his face. He blinked as they slithered off his forehead. She gaily chewed on a mouthful of popcorn.

His face leaned towards her. "You're a mean woman, Mandy."

She smiled mischievously, swallowing her popcorn, her own face leaning close to his. "I had a good teacher," she whispered.

Her eyes sparkled with hint, and he grinned, marveling in the seductive way she could tease him. Their faces were close and he could smell the salt and corn on her breath, her lips shining with butter. His craving for buttered popcorn stirred him senselessly, and he would've helped himself to much more than those popped kernels in her lap had Dan not cleared his throat, causing him and Amanda to snap to attention.

Dan observed them with a quizzical eye. His brief glance at Garry showed that he'd seen every bit his pal had relayed to him. *Poor buddy. Helplessly smitten!*

But Garry's relationship with his nurse wasn't the only significant change Dan had witnessed this day. No matter how wrong he felt Melissa was in bringing Amanda under such false pretenses, he couldn't deny the fact that his wife had chosen the perfect woman for the job. The changes in Garry were miraculous. Like a doubting Thomas, he wouldn't have believed it without seeing it. Amanda had somehow revived Garry's desire to live and had rekindled his belief in himself as a musician. To see Garry at the piano again had Dan so choked with emotion, he almost left the room to save himself embarrassment. When Garry began expressing ideas for a future album, Dan was ecstatic. *Unbelievable!*

Emotionally and physically stronger, Garry had accomplished much in the past week. He'd mastered the art of getting in and out of his wheelchair within a couple of days. He'd practiced to and from the floor, as well as to and from the bed. He regained stamina by exercising eagerly and with confidence. He proved he could overcome obstacles that used to overrule his will.

Dan's half-day visit with Garry was well spent and worth flying over a thousand miles for, and with those crutches he'd brought on the plane, he wasn't about to leave until he saw Garry's first attempt at using them. Melissa totally agreed. Excited about the event, Amanda hollered out, "Nicolas, Nicolas! Come quick!" Nicolas was there in an instant, the whole gang gathering around Garry's wheelchair with breathless enthusiasm.

Garry had the crutches, but he wasn't moving from his seat.

"What's the matter?" Amanda asked, bobbing her chin to ignite his motivation. "What's the wait?"

Garry frowned. "I didn't expect to have an audience."

It wasn't so much the audience he minded as it was in knowing he hadn't practiced first. What if he fell on his face or some other fool thing?

"Oh, good grief, Garry," Melissa said exasperated, "we're all family and we're all anxiously waiting. Just do it." She grabbed Amanda's hand as though to stress her point. Garry noted the gesture as Dan announced with elaboration, "Ladies and Gentlemen… *Garry Danzlo.*" Then came whistling and cheering and clapping so loudly, one would think no less than a dozen stood around the reluctant performer.

Garry had everyone's attention, but only one had his—the one with the pretty smile on her face and near tears in her eyes. He was hearing her silent encouragement, feeling it deep in his bones. "Alright, alright, I'll do it!" he finally said.

Rising from the chair, he balanced well on his left foot, Nicolas standing by with the crutches. Silence gave way to suspense as Melissa removed the wheelchair. Amanda guarded his front, and Dan, his back, Nicolas assisting with the supporting sticks beneath his arms. Then everyone stood back.

Garry made several steps forward, fairly steady, yet that's all it took for the cheers to rise to another crescendo, though this time with tears and laughter. He held on for dear life to those crutches as he was suddenly bombarded by all of them, giving him kisses and hugs, slaps on the back and cheers in his ears. But it was Amanda's hands and her kisses that made all other touches seem dim. Tears poured down her face as she embraced him with arms full of happiness. She squeezed him and kissed him with her candied lips brushing pure confection upon his neck and jaw and chin. Whether she had willingly brought those lips to his mouth, or he actually captured them, he was uncertain. He was only aware of suddenly tasting their goodness, then craving them as they were quickly robbed from his reach.

"This calls for a celebration," Nicolas shouted to all. "I say we celebrate with generous slices of my freshly baked apple pie. Sorry, no ice cream available, but there is Cool Whip!"

"Hmmm, Cool Whip," Melissa and Amanda responded in unison, licking and smacking their lips deliciously. Garry was drawn immediately to Amanda's mouth, his mind recalling Melissa's titillating confession, *you can imagine what wild things she did with a bowl of Cool Whip one night.*

The forbidden fruit in Garry's pants petrified like a rock in a hard place; it couldn't move, nor could he from the place he stood. Everyone was heading for the kitchen except Amanda, who was the first to notice he wasn't going anywhere. Her eyes met his. "What's the matter?" she asked. "Can't get those feet moving? Need some help?" She was before him in seconds, her face smiling up at his. Her sunshine permeated his skin like a warm bath. She was very potent to his senses today. *Watch it*, he warned. *Just say something nice.*

He looked down into her face. "Perhaps I don't want to walk without you, Mandy."

He hadn't intended to say something *that* nice, but the words kind of erupted out of his heart. It was by far the nicest thing he'd said to her in days. An appreciative glow shone in her eyes. She took his crutches away and leaned them against a wall while he balanced himself on his good leg. She placed herself underneath his right arm and smiled up into his bewildered face. "Who needs crutches?" she said. "Pretend I'm your right leg, and believe like I believe. Follow your dream, Garry, and someday soon, you'll walk without me." She nudged him forward, and he took a step with her. And then another. He tried to concentrate on the steps and not her words, but they tended to stay with him.

*Follow my dream? Walk without you, Mandy? What a contradiction!*

The next hour was pure agony. No matter how hard Garry tried to avoid Amanda, his body wouldn't cooperate. She sent sparks careening through his loins with every word she spoke, whether she was talking to him or not. And her laughter—an instant earthquake! He need not even look at her, for her very fragrance emanated up his nose and sent adrenalin into his blood. It sauntered through his body like the plague.

Dan and Melissa, who couldn't keep their hands off one another, only worsened Garry's distress. An hour after the pie feast, Garry was deliriously happy to see the door shut behind them. That is, until he turned to see Amanda with tears in her eyes. He was glad he'd given up the crutches and gotten back in his wheelchair. Standing would've given him too much of an advantage to comfort her physically. And he was too vulnerable this evening. One kiss and he'd be asking her to come to bed with him. So he tried another comfort measure.

"It's miserable with just me, isn't it," he said, feigning disgust.

She gazed down at his repulsed, exaggerated expression. She sniffed and wiped her tears. "Miserable, indeed," she said, stomping her foot for effect. "What shall I do with you?"

He grinned, taking her hand lightly in his. "Would you like a list?" His words came out as a whisper, although he hadn't meant for them to.

Their gazes grew serious, and then their fingers entwined. Both heartbeats pounding, they spoke in unison, "We need to talk."

They swallowed uneasily, seconds passing in silence. Then they tried again, their sentences clashing together.

"I want to explain—"

"I need to tell you—"

The dog had drowned them out, her fierce growl aimed at something upon the floor. Bagel stood on all fours, poised over a newspaper she'd dug from somewhere, her paws crushing one end of it as she glared down at a photo. She barked ferociously.

"What is it, girl?" Amanda asked, bending down to get the paper. She paused as she recognized the photo. Picking it up, she scanned the article, her brows wrinkling inward. Then her eyes met Garry's with affliction. "Your engagement," she said.

He hesitated before taking the paper she proffered, cursing himself for not destroying it the other day. But he'd kept it hidden, or so he thought. He glanced at the dog saying a silent *thanks a lot, pal,* and took the newspaper from her hand. "Hmmm, so it is. Old paper."

"Old? Couldn't be very old, else you'd be a married man."

Garry moved uncomfortably in his chair. "Wonder where today's paper is?" He looked around like a jackass, and felt like one doing so. Only minutes ago he was ready to explain why he'd been avoiding her these past few days and how he wasn't able to avoid her today. How he didn't know what to do about it, though he knew what he wanted to do about it. He wanted to pull her into his lap and kiss her worries away, tell her he couldn't marry Daphne because he was in love with her. Let her know he didn't care that she wasn't Jewish, for it didn't change the way he felt about her. The problem lay with his Mom. So why wasn't he telling her all this?

"I'll tell you what," she said, not smiling, "You go look for today's paper while I turn in for the night. It's been a long day. I'm rather tired. Perhaps we'll talk some other time. Goodnight, Garry."

She left without a backward glance. He flung the paper across the room, purely disgusted with himself.

# 32.

# YOU COULD SHOW ME

AMANDA SAT ON the window seat in her bedroom, her arms curled around her legs, her feet flat on the seat while she stared out at a nighttime paradise. Walt Whitman was right, she mused thoughtfully, Colorado's beauty did awaken "those grandest and subtlest elements in the human soul." To look upon this sweet fragment of America was to know what the great poet meant when he said: "the proof of a poet is that his country absorbs him as affectionately as he has absorbed it."

She was absorbed now, affectionately by this place she'd come to know. She felt poetry in her heart. It sang a sweet melody, urging her to write the words down that would later, through time, awaken the memories of her moments here with Garry and bring them back to life. But she picked up no pen, only stared out the window, knowing she'd never see Colorado in the midst of spring. Soon, she'd be gone, and Daphne would take her place.

She suddenly wished it was Eddie she was in love with, not Garry. Eddie had proven his love time and time again throughout the years. He'd never been afraid to tell her. The changes in him were surely the result of Paul's doing, leaving too many unpleasant memories between them. Paul had spoiled everything.

And now, yet again, she'd chosen the wrong one to love. Garry had no intentions of professing his love for her, for he had no plans to break his engagement to Daphne. In less than a week, Daphne would be in his arms. And Amanda would be out his door.

She closed her eyes, trying to concentrate on the jazzy blues music playing softly on the cassette player by her feet. But the only sound she could hear in her ears came from Garry, the silent words she thought she'd kept seeing in his eyes

241

today. *I want you, Mandy. I want to kiss your lips. I want to touch you where no other man does.*

She covered her face with her hands, weeping silently, rocking back and forth. *Why, Garry? Because you're lonely? Because I'll do until Daphne gets back? You torture me with your silent words. You've got to stop. Please stop.*

She leaned her head against the cool glass pane, looking out at the white blanket of snow covering the ground that lit the wintry night sky. Another song began on the cassette player, the jazzy rhythm of piano, bass, violins introducing the 1945 Decca recording of *Lover Man (Oh Where Can You Be)* sung by Billie Holiday. Amanda sighed, allowing the melodic blues to sing through her mind and fill her soul. Her own voice began to unite with Miss Holiday's.

GARRY FELT MISERABLE. He didn't love Daphne! His feelings for her would never compare to the potent, and reeling ones he felt for Mandy. Yet he continued to deny the woman he knew he loved, and played foolish games, or just plain acted stupid!

God, he was supposed to be angry and hurt that she had deceived him, had kept secrets! Where was the resentment, the bitter emotions? All he could feel was affection.

So why deny her? And himself? Why couldn't he just admit that he'd made a mistake and asked the wrong woman to marry him?

*Just tell her the truth, Danzlo! And tell Daphne the truth. Else, lose the best thing you've ever had.*

Yet his mind countered with a question: *was he the best thing for Mandy?* The question was like a thorn pricking deeply in his conscious, leaving doubt and fear. He knew that she knew nothing about life with an acclaimed singer and musician. The lack of privacy it involved, the millions of fans she'd be sharing him with. Daphne loved the spotlight, craved the attention their marriage would afford her. He had no doubt Daphne would fit in just fine as his wife.

Yet it was Mandy he wanted.

He could never just ask her to live with him. She deserved more than that. He wanted her to have more than that. Maybe it was good that his mother was coming for a visit. It was time to face some facts with everyone.

Although Amanda and Nicolas had said their goodnights near thirty minutes ago, Garry had stayed up. He'd been practicing with the crutches. He was up on them now, facing the door in his room. He opened it. He saw the light beneath Amanda's and hobbled toward it. He stood in front of it, trying to find enough courage to knock. Music played softly in her room. *Was that her voice singing?* He lent his ear a bit closer, trying the knob to see if it was unlocked. He shouldn't just walk in. But he did.

He opened it slowly, though not too wide, for the door would creak when it was halfway open. He slid himself through, just enough to spy her upon the window seat. Her eyes were closed, her head leaned back as she sang with a voice he'd never heard. It was low and dulcet, and smoothly seductive. Much different than the one she used for the little ditty songs she'd sang. No, this was the voice of a woman who was born to sing the blues. He stood mesmerized, not only by her voice, but by her beauty. She wore a gown of icy pink, silky and sheer. A brief moment of betrayal singed through his chest as he was reminded of the not-so-delectable Ms. Fields. And yet, this was the lady with whom he'd made love to the other night—the intimately familiar and passionate Mandy whose hidden qualities took him unexpectedly, and beyond anything he'd ever experienced in his life. No, it wasn't betrayal he felt this moment, but rather pure gratitude.

He should leave before she saw him, only he lingered, listening, feeling the words. It was strange, yet tantalizing to hear her sing of romance, and wanting to be made love to.

He definitely needed to leave. But as he started to make his move, he observed a note atop the bedside table, his gaze catching the name *Eddie*. Curiosity had him leaning over closer to read the last couple of lines. *Just ask and I'll give you the world. I love you. I always have. Please call… Eddie.*

Jealousy tugged at his heart, a sudden feeling of loss tearing through his body as he realized Amanda was thinking about Eddie and not him at all. Had she talked with him tonight? The note sat next to the phone.

Amanda was finishing her song, deep emotion seeped in every last word.

Garry scooted out the door, closing it gently. His limbs were trembling, his hands sweaty on the crutches. He suddenly felt drained of energy, his eyes burning, his head achy and light. *Eddie, I need you,* her voice rang in his ears as his mind recalled words she'd spoken to that hero who saved her from the pond.

He returned to his room and lay down on the bed, his heart pounding in his ears. He tore open his shirt. His skin was hot and wet. A bead of sweat rolled across his nipple. *Touch me. Touch me, Garry,* her voice slithered with it.

*God, help before I go insane!* he beseeched in prayer. *You dared to let me have her when You knew I couldn't keep her. Or was it I that dared to take her, and this is my punishment for playing David's role with Bathsheba. She belongs with another man… a man more worthy of her love than I. A man she possibly did love, until I came along, confused her heart and seduced her away from him.*

Garry sat up, reaching over into the drawer by the bed. Nicolas had placed a small bottle of brandy there. He grabbed it, uncapped it, brought it to his lips, and then paused. He started to return the bottle to the drawer, but weakness and loneliness grasped him. He took a swig of the fiery liquid.

This was his father's fault, he decided. This present suffering. Wasn't it enough that the man had destroyed his childhood by walking out on his family, leaving them to live in poverty alone? Jonathan Danzlo had no right to return when he wasn't wanted.

*Papa…* the handwriting on the wall that began the chain of events that would cause dear ole son to suffer guilt and pain the rest of his life. The guilt that would take birth with the suicide, which instigated the car accident, which brought Mandy into his life, which began the merry-go-round of agony that had yet to have an end.

At first he'd wanted her to go, and she wouldn't. Now he wanted to her to stay, and she couldn't. He'd kissed a clown, who had turned into a princess. But this fairy tale wasn't typical of the usual swoop upon the white horse and a gallop to the castle to marry and live happily ever after. No, if he wanted the princess for his bride, he'd have to fight another man for her love, and his own mother whom he'd made a holy vow to—whose descendants had never broken such vow, for generations upon generations.

He took another swig from the bottle, capped it and placed it back in the drawer. He lay down and closed his eyes. An image of Eddie appeared beneath his lids, the dark and handsome knight sitting upon a white steed, and Mandy, the princess, cuddled against him. They were waving good-bye as they rode off into the sunset.

Garry's lids flipped open. He reached over into the drawer again.

"One more sip," he said. But it was a guzzle. He lay back down, praying for sleep as the heat of the brandy simmered through his body. He felt its warming ache run slowly down his arms as he unbuckled his belt and pulled it from the pant loops. He discarded it to the floor. Unfastening his pants, he laid his hand across his bare navel, his shirt splayed wide open. He was asleep in seconds.

The dream began differently. He was in a grungy motel room in L.A., his own voice shouting angrily.

*"Don't talk to me of love. You know nothing of love, old man. Get out of my face. You make me sick."* Garry shoved his father away from the door.

*"No, son, please. Don't go. I do love you. God knows I do! If you'd just give me one chance, one moment to explain!"*

Garry spat in his face. *"You're not worth it. You haven't changed. You're still a lowdown bastard!"*

*He slammed the door in the old man's face, hurrying across concrete, clanging down the black, wrought iron steps leading out from the shabby motel building where his father stayed. Garry was determined to break clear from the old man, once and for all.*

*But darkness grew quickly, and he was suddenly cast among shadows that towered upon brick walls like giants. He was in an alley, so familiar, so bleak. And in his hand was a gun.*

*Garry looked up. There stood his father, smiling at him, his eyes bursting with pride. It was the same expression he'd seen over the past couple of weeks from that old fellow he'd befriended—Jake Fayman, the alias.*

*Those eyes were a familiar topaz blue, shaped like large almonds like his own. Why hadn't he noticed before? It was as though they truly held love, glittering with pride and joy. "Damn you, damn you! Stop looking at me like that!* His hands shook on the gun.

*"I love you, son. I love you."*

*"For the love of God, stop it, stop it!"*

*But the words of the old man kept echoing in his head, till at last the gun exploded in Garry's hands. He had pulled the trigger.*

*His eyes blurred with tears. They strained through the fog of smoke enveloping his victim. But he was unprepared for the terror that scorched his eyes when the fog disappeared. It was Mandy, blood oozing from her side, her body limp in the old man's arms. His father's eyes were now stricken with sadness and pain, tears rolling down his face.*

An agonizing howl vibrated the walls of the Colorado home.

Amanda hurried through the bedroom door, Nicolas behind her, both dashing toward the bed, dodging his flailing arms, and fighting them while trying to bring him back to reality with soothing words.

Once Amanda's voice penetrated his ears, Garry's eyes opened, his lips crying her name. His arms circled her, clutched her, afraid she'd disappear if he let go. His dampened face nuzzled her neck and he reveled in the warmth of it, the delicacy of her skin. The pulse in her neck thumped against his cheek, bringing him relief and assurance that she was alive.

"Nicolas," she said, her voice vibrating against Garry's forehead as her fingers interweaved through his hair, "perhaps you could make some hot tea."

Moments later, Garry sat up, still clinging to Amanda, her arms now wrapped around him. Nicolas returned with the tea, placed it on the bedside table, leaving her to care for her patient. The door closed behind him.

Though Garry found peace in the arms of this woman, he suddenly felt like a child. He released her, lying back on the pillow. He couldn't look at her, too afraid he'd cry.

He closed his eyes, an image waiting for him—an unopened envelope lying on an old Formica kitchen table—his father's handwriting on the back of a monthly bill. He had discovered it, before his mother had. *I can't take it anymore*, it read. Signed, *Jonathan*.

He opened his eyes.

"Come, sit up, Garry. Drink some of this tea."

Urged by her voice, he straightened, took a sip, and placed the cup back on the night table. "You can go to bed now," he said, avoiding her face. "I'll be alright. I'm sorry I—"

She hushed his words with gentle fingers upon his lips. He responded to them, taking hold of her hand, his eyes finding courage to look at her. "Talk to me," she whispered. "Tell me about your dream. Your fears."

"I can't." His eyelids lowered despairingly.

"You can. You've got to. Please, Garry. I'm your friend."

His eyes lifted, feeling joy in her words. "Yes, Mandy... you are my friend." He touched her face with his fingers, his thumb tracing the side of her mouth. "I've wronged our friendship. Taking advantage of you seems to be a bad habit of mine. I speak to you when I want. Avoid you when I want. You're like my puppet on a string, and I manipulate you any way I like, anytime I like. I even took you to my bed, when I promised to marry another."

She sat quiet, still, and then said, "Is that what this is about... *guilt?*"

"I would never hurt you on purpose, Mandy. Not you."

Amanda paused, reading his thoughts. "Not me, but maybe your father?"

His eyes hardened. "I don't care to talk about my father."

"No, but you need to. He's been a focal point of your problem. Has been since the accident. He was in your dream, wasn't he?"

"Go to bed, Amanda."

"Ah, you're mad at me. No more Mandy. I'll go to bed after we talk."

"You'll go to bed now."

"Fine. I'll sleep here tonight." She moved up on the bed, jerking the covers out from under him.

"Woman, you're irking me."

"Hmmm, I've heard that line before. Now, where were we? Oh yeah. I think you loved the man, but you won't admit it."

"Loved him? He betrayed me. What he did was unforgivable!"

"I see. So if I ever betrayed you, you would never forgive me. No matter how much I believed at the time I was acting in your best interest."

Her eyes flickered apprehensively, and in them, he saw her own guilt and remorse shining through. A bit of makeup and reading glasses hardly compared to what his father had done.

"This is totally different, Mandy. His actions stem from a cowardly and selfish act. There's not a coward or selfish bone in your body."

"Hmm. Perhaps we need to analyze this better. Your father, being the weak man he was and burdened by poverty and a great sense of hopelessness, decided one day to leave his family. Considering his failure as a father and husband, we might assume this is why he never remarried—this little fact was relayed to me by Melissa. Of course, it could be that he never found the happiness he was searching for. How unforgiving is that? It doesn't matter that he wanted to see his son again and found enough courage to face him after nearly thirty years."

Garry's face hardened. "It was more than that. You don't know the entire story."

"Then tell me, Garry. You said I was your friend."

Her pleading face was agony, doubling his hurt, and his pain.

"He pretended to be someone he wasn't," he said, his voice raised as he looked at her and slammed his hand on the bed. "A fan, who claimed to have sneaked behind stage to steal an opportunity to meet me. He told me his name was Jake Fayman, and I believed the bastard. For two damn weeks he played me!"

He was shaking; Amanda was crying. Her hand reached out and touched his. He grabbed it, his fingers entwining with hers. His gaze lowered, locking on the comforting image.

"He rode three thousand miles across the states on a bus, just to come see me, Mandy. I felt touched. I invited him to come to a party after the show, allowed myself to become close to him those following days. I don't know why! I thought it was because he was from Brooklyn, my old stomping ground, and I could relate to some of his hometown stories, add to them. He filled me with memories I'd forgotten, the good ones and the bad." His face lifted to hers, whose eyes never wavered from him, listening to his every word. "I saw him as a lonely man who had no one to talk to, who needed someone like I once did. I gave into that need, perhaps feeling sorry for him, but mostly, I think, because I respected him for who he was, or at least who I thought he was—an elder who had struggled through life the best he could and found joy in a little thing like being with me."

He swallowed the tears congealing in his throat, looking away.

"Oh, Garry," she softly said. "His joy was with you. He finally did have that happiness he'd been searching for. You just have to see that truth and somehow find it in your heart to forgive."

"I can't teach my old heart new tricks, Mandy. I'm not sure I can even try. Maybe you could show me how."

His voice was genuine. She nodded, her lips curled inward against her teeth. "I'll try," she said. "You know I will." She paused. "You need to tell me what happened that day, Garry. The day of the suicide. Was that the day he confessed?"

His throat tightened. He could barely get the words out. "The old man was leaving town," he began. "I wanted to give him a keepsake, of our friendship. It was my prized harmonica—the one I had as a child. The very one he'd given me and taught me to play." He swallowed with difficulty. "I didn't know *then* he was my father. When I handed it to him, he got emotional, and I realize now he probably never meant to tell me. But the sight of the harmonica broke him to pieces. I couldn't understand what he was saying at first." Garry's respirations grew rapid as he remembered the horrific moment that sent him over the edge. "I got angry. So damned angry I felt ill! And then he kept begging, crying out those words that weren't true! 'I love you, son, I love you' and I kept telling him to *shut up! Just shut up!*"

He was vaguely aware when Amanda adjusted her fingers, her hold slackening only enough to tenderly comb his knuckles with affection. The convulsive tension loosened in his hands, yet his eyes continued to stare, strained and glazed. "When they found him, Mandy, he was clutching the harmonica. It lay against his heart in a pool of blood."

He bent toward her, his hands reaching, wrapping around the back of her head. His fingers interlaced in her hair as he laid his forehead against hers, his nose touching hers. He tried to suppress the tears that welled inside him, using her as his strength to hold them back.

"It's okay to cry, Garry. Sometimes we have to."

"I'm not much of a man, Mandy. Real men don't cry."

"That's not true, Garry. David in Scripture was a real man. He was a man of music and song just like you. He wept before the Lord, and God saw that he was good."

Garry flung his arms around her and held her with all of his might. And then he cried. And she cried with him.

They stayed wrapped together for a long while, the tears finally subsiding. Amanda was the first to speak.

"He loved you, Garry. Don't shut him out. It's not too late. It's never too late."

He gently unlocked their embrace, staring into her face as if seeing her for the first time. Somewhere in the back of his mind, he felt he'd heard those same words before. It echoed through him with *déjà vu*.

"If you could just see the truth, Garry, you'd realize that you loved him too… enough to give him a special gift, a token of that love you keep denying. What does it matter that he was your father? What a blessing you gave him! Two weeks of memorable joy in his life. And though he chose the wrong way out when you denied him—because some people just aren't strong enough—he blessed you too, with two memorable weeks of joy! Take it for what it's worth. As for his death, he made that mistake, not you. He's paying for it on the Other Side, and I do believe there is a world beyond us far greater than we could ever imagine. I just know it's filled with All-Loving Power, love so Unconditional and Divine we can't possibly comprehend it. I believe he's trying to learn from his mistake this very moment, and you could help him if you could just forgive him."

"He hurt me, Mandy."

"And you hurt him."

He paused, feeling somewhat perturbed. "How come you always have to be right?"

"I'm not always right. Only most of the time."

He cracked a smile. Then he grew serious, waiting, knowing she'd help him say the words.

"Close your eyes, Garry. Picture in your mind your father. See what he's doing. What does he look like?"

He closed his eyes. "He's sad. He's looking at me. I've disappointed him."

"Talk to him. Silently, he's telling you he's sorry for leaving you those many years ago. He says he was weak; he couldn't give your mother the things he wanted to. He was afraid and too proud to admit his failure, too unwise to reach out for help. Perhaps he didn't know how to love, and he learned how the hard way. But he's here now, in search of love and forgiveness. *I'm sorry it took so long, son*, he says. But *I do love you. I always will. Forgive me. Please.*"

Garry tried to speak, but no sound came from his mouth.

"*Tell me you love me, son*, he's saying. *I need to hear it. Bring me honor, I need it. I need you.*"

"Yes!" he cried out, the pain he saw in the old man's eyes now his own. "When I wanted you, I needed you. And when you hurt me, I wanted to hurt you back. It's true. I do love you, Papa. I forgive you for hurting me. Please forgive me for hurting you."

Silence pervaded the room, and he somehow felt lighter. His eyes opened to see Amanda sitting before him with a tear-streaked face and a smile curving her lips. He smiled back.

Then her arms reached high into the air, her voice shouting, "Yes, he forgives you! He does, I do, you do… we're all forgiven! What a storybook ending. I just love happy endings, don't you?"

Garry's pillow smashed across her head, and she fell sideways on the bed. He took hold of her rust-colored robe, dragged her toward him, his hands holding hers tightly while her head lay captive in his lap. He hovered down into her laughing face.

"Feeling better, aren't you?" she said happily.

"Much better. Thank you, Mandy."

"Thank you? What kind of appreciation is this, holding me hostage upon your lap?" She raised their hands, high up in the air. "I demand better satisfaction. Release these chains, sir, or you shall find doom upside your head with a heavy pillow."

"My sweet damsel, if your hands are chained, you'll reach no pillow."

Amanda brought one of his hands down to her mouth and clamped her teeth hard on a knuckle. "Ow," he screeched, releasing his grip. "You little—"

She waylaid him with a king-sized pillow, rolled quickly away and jumped off the bed. "Now what were you saying?" she asked primly, gasping for breath as she stood several feet from the bed, her fluffy weapon dangling at her side in one hand, the other hand resting on her hip. She was unaware that her hair was a wild mess and that her robe had spread open across one breast. Garry had a fetching view of a taut nipple straining against icy pink silk.

He cleared his throat, his eyes unwavering from the feminine sight of her. "I, ah… don't remember what I was saying to be quite frank."

Realizing her state of undress, she jerked her robe together, the pillow dropping to the floor, her face growing crimson. "It's late, we should get some sleep." She looked over at the clock beside the bed. "Three o'clock. Very late." She turned to leave.

"Mandy, wait. Come here." She slowly faced him, never moving from her spot. "Come here, Mandy," he urged again.

Timidly she stepped forward. "Yes, what do you want?"

She stood nervously before him, knowing he'd seen her flannel-less wear. No eyeglasses tonight, no makeup. She was getting bolder by the day.

"I want your hand," he told her, and reached out and took one in his own. "Thank you, for tonight. Like always, you were here for me." He kissed her hand gently. "I made it through the rain… with you. I'm glad fools get lucky sometimes. Goodnight, Mandy."

"You're welcome. Goodnight, Garry."

She was almost out the door when he called her name again. She turned. "Yes?"

"I was just wondering if you'd heard anything from your friend. You know, Eddie. Perhaps you called him? He was worried about you when he left."

The inquiry seemed to surprise her. "That's sweet of you to ask, Garry. But no, I've not talked with him. He called to check up on me the day after my fall, but I was napping and Melissa relayed that I was fine."

"Good," he replied, sending her a counterfeit smile.

He watched her exit and laid back on his pillow, realizing how lonely his room felt without her in it. He gazed over at the phone, his focus on a group of buttons beside the receiver—an intercom system that could enable him to communicate to any part of the house. He tried to fight temptation, but it overtook him. He pushed a button and spoke her name. He sat breathless, waiting. No answer. He thought to abandon another attempt, but once again said, "Mandy… the intercom…"

"Garry?"

He was suddenly speechless, his name on her lips sending jelly sluicing through his body, a fat wave of it settling atop his feet.

"Are you alright? I'm coming to your room."

"No. I mean… not necessary. Can't sleep. Know any lullabies?"

Amanda paused, and then giggled. "Surely you don't want me to sing you to sleep."

"Why not? You have a nice voice. Heard you singing in your room. It doesn't have to be a lullaby." Did he sound too urgent?

Another pause. "All right, get ready to hang up the phone. Little Ethel Merman is on the air." But her voice wasn't boisterous at all like the great Ethel Merman's. It came smooth, with the same soft and low tone he'd heard earlier. *Sexy.* He liked it a lot. He smiled as he recognized the song she sang—*Bella Notte*—from the Disney movie, *The Lady and the Tramp*.

If an ear could be mesmerized, his was as it tarried on the line, listening, her voice drifting in, dispersing its essence within the divisions of his body.

She finished the song, and a moment of silence followed. Then she whispered, "Are you asleep yet?"

"On a cloud," he answered.

"Goodnight, Garry."

# 33.

## SHADOW MAN

*"GOING SOMEWHERE, BUD?"*

Max halted with the evening newspaper in his hand, his hurried steps from the hotel elevator severed by a human stone wall. "Get out of my way, Chandler. You don't scare me."

He stood unblinking at Eddie's formidable stance—dark gloved hands at his side, a London Fog raincoat opened at the front; a powerfully built chest strained menacingly against a white shirt. Refusing to be intimidated, Max moved around him toward Daphne's hotel room, but Eddie darted in front of him. Max glared up at the saber eyes that warned him against going anywhere, particularly to Daphne who was preparing herself for a hot evening out on the town.

"What's the matter, Max? Don't you like me?" Eddie's tone oozed with sarcasm.

"I don't trust you, Chandler. You're up to something. Daphne might be blind to it, but I'm not. My eyes have seen."

Stepping back, Eddie lightly laughed. "Seen what, boy?"

Being called a boy displeased Max worse than the sarcasm. But compared to Eddie, Max was a boy, no more than twenty-four in age, barely hair-growth on his face. Eddie stood a good four inches above him, and had a chest twice his size.

"You let her fall yesterday. You stepped aside and let her fall."

"You crush my heart, Max. Why would I do such a thing?"

"Because you knew who she was when you walked up to her."

Eddie cocked his head back in surprise. "Tell me more, Max. You've got my interest."

253

Max shifted his feet. "You were there to save the boy, because that slut Amanda—"

Max was suddenly slammed against a wall, his legs buckling beneath him when his right hip rammed sharply against a hall table, his body folded awkwardly, his neck cupped tightly in Eddie's hand. He couldn't breathe, his face quickly turning a reddish blue.

"Would you like to rephrase that remark?" Max nodded his head best he could. Eddie backed away as Max hefted himself upward, coughing, massaging his neck. The Palm Beach Evening Post lay open on the floor where it was dropped in the struggle. The scandalizing article stared Eddie in the face. He'd seen it in the lobby before taking the elevator up to Daphne's hotel room. He flinched as he read the headlines again, an uncomfortable reminder that Amanda was with another man. But the fact that her name was being slandered across the nation was of greater concern.

**PLAYMATE NURSE HEALING DANZLO**, read the headlines.

"A pain in your heart?" Max dared to say.

Eddie's gaze rose to the punk kid who didn't know when to shut up. A twitch ignited in Eddie's cheek, his eyes darkening dangerously.

Max bent down to retrieve the paper. He held it folded in one hand, slapping it against his other. "Yeah, wait till Daphne sees this. She'll drop you so fast, you'll have to call her on the phone to say goodbye... if she doesn't kill you first, and maybe even that jerk-face Danzlo.

Eddie clucked his tongue. "The only *jerk-face* alive is you, Max. The way I see it, you're the one with the short life." Within a split second, a knife shot out and whipped across Max's windpipe, a cut so clean and precise, it took only one gloved hand to obstruct the bleeding. Max never blinked as he took his last breath.

# 34.

# JUMP SHOUT BOOGIE

NICOLAS'S PREMONITION BEGAN as a small annoyance upon awakening. He didn't dare spoil the cheerful atmosphere at the breakfast table so he kept his sense of foreboding to himself.

His boss was in exceptionally good spirits, thanks to Amanda who had somehow brought him out of his burdensome cave and into a new world filled with hope. Whatever happened last night, Garry Danzlo awoke this morning as a new man with an aspiring goal.

No longer was he avoiding the woman, but rather he was so daring in maintaining close proximity with her that after the meal, he had the poor girl in a nervous tizzy. She could barely catch her breath when the boss drew so near that he blew down her neck!

*Too skilled on crutches already*, Nicolas realized. The man was acting like a fiend on them.

It was a little embarrassing for Nicolas. The obscene maneuvers done right under his nose. He should've declined Miss Amanda when she volunteered to help him prepare a couple of pies from scratch after the meal.

Mr. Danzlo wanted to help. In fact, he insisted on helping. He kept himself a mere five inches from the woman the entire time she was trying to gather ingredients. As she reached into the cupboard to take down a canister of flour from a high shelf, instead of offering to reach it for her, considering his taller height, Danzlo clasped her waist from behind and whispered close to her ear, "Here, I'll steady you."

Her hands tipped the canister one hundred-eighty degrees, its loose lid plopping onto the counter as a half a pound of flour spilled atop her head.

Garry had let go just in time to miss the spill. Standing back on his crutches, he burst into laughter. Without warning, Amanda tossed the remaining half-pound of flour into his face. His laughter ceased while he sputtered white powder that snowed down his shirt and pants. Spitting a glob of floured paste into his hand, he threw it at her, hitting her shoulder with a splat. "Ooo," she puffed powder. Nicolas was beside her with a full glass of water, and said, "Quick, here!" Amanda took it gratefully. She aimed well.

Garry accepted the towel Nicolas proffered with a calm "thank you," wiping gunk from his face, while wet-flour droplets splat on the floor. "I lost. You win," he told Amanda. "You deserve a hug." Before she could stop him, his left crutch fell to the floor and he grabbed her around the neck, the front of their bodies pasting together. He looked down into her white powdered face, saying, "I can kiss you, or you can make my bath. Your choice."

Amanda blinked white flakes off her lashes. "I'll make your bath," she said hastily.

"Bubbles would be nice," he yelled, watching her fly out the kitchen.

Bending down to hand Garry the fallen crutch, Nicolas said, "I hope you know what you're doing, sir. I'm glad to see you're not avoiding the poor girl this morning, but to be so overindulgent in the opposite! I hope you have realized which woman you're in love with and what one you need to marry."

Garry's response was to wrinkle his nose and grimace.

"I see. No plans to marry the girl, just plans to use her."

"Don't," Garry said. "Don't accuse me of not loving or caring. All I know is that I won't be wasting the days I still have with her. I don't know what the future holds. This isn't the future. This is now. And I need her now, Nic."

"I'm sorry, sir. I shouldn't have—"

"Just leave it. You have a right to your opinion." He shifted his feet, the crutches shuffling under his arms. He glanced at the kitchen doorway where Amanda had taken her exit. "Mom will be here Sunday."

Garry said no more. He didn't have to. His very future could depend on this visit from his mother. Nicolas knew it as well as he did.

"Yes, sir. And we'll be ready."

Amanda's voice intruded from down the hall. "Hey, you abominable flour-head! You getting in this bath or what?"

Garry smiled. "See ya, Nic. Trouble calls. Hmmm! I love trouble." He glanced over his shoulder at the older man and winked just before he headed out the room.

Bagel came trotting in the kitchen directly after Garry's departure. Nicolas reached down and grabbed the morning paper from her mouth. One look at the front page and Nicolas said aloud in the direction Garry had gone, "Glad you love trouble, sir, for it's growing like weeds in a flower bed."

Two minutes later, someone knocked at the front door.

"Mrs. Borowitz," Nicolas exclaimed, opening the door with joyless shock. "We thought you weren't coming until Sunday. But glad to see you, Madame. Let me take your coat."

Garry's mother trampled in, killing the snow off her boots. She chucked them off at the door. "*Oy!* Stop the 'glad to see you' crap, Nicolas." She threw her coat into his arms. "You'd think I smashed a pan upside your head the way you're gawking at my face, and don't think I don't know why. Where's that undisciplined son of mine and that frolicsome nurse of his? Just point the way."

Nicolas stood with mouth wide open, the hidden newspaper stuffed tightly under his vest, *all for naught!*

"Close your mouth, Nicolas, and give me that paper. *Feh!* You look like a stuffed crab."

Nicolas did her bidding, quickly.

She unfolded the paper, glancing down the front page. "A disgrace to the family. *Oy vay.* All of New York, all the world thinks my son is a homebound playboy with his own personal bunny for a nurse. Where did I go wrong? Just tell me where I went wrong? Where is he Nicolas? In his room? *Nu?* I'll go to his room." She flew down the hall.

Nicolas slowly padded into the kitchen like a walking corpse. "Weeds in the flower bed," he spoke. "Weeds, weeds, weeds."

BUT WEEDS WERE not what Miriam Borowitz saw when she came upon her son in the bathroom. *Bubbles, bubbles, bubbles.* They were everywhere! On the floor, in the toilet, in the sink, and particularly in the tub where they percolated amply. Somewhere within that pyramid of soapy globules was her son, a gurgling and laughing buccaneer plundering his bubble-ship for his prize booty—no doubt, it was that frisky little bunny she saw walloping about in the frothy tub, shrieking out for freedom. Wet cloth slopped the tub's edge as one leg flew straight up in the air, another slung over the tub's side.

"Garry!" she cried. "Have you no shame? Did I not teach you better?"

"Mom!" chirped a sea bird among the burbling froth.

"*Mom?*" choked the other water creature.

"Garry. Oy! Get out of that tub this instant," mother whale commanded.

No smooth landing for the soapy two who suddenly splish-splashed and dove overboard, plopping into the shallow watered floor. Miriam Borowitz, stepping back, received a giant bubble burping upon her red wool skirt. Miriam stared down at the two foamy critters, with her face wrinkled up and her head shaking. Her only consolation was that both, male and female, were fully clothed.

"Mom, I thought you were coming on Sunday," Garry said, as he allowed Amanda to help him up. Amanda splashed through the shallow pond, grasping and lifting, an arm about his waist, his arm around her shoulders. After swiping a few foamy bubbles from his eyes, his gaze lifted to his mother. "Ah, Ma, don't cry. It's not what you think. We were just having a little fun. You didn't fail as a mother. I'm still the respectable son you brought up. I know what you see doesn't look too respectable, but—"

"Oh *shah*! Can't a mother cry because she's happy to see her son up and on his feet again? As for your behavior, I'm sure the trollop beside you was debaucher of that little game of pirate."

"Mother!" he shouted embarrassed and angry. "She didn't say that," he said to Amanda, distress on her sudsy face. She was biting down on her lower lip. He realized now he should've warned her about his mother's boldness. "The blame is mine," he defended Amanda, turning back to Miriam. "I pushed her into the tub and fell in behind her."

"No," Amanda said, "my fault. He wanted bubbles. I gave him bubbles. Lots and lots of them."

"Yes, she used the whole box," he added, "*Mr. Bubble all gone.* So we really should blame Nicolas. He gave her the box."

"Indeed, Madame," Nicolas said from the door, catching the tail end of the bubble story. He'd heard so much banging and sloshing moments earlier, then yelling, he felt it his duty to see if everyone was alive. "One doesn't give Miss Amanda a whole box of Mr. Bubble, Madame. Truly my fault."

"Mischievous, but not a trollop," Garry added.

Nicolas skidded back on his feet at the word, "A trollop, sir? Certainly not.

No, no." Nicolas looked at Mrs. Borowitz. "Miss Amanda is an angel of mercy, a blessing in bubble disguise," he said with an amused glance at his soapy companion. The poor girl was shivering. As Garry drew her nearer, Nicolas sloshed through water to fetch a dry towel off the rack. Taking it, Garry wrapped Amanda securely, whispering words of comfort to her. Miriam stood by, arms folded beneath her ample breasts, one wet shoe tapping impatiently... *spit, spat, spit, spat* in the shallow bathroom pond.

In some remote, distant locale in Garry's mind, the *spitter* and *spatter* of his mother's impatience echoed upon his brain waves, signaling *Warning*. He lifted his eyes, paralyzed by her accusing stare.

"Are you not engaged to Daphne Dimont, son, or was I just imagining the article I read in the paper a few days ago? Maybe we've changed partners? Or perhaps the nurse plays when Daphne's away?"

Anger and resentment seared Garry's senses, but the most disturbing emotion was the embarrassment and humiliation he knew Amanda was feeling beside him.

"I think we can find a better time and place for this discussion, Mom. This is hardly the place for a serious conversation. As you can see, I'm a little wet. Wouldn't want your son to catch pneumonia, would you?" An etch of a smile curved his lips, but Miriam didn't smile back.

"Well, while you get yourself together," she said, glaring at the woman beside him, "Think on how you plan to get out of this one!" She tossed the morning paper at Garry, but his scant grasp sent the mid-sections of the newspaper crumpling loose to the floor and finding doom in the sudsy water. However, he had the front page.

Miriam left. Nicolas trailed behind her, shutting both the bathroom and bedroom door. Garry stared locked-jawed at the scandalizing news article at the bottom of the page.

"Oh my... oh good grief!" he heard Amanda say beside him. He jerked the paper from her sight. She fought to get it and won, his balance no longer supported. While her eyes scanned the appalling news column, his hands grappled her waist from her side, his knees straddling her legs while he struggled to stand on slippery feet.

"Oh... good... *grief!*" she cried, her eyes never leaving the paper, her body stiff as a flag pole.

"It's just rumors, Mandy. Not everyone will believe it," he said.

Tears brimmed her eyes. "No wonder your mother is upset. No wonder she hates me."

"She doesn't hate you. She doesn't know you."

Amanda shoved the paper between their faces, the backside smashing Garry's nose. She began to read, speedily, loudly, swallowing deeply at intervals.

*"If anyone wonders how the heartthrob musician Garry Danzlo spends his time these days, wonder no more. Worried he's having a hard time recuperating from the tragic car accident he had five months ago? Worry no more. For according to a close personal source, deep in the Colorado woods, Garry Danzlo has a playmate, his frolicsome nurse, Amanda Fields. Ms. Fields was said to have been in Danzlo's bed, and naked in his arms, when paramedics came to tend her after an accident in his icy pond some days ago. Asking those three paramedics (who wish to remain nameless) to verify this bit of naked news, they refused comment. But isn't it great how gossip will travel? Wonder if Mom knows her son is playing doctor in the woods. Did she not teach him that such games were naughty—"*

Garry yanked the newspaper from her hands, shreds of it scattering to the floor. He watched her distress turn to fear within seconds, not knowing that her angst stemmed from Daphne's threat. "I've got to go," she said, attempting escape, "I need to see Robbie, get back to Florida!"

Garry grabbed her, his arm circling her waist. He brought her wet body hard against his own. The corded muscles in his arms swore victory as they clung to her, sapping her strength.

"Mandy. *Baby*, settle down. Robbie's fine. Trust me."

She gazed up at him, sniffling, nodding. Eddie had promised. "But Garry, everyone—"

"Who cares what other people think? What matters is the truth we know." He had both her hands clasped in one of his own, enfolded on his chest. The wet shirt was no mask for the quickened beats of his heart thumping against her curled fingers. "These kinds of articles are written every day, a sick way of entertaining the public with rumor and gossip. It's all part of being a celebrity. I'm just sorry you had to be a part of it."

"But everything they wrote is true and—"

"No, Mandy, it's not. For one thing, I'm not marrying Daphne… because she's not the one I'm in love with." He drew her closer, his breath a warm breeze against her lips and damp skin. "We both know what's going on between us. Should we be ashamed of our relationship? No one else counts here, except for you and me."

Water dripped like gold droplets down his face and gilded his hair. Heat throbbed between them, his male staff branding itself along her pelvis. She melted against him. Against *it.* He groaned.

Her lips quivered. "But others do count Garry. Your mother and..."

"And who, Mandy. *Eddie?*" His words came out sounding like an accusation, his jaw twitched.

She studied his expression. "We're old friends, Garry. I can't help but feel—"

"Feel what?" he said, choking out the words, his eyes searching, demanding, yet at the same time, not wanting to know. "Does he make you feel anything like this?" His lips descended on hers greedily then, nearly toppling her backward, her knees buckling beneath her. For once, Garry was in full control of his balance as he held her up close, tight, strong in his arms, a mighty hand binding her even closer— as if there were a space to be had. She moaned as her mouth opened to his passionate onslaught, his tongue finding hers, entwining with hers, hungrily, taking the kiss with purpose. He was trying to prove that no man, save himself, could grasp the emotional chord within her and touch it with music, pluck it, while staying in tune with the orchestra that played throughout the rest of her body. He kept harmony with the waltz he played within her, and then a rumba, a swing, and a boogie-woogie with a jazzy beat.

He backed her against the toilet bowl while she held on for dear life. Her upper body was suddenly suspended over the commode seat, the swoop of Garry's tango causing one shapely leg to fly up into the air, attaching like glue to his waist. A muscled arm caught her calf underneath, a warm hand sliding like a violin bow beneath her spongy wet skirt and making its way to the string-laced panties she wore. He plucked the string, grasping a hand full of bare buttocks, pulling her against him, against that hard instrument, the trombone, as it played a rock and roll number against her hot *sex*ophone. Electrifying, he thought.

His fingers embraced her like an accordion—she, his squeeze box as he leaned her back against the toilet tank and moved upon her with a slow rhythm. She was his baby grand, his mouth tapping staccato kisses down her moist neck and blouse. A minuet flowed when his hot tongue grazed the nipple he found taut against her clinging sodden shirt. He performed a ballad with his teeth, plucking the wet fabric, blowing hot air upon the budding fruit, swollen and ripened to taste. With talented fingers, he flung open her blouse, the performer gazing down, glazed-eyed, possessed by the bountiful display—that song he named *Woman.* He cupped one breast, seductively covered in white lace, and he squeezed it, massaged it, his thumb grazing the sprouting summit protruding from the mesh fabric. *Hmmm,* like a bride, he mused, as he yearned to lift her veil and kiss her, suckle her honey. His focus lifted, hot waves rising above the voluptuous song as his blues met two pretty brown eyes. "Say you want me, sweet woman... like I want you," he whispered.

"Oh, yes, I do, I do," she cried shamelessly, pulling his face to her face, fastening his lips with her own, plundering hastily with her tongue for its sweet pleasure. She became wild and untamed with her clothes half-hanging off, the heavy wet skirt yanked up to her waist, her soaked blouse off her shoulders, binding her arms back as she tried to envelope him fully. "Come closer," she begged, though any closer, he'd be saran wrap. But he tried, their feet slipping beneath them, his shirt tearing from his tight chest as she held on, her rear dropping down with a plop on the closed toilet seat. His hand was squished between her buttocks and the lid. He kissed her harder, neither caring how awkward their post while they laughed and kissed and squirmed and danced their bodily parts.

How they maneuvered her atop him without a splash on the floor, they'd never know. Yet with a few flailing kicks on the tub nearby, she was suddenly straddling him, undoing his pants, that male instrument popping out, throbbing like an unfinished symphony in her hands. Her fingers kneaded its moistened head while her lips kissed his mouth lovingly. Garry thought he'd die if she didn't sit and envelope him soon. And like an answer to his call, she did. Her instant orgasm took her to extremes... took *him* to extremes. Hers was the overture; his, an overtone, the finale, the euphonic ending to the opera. Their insides clapped with joy and celebration, the standing ovation coming as Mother shouted through some distant door.

"Garry! You still in there with that bunny?"

Silence gripped them both.

Then Amanda rocketed off Garry and he flew seconds behind her, grabbing the towel rack. His feet slid beneath him and glided him backward. His pants were now down around his knees, cushioning his legs on the slick watery floor. Amanda snatched a towel from a shelf, flung it around herself, her focus zooming on Garry, or rather that glistening trombone that stood patriotically in the wind. "Oh my stars," she gaped in horror. "I really *am* a hussy!" She looked shamefaced, as though she'd just awakened from some erotic dream.

*Bang, bang, bang* went the door in Garry's bedroom. Keen ole Nicolas must've locked it, they both realized. "Garry! Garry, open this door this minute!" His mother thundered from beyond.

Garry swallowed with difficulty. He was no longer worried what his mother was thinking, but what Amanda was thinking. "Mandy… baby" he said cautiously, realizing he didn't know what to say while he sat on his knees with his pants down. No time to say anything. She was standing, now frantic, afraid his mother would walk in. "The guest room. Go through the guest room," he told her.

She turned, bewildered, her mind half-registering, half-remembering there was a guest room exit. She was behind the closed door so fast that one might think she'd walked right through it.

"Garry!" *Bang, bang, bang.* "I'm going to count to three. One—"

Garry fell over like a tree, his hands grasping the waistband of his pants, jerking them up while splashing through the stream in his bathroom.

"Three," The jingling of the keys in the lock rang toll bells in his ears, his heart pounding with the rhythm of the clang. He was fumbling and fighting with his pants zipper, his fingers wet, cold, and numb.

*Stomp, stomp* came the footsteps through his bedroom, his mother gasping back with fright when she entered the threshold of the bathroom to find her son helplessly on the floor.

"What kind of nurse would leave my poor son like this!"

Garry, worn out, spoke with a wearisome sigh. "Ma, first you're screaming because you think she's in here, and now you're screaming because she's not. Could you make up your mind, please? Frankly, I liked her in here. I need her, Mom."

"I know, darling," his mother responded sympathetically. "You need her and she abandons you. *Oy!* It's the way of women like her. Pay them good money to do a job and then they don't do it."

She bent down to help Garry up, Nicolas standing beside her, jingling the keys. He was gazing down at his boss.

"Nicolas! Don't just stand there. Help my son!" his mother barked. "Hmmph. I tell you, Garry. We're living in a pitiful generation of servants… a pitiful generation."

# 35.

# ALL I NEED IS THE GIRL

AMANDA SOARED THROUGH her room, her bare feet zinging this way, then that way, two hands pitching everything she owned into two suitcases—socks, underwear, pencils, stationary, sweaters, shirts, makeup...

A floozy, she accused herself, sweeping hurriedly about, not nearly packing fast enough. *Miss Trollop U.S.A.!* The strumpet of Danzloville. To think she acted like a horse in heat, galloping for her stud. No, *on* her stud! For shame, for shame.

"Have mercy on me, oh Lord I pray, for troubles surround me, and I've sinned big time," she cried on a breeze, making steady trips to and from the bed.

She had barely dried off from her shower when she'd marched to the closet to retrieve those suitcases she flung on the bed, her dark hair slicked back after a quick combing, the wet mass still dripping down her back. She wore nothing but a rose-colored towel.

Her chore done, she mashed down the lids of the suitcases, locking one case and then the other. Stepping away from the bed to get the clothes she'd laid on a chair across the room, the towel, which had gotten tucked into a case, slithered from her body, the terry cloth as good as silk the way it slid so sensually from her clean velvety skin. No less than the feel of Garry's hands against her body. Pivoting quickly, she saw her towel dangling from the locked suitcase. The keys, the keys, she thought... are in the suitcase. *Locked in the suitcase.* She tried to open the thing without a key but to no avail. Then she hurried across the room to the chair where the one set of clothes she thought was there was not there. Not there. She'd put them in the suitcase.

A knock sounded on the door. She jumped.

Flinging around, she faced it stark naked, a cool breeze circling her legs, feathering between her thighs, prickling the dark curls of her womanhood. Air nipped her breasts sensually, peaks sprouting forward in haste at Garry's mellow voice only feet away. She covered herself best she could, one arm slung across two breasts, one hand concealing her crotch as if Garry could see beyond that wooden closure. She stood glued to the floor, her heart pounding in her feet.

"Mandy, open up. We need to talk. Before lunch."

"I'm not eating lunch. Not hungry!"

"If Mom catches me outside this door, she's going to have me for lunch. Now open up. I've got to talk to you. It's important."

"Later."

"Now, Mandy. I've got a key. Don't think I won't use it." He tapped it on the brass knob—with great cheer, she was sure. She didn't think he would use it. *Wrong!*

"No!" she screeched, hearing the key in the lock. She snatched the fastest thing she could get hold of—the covers on the bed beneath her luggage.

As GARRY ENTERED the room, two suitcases zoomed off the bed, flying through the air like trapezes. One landed haphazardly against a wall, the other flew dangerously at Garry. He closed the door just in time to miss the big boom. As he heard the suitcases drop to the floor, he flung the door open to find Amanda hiding behind a heap of bed linens—a comforter, a blanket and a sheet—half on her, half still attached to the bed. Thanks to the queen-sized bedcovers, she'd managed to conceal herself from sight, ridiculously so. The only things in view were two beady, scared eyes peeking through a hood.

Garry, supported by crutches, walked into the room and quietly closed the door. He glanced down at her poor beaten luggage on the floor. "Hallelujah for Samsonite," he said, turning his attention back to the blanket queen. "You cold, dear heart?"

Amanda's blanket nodded vehemently. He choked back the laughter threatening to burst his lungs. He glanced back around at the luggage on the floor, then back at her. "Planning to go somewhere?"

"To Florida," she answered shakily. "Where it's not so cold."

His face strained as he slowly approached her.

"Don't come any closer!" she warned.

"No? How come? Whatcha got hiding behind the blankets, Mandy?"

She backed up against the bedpost. "I said don't come any closer. I'll scream."

He smiled. "Like you did earlier in my bathroom. You're a wild woman, Ms. Fields."

"Get back I said!" She tried to shuffle back herself, but her covered backside was slippery against the bedpost. She stumbled sideways, her feet tripping on the bulk beneath them. She made like a tumbleweed across the floor. Garry threw his left crutch on the bed, and using his right for support, he hefted the covers up with Amanda swimming ferociously in them, her security blankets all gone and lying like a hill on the bed. She had leaped into the air, the little naked jaybird landing right in the crook of Garry's arm. Seconds ticked by as they stood like stone statues attached to one another—she, revealing crazed shock at being caught in the nude, and he disclosing surprise, for he hadn't expected her nudity, only to catch her in her underwear.

"Why, Ms. Fields, you have no clothes on," his voice said huskily.

She swallowed several times, unable to move anything but that Adam's apple bobbing in her throat. His gaze stayed steady on her face while she stood on the balls of her feet, his left arm sturdy against her back. Her knees knobbed against his. "My clothes are locked in the suitcase."

A slow grin formed on his mouth, a brow arching. "I've often wondered why they call me Mr. Lucky. Now I know. So where are the keys, Mandy?"

"In the suitcase… w-with my clothes."

A chuckle escaped him. "How much more can a man take?" His grip loosened on her back, and she eased down on her heels, her womanhood sliding against the firm male rod in his pants.

"Garry," she whimpered, making a mere attempt to push him away. His arm tightened around her. *Ah, Mandy,* he thought, gazing down into her face, *how easy it would be to fall on the bed and make love to you again, for I see that you want me, those pretty brown eyes steaming with ardor. But I also see uncertainty there, fear. I won't frighten you.*

His hand slid tenderly up her back into her hair, his fingers entwining with the damp tresses at her shoulder. "Mandy, we have so much to talk about, so little time," he said gravely, his breath warm against her quivering lips. "Remember what we shared some nights ago and how I said it would never happen again? Yet this morning, it did. I wanted it to." He paused, allowing his words to penetrate her thoughts. "Don't get me wrong. I'm not apologizing. Just believe me when I say you're not a hussy or a trollop. You're beautiful and desirable to me, whether you're wearing tank dresses and flannel gowns… or nothing at all." He smiled down into her face. "I admit it, I'm crazy about you. Yet I've foolishly made promises to others, unable to make one to you. Even this moment, I'm lost to give you one." He smoothed down a stray strand of her hair. "So much to consider, so much I haven't told you about myself, my work as a musician, that fame game you know so little about, the excitement, the turbulence, the hectic life it entails. Nor have I told you about my very *Jewish*—"

Garry's words were disrupted by what sounded like a stampede of cows rustling up the hall, that all-familiar voice of mother Miriam blasting too close for comfort. "Now where's my son, Nicolas! I can't leave him alone a minute without him struttin' his stuff. Doesn't he ever get enough of that harlot nurse?"

Amanda pulled away from Garry so violently he stumbled back. He grasped her arm to maintain his balance, but she fell backward across the bed, his right crutch stealing away from him while his own body tumbled atop her.

"Garry!" A rapid knock sounded on the door. "You in there? You may as well answer me. The noise is revealing. Just keep it up. Keep shaming me, son. This is her room, isn't it, Nicolas? I knew I shouldn't have left him alone."

Amanda was desperately trying to get up while Garry was trying to pin the girl down, the bed creaking and squeaking, she moaning and groaning in protest beneath the hand he lightly clamped over her mouth.

"You're disgusting, son. You can't even do it quietly, can you? And right under my nose. Where did I go wrong as a mother?"

Amanda's struggle turned to tears.

"Mother, go away," he shouted, fingering Amanda's tears tenderly from her face. "It's not what you think. I just need to talk to her."

"You can talk with the door open."

"Blasted, Mom, I'm thirty-eight years old. I'm not a boy anymore." He looked down into Amanda's face. "I'm glad I'm not a boy anymore," he said much more softly, a twinkling of mischief in his masculine voice as he attempted to make her smile.

"*What?* I didn't hear that last part, son. You saying something smart to your poor old mother."

"Oh, go eat a bagel, Ma, and give me a few moments with my nurse. I'm being good. Trust me."

"Ha! I bet she thinks so."

Nicolas on the other side of the door exclaimed, "Mrs. Borowitz. Here, here. You have Miss Amanda all wrong. And your son… he just wants a private moment with the dear woman. Let's respect that wish. Now come, Madam, and I'll fix you a cup of hot tea, or coffee if you choose. We do have fresh bagels in the kitchen, and I must say, they're quite good."

"Oh, stifle your tongue, Nicolas, and lead the way to the kitchen. You had better have lox and cream cheese. I don't eat bagels without lox and cream cheese!"

"In the refrigerator, Madam."

"And Garry," she shouted going down the hall. "You have five minutes of privacy!"

Garry gazed down at Amanda's stricken face, his thumb grazing her cheek. "Five minutes, the old bat says. Hardly enough time to—"

"Garry, you shouldn't call her that. She is your mother." Her hand rose to his face. He took it, kissing its palm delicately.

"And we should respect our mothers, right? And so few do these days, agree?" She was nodding her head and eyes closing dreamily as he feathered kisses up her arm, upon her shoulder, her neck. "Actually, baby, that's my problem. I do respect her. I owe her a lot. For who I am, for what I am. She always wanted nothing but the best for me. Only thing is, she can't see what's best for me right now. And that's what I'm afraid of."

His lips hovered over hers. He needed to talk, not kiss her, yet his lips descended on hers helplessly, tasting the honey upon them, drinking the salty tears that drenched them so fully. His tongue plundered in, parting her lips to taste her sweet wine.

For Amanda, sexual hunger, stronger than any she'd ever known, arose inside her. The tremendous emotion of loving him burst to surface, and desire undulated through her body. That place between her legs was hot and moist, *waiting*, wanting. She clasped her hands on either side of his head, deepening the kiss, her naked breasts arching against him, warmth pulsating from deep in her throat, down to her legs as his hands traveled up her silken skin. His warm fingers feathered her hips, her ribs, the sides of her breasts. She felt the rigidity of his manhood pressed against her, moving against her, her naked limbs circling him in haste to accommodate the need to feel him tight and firm between her legs. His knees inched like a worm upon the mattress. She rolled him down the hill of covers, having her way with him, smothering his laughter with her salacious kiss.

"A little lioness," he said breathily as she gave him some air. He basked in her passionate garden, soaking up her naked wilderness. And then he reveled in more of her sweet kisses. "Good Lord woman, you give me a desire to explore that rainforest between your thighs in a way I've never done before." He kissed her fully, hungrily, "but baby, as I much as I want you, we need to end this exciting safari." He bit her lower lip seductively, "There's a, a, great beast lurking in the kitchen and…"

Amanda's hot smooching ceased swiftly as she snatched a pillow from somewhere above his head. She covered her chest quickly, her face feverish with embarrassment. In less than a whipstitch, she was off his belly, hovering behind the pillow like a frightened kitten. Her lips were quivering, her eyelids batting nervously, a few tears seeping down her cheeks. "I'm a… *wanton*, aren't I?" she said with chagrin. "Your mother has every right to think I'm what she thinks I am."

"Ah, Mandy, sweetheart," he said, raising his back from the bed, pleasure and concern etching his features. He reached out for her, but she backed away.

"No, Garry, it's true. I'm so ashamed. I'm as loose as a goose. I don't know what's come over me. I mean, I was never like this before. Never the wild thing. I've only been with one man in my whole life."

Garry's brow raised in stunned surprise.

"It's true. I was a virgin when I married, can you believe it? I was such a romantic in my adolescence. Read a lot of romance novels back then," she said, her eyes shining while her smile was wondrously I. "Those virginal heroines were always getting swept up by some robust man who became their only true love." She shrugged her shoulders, the glow in her eyes now sparkling.

Garry was amused at her confession, and deeply touched by the innocence with which she spoke it. He would have liked to be her only true love, but how does one compete with a dead man and past memories? Surely there were good memories with the bad. He wanted to say something special to her. He spoke the words softly and tenderly.

"I love you, Mandy."

Seconds ticked by wordlessly, Amanda afraid to speak, afraid she'd heard the words wrong. Happy tears burned her eyes, and just as she was about to break the silence with a similar phrase, a knock sounded on the door.

"Mr. Danzlo, I'm sorry to interrupt," Nicolas's voice came from beyond. "I hate to be the bearer of bad news, but I'm afraid I can't hold your mother in the kitchen too much longer and, sir… Miss Daphne's on the phone. She wishes to speak to you. Says it's urgent. She called on your private line. Should I transfer the call in there?"

The atmosphere stifled the two on the bed, one gazing at the other, wary of some formidable doom forthcoming.

"No, Nicolas. Tell her I'll call her back."

"Yes, sir," Nicolas said and retreated down the hall.

Amanda touched Garry's face softly, her forehead lined with concern. "Garry, he said it was urgent. You should've taken the call."

"No, Daphne said it was urgent. There's a difference. Besides, I need to talk with her in private. We have things—"

"You don't have to tell me. It's none of my business, right? I shouldn't be so bossy. Bossy in bed, out of bed. I'm disgusting."

"You're exciting," he said, grinning. "I've never had so much fun in bed or out of bed in my life. What will I do without you?"

The question came like a shooting arrow piercing her ears, the sting reaching her heart. He still expected her to leave? "Evidently, you'll continue the fun with Daphne." She stumbled off the bed, covers and all, heading resolutely toward her luggage.

Garry grappled for the crutch strewn on the far end of the bed. "Mandy, baby, I didn't mean it to sound that way."

"Don't Mandy-baby me while Daphne-darling waits by the phone!" She threw the covers off her, not caring about her nudity and Garry's goggling eyes while she separated the sheet from the comforter and blanket. She folded it neatly and flung it around her nude body, wrapping and tucking until she was satisfied with the seamless dress she'd made, the last bit of the flowery material flung over her shoulder drape-style. She picked up her suitcases and headed toward the door. Garry was suddenly in front of it, standing lopsided on one crutch.

"I *know* you're not going out like that." It was a warning.

"Bet me, you… you two-timing stud." Her suitcase kicked him in the shin.

"Ouch," he yelled, lurching sideways. It gave Amanda a free chance at the doorknob.

"Blast it, woman! Robbie's coming. He'll be here Sunday."

Amanda froze, the suitcases tight in her hands. "What?" she said, staring at the door. Garry rubbed his shin.

"It was supposed to be a surprise. Melissa and Dan are in Florida right now meeting up with Dr. Conyers. They're making the necessary arrangements with the

Children's Home to release him. Put the suitcases down, Mandy."

They dropped to the floor. She turned, watching as he reached into his pocket and pulled out a small metal gadget resembling a pick. "The key I opened your door with," he said, holding it up for her to see, "and capable of opening any lock I put my hands on. Had it since I was a kid." He lowered onto his good knee, working the pick into the suitcase lock. "Takes skill to open some locks, skill I obtained in my youth," he said with a sly grin. "It earned me a title. The 'Lock-nose Kid' my friends called me. You'd think such a name was a mock to this big schnozzle I've inherited from my Grampa, but the truth of the matter... I've always had my nose in locks. They fascinated me." Two clicks and both suitcases were open.

Garry climbed up his crutch. "You can put some clothes on now, though I think you look mighty fine in that sheet dress."

Amanda blinked twice. "Is it true? Robbie's coming here?"

"In the flesh. He's one of the three things I sent Melissa to Florida for. I knew that having Robbie beside you would make your leaving easier."

Amanda stiffened. There he went again about her leaving! "Your reasoning sounds arrogant, Garry. Think I'll suffer without you? Well, don't hold your breath. Blow it on Daphne." She picked up the suitcases and walked to the bed, never looking back. "I'd like to get dressed now. Please leave."

"Mandy, you don't understand the situation."

"Don't I?" She turned and faced him, trembling, crying. "I'm the playmate they mention in the world news these days. Rumor has it that the renowned musician could possibly be in love with his little playmate nurse, except it contradicts the fact that he's marrying the elegant Daphne Dimont very soon. Just as well, because mother Miriam is abhorred with the little harlot nurse and disgusted with her son who can't seem to keep his hands off her."

Chagrined by her anguish, he sighed. "I told you I wasn't marrying Daphne. If you think I possibly could now, then you don't know me. I'm in love with you, Mandy. I think I knew it the moment you toddled off-balanced, landed in my wheelchair and straight into my lap. I wanted to lick the boysenberry right off your lips." He cupped her cheek with his hand. "I realize I've made promises to others, and I've never given you one. I can't, Mandy. When Daphne finds out I'm breaking the engagement, you can bet sparks will fly. I'm afraid to think what she might do, but more afraid of the fireworks my mother can cause. If you think she's upset now, you've not seen anything yet. God forbid I find love with a Christian woman." He wiped her tears with his thumb. "There'll be fewer tears if you go home."

He twisted in place with one crutch, saying no more. The other crutch lay somewhere in the room. He left it, and her, as he made his way out the door, shutting it on his way out.

When Garry exited Amanda's room, his mother was standing in the hallway. He halted before her.

Miriam was taken aback by the misery she saw in her son's eyes. "Are you all right, son?" she asked. He didn't answer. "How about a bagel with your old ma? I've eaten one, but I'll eat another. I'll worry about losing weight tomorrow."

Garry smiled through his pain. "That's okay. I'll wait for lunch. Gotta make a call." He made a gesture with his head toward his room. "I won't be long, then we'll visit as long as you like."

She hesitated, and then forced a grin. "Sounds like a sweet deal. I love you."

"I know. I love you, too." He took the remaining steps to his room and shut the door.

MIRIAM'S GAZE WAS riveted to the door across the hall from her son's. She realized that Garry's little bunny was much more than she assumed. Her son was in love, and it wasn't with Daphne. Melissa was eating that up, she imagined, and the way she raved about Amanda Fields, one might think the girl walked on water. True, the miraculous advancements concerning her son could not be denied—for that, she was indebted to the girl—but something wasn't right here. Too many tension-filled vibes in the house—*secrets*. She planned to find out what they were. Garry's affliction from moments ago stood clear in her mind. Was this woman playing shenanigans with her son? Miriam saw it her caring and loving duty as a mother to do a little investigating. Yes, before Melissa arrived on Sunday, she'd know all.

GARRY'S PHONE CALL to Daphne would not be pleasant. She wasn't one to let bygones be bygones. He dialed the number with a trembling hand.

"Garry, darling, it's you, I'm so glad," she answered. Her tone was a mixture of happiness and concern, neither of which indicated that she'd read the scandal in the papers concerning his licentious involvement with Amanda. "I've so much to tell you. Things you need to know, Garry."

"I've things to discuss with you, too. Where are you?" He felt he had a moral obligation to at least break the news of their severed engagement in person.

"I just arrived in Boca Raton this morning," she said excitedly. "It's one of the grandest, richest cities in South Florida. Both exotic and beautiful, darling." No doubt costing him an arm and a leg, he thought. "Max is spoiling it, however. I sent him on an errand hours ago and he's yet to return. Undependable, just like you've always said." She paused. "You're not saying anything, Garry. You're not angry with me, are you?"

"No, Daphne. It's not that. We need to talk."

There was an awkward silence on the other end. He could almost see the hard, cold look rising in her eyes, feel her muscles quivering through the telephone line, his ears zinging with the energy of her fury as it thickened. His own body grew tense, compressed with his own inability to speak.

"It's about *her*, isn't it? About us," she said in a controlled voice. His hesitancy to answer spurred her into a harsher tone. "You're making a grave mistake, Garry. She's a fraud. A fucking whore! She's been—"

"Shut up, Daphne! You don't know anything about her."

Daphne laughed. "That's what you think, darling. She's the very reason I called you to begin with. I've found a lot about your little Ms. Fields while I've been away."

Garry's right hand tightened into a fist and loosened. His nostrils flared. "Stick to your own business, Daphne. And leave her the hell alone."

"But she is my business," she said with a sardonic chuckle. "She's taken what's mine."

"You never owned me, Daphne, and I was wrong in asking you to marry me when I was so emotionally unstable. I'm deeply sorry about that. I know you can find someone else."

A crazed type of laughter circled through the phone line. "But darling, I have! If you only knew who it was." She laughed again. "What a fool Amanda was in choosing you. Her tough luck. I have him now."

"What the hell are you talking about, Daphne?" Garry's teeth clenched as tightly as the hand that gripped his phone.

"Oh, you'll know soon enough, darling. I'm not even near done with you. Or Amanda. I'll see you on Tuesday."

The line clicked loudly in his ear. Its sound was like a gunshot that tore through his head, deranging his mind with chaos. He felt totally alone, and so damned confused. It took several minutes for him to sort out everything Daphne had said. Whatever she'd been doing over the past days, whatever she was up to now could only mean trouble of the worst kind.

Melissa, Dan, and Nicolas had all tried to tell him about Daphne—things he pretended not to see. But he didn't have to see now. He sensed it, his gut wrenched with uneasiness.

It was one thing to have Amanda's dignity crushed by his mother, but he would not allow Daphne to destroy what dignity she had left. Amanda needed to go home where it was safer, saner. Yet Daphne had said *she* was in Florida, so sending Amanda home at this time might not be the wisest move. There's no telling what Daphne's jealous connivance might entail. Words that Nicolas had once spoken intersected his thoughts. A threat. Blackmail.

*Who else but a jealous female, sir.*

Garry slumped over, threw his head in his hands. "Dear God," he spoke under his breath, spinning in a turmoil of realization. "This can't be happening. What next?"

# 36.

# BRING HIM HOME

DAN HAD MELISSA laughing in his arms as they approached their room at the Royal Poinciana Hotel in Palm Beach. He sat her down at the door, his hand scrounging into his pocket for the room key while her loving arms circled his neck. She was kissing his face, his chin and mouth, the little minx driving him mad till he could stand no more. He grabbed her waist, hefting her up against the doorframe, his mouth teasing her neck with kisses and licks.

Shouting for release and laughing all the while, she managed to say, "The door, Daniel! Open the door!" Doing his bidding, they tumbled in, an elderly couple outside, gaping in at their rolling bodies on the floor. Dan kicked the door shut as Melissa crawled on her knees to escape. "You'll not escape me, *my little pretty*," he said. He grasped her ankle, dragged her downward and pounced on top. "Now what are you going to do?" he asked.

The phone started ringing. "Answer the phone?" she responded.

"Not what I had in mind."

The phone continued to ring and Dan hadn't budged an inch off her.

"The phone, Dan. It might be important. Fourth ring and—"

Dan rolled over, jerked on the telephone cord nearby. With a crash, the phone came tumbling into the floor near their bodies. The receiver flew toward them, bouncing just inches from Dan's hands. He scrambled to get hold of it. "The honeymoon suite," he answered with breathlessness. "Dan Juan is my name and romance is my game. This had better be important."

"Dan!" Melissa screeched, slapping him on the shoulder.

"What? Just calm down, Garry. Talk more slowly. Your mother is there?" Dan sat straight up. Melissa did the same. "Yeah, we saw it in the paper this morning. No, she didn't. You didn't! She did? You're kidding?"

"What, what?!" Melissa was saying beside Dan, shaking his arm vigorously.

"Hold on, Melissa! Now what, Garry? You think Daphne's involved in what? Oh yeah, trouble. You better believe that. You want Amanda to leave on Tuesday? I don't get it."

Melissa, getting hysterical by the second, smashed her head against Dan's, their ears sharing the receiver. "Don't you dare ask her to leave," she commanded into the phone. "If she leaves, I'll never speak to you again as long as I live!"

"Melissa!" Dan jerked the phone from her ear. "You're as bad as Garry. Now calm yourself! Garry, you still there? I've been telling you all along that Daphne isn't the woman you think she is. I guarantee she's got something up her sleeve, else she'd be on a plane to you this very moment. She won't say goodbye without a fight. She proved that by blackmailing Amanda. I'm just glad Robbie's fine. We saw him this morning and—"

Garry's voice boomed on the other line. Dan yanked the phone from ear range hoping to save himself from a busted ear drum. He forgot Garry didn't know about the blackmail, or at least that *he* knew that Daphne was behind it. "The boy's safe, Garry, I assure you. I know it's hard to believe. Now don't blame Melissa or Nicolas. They knew you wouldn't listen to reason, so they led you to believe that Eddie… that his girlfriend was behind the blackmail. Does he have one? A girlfriend? Garry, who cares? I think he's in love with Amanda! No, she's not in love with him, at least I don't think so."

"She's in love with you, ya big dummy!" Melissa screamed into the phone. "And you had better tell her you love her, else I've gotta eat pig's feet!"

"He says he did tell her," Dan said, surprised. Melissa, deliriously happy, flung her arms around Dan, squeezing his neck, both of them tumbling down upon the floor. Dan captured the runaway phone. "What? Daphne and Eddie? Are you sure? That's pretty farfetched, Garry. What, today? Impossible!" Dan was trying to shove his prying wife off his shoulder. "No way we can get Robbie there today. We saw him early this morning before school. Adorable kid. Smart. Excited to be seeing you as well as Amanda. Yeah, the legal papers won't be ready till morning. Tomorrow night? All right, I'll make arrangements. See you then. Stop worrying about Robbie and don't be making any rash decisions concerning Amanda till we get there. I can't imagine Daphne doing anything fast."

Dan hung up the phone and turned to Melissa, "I smell a load of trouble.

Almost makes me wish we didn't leave Robbie this morning. Daphne's in Florida."

"That means Eddie's in Florida. He's luring her away from Robbie."

"You know this for a fact?"

"I'm pretty certain," she said, nodding. "Amanda asked for his help. I don't think he would let her down. Amanda should be the one we should be worrying about now. Who knows what might be happening this very minute with Mom in the house. You know how she is."

"All too well. How much do you know about this guy Eddie? Is he trustworthy?"

"He saved Amanda's life. Saved mine. I know he believes in justice." Melissa paused. "Robbie's a wonderful little boy, isn't he? Garry's going to fall in love him, I just know."

"I'm thinking you just know a lot of things, my little pumpkin." Dan pushed her back on the floor, his face hovering over hers. He kissed her hard and long on the lips. "Do you just know what's coming up next, here on this floor?"

"Hmmmm," Melissa mused, her chestnut eyes sparkling with love and delight. "Our own TV series? *Have Buns Will Travel.* Nothing less, please."

His clothes flew off, hers with them. No worrying about Garry, Amanda, Miriam, Robbie, Eddie, or Daphne. They just wanted one glorious hour to themselves. Maybe two.

# 37.

# GIVE MY REGARDS
# TO BROADWAY

WHEN NICOLAS CAME knocking on her door to announce that lunch would be served, it took effort for Amanda to leave her room and approach the kitchen. The moment Miriam took in her state of wear—no soapy bubbles camouflaging her ugly clothes—Miriam looked at her son like *you've-got-to-be-kidding!* Surely she was thinking to condemn her son to the helplessly tasteless and throw Amanda alongside him. Only, that's exactly where she wanted to be. *Beside Garry.*

As though he had heard her thoughts, his hand reached out for Amanda, nudging her toward the seat that was next to his. Though his face seemed strained, unsettled somehow—perhaps because he'd spoken with Daphne—he smiled into her eyes, sending her silent affection. It was as if an angry word had never passed between them.

Nicolas approached the table with a basket of hot cross buns. He was behind Miriam as he did so, mouthing to Amanda, "Just be yourself." Sweet Nicolas. She took his advice and before the end of the meal, she'd actually gotten a laugh out of Miriam and a few appreciative smiles. However, those smiles were short lived by the time lunch was over. Amanda had insisted that Miriam visit with Garry while she and Nicolas cleaned up the dishes. Innocently, she praised Nicolas' knack for planning ahead and mentioned that his Friday evening suppers were particularly special.

"I should certainly hope so," Miriam responded condescendingly, sending her son a frown. "What else would one do on the Shabbat?"

Garry quickly rose from the table, his crutch in one hand, the other reaching for his mother. Hoping to save Amanda embarrassment, he said, "Come, Mom.

Let's go into the music room. I want to show you something."

Miriam hesitated suspiciously. "And what of your exercise, son? Does your nurse not work on that duty each day?"

Garry sighed. "My nurse has a name... it's Amanda, and she's standing beside you."

Miriam just waited, unblinking. He began again more calmly. "I'm sure *Amanda* would be pleased to answer any questions you might have concerning my health. Daily workouts are scheduled several times a day. We've had our morning one. I mean, I had mine!" he rectified.

"I'm sure she had hers, too, son." Miriam frowned, an evil eye aimed his way. "Take me to the music room."

With Garry and Miriam gone, Amanda turned to her friend. "Oh, Nicolas, how will I ever get through this day, this entire weekend?"

"With my help," he said. "Somehow we will all get through this. Mrs. Borowitz might act like she dislikes you, but inside, I think she is moved by your ability to enlighten her son's life. She can't help but see the wonderful changes in him, on an emotional level as well as a physical. I'm sure she can't deny the love Mr. Danzlo has for you, or you for him. It was quite evident while she watched the two of you at the table. Her eyes were as keen as a hawk, not missing a thing. I might add, too, when Mr. Danzlo told her he'd broken his engagement with Miss Daphne on the phone, she seemed relieved. She's never been very fond of her."

"He broke his engagement? Oh, Nicolas, do you know what this means? With Daphne out of the picture, I'm finally free to come clean with Garry. I can..." Amanda paused as she took in the harsh, concerned lines on Nicolas' forehead. She swallowed. "I see. It's not quite over, is it?"

"The engagement, yes," Nicolas assured. "Quite over, but I'm afraid we've not heard the last from Miss Daphne. As for your confession, I suggest you make that sooner than later. She's held off from telling him herself, but..."

Amanda heard the hint. "Yes, tonight. It's got to be tonight, Nicolas. And I need to be honest with Mrs. Borowitz, too. Maybe if I could show her first that I respect and have some understanding of her religion, she might learn to accept me better. Only, I actually have very little knowledge." She sighed heavily. "Oh Nicolas, what am I to do?"

Nicolas loosened his posture for a moment, a grim twist to his mouth. Then his eyes lit on her. "What you're going to do, Miss Amanda, is listen to some Jewish music while you help me clean and prepare a very special *Shabbat* dinner. One must create a *Shabbat* atmosphere. *Shabbos,* it's called in Yiddish. Did Mr. Danzlo ever tell you his grandparents were Yiddish? Immigrants from Russia. Ah, a story in itself, but no time for that now. We've much work to do. Lots to cook. I'm afraid the white linen tablecloth needs cleaning. I'll have to wash it and press it. We'll use the good china and flatware. Now let's see. Candlesticks, candles, the *Kiddush* cup—we'll use the silver one in the dining cabinet—and wine, a *challah* cover, salt... what else am I forgetting?"

Smiling, Amanda said enthused, "Music? Flowers?"

"Ah, flowers! Fresh flowers makes the house more *Shabbosdik.*" Nicolas winked. "And music. I'll go get the music on, you call the florist. While we work, you can learn some of the blessings of our ceremonial dinner, particularly the candle blessing. It's traditionally recited by a woman, though in some families, recited by all. Same goes for *Kiddush,* the wine blessing, though that's traditionally recited by the man of the house. I'll try to teach you all I can, what little time we have. Before evening, you'll be quite the Jewish princess."

In the music room, Garry was trying his best to conjure the nerve to tell his mother the truth about everything. About Amanda. Miriam read into Garry's discomfiture. She gazed gravely at her son. "I already know, Garry. She can't hide it. You can't hide it."

Garry yanked at his collar, trying to swallow. "You do?" his words thumped out. "And?"

"And I swear I don't see what you see in that girl. Well, she does have a personality. That is, what little I've learned of it at the kitchen table. Okay, I'll admit when I'm wrong. She's proved to have a dear personality, which is more than I can say for some of those other women you've dragged into your house. Get rid of the glasses, throw in some contacts, buy her a decent looking outfit, she might pass for a young Vivian Leigh. Of course, Vivian wasn't Jewish, but you're not marrying Vivian. You want to marry Amanda, right? You love her; she loves you. One would be blind not to see that. You want my blessing? Well, all I can say is, thank God it has finally happened, son! A mother wants grandchildren before she dies, and Melissa's taking her dear sweet time about it. Maybe you won't put me through all this waiting, huh?"

Garry tried to speak, even gestured with his hands in hopes to ignite his voice, but nothing was coming out. He wanted to tell her that he never dragged women into his house, nor did Amanda look like Vivian Leigh. But heaven forbid he ever tell her that, for *Gone With The Wind* was her favorite motion picture of all time and

Vivian Leigh, her favorite actress. Never mind that "dear Vivian" was Catholic… a fact that was *hush-hush* in their house. Amanda was neither Jewish nor Catholic. God resided in Amanda's heart—in the earth, in the sky, in all things everywhere where anything was, Nicolas had told him. She was Christian, yet her religion was nondenominational, her church, in the center of her being.

"Garry, dear, are you trying to tell me something? It's Daphne, isn't it? You're still afraid she's going to cause trouble now that you've broken off with her." Garry had his mouth open. He shut it. "Don't worry, I'll stand by you. She wasn't right for you. Too selfish and vain. True, she's Jewish and beautiful, but best you stick with Amanda. Not often you'll find such a good-hearted Jewish woman to please you like she does." She patted him on the knee. Garry groaned. "I was beginning to doubt Melissa's praise for her when I came, but the girl has proven her goodness by the miracles she's brought about in you. You're walking, son, and," she started to cry, "and that's enough to hug her. Not only does Melissa highly praise her, but Nicolas thinks she's some kind of saint. He was so adamant I give the girl another chance that he got down on bended knee while we were in the kitchen eating bagels. What's gotten into that man, son?"

Garry shrugged his shoulders. He didn't feel so good. His stomach was rolling.

"Dear, are you all right? You look a little pale." Of course, she would notice, he thought. She placed a cool palm on his forehead. "It's a bit stuffy in here. Let's go into the family room, son. I hear Jewish music. Leave it to Nicolas to put one into that *Shabbos* mood."

Garry doubled over in grief. The ceremonial *Shabbat* meal. Oh God!

"What is it, son? Your stomach upset? You always had stomach problems as a boy. Stress. Does it every time. You worry about the marriage already. *Oy!* You haven't proposed yet, have you? We'll see if Nicolas can find some Alka Seltzer." Miriam began the plop and fiz jingle, retrieving a groan from Garry before she could finish. "I know, son, you don't like my singing. Be a good boy, and don't blame your mother for trying."

Garry wondered if an asylum for the mentally distressed could provide the answer to his problem. Committing himself to a locked cell sounded better than facing what lay outside the music room door—the evening meal sure to be a ceremonial disaster! Amanda knew nothing of the Jewish way. She proved that with her naive remarks concerning their special Friday night dinners.

"Mother," he said, wagging behind her on one crutch, heading up the hall, "there's something I've got to tell you about Amanda."

They approached the family room, music blaring from a boom box sitting atop the end table by the sofa while two voices in the kitchen sang out joyously. Lyrics were sung off track with the song, a bit off harmony, but laughter rang through, a joke, the creak of the oven door opening, the chop of a knife slicing upon a cutting board. Determined to get the confession off his chest, Garry yelled over the music, "Amanda is not—" a breeze flittered across his face as Miriam passed through the swinging door to the kitchen. "—Jewish," he finished in solitude.

*"Ai-yi-yi!"* Miriam sang out happily from the kitchen. "Nicolas, how you shock me this day! Two-stepping with a casserole! And poor Amanda at the sink crying. How thoughtless not to ask her to dance." Garry peeked inside the room, his sight catching the one by the sink chopping onions, tears rolling down her cheeks. "Yes, thoughtless," Amanda said, crying to his mother. "Ordered me to stay put by the sink with my onion. 'Shut up and finish my dinner!' he said. Can you believe such cruelty? Accused me of being a rotten dancer without any proof whatsoever, so I zapped him one, cursed him with a casserole dish. 'Dance till you drop,' I said!"

Amanda stomped her foot so hard, her glasses fell off her nose onto the floor. Laughter roared through the room while Amanda stood with her onion, its stinging aroma like a waft of fire in her eyes. She tried wiping them with her forearms, but it was useless. Her face was a sopping mess. Her eyes were closed now, the stinging sensation torturing her while she laughed and dropped her onion upon the kitchen counter. She heard it roll into the sink, her hands reaching blindly for a towel, but then Garry was in the way. Yes, it was Garry, she realized quickly as her onion-juiced fingers surveyed the contours of his face—the hard cleft of his chin, the thin lips, the strong nose, the slanted cheekbones.

"Don't touch my eyes," he pleaded softly, "they get kindled enough each time they look at you."

His voice spoke through her, and she trembled as he embraced her wrists with one hand, guided them to the sink, turned on the faucet. Water splashed across her hands as he leaned forward against her back to prop his crutch against the counter edge. His breath blew warm in her hair, tickling, and she laughed. He moved snugly against her to place the soap in her hands. His fingers began soaping her fingers as he sang close to her ear, *"This is the way we wash our hands, wash our hands..."*

Amanda heard Nicolas chuckling nearby, but what of Miriam? Amanda tried to open her eyes so she could peek at Garry's mother. Then came a gush of water, sloshing into her face, and then more gushes, Garry's hands mopped her cheeks, her nose, her eyelids, swishing and swashing. She squealed and squirmed for dear life.

Amid the squeals and laughter, Miriam's voice came through like a dream. "That's right, son, scrub it good and clean! Watch it, now, don't lose your balance." Seconds later, "Here's a towel. Hurry up. Now, give her to me, son."

Amanda was suddenly confused. One moment, her head was besieged by a towel, and then her face vigorously run over by a hand buffer. Next, her body was pulled from place and dragged down the hall, the towel flapping in her face. Garry no longer had her; his mother did. Thrown into a room and up against a bed, she heard the door slam.

She swallowed hard as she cautiously lifted her towel veil. She stared into two condescending eyes.

"Just what are you trying to pull, young lady!" Miriam's voice boomed forth. "You think me a simpleton, a fool? I'm no *golem!* You may have deceived my son, but you don't deceive me!"

"E-Excuse me?" Amanda spoke shakily.

"Oh, lay off the innocent act. Cough it up, girl!"

Amanda felt doomed. "W-Which part first, ma'am."

"Why don't we start with these?" Miriam lifted Amanda's glasses from her pocket and placed them upon her nose. She had apparently picked them up from the kitchen floor after they'd fallen off Amanda's face earlier. "*Oy!* If these aren't the most godawful looking things I've ever seen, then I've never seen! Funny how I can see through them quite well, particularly if someone handed me a book. What magnification are they? One point two five at the most?"

"Y-Yes, ma'am. It's really quite a simple story actually."

"*Bubkes!* Nothing Melissa ever concocts is simple. She might think it simple, *hoo-ha!* Oh, yes, don't look so surprised. You think I don't know my own daughter is behind this little charade you play under my son's nose?"

"Mrs. Borowitz—"

"*Shah!* Let me finish… and call me Miriam. Listen, *bubele*, I don't completely blame you. I should live so long after housing that child for so many years. I should live to a hundred and twenty. You should live to a hundred and twenty. We both deserve it. But to put you in that nothing of a dress. It's a *shmatte*. *Oy vay!* It shouldn't happen to a dog."

Amanda gazed down at her dress, disheartened. She had thought it one of her better ones.

"But she's a regular genius, that daughter of mine. Plain talk, she's crazy. Loaded with sense but sadly, she doesn't always use it." Miriam shook her head.

"She felt threatened by Daphne while she was out on her nurse search. I never doubted my daughter's ability to overcome that obstacle. I expected to come here and find some secret she was holding back from me. But this madcap thing!" She put her hands to her head. "*Oy-oy-oy*," she said, tilting it side to side like a seesaw. "And my son," she added, her hands crossed on her chest. "He's living proof that love is blind." She grabbed Amanda by the shoulders, looked her up and down. "Despite your horrid appearance, dear, he has found deep love and respect in you. Infatuation I thought. I couldn't understand his attraction at first, but then, during our lunch meal I thought to myself, 'such *edelkeit!*' A sweetness of character if ever I saw one." She smiled and tucked a finger beneath Amanda's chin. "Gentleness and sensitivity is within you —something I'm sure my son quickly learned. He needs that. A warm and kind woman. My bet, he'll fall on his face when he sees you tonight. Sit down, dear."

She pushed Amanda into a nearby chair. *Plop* went her tush. Miriam pulled the Bobbi pins from her hair, the dark strands springing to life from its pinned up state. Amanda sat paralyzed before the vanity table and mirror in the guest room, now Miriam's room. Miriam wore a frown that wouldn't quit. *"Feh!"* she said, baring her teeth, wrinkling her nose. "Where did Melissa buy this *dreske?* In a *shlock-house?"* In seconds, Amanda's dress was unzipped, the ugly tan collar around her neck suddenly resting low upon her breasts. After a quick combing from Miriam's brush, dark chocolate hair fanned deliciously about her bare shoulders, the ones Garry kissed earlier that morning. Amanda closed her eyes, her breath slightly sighing.

"Are we thinking about Garry, *bubeleh?* Or are we praying?" Amanda opened her eyes to Miriam's questioning expression in the mirror. *"Aha!* Already you worry what he will think when he sees you differently tonight? You won't worry, *bubelah*, when it's time to face him. You'll be happy he doesn't blame you for deceiving him. He'll think his good ole ma created a miracle, thanking me for bringing out your loveliness. *Oy!"* she lowered her head, holding Amanda's chin with her fingertips and evaluating her looks in the mirror. "Maybe not so much Vivian Leigh," she decided, noting the brown eyes and olive complexion and those native-like features of her face, "as say, Natalie Wood. Always thought she was pretty. She played in *West Side Story*, remember? Saw it opening night. Won an Oscar for Best Picture of the Year, 1961 it was. Of course, you were barely born then." Miriam went back to brushing Amanda's hair, lifting strands with her fingers for style variations. "I adore motion pictures. Love Broadway. Ever been to a Broadway, dear?"

Amanda shook her head. "No, I, uh… Mrs. Borowitz. I mean, Miriam," she corrected after receiving a reprimanding glance. Then Miriam jerked her hair and twisted it in the back, away from her face.

"I really want to be honest with Garry, tell him the whole truth. I appreciate your thoughtfulness in helping me mend the situation, but—"

"You will tell him, *bubeleh*! I'm sure of it, but tonight... he'll thank me." Miriam left her side for a moment to retrieve some things from one of her unpacked suitcases.

*In other words*, Amanda thought, *I'll have to tell Garry in my own way some other time.* Well, she couldn't wait any longer. Somehow she'd have to make Garry realize that Mariam's surprise was the real her. That didn't make her confession any less difficult.

A couple of jars plopped on the vanity before her. Cleansing cream, a clay pack...

"Miriam, I'm really glad you've changed your mind about me. That you accept me for who I really am, not who or what you thought I was. But there's more about me you should know and—"

"*Shah!* Enough, girl. I trust my son's judgment. I've never seen him so smitten with a woman. I hate to say it, but he's had many at his doorstep. But none like you, *bubeleh*. You're different, be assured. You're the one he plans to marry."

She could barely breathe. "I am? He said that?"

"Do you *not* think he'd carry you, lame or not, to the synagogue this very night if it weren't for being the *Shabbos?* You need only say yes, dear *bubeleh,* and he'd carry you across the world." Miriam's eyes glazed with tears. "*Ha Shem* has shown mercy upon my son and brought to his life a Jewish princess. And blessed am I to receive such a daughter-in-law."

It was Amanda in tears now, distressed to the max. "Miriam, I'm not—"

"Such sentimental fools, we women. Now talk no more, child." She slapped some clay from a jar onto Amanda's face. "This clay needs to harden. I'll do the talking for both of us. Good thing I shopped this week for Melissa, bought her a beautiful magenta pink cashmere sweater dress that will look lovely on you. *Oy!* Don't talk, *bubeleh*. So I'll buy her another dress. No skin off my back. You like musicals? I love musicals. *Bye, Bye Birdie... Hello Dolly... Fiddler on the Roof...*"

Amanda felt the plaster on her face slowly cracking with every deep swallow she took and every blink of her eyelids. She was trying to remember the *Shabbat* blessings Nicolas had recited and what she was supposed to do and not do, when and how and why.

# *38.*

# OH, MY LADY

GARRY'S KNUCKLES RAPPED on the door.

"Alright already! We're almost done, son! Nozzle your *shnozzle*. We'll meet you at the table in three minutes."

Garry turned not so suavely, his right leg weak and tired. His armpits were sore from using the crutches for hours on end. He'd made several hundred tracks to and from the guest room, his temptation to knock the door down nearly driving him insane. The moment his mother decided to kidnap his precious nurse, he'd already been late for his 2 p.m. workout. With Nicolas' encouragement, he finally decided to do it on his own, if only to keep his mind off of whatever was going on behind those closed doors. He'd gone into Amanda's room more than a dozen times—stood, walked, sat. On his first trip there, he'd found his other crutch lying near the bed. It took the third trip before he'd decided to pick it up and use it.

He was in the dining room now, Nicolas stirring about the table, doing last minute touches to the elegant setting of china, glass, and flatware. "You think she knows, Nic?" he asked for the thousandth time, following Nicolas around the table. "I don't think she knows yet. I think the least we could expect is a scream. But not even a yell came from that room. What could two women who hardly know each other talk about for so long? And laugh about it, Nic? I heard laughing."

"Sir, please sit down! Here, let me take your crutches." Nicolas took the crutches by force, pushing his boss into the head seat at the table. "The women will be here soon. The hour is approaching. Has your mother ever been late for a *Shabbat* dinner? No, and she never will, sir, so stop worrying. You're dressed much

286

too handsome tonight to run your face ragged. Three lines I see that weren't there two hours ago."

"You're right. I'm getting too old for this. I don't have the patience I used to have. I love Mom, but…"

A lovely vision, standing demure and uncertain, appeared in the entryway a few yards from where he sat, stealing his eyes, subduing him and his words. He got up, though clumsily, spilling his chair over onto the floor, his hands grasping the table for support. "Mandy," he whispered across the long table that separated them. She smiled, her eyes twinkling under a chandelier light as she advanced into the room. *Oh God*, he thought, *my God*.

He tried steadying his hands on the table as she approached closer, her hair shining with dark luster, bouncy and soft across her shoulders. One side was lifted and brushed back with a pearled comb. Dainty pearls decorated her earlobes. Her face wore a healthy glow, her cheeks rosy. Her eyes were enhanced softly with shadow, yet seemingly bigger, more expressive as she focused on him. She was but a touch away when she said, "Hi," his gaze capturing those lush lips, drenched in gloss. "Hi," he responded, too benumbed to say more.

"When you're done drooling, son, you can offer her a chair. Then you can thank me for bringing such a lovely woman to dinner."

His focus didn't waver from Amanda. He smiled at his mother's remark, answering her with, "Just gazing, Ma, not drooling. And I thank you for bringing this lovely woman to my dinner table. Who is she? Have we met before?"

Amanda's eyes sparkled. "On occasion, Mr. Danzlo," she said. "Several of them actually." She held out her hand. He took it and kissed it. She watched and sighed.

"Ah, it is you, Mandy. No other woman is so sweet on my mouth." He smiled, and then pulled out a chair. "May I be so honored as to have your presence beside me?"

She glimpsed Miriam across the table, tears bubbling her eyes. It caused Amanda's to do likewise. She slowly sat down, Garry's eyes never wavering from her face. Then his voice touched her ears and tickled her senses.

"I must say, you're looking *hot* tonight, Ms. Fields."

His gaze wandered appreciatively to the pink cashmere that hugged her form nicely. It left her neck bare, unlike the many high-necked clothes he was used to seeing on her. He touched her sleeve, his fingers reveling in the soft wool.

"You look rather hot yourself," she dared to say, admiring the fine black suit he wore: slacks pleated at the waist; a two-toned striped vest worn over a white linen shirt; and a black cravat at the neck. The vest was topped with a silk-lined dinner jacket. "A bit overdressed, aren't you?" she teased lightly, considering this was only dinner at home.

He bent down, his voice for her ears only. "Shall I take something off? For you, anything." She blushed.

"Not fair, son! I didn't hear that. Best you behave. The *Shabbos* approaches." Miriam glanced down at her wristwatch. "*Oy!* Seventeen minutes before sundown! *Ai-yi*, quickly Amanda. Light the candles and begin the blessing."

Reality came crashing back, and if it weren't for Nicolas behind him tending to his chair, Garry would've landed on the floor. His left hand mightily gripped the lapel of his jacket as though to stop that racing thoroughbred from leaping out of his chest. "Don't you think you should say the blessing, Ma?" he nearly screamed.

"Nonsense! Am I the woman of this household? *Nu?* Has Amanda not lived here these past weeks? Amanda, say the blessing. Hebrew would be nice, dear."

Garry's fear rose as she picked up the matches. "Mom!"

"*Shah,*" shrieked Miriam.

Amanda opened the match lid and glanced at the kerchief by her plate, the one she was to cover her head with before lighting the candles. She reached for it and exchanged a glance with Nicolas, who sent her an encouraging smile.

Garry sat dumbstruck.

She lit the candles and began the blessing, waving her hands about the flames—to spread the *Shabbat* light and draw it close to yourself, Nicolas had reasoned for the centuries-old custom. "*Baruch Ata Adonai, Elohenu Meliech ha-olam,*" she chanted in not too perfect Hebrew, then she shielded her eyes from the light— seeing not, enjoying not, until after the blessing, which she continued with, "*asher kid'shanu b'mi... b'mi...*" b'mi—what?! She coughed and began again, "*asher kid'shanu b'mi...*"

"*B'mitzvotav,*" Garry quickly filled in, his Hebrew much better than hers. Her voice blended with his as her memory found revival. Garry finished the blessing with her, "*v'tzivanu l'hadlik ner shel Shabbat.* Amen."

Amanda uncovered her eyes and looked at the light. Everyone around the table was wishing the other *Gut Shabbos* while she kept looking at the light, not because she was supposed to, for in truth she should've been wishing the others *Gut Shabbos.* "Amanda," came Miriam's voice, jerking her from her trance-like state. "*Gut Shabbos,*" she said hurriedly, her face meeting Miriam's.

"*Oy, doll!* Don't beat your brain against the wall over a little forgetfulness. You see me worrying over a little word. *Eh!* Worry, who needs it? I need it like a hole in the head, so why do you? Look there," Miriam nodded toward Garry, Amanda's head turned, catching those blue eyes aimed at her with adoration and pride. She basked in the brilliant smile curving his lips.

"My son, the musician," Miriam said. "Memorizes notes, memorizes a zillion songs. From that he makes a living? I should have such luck! He knows from nothing it seems. *Oy vay*, that some should call him a *Shabbos goy!* True, he doesn't observe like he should, *nu?* But his Hebrew he remembers; holy blessings he remembers. No *shlemiel*, my son. He's—"

"Mother!" Garry's face warmed.

"Alright already! Can't a mother brag when she wants to? Start *Kiddush*, son."

Garry pulled off his black jacket and hung it across his chair back, heat consuming his body. After donning the *yarmulke* cap on his head and *talit* scarf on his shoulders, Garry stood from his seat as was the custom for this blessing over wine to welcome and sanctify the Sabbath. Garry reached for the goblet, which was ready with wine. Nicolas stood and so did Miriam, Amanda following suit, assuming she should. Garry sent her an assuring nod. In a low voice, he began, "*Vahhi erev vayhi voker…*"

Amanda listened, enthralled by Garry's ability to recite in Hebrew the words from Genesis 2:1-3. She did not know *Kiddush*, only the one that followed the passage in Genesis. There would be two blessings, *broches*, Nicolas had called them: the first a praise to God for having created wine; the second, thanking the Lord for the holy Sabbath "as an inheritance" and "memorial of Creation" and "in remembrance of the Exodus from Egypt."

After Garry finished *Kiddush*, he toasted the wine cup saying, "*Lechayim*. To life," he translated for Amanda, his eyes never leaving hers as he sipped from the cup and passed it to her. She was near tears as she sipped from it also, and then in turn, passed the cup to Miriam.

They exchanged nervous glances, a feeling of doom engulfing them both by the time they all recited the blessing on washing the hands, which Amanda could only mimic as best she could, followed by the blessing over bread called *Motzi*, which Garry recited.

The two *chalot* was uncovered, one loaf placed on top of the other prior to the blessing. The bottom loaf with a slight incision, was now sliced and served. The *challah* were light and fine-braided loaves of white bread, glazed with egg white, its crust crisp, its inside texture almost like cake. Perhaps he and Amanda would've enjoyed its hint of sweetness, its delicate flavor, had it not been for the anxiety steadily rising in their throats. Amanda raised an inquiring brow as she watched Miriam sprinkle salt upon hers, Miriam passing the shaker to her when done. Amanda took it hesitantly.

"Do you not use salt, *bubeleh?* Remember the Jewish teachings of why we use salt? A valuable commodity in Roman times and available only to free people. To eat it is to emphasize we are free people serving God. But of course, you learned all this through your Jewish teachings. Where did you go to school, dear? What synagogue do you attend? I have friends in the Palm Beach area. Perhaps you know one of them. Naomi Heschel... David Schauss... Agnes Patz?"

"Mom..." Garry intervened.

"No? How about Samuel Gittelsohn? We worked together at the plant years ago. He goes to one of the synagogues in West Palm Beach. Perhaps you've—"

"Mom!"

Miriam looked over at her son with reprove. "Garry, am I not talking to Amanda? *Nu?* What do you want? The salt? Amanda, pass the salt to Garry. Now, *bubeleh*, what was the name of your synagogue?"

Amanda glanced at Nicolas, his gaze filled with empathetic compassion.

"Amanda, dear?" Miriam urged, a little concerned by her hesitation.

She started to speak, and so did Nicolas, but it was Garry's voice that boomed forth. "For the love of God, mother, will you listen to me? She doesn't go to any synagogue!" He was now standing, his thighs firm against the table, his hands spread atop it. His face burned with agitation, yet inside, his body trembled with apprehension.

He expected horror to mar her features, but Miriam kept talking. "Well, of course she does, son," Miriam said nervously. "Any Jewish woman with her sweet disposition would visit one, at the very least on the high holy days. How can you sit and say such *shmutz.*"

"Because she's not Jewish, Mother!"

The air was stifling for long seconds as the truth sank in, Miriam's expression quaking with shock, distress, denial, skepticism, and then reproach.

"A *shiska?!* You keep this from your mother? *Riboyne Shel O'lem!*" she screeched. "*Ai-yi*, and you talk to me of love! *Oy vay iz mir!*" she cried. "Your *kalleh*, she will *not* be! Do not even think it! Do you not remember the vow you made before *Adoshem?* You will not marry this... this *goy*, though *futz* as you may! Fool around as you like, son, for I cannot stop you from climbing into her bed, or she into yours."

Garry's face hardened. "Vulgarity doesn't suit you, Mother, nor is it called for at this table, particularly this night. Should I remind you what we're gathered here for? You need not apologize to me. But you *will* apologize to Amanda."

"*I* will apologize? Who deserves apology here?"

Amanda stood. "You do," she said softly. "From both of us." She looked to Garry for agreement, his eyes meeting hers. He moved beside her.

"Okay, Mother, you want an apology? You have two of them. In fear, we kept a secret. I love her like I've loved no other woman. If I could have my wish, I would marry her this very moment... if she'd have me."

He gazed down into her brown eyes then. He caught her tightly against him. "It's true, Mandy. I want you that much."

"*Gevalt*, Lord, enough already!" Miriam cried, scaring them both to attention. "This is not happening! That my own son would think to betray me! And he expects acceptance, *noch*? I will not, *cannot* accept! *Oy, Gottenyu!* That I should be put through such pain!"

"Mrs. Borowitz, if I should say something," Nicolas said.

"*You*, Nicolas?" Miriam looked disgusted. "It is you I should blame for letting this happen! You saw, yet did nothing to save my son from this *averah*. O-O-O-o-o-oy vay! I-can't-stand-any-more!" Miriam burst into tears. "Son, my son, where did I go wrong? May God forgive you if you should marry her, but I can't forgive! I can't even finish this *Shabbat* meal."

Miriam staggered from the table, one hand across her mouth, the other pressed to her heart as she rushed out the room. A door in the distance slammed.

The three at the table stood frozen, except for the tears pouring down Amanda's face, and one that crept down Nicolas's. As for Garry, shock and wretchedness stripped him dry. He felt Amanda slipping from his arm. He tightened his hold and brought her hard against his chest, his breath breathing hers as he murmured against her lips, "I love you, Mandy. Never forget that."

His words hinted warning. He lowered his head to brush a tender kiss upon her lips, but her whimper crushed hard against his mouth and he took her lips, helplessly, rapaciously, surrendering his reckless need to those arms that wrapped lovingly about his neck. He broadened the kiss as if it might be their last. Then he released her abruptly, shoving her back, his smoldered gaze kindling her for one poignant moment before he snatched up his crutches and walked away.

Amanda stood devastated, her lips bruised and throbbing.

"I'm sorry, Miss Amanda," Nicolas said, coming around the table. "I hate to see the both of you so hurt. I was afraid something like this—"

Her arms flew around his stout body. "I've lost him, Nicolas! I have him, yet I don't. I have his heart, but not the rest of him. I want the rest of him, Nicolas! I want to spend the rest of my life being where he is!"

"Shh," Nicolas said. "You've not lost him yet. Keep faith. Miss Melissa will be here soon with your little boy. That will make you smile, and somehow things will work out."

GARRY WAITED NEARLY two hours before attempting to reason with his mother, only to get angry all over again. By 10 p.m., he was at the adjoining bathroom door, knocking, apologizing to his mother for all the yelling he'd done. He'd spoken in a most respectful way then—for he knew Amanda would want him to—and asked Miriam to open the door so he could kiss her goodnight. They would talk later when both their heads were cooled.

"No, there's nothing further to discuss," she said, her refusal abrupt and final.

Afterwards, he looked for Amanda. She had retired for the night. He felt miserable that he'd denied her his presence for the remainder of the evening. He exited his room and stood outside her door for a long while, unable to bring himself to knock. He knew full well that if she answered, he'd take her into his arms and want to make love to her all night. So he just stood there and leaned his head against the door frame.

*I don't want to lose you, Mandy,* he said silently to the door. He raised his palm and laid it flat against the wood, hoping she might hear the energy of his words, or at least, somehow feel it. "There's power in intention," she'd recently told him while demonstrating the work she did energetically. He'd allowed her to integrate some of her healing work into his daily exercise after the pond accident, and he truly felt it had made a difference in his own health. "Whatever energy you want to send someone," she'd said, "whether to heal a physical condition or to simply send love or gratitude, one needs only to do it with intention and love from their heart."

*I'm sending some now to you,* he told her soundlessly. *I send you healing… my love, and my gratitude. What I can't give you is a promise. I could marry you and we could forget I have a* mother, ignore the fact she won't accept you. Then I could throw you into a world of fame and fortune, a crazy world of entertainment you know nothing about—unlike the quiet world you're used to. Not a very stable life, Mandy. It's scary out there. Sure, there's laughter and wonder, but there's also grief, disappointment, and confusion. Where will you be, Mandy? Beside me? Or at the house, waiting and wondering when I'll be home?

From behind Garry, a door eased open. Miriam gazed dejectedly at the lone figure standing at Amanda's door—her beloved son, slouched against the doorframe, one hand upon the wooden closure. Would Amanda not let him in? Or was he too afraid to knock on the door? An image of Garry as a young boy flitted through her mind. "Come, *tatteleh*," she'd say on many a hot and lonely night, "let's go sit on the fire escape and look at the stars." They did so, and she'd hold him all the while.

*This is best for you, son*, she silently said. *Your mother knows best. Amanda doesn't belong in your life. You'll see. You'll be happy again in time.*

Miriam backed into her room and quietly shut the door.

# 39.

## HE LOVED ME

"SHE DOESN'T BELONG in his life! I do, goddamit, I do!"

Daphne's hysteria had her hands pummeling at Eddie's shoulders, real tears scorching her cheeks. Her crazed screaming amidst a convulsion of sneezes had brought Eddie storming through her penthouse suite just moments before in an attempt to calm her down before hotel management was contacted.

"That bitch! I knew I shouldn't have left them alone. I hate her, I hate him."

"Shhhh," Eddie said, pulling her head against him. "You don't need him."

Daphne thrust back in bitter defense. "You wouldn't know. He wasn't like the rest of them. He saw things in me no one else did. He gave me chances. He cared, he loved me. I know he did. But that damned accident. It changed him. It changed everything." Her breath released in a long shudder. "I had dreams, I had dreams. I wanted him to be a part."

Eddie gazed at her downcast eyes observingly. He lifted her chin and discovered that shining behind all those self-seeking dreams of hers was the capacity to love. Danzlo had been her closest ticket there. "We can't always have the ones we love."

Eddie didn't mean to set off more sparks, his mind engaged elsewhere for a moment. Daphne stumbled backward, her eyes transforming into frenzied suspicion.

"You do love her. How did you get in here? Where's Max? I should've listened to him. Max!" she called out in near madness. "I need Max!"

Eddie took a step forward. She took one back. He grinned handsomely, his voice calm and soothing. "I'm not here to hurt you, Angel. I'm here to help you. As for Max, maybe it's not Max you need."

The lewd hint threw Daphne off-guard, Eddie's intention to seduce colliding with her logical conclusions. His sturdy attractiveness was potent and demanding. Her face grew flushed, her nipples hardening against the silk robe she wore. She shook her head. "Don't confuse me. I know you want her."

"Do I?" he said huskily. "When there's you?" His warm eyes never wavered from hers, again an unexpected signal, for wasn't it just her body he was interested in?

Daphne blinked, swallowed. "Max says you're just using me to get what you want. That you can't be trusted. What you really want is Amanda Fields. Isn't it?" she said harshly.

"Jealousy doesn't become you, angel. Although you're still beautiful when you're angry."

"You're avoiding my question. I think you might change your mind about calling me angel if you don't answer it."

His gaze fixed on her, wickedly. "Forgive me. You and I both know you're not an angel, so let's cut the bullshit and get down to what we really want. You first."

Disappointment dimmed the blue radiance of her eyes. "So Max was right," she muttered, turning, sitting down at the vanity table facing the mirror. Within seconds, that dim light in her eyes turned dark with hatred. "What I want is money," she demanded, watching his reflection warily in the mirror. "I want lots of it! You want Amanda, it's going to cost you."

"Just money, angel? You sure that's all you want?" He leaned against her, his groin hard against the back of her head, his hands moving upon her face and neck. He pushed at the thin fabric across her shoulders, the silk robe slipping off her shoulders, her naked breasts dancing in the mirror. "Who do you think I really want, Daphne?" Her eyes met his in the mirror. Hers were filled with uncertainty, yet suffused with lust as his hands and fingers kneaded her breasts. She watched in the mirror, an intake of breath revealing the effectiveness of his touch. "You doubt me?" he whispered against her neck. "We make a good team, angel. *Revenge* is our game." He glanced up to her reflection in the mirror. "What do you think?"

Daphne froze, unable to breathe for seconds, and then jumped up in all her naked glory. She tripped over the robe tangled in her high-heeled shoes. Eddie caught her in his arms. "We really must stop meeting like this," he spoke to her gruffly.

"Oh Eddie, you want… you want Amanda punished? *And* Garry?"

"Did I say that?" But the devilish grin on Eddie's face was all Daphne needed. She was ecstatic! "To hell with Garry and his measly millions. You're filthy rich, right?"

Eddie couldn't keep his laughter from exploding. "A true fucking bitch."

She had humored him, and his vulgar verdict excited her beyond means. "Let me prove it to you," she said breathlessly. She began to unfastened Eddie's pants, and then started on his shirt. "Max," she said suddenly. She'd almost forgotten him.

Eddie smiled into her flushed face. "Max won't be coming back," he informed her. "Hope you don't mind but I took the liberty of getting rid of him. I wanted to be alone with you."

Elation glimmered in her eyes. "Eddie, you're so brilliant. Max is a sucker when it comes to money. Did you pay him well? Enough to keep him away a long while?"

Eddie grinned. "Max was well paid. He may never come back. Would you care?"

Daphne's lips curled into a seductive grin. "As long as you're not going anywhere, I could care less when he comes back."

Eddie clasped her hips and thrust deep inside her, smothering her cry with his mouth. He closed his eyes, thinking of his plan for this one. He'd promised the Shark a game.

He threw her on the bed and ripped off his shirt. "I'm going to slam you to hell and back, angel. You ready for some banging?"

Daphne's jaw dropped, her hungry eyes plastering on a Herculean chest, then downward to a magnificent V where pants splayed open to what was nothing less than exceptionally *well-hung*. She swallowed hard, whispering. "Rocky. I'm going to fuck, Rocky."

# 40.

# STARS IN THE NIGHT

AMANDA SIGHED HEAVILY as she realized another day had passed without confession. She donned her usual unflattering garb the next morning, for at this point, what else could she do? The tension surrounding Mariam was more than enough stress for Garry to handle right now. Yet, after his confession the night before concerning his father's betrayal, Amanda's anxiety was at a peak. She was starting to think that Garry wasn't meant to know everything. Nicolas, so concerned about her last night, admitted what she'd suspected—Garry knew half the truth. It was the reason he'd not spoken to her for several days following the pond accident.

She chucked the glasses and placed them in the pocket of her skirt, wearing makeup to a minimum to bring out more of her natural coloring. She was tempted to wear something nicer from her original packed suitcase, but realized it would only make it difficult for Garry to keep his eyes off her. Not a good thing with mother Miriam around, not to mention the questions it would arouse in Garry's head. The pink cashmere dress came from Miriam, he knew.

It was later that morning when Amanda attempted to give the dress back, but Miriam told her it was a "going away" gift. Garry tried his best to bring harmony between all of them during the day, but Miriam wasn't having it. When at all possible, she'd mention Daphne's name in some positive light, just to stir trouble. Twice Garry had taken his mother in the other room for a long talk. Twice he'd returned, unsmiling.

Evening now upon them and the Sabbath finally over, Garry had a big surprise for Amanda. Melissa and Dan had taken an evening flight. They were on their way with Robbie. Happy tears and a squeal preceded the best bear hug a man could possibly get.

The next hours dragged on endlessly for Amanda. She couldn't wait for Garry to meet Robbie, sure that the two would get along wonderfully. When time drew near, Garry excused himself to the bathroom. He returned on one crutch, leaning on it, peeking around the corner facetiously. "What? Still no Robbie? If he doesn't get here soon, I'll need to replace the floor from all that jumping and running to the window. I think we need to tie you down to a—"

He was suddenly wearing Amanda, stuck on him like flypaper. She squirmed and kissed and hugged while he fought to stay balanced on the one crutch. "Thank you, thank you," she said, just before Melissa entered the front door. Robbie followed behind in his wheelchair, pushed by Dan. Then the real squealing began. Tears, hugs, and lots of kissing intermixed with laughter galore. Even Miriam was smiling, the joyous reunion all too contagious not to react. Robbie's face glowed with sheer happiness, his eyes sparkling and dancing. He kept stealing peeks at Garry, his curious expression filled with awe and excitement. He appeared especially happy when he saw Amanda fling herself at the famous musician, hugging the man with all of her strength. Garry teased Robbie with silent hints of having some crazy woman in his arm. Then, all of a sudden, she hauled Garry by the waist, dragging him closer to the dark-haired boy in the wheelchair.

"Garry, this is Robbie. Robbie this is Garry," she said with a gasp, as if they couldn't guess who each other were.

"A pleasure to meet you, Robbie," Garry said, offering his left hand since Amanda was clinging to his other arm, his right hand grasping his crutch.

"Likewise here, sir," Robbie said maturely. He happily shook Garry's hand.

"Robbie's left-handed too," Amanda said. "You have something in common!"

Garry chuckled. "And you thought we wouldn't? We already knew we had something in common. Tell her, Robbie."

Robbie wrinkled his nose in question, though trying not to appear overly unknowledgeable. He caught the hint when Garry gestured with a nod of his head toward Amanda, his eyes making silly rolls in their sockets. "A simple observation!" Robbie stated with scientific intelligence. "Both of us guys are crazy to have you in our lives!"

"What?" she said playfully, her eyes shining with a silly pout on her mouth.

"Of course, there's the part about liking you a lot," Robbie added.

"Yeah, a whole, whole, whole lot!" Garry put in, sounding like a child himself.

Amused, Amanda glanced at Melissa, who had to put her two cents in. "Count me in! I believe that makes three crazy people in this room who like Amanda a lot."

"Four!" Dan rushed in.

"Five!" Nicolas cheered.

Then silence.

Miriam sat on the sofa, quiet as a mouse, pretending to pick lint off her black skirt while the others stood by waiting. Melissa took it upon herself to remedy the moment. "Amanda, Robbie's got a surprise for you."

"Another surprise? Your presence has already spoiled me to the core, Robbie."

"Should I show her now, Aunt Melissa," he said, glancing over his shoulder. His title for Melissa got everyone's attention.

"I told him he could call me that," she quickly said. "By all means, Robbie, show Amanda now."

"Stand back," the boy announced. Robbie grabbed hold of two walking sticks attached to the sides of his chair. He placed his hands inside the cylinder discs, grasping the handles. He stood with little difficulty, the braces on his legs giving him full support. He took the first steps Amanda had ever seen him make on his own. So overwhelmed with emotion, after just a few steps, she ran and scooped him up in her arms, twirling him excitedly around. She was laughing; he was laughing, and Garry never lost his smile, even while he dodged one of Robbie's walking sticks that zoomed dangerously toward him. Everyone laughed and cheered while Amanda began kissing Robbie ridiculously all over his face and neck. The boy screamed with glee as he tried catching her face in his small hands. Eventually, he accomplished the feat.

"Well, how did I do?" he asked proudly.

"You were magnificent, fabulous, terrific, and all that jazz!" she exclaimed.

"And Garry? Was he terrific when you saw him making his first steps?"

Garry grinned at them. She knew that Robbie's fascination was mostly due to the letters she'd written him, creative stories she had filled with adventure where Garry was sometimes the outlaw, yet always the hero in the end. She had hoped that in some small way, she could reach Robbie through her stories, help him find the strength to overcome and conquer his own inabilities. For Garry, there was no need for heavy braces on his legs, but Robbie, there was no standing without them. His legs were paralyzed.

"I think you both played a pretty mean game of first-time walking. No competition. I hereby pronounce you both equally terrific!"

Robbie's smile grew wide and bright. He hooked his arm around Amanda's neck straightening his shoulders. He looked pretty proud of himself. Garry chuckled. He, too, was proud, his attention aimed on Amanda. His eyes gleamed with love and respect.

"The hour is late. Should we not get to bed? Nearly midnight, and the boy is still up," Miriam butted in.

The room hushed for the next few seconds, and then Amanda put Robbie back in his chair, Nicolas rushing to help her.

Robbie looked at Nicolas with a wry smile. "I know who you are. You're Amanda's Kemo Sabe. She tried to draw a picture of you on a horse, but you look better than her silly drawing. But… who is that?" he asked, pointing in Miriam's direction.

"It's not nice to point," Amanda whispered beside him.

"Robbie," Garry's voice boomed in, coming up behind him, "meet my mother, Queen Miriam."

"Your mother's a queen?" Robbie exclaimed, his brows arching with excitement.

"Garry!" Miriam scolded.

Melissa giggled. Dan and Nicolas held in their chuckles. Amanda stood tense.

"Pay him no mind, boy," Miriam told Robbie, lifting from the sofa. "I'm no queen. My son is just being a *shtunk!*"

"Being a what?" Robbie asked, squeezing up his nose.

"That's right, little one, wrinkle that nose. A *shtunk* is a stinker. And my son's being a big one. Best not to learn from that one. Better to listen to me than to listen to a *narr.*"

"Huh? I mean, ma'am? A *narr?*"

Dan broke in. "I think we should get ready for bed now."

"A *narr* is a fool," Miriam answered. "In this case, a clown!"

"Sleeping plans, anyone?" asked Melissa.

"Are you being a stinking clown?" Robbie inquired of Garry.

Melissa held Dan by the arm. "We'll sleep upstairs, in the larger loft bedroom. Robbie should stay downstairs near Amanda so she can tend to him. There's a small sleeper in the music room."

Garry smiled down at Robbie. "Afraid it's true. I'm a nasty ole stinker of a clown!" he teased.

"It's quite cold upstairs," Amanda said to Melissa. "Nicolas, you didn't think to turn the heat up upstairs, did you? Why don't I sleep in the music room and the two of you can have my bed."

"Where do I sleep?" said Garry's voice beside her, causing her to jump as he touched her back.

"The boy could sleep in my bed, more room." Nicolas suggested. "I can sleep in the music room."

"Can I sleep with the *narr*?" shouted Robbie above the others.

And so it was—a battle for the beds.

"Now listen up," Miriam ordered. "Nicolas and Garry will sleep in their own beds. Amanda doesn't mind sleeping in the music room and will happily give up her own bed to Dan and Melissa. And you, *tatteleh*," she said looking down at the boy wearing the hopeful expression on his face, "can sleep in that king-sized bed with the *narr*." Robbie was all smiles. "Now children, Queen Miriam is tired and would like to go to bed." She looked to Amanda gravely. "I take it you'll assist the boy?" Her eyes had fluttered disconcertingly at the braces on Robbie's legs before returning to Amanda's face.

"Of course," she said, half-smiling, but Miriam wore no smile. That is, not until Robbie yelled out to her as she was turning to leave.

"Queen Miriam!"

She turned to look at the little boy with the giant grin on his face.

"I'm glad you're here with us," he told her. "You remind me of my Gramma. She was funny like you. She knew how to break up a fight."

Miriam lifted a brow. "And you loved this Gramma? You were good to your Gramma?"

"I wasn't always a good boy," Robbie confessed, "but I loved her this much!" He spread his arms as wide as he could. "That's much bigger than my heart."

Miriam chuckled. "Physically, yes, *tatteleh*."

"You talk weird. Does *tat… tat-teleh* mean Robbie?"

"*Tatteleh* is a Yiddish term of endearment used to address little boys. It's like calling you dear, child, sweetie."

"Cool! Is there a Yiddish term I can call you?"

"How about *bube* or *baba*," Garry offered.

"Booba or baba?" Robbie said, looking wryly at Miriam. "Is he being a *shtunky narr* again?"

Miriam paused uncomfortably. *Bube* was a term for grandmother. *Baba*, a Russian term, also used for grandmother, though often used to address any old woman. "I think not a *shtunk* this time," Miriam informed, though she threw Garry a critical eye. "Bedtime. We'll save talk for tomorrow. *Nu?*"

"Goodnight, booba!" Robbie shouted as she walked away. Miriam paused in her step.

"That's spelled b-u-b-e," Garry said. "The 'u' sounds like put or hook, not 'oo' like boo."

Robbie smiled. "I mean, goodnight, bube!"

"Goodnight, *tattelah*," Miriam said, heading for her room.

GARRY LAY IN bed, his eyes open in the semi-darkness. The royal blue drapes stood halfway drawn, a full moon shining in through the glass. It cast large shadows on the wall. The drapes were drawn partially open per Robbie's request. Amanda had obliged the boy's wish to view the night sky prior to tucking him, and then Garry, into bed. Garry could still feel the warmth of her goodnight kiss, brief though it was, yet smack-dab on the mouth—unintentional on her part, for she'd been leaning in for a chaste kiss on the cheek when Garry swiftly caught that kiss on his lips. "Gotcha," he teased with a wink of his eye. Nervously she smiled, Robbie lying beside him, grinning. "That's lesson number one," he told Robbie. "Want more from a woman, you've gotta be sneaky about it." Amanda didn't look too pleased with this male advice; she frowned while Robbie laughed, enjoying it thoroughly. Robbie enjoyed anything Garry had to say. It was the boy's conversations that intrigued Garry though. He found him to be quite an intelligent youngster.

"Did you know that the moon is approximately 238,857 miles from the Earth and that it moves about our planet at an average speed of about 2300 mph?"

They were Robbie's first words when Amanda left, the door shut and his eyes toward the window. He continued on and on about space ships and past explorations, and his dreams for the future.

"Yep, I'm going to fly to the moon one day. Be the best astronaut there ever was!" Then out of the blue, he said, "Do you love Amanda? She loves you. She hasn't really told me so, but she doesn't have to. I can just tell. I can't wait till she finds out I'm going to be her son. Aunt Melissa told me you're getting everything arranged so Amanda can adopt me. I've never had a mother before. At least I don't remember her. But I prayed for one. Wouldn't it be neat if you could be my dad?"

Garry was lost for words. A strange emotion whirled inside him, somehow pushing and pulling at the same time. He gave no response to the boy, yet felt impelled to touch him. Reaching across the bed, he touched a shoulder. Robbie took his hand, squeezed it, held it for a while, and then fell asleep.

Garry lay for a long time, listening to the gentle snooze of Robbie's sleeping form beside him. Already he felt a bond growing between them. Mandy was responsible, for he lived her excitement with each mention of the boy's name. She'd told him about their make-believe trips to the Milky Way, and she'd shared some of their tales of galaxy adventures. *Robbie's Starmate,* she had called herself.

Starmate… soul mate… what was she to him? His future or his past-to-be? Right now she felt light years away, though she was just a few feet down the hall. He could only imagine that she was hurting from his mother's rude remarks, Miriam far from being convinced that Amanda should be part of the family. He loved his mother, respected her for many things—for loving him, teaching him, and always believing in him. He knew Miriam was doing what she thought best. For her to give in meant to give up on her son.

What of Mandy? Was he giving up on her? His choices were few. He could just ask her to live with him, but then there was Robbie to consider and what kind of moral example would that set? As for marriage, why would he throw her into such when great risks were involved? It was one thing to be thrown into a busy world of entertainment. And yet another to put up with Miriam's destructive grievances. And then there's Daphne's promise for revenge. Those latter two reasons alone would bring more heartache than he'd ever want Amanda to bear.

Two days and two nights, and he would send Mandy away. He and Dan had discussed the situation further on the phone last night. They both agreed that Amanda and Robbie would be better off in Florida, far away from him. Once Amanda was no longer in the picture, Daphne's little war need only be with Garry. Daphne just needed to be swayed in his direction.

God help, but he would make these two days memorable! For Amanda, for Robbie, and for himself. They'd get out of this house, explore a bit of Colorado, something he hadn't done since he had bought the place. And Monday night, they'd throw a party, celebrate their time together… for who knew what Tuesday might bring.

# 41.

## LET'S GO STEPPIN'

SIX O'CLOCK IN the morning and Garry was banging on all doors in the house. "Up, up, you sleepy no-counts! Time for fun and adventure! Today, we explore Colorado!"

Dan wanted to explore Garry's face. Break his nose in a couple places. "He's got to be dreaming," Melissa said, lying beside her husband. "Honey, go put him back to bed." She fluffed the covers and turned over on her pillow.

"Mandy, girl, you up yet?" A loud thump echoed from the music room as Garry opened the door. "Woman, get off that floor and get moving! Robbie and I don't have all day." Then the door slammed shut.

"I'm going to kill me a son!" screamed the woman no longer asleep in the guest room.

"Sorry, Ma, but like it or not, you're going to be a tourist today." Then, "Nic, ole boy, I knew you wouldn't disappoint me. Dressed and ready to go I see."

"You wouldn't disappoint *us*," Robbie corrected, rolling his wheelchair beside Garry. "We're gonna have a blast today, Nicolas!"

Several Yiddish words exploded from the guest room.

"A blast," Nicolas said, clearing his throat. "Hmm, yes, to be sure, Master Robbie. "I'll go pack us a picnic lunch. Would you like to help?"

"Cool! A real picnic! The closest thing I ever came to a picnic was eating on the back porch with Gramma. Gramma used to call it a picnic, but we didn't eat on a blanket or anything? Can we sit by a lake? Amanda says there are lots of lakes in Colorado." Robbie knocked on the guest room door. "Hurry up, *bube!* We're going on a picnic!" Robbie grabbed his chair wheels and headed toward the kitchen,

Nicolas following behind the excited boy. "I hope we get to see some cowboys and Indians today. That would be the coolest! Maybe even see a ghost town. Maybe we'll get spooked."

"Spooked to boot," Nicolas said with chagrin, thinking solely of Miriam Borowitz and the day to come.

"Yeah boy, we'll boot 'em right out of town! Do you own cowboy boots, Nicolas? Garry said he was going to buy me some today. He's a cool guy, isn't he?"

"The coolest," Nicolas agreed, chuckling, heading for the paper plates, cups and plastic utensils stored in one of the kitchen cabinets. "You're quite a cool guy yourself," he told Robbie. "Miss Amanda is a lucky woman."

Robbie grabbed a stack of napkins from their holder on the table. "Nope, I'm the lucky one. Amanda is going to be my mom. I wished she'd marry Garry, and then I could have a mom *and* a dad. And *wow*, the neatest parents in the world!"

"Not an impossible dream, Master Robbie." Nicolas stuck his head in the refrigerator, searching for lunchmeat, cheese, and leftovers that might be a good add for their picnic spree. "If only certain others believed in such a dream, it might come true," he said under his breath.

"Like *bube?*"

Nicolas moved his head aside the refrigerator door, gazing across the room at the boy who was busy looking through lower cabinets and drawers for anything he thought should be included in a picnic basket. The boy had good ears, Nicolas realized. And a bright head on his shoulders.

Robbie circled his wheelchair and sent Nicolas a mischievous grin. He began a cheerful little beat against his chair arms, with lips pursed for whistling. That whistle became a tune well recognized as Bobby McFerrin's hit song from the year before, *Don't Worry Be Happy*. Robbie's confidence shone through in every sparkle of his eye as he sang and rocked in his seat to the beat. By the time he maneuvered his chair toward the table with a loaf of bread and a butter knife in his lap, he was back to whistling.

Nicolas's mouth curved into a giant grin, his concern over Amanda and Garry lessening considerably. He had the oddest feeling Robbie would handle everything. He happily joined in with a bit of whistling of his own, all worry placed aside.

Amanda was never happier than she was at that moment, with Garry and Robbie by her side under the big, blue Colorado sky. Everyone was enjoying the mild climate of the day, breathing in its dry, fresh air. Although snow still covered a great part of the land—particularly along the mountain range—the temperature was amazingly high for the end of March—63 degrees Fahrenheit. It was a perfect day and Garry had amazed everyone with his last minute plans, the tour guide showing up at the door at seven o'clock sharp taking them all by surprise.

How Garry just happened to be acquainted with one of the best guides in town—Sweetwater Jones, a Cheyenne Indian who stood as tall as Garry—no one knew. Sweetwater had a medium physique, a little on the heavy side, his coarse, salt and pepper hair resting upon his shoulders. His face was well rounded, his nose rounded and flat, and his jawline strong and squared. Was it Garry's money, or his charismatic effect on people to drop everything and provide assistance—even when awakened by a five a.m. phone call—that ushered this guide in on such short notice?

The trip was so proficiently planned that a handicapped van waited outside, ready to take the dog to Yancey's ranch for the next two days, and to lug all eight of them on an excursion through what Sweetwater termed as *the land of legends*, a majestic sight so impressive, no wonder Colorado was sometimes referred to as "The Switzerland of America."

According to their guide, this two-billion-year-old land mass was uplifted by primeval oceans that stirred the earth with its vigorous waves. Its turf boomed forth volcanoes and was sculpted by the effects of ice, snow, rain, and fog. Many great waterfalls chiseled its prehistoric form into a splendorous panorama of craggy peaked mountains.

Amanda was captivated by the amazingly beautiful vistas and its magnificent steep canyons that burst of pink and mauve colors. But her fascination paled against Robbie's. It was one thing to spend an entire day with a real live American Indian and get to ask him a zillion questions, but another thing to see such a spectacular wonder. Nothing like flat Florida, which was the only place Robbie had ever known. He thought the jagged cliffs and granite-walled canyons were "cool," and admired the Engelmann spruce trees, the Douglas firs and lodgepole pines. Most were cottonwoods and aspens. Sweetwater Jones said that cowboys had a nickname for aspens. "Quakies" they called them—due to the glimmering tremor of their leaves so brought to life by the sun and the breeze. Robbie would be calling aspens "quakies" from now on.

Colorado's many valleys were home to historic ghost towns, and scattered all over the land were remnants of abandoned old mines. Due to their limited time in exploring, they'd not be able to visit any of the Old West towns, but Robbie was more than satisfied with the sights they were seeing.

The Western Museum of Mining and Industry allowed for a hands-on experience for all, Robbie the one most intrigued. He learned how to pan for gold and observed mining displays and how they operated. His real fascination was the United States Air Force Academy just across the interstate. Robbie tried not to think too much on the fact that only the most intelligent, healthiest, and sturdiest young people were admitted to this fine academy. Tough physical training was required, far from his ability to accomplish. His unusual silence prompted Garry and Amanda to make several witty comments during the tour, somehow helping to push away those discouraging facts. Robbie refused to believe he'd never be a space cadet. He'd pinned his faith on the belief that all things were possible. His Gramma and Amanda were two firm believers in that same sentiment.

Saddles and ropes, boots, buckles, spurs, and hats were just a small part of the exhibit at the *Pro Rodeo Hall of Champions*, the only cowboy museum in the United States devoted to the men and women of the rodeo. The whole Danzlo gang got to experience the jolting sensation of a bucking Brahma bull ride through film and stereo sound. "Let 'er buck!" Garry yelled. "Yee-hi!" Robbie shouted, his face turned toward Miriam's. "Ride 'em cowboy, *bube!*"

"*Ai-yi-yi!*" Miriam said, pale-faced and wincing.

Miriam may have acted like she was having a bad time, but in truth she was enjoying their day outing, especially once they left the museums to explore the natural wonders. It opened to such haunting beauty, it took one's breath away. One such sight came on horseback through the Garden of the Gods—a national park displaying abstract rock formations of red sandstone. It was a fun experience for all since none of them were familiar with horses, except for Sweetwater Jones. Robbie rode double with him, the boy's paralyzed legs keeping him from experiencing a solitary ride. But that was okay with him, for they were riding the biggest and most handsome stallion in the stable called Star. "Wow, a white stallion like Silver!" Robbie exclaimed. To him, it was like riding the Lone Ranger's prized possession.

Late afternoon, the van drove up in front of the huge pink-and-ocher building offset by large Mediterranean-style towers. The famous Broadmoor had three world-class championship golf courses and an indoor ice-skating arena. It also had its own private lake, horse stables, an exquisite carriage house, two museums, eight restaurants, a mountain zoo, a ski slope with chairlifts, and shops galore.

Melissa noticed right away that Amanda was unusually silent. She made a quick excuse to visit the ladies' room and grabbed and towed her across Puerto Rican carpets, past Italian marble furnishings and authentic Chinese antiques. They stepped into the restroom to have some girl talk, but unfortunately, Miriam followed behind them. Melissa practically shoved her mother into a stall, reminding her how long they'd been on the road and that she needed to take her time. Amanda was suddenly against the farthest wall, Melissa's hands on her shoulders.

"Out with it," Melissa said, her voice in a loud whisper.

Amanda blinked several times, naiveté painting her face.

"You don't fool me. Okay, I'll guess. It bothers you that Robbie is paying most of his attention to Garry." Amanda's brow wriggled upward, appalled at such a notion. She shook her head vehemently. "Okay then, it's got to be Robbie's growing relationship with Mom, something you're not having much luck with."

Amanda paused, and then shook her head again, this time looking toward the mirror, a forlorn reflection staring back at Melissa. Although she looked cute today in a baby-doll dress with a satin-edged hemline, the patterned tights with the woolen stockings crouched in ankle boots did appear a bit college fashioned. But Amanda was thinking more on the line of Pipi Longstocking. She crumpled the cloth of her dress in her hands, a stray hair falling across her nose. She blew it upward with one puffy breath, frowning when it landed inside her mouth.

Melissa stepped back. "Hmm. Don't look very classy for a joint like this, huh?"

"I don't just feel out of place, I *am* out of place, Melissa. I'm not who I seem to be! I've yet to make my confession to Garry. I appreciate that you finally told me today that he knows about the glasses and makeup, but the fact that he only knows half the truth bothers me. He deserves to know everything, and from my own mouth. I thought I was going to do it the other night, but the stress level with your mom was just too much for everyone. It's never the right time to reveal who I truly am…"

"Because he doesn't need to know," Miriam finished for her, springing forth from her stall. "Why tempt a man's lusts more when he's going to tell you to leave."

"Mother!" Melissa reprimanded, looking at Amanda apologetically. "He's not planning any such thing!"

"There, you are wrong, daughter. You disappoint me. Where are your Jewish values? You know he has no choice but to tell her to go."

"No choice? If he's in love with Amanda, then he should be with Amanda! Times are changing, Mother. It's time you did. And he does have a choice."

"A *wrong* one? My son will not pick!"

"How can you stand there and talk like that about the person who came and brought life back into Garry's broken body? Did we not pray together? Did God not answer our prayer? Perhaps it doesn't matter that your son walks again, and while he does, his heart lay in pieces on the floor. He's finally found the love of his life, and he can't have her? Is that what you want?"

Miriam grew pale. "A cruel game you play with your mother. Perhaps if *someone* had told the truth from the beginning, there would be no need for this foul play, and Garry—"

"Would've still fallen in love with her!"

"Melissa, stop! Please," Amanda shouted. She was hurting enough that she'd caused Garry and his mother to argue. But now, she'd caused friction between Melissa and Miriam as well. "We shouldn't spoil our good time with fighting. Garry has provided us with this wonderful day, meant to put smiles on our faces and a memory in our hearts." Amanda's gaze collided with Miriam's.

"The wise in heart are called discerning," Miriam quoted gently. "In that, I respect you. I'm sorry, Amanda. Deep down, I wish, well, it doesn't matter what I wish." Miriam turned and walked away. She left Melissa and Amanda staring at a closed door. Melissa turned to Amanda.

"What did she mean by that? The wise in heart...?"

"It doesn't matter."

"Of course it does! You know something I don't. What is it?"

Amanda backed her head against the wall, her eyes closing, warding off the tears she felt welling up inside her. "This trip Garry has planned," she began brokenly, "with all of its sweet memories, is Garry's way of saying goodbye to me. Kind of like the Last Supper. That's what it feels like, Melissa. Knowing soon I'll be going away." Amanda opened her eyes. They were misty and grave. "But I know Garry loves me. That, alone, will be my comfort."

Melissa stared horrified. "Garry wouldn't do that! He could never let you walk out of his life, not after everything the two of you have been through. He'd be a fool!" Melissa began to cry. "I want you to be my sister. I want—"

Amanda grabbed her around the neck. "I love you, too, Melissa. Let's not talk about it anymore, okay? Let's just have a good time. And let's stop squeezing each other, because I've got to pee."

Both girls giggled, dabbing their eyes with their fingers.

"Tell me about your trip to Florida," Amanda said, going behind a stall door. "Did you and Dan get some time alone together?"

"Romance was our dance!" Melissa said, entering the stall beside hers. "We stayed at the Royal Poinciana, rented a car, traveled down A1A along the beach shores, took a short cruise on the Intracoastal Waterway upon the *Manatee Queen*, and had an intimate candlelight dinner at *Jo's*. Oh, and while we were dining, some stranger came up to us and asked if we wanted to two tickets to the theatre in Jupiter. For free. We couldn't believe it! A special presentation of *Hamlet*. It's always been my favorite Shakespearean play. So we drove to Jupiter and saw it! Burt Reynolds has a ranch in Jupiter, you know. We went right by it."

"*Hamlet?* That's it!" Amanda began pounding on her stall wall, scaring Melissa straight off the toilet seat. Fortunately for Melissa, she'd finished her business. Jerking up her pants, she flew out the stall to find Amanda outside it, grinning, her face all aglow.

"What? *What!*" Melissa urged, bobbing her head to get an answer.

Amanda's glow ebbed. "No, that would be a cowardly way to show him, to confess my true self on a stage. However, to get Garry on stage... *that* would be brilliant!"

Melissa paused only a second. "I get it! *Hamlet*—the play within the play. Reveal all by putting on a show. How ingenious! We could've called it, *Amandlet: The Nurse Trap*. 'To be or not to be, that was the question.' Go on!" Melissa bobbed her head again, expectantly.

"I'm thinking, I'm thinking." Amanda's eyes were downcast, her weight against a wall. She drummed her fingers on her thighs. "If we could get Garry in front of a quaint group of people... you know, start off small and..." Amanda's pause became a sigh. "Oh Melissa, we're asking for a miracle here. How could we ever pull off any kind of plan so late in the game? Our time is just too short."

The bathroom door flew open and in rushed a freckled-face, redheaded woman hurrying toward a stall. She stopped short in front of the girls.

"Amanda? O-M-G! What a small world. What are you doing here?" She reached for a quick hug around Amanda's neck before going behind a stall door. "Sorry, I'm in a big rush. I'll just keep talking. I can't tell you how much I appreciated you caring for Joe when he was in the hospital. We'd almost given up, believed the worst, but your encouragement and tender ministrations was a godsend. We live in Los Angeles now. Joe's playing again. He's part of a jazz gig tonight, here at the Broadmoor. It was supposed to be an open talent show to raise money for a needy cause, but nearly all of the acts cancelled on us and now the band's main singer has been coughing horribly all morning..."

The toilet flushed and as Amanda's acquaintance, Bobbie Lee, exited her compartment, she came face to face with two wide-eyed women, their mouths agape. They turned to each other, saying simultaneously, "Not a coincidence!" They pivoted to Bobbie Lee.

Bobbie Lee laughed. "You know someone who might cover the loss?" She turned to the sink to wash her hands.

"Do we know someone?" Amanda said, incredulously.

"Boy, do we know someone. Wait till you find out who it is."

"Bobbie Lee, this is Melissa. Melissa Bobbie Lee."

Bobbie Lee began rummaging through her pocketbook and pulled out a crinkled flyer. "Sorry, Joe's waiting for me in the car. Lots to do. She slapped the flyer on the sink counter. Be there, 2:00 p.m. rehearsal. Talk more then." She grinned. "Joe will be so ecstatic to see you."

As Bobbie Lee left, another woman entered the restroom, passing the two who were squealing excitedly. Amanda spoke first. "Robbie and Nicolas can help us."

Melissa nodded. "All we have to do is get them alone long enough to tell them what, when, and how."

The clearing of a male voice outside the restroom door sounded. "Miss Amanda? Miss Melissa? Is everything all right? Mr. Danzlo has sent me to—"

The door flung open. Nicolas, caught off guard, was suddenly snatched by four female hands. The next second, he was flushed and sputtering, appalled to find himself in the ladies' powder room of all things!

"Nicolas, we have a plan!" Amanda announced.

"The plan of the century!" Melissa added.

"Might we discuss this elsewhere?" Nicolas swallowed his discomfiture as his stare shot to a lady exiting from a more private part of the restroom, her face astounded by the sight of a man where he shouldn't be. Nicolas squeezed his eyes from the horror of it.

"We need privacy, so this is a good place," said Amanda.

"This is a bad place! A bad, bad place!" Nicolas said. His eyelids were so tightly shut, a crow bar couldn't pry them open.

"Then Garry should've sent his mother to do his bidding," Amanda said, smiling.

"Oh, that I could be so lucky! She's gone off with Mr. Borowitz, his surprise arrival from New York another one of the boss's last minute plans. *Thank you, Mr. Danzlo!*"

"That's wonderful!" Melissa said. "Mom will be out of the way. Now, listen up, Nicolas, this is what we need you to do…"

# 42.

# I SHOULD CARE

"ALL RIGHT, DAN, where are they? And who are all these people? I thought this was supposed to be a private gathering."

Dan only shrugged as Garry's gaze surveyed the luxurious room, richly decorated in pastels and silver. Tables sat covered with fine linen cloths in mint tones. Buff-colored candles ensconced in silver platforms and glass domes made centerpieces for each setting, their flickering lights glittering like diamonds upon the lightly patterned wallpaper in the huge room.

Their table was large. Dan sat to Garry's left, dressed in a crisp white shirt, his silver cuff links reflecting light off the dancing candle flame. He looked quite fine in his gray pin-striped vest and matching slacks next to Garry, who was handsomely dressed in white from neck to toe, except for a few silver accessories—a deep pink cravat and a silk lapelled vest of deep pink and white. He wore it thinking of the pink cashmere dress Amanda might wear, his mind conjuring up her lovely visage.

He glanced at the empty chair next to Dan, and the one to the right of himself. Melissa and Amanda had yet to show up. Suspicion had stirred in his head earlier when the two women had finally returned from their long visit to the restroom. Nicolas had looked less than calm after his venture to fetch them, his face pale even as he made an excuse to take Robbie out for some fresh air. Garry had intended to follow them, but Melissa had grabbed his arm, flinging him backward upon his crutch. She announced that The Broadmoor was much too varied with recreation— shops, museums, spas, sports, et cetera. She and Amanda wanted to shop.

Disappointment had swallowed him then, for he'd hoped to spend some quality time with Mandy, and hopefully alone, but her face was so aglow, her eyes sparkling with the prospect of shopping, he could only respond by saying, "Sure, have fun without me."

"Garry, where's your smile?"

The voice belonged to Frank, Miriam's husband of three years. He sat next to the empty chair reserved for Amanda. Miriam on the far side of him. Garry's gaze shifted, welcoming the older man's smile. Frank's eyes were an aquamarine. One could see an ocean of sincerity in them. Though not a handsome man, his warm smiles and sea-sparkling eyes had a way of grasping one's attention. "Dan, ole boy, you're not looking too happy either. Think the women have stood you up? They're probably just lost. Big place, you know."

Dan frowned. "That's unlikely since they're the ones who planned this little party, or so we were told. They know exactly where we are."

"That's true, Frank," Garry said. "They told us where to come and what time to be here. I'm afraid those two are up to something. Get them together, watch out. To tell you the truth, it's starting to scare me."

Frank laughed. "Now I'm really curious about this nurse of yours! I shouldn't have let your mother drag me to the newsstand as soon as I got here. One minute sooner and I could've met—"

"Just be thankful we saw no more scandalizing articles about Garry," Miriam burst in, "though I'm sure half the people here already know about his live-in playmate! Just look around at those peering faces."

Garry half-embarrassed, glanced around the room. Several people were looking at him, smiling, waving. Garry smiled back wryly, nodding his head in recognition. "Who *are* these people?" he asked the waiter who stopped at their table to unload a tray of drinks they ordered. "Wasn't this to be a private party?"

"Well, yes, Mr. Danzlo," the waiter assured. "Your sister made it clear that no one was to be allowed in without a personalized invitation, this reserved table the exception."

Garry sent Dan a solicitous glance. Dan cleared his throat. "Exactly what do these invitations look like and what do they say?" he asked uneasily.

The waiter, who appeared reluctant, looked askance toward the large dance floor in front of their table. As though receiving some cue from another waiter standing by it, he turned back, saying, "Just a moment, please." Leaving, he returned with what looked to be a business card. He handed it to Garry. Garry took it, his eyes growing larger with each printed word he read aloud.

"This card cordially invites you to the *Wing-Ding Jazz Fest & Talent Show,* sponsored by the Danzlo Group Performers, helping to end the devastating effects of ALS—more commonly referred to as "Lou Gehrig's Disease."

Garry's focus shot to the dance floor. Velvet green curtains opened to an orchestral platform, decked with musical instruments, but no musicians. At center stage, stood Melissa wearing a black theatrical warm-up wrap top with ankle length leggings. She stepped forward.

"To be or not to be… that was the question," she said to the audience, her arms outstretched in dramatic show. She slung one hand across her chest. "Whether 'twas nobler in the mind to suffer the slings and arrows of outrageous deceit, or let a sea of troubles stir—recklessly, carelessly—within the heart of an opposing man. Let die, let sleep—"

Amanda stormed across the stage from behind the curtains, clearing her throat exaggeratedly. She, too, wore black, a three-quarter sleeved sweater over capri leggings. "Excuse me, but I believe that's *my* line. You're always hogging the stage. *Geesch.* Can't a girl get a word in edgewise? How will I ever confess?" Amanda's focus zoomed on Garry's face, a spark of desperation in her eye, yet humor too.

"Confess, what?" Melissa asked. "That you have no talent?" She snorts unladylike to the crowd, causing them to laugh.

Amanda frowns. "I have talent! I have lots of talent." She stomped the floor with her soft leather jazz shoe. "I need only a chance. That's all it takes to prove what I can do. Belief in myself, belief in… you," she said to the audience, her gaze moving slowly until it settled warmly on Garry. "Okay, so I need some guts," she blurted suddenly. "Give me a prop, any prop." Her hand flew out beside her, and someone backstage threw her an umbrella; it landed conveniently in her outstretched hand. Another one appeared for Melissa. Melissa began a solo, her voice in tune with "Singin' In the Rain." Then Amanda's voice blended with hers, both of them tapping their feet to a rhythmic beat, their umbrellas opening and swinging as they shuffled and danced in set patterns across the floor. Meanwhile, a band began to gather, one by one, providing the background music for the duo. As the song wound down, the girls tapped their umbrellas in sync with the beat and then sashayed off stage behind the curtain.

The crowd cheered with appreciation. Then Bobbie Lee appeared, announcing that more entertainment was yet to come. She thanked everyone for joining them and supporting an important cause. She introduced the members of the jazz band, indicating that a couple of musicians would appear later as they had delayed flights into Colorado. She humored the audience with an amazing little story of how all seemed lost in providing a variety of entertainment tonight, and how a bunch of talented performers miraculously appeared, volunteering not only their time and talent, but supporting graciously and generously to this progressive neurodegenerative disease that affects thousands of people each year, leading to death only two to five years after diagnosis.

"On a more happy note," Bobbie Lee said, "we have a special guest among us who doubly proves that miracles do happen. A survivor of a tragic and debilitating accident that took his ability to walk some months back, the talented musician and singer Garry Danzlo sits among us. Only today, he can…" Bobbie Lee paused as her emotions began to get the best of her. "He can *stand* among us," she finished tearfully.

A lot of whooping and hollering infused the room, joyously edging Garry to stand. Garry was embarrassed, yet too overwhelmed by the emotions bubbling up around him, and within him. He felt the energy of pure love around him. He was missed, and of a sudden, all those poignant memories of what was most important came flooding through his senses. They all believed in him; they all appreciated him, respected him. He saw it in everyone's eyes. It initiated his courage to stand with the help of his cane.

The room quieted long enough to see if Garry would speak. All he could do was nod his head in acknowledgement. But then he somehow managed a "thank you" and suddenly said, "I'm not singing tonight." He smiled his handsomest smile and sat down, and a roar of "aww" and "come on, Garry!" and "why not? You can do it!" intermingled with clapping and laughter.

Saved by the loud drumming of an instrument backstage—the cue that another act was about to begin—the roaring crowd soon settled down. Behind the curtain came a child actor – Robbie. He entered the stage in his wheelchair, a bongo drum in his lap. Garry had been overly touched and proud by the prior performance involving Melissa and Amanda, but nothing prepared him to the emotional shift he felt in seeing Robbie on stage. Robbie looked straight at him with a big grin on his face as he began a quiet *rat-a-tat-tat* on the drum. His small hands began to play in talented rhythm on the drum, his focus now immersed in the beat he was playing. As his volume increased, the beat suddenly transformed into a Native American rhythm that introduced Sweetwater Jones to the floor. A long feathery headdress adorned Sweetwater's head, his clothing made of leather and turquoise jewels. Sweetwater stepped to the beat of Robbie's drum, reenacting an old rain dance—full of zigzagging movements that were both beautiful and moving.

Surprisingly, the next performance began with Nicolas, the start of an a cappella quartet where his voice took on a drone of two "bum" beats, his knees bending in rhythm with each ignited sound. Moments later, Robbie rolled up beside him, clicking his tongue with another faster rhythm, his hands clapping at alternate beats. Next, Amanda joined the line with her own unique tempo, a squish-squash sound that had her body moving in opposition to Nicolas'. Then the last of the living quartet instruments was Melissa, her cadence of mouth noise completing a musical blend of regularity.

The ensemble performance was thoroughly entertaining and uniquely fun. Toward its end, each quartet member began to make their way off stage. Amanda stepped away first, slipping behind the curtain, and then Melissa, followed by Nicolas. Robbie closed the act by sounding a melody that led into a jazzy beat, whereby the band of musicians behind him began to blend in, incorporating the sounds of bass, guitar, trombone, saxophone and drums.

After their piece was finished, silence fell throughout the entire room, for Amanda entered the floor, dressed in a floor-length, white chiffon evening gown. Her heeled shoes clicked against the wooden surface as she strolled across the stage to be closer to the band of musicians. There she stopped and leaned against a pillar. Closing her eyes, she waited as a saxophone played a brief intro, providing the key that would assist her to begin in solo a very spiritually stirring version of George Gershwin's "Summertime" –lyrics written by DuBose Heyward back in 1935 for the opera *Porgy & Bess*, known to be some of the best written material of its time. Amanda's slow tempo and style was unique and evocative, her dulcet voice transforming this old, favorite jazz tune into a soul-felt and passionate one. As she finished the first stanza, her gaze fell on Garry, and she began to walk toward him. The music stopped. Her singing had stopped.

It wasn't a time for confession, not in front of all these people. The secret she'd been keeping for weeks from him deserved a more intimate moment. She would try to confess all, sometime after the show. This moment was for Garry. To bring him back to those who loved him. Back to a world he knew well, to the one thing he'd been destined for and that he loved beyond mere words. *His music.*

"I could really use some help here," she said as calmly as she could. She was taking a big risk in asking him like this, putting him on the spot in front of so many people. But it was her only chance to get him back on stage. And it would be his chance to prove he could do what she believed he could. "We've made a pretty good team so far," she coaxed. "We could do it together? Wanna sing with me?"

Garry's expression was as stark as his body. He wasn't saying anything. And surprisingly, no one else was either, for they all waited with bated breath for his next move.

# 43.

## WHY DON'T WE TRY
## A SLOW DANCE

GARRY'S WORDS WERE wedged in his throat, his insides twisted in his chest. He struggled between discontent and wanting. Discontent because he was afraid, so damned afraid to do what she was asking him to. For what if he failed? Yet a part of him wanted it badly, to be able to sing this type of music and work with a crew of talented jazz musicians. It had been a dream he'd always pushed aside, again and again. And here was Amanda, standing before him, being the loving encourager she was, believing in him. She was not so much the calm and self-assured performer from moments before, but rather a lady in white whose eyes sparkled with tears while trembling in her gold sandal heeled shoes as she waited for his reply. All he could see was this beautiful creature God had given him to experience in this lifetime; and now she was trying to give him a gift, if only he would take it.

"I don't know all the words, Mandy," he managed to say. The moment he said it, Melissa was there with sheets of music, slapping them on the table in front of him. The silent plea on her face ignited his move.

He shook his head, giving up, and lifted himself to stand. With his left hand steady on the table's edge, his right arm outstretched to the crowd. "Women. How do you say 'no' to them?"

Laughter filled the room. A big round of clapping hands, encouraging words, and Amanda's extended hand reaching out for his own brought him onto the stage beside her. Someone took his cane while another provided him a stool close to the band. He scanned the music quickly and spoke to the musicians about a few changes he'd like for them to do. He asked Amanda to start from the beginning,

318

with the same tempo and passion she'd originally had in her voice, and he'd join in when the time was right.

He was good to his word, singing the next stanza in solo, and then their voices united, creating an amazing blend of harmony and flair. Only one little measure had them a little out of sync—both of them grinning as they managed to cover it up quite cleverly. Their duet was surely the most memorable part of the evening for everyone. The moment their song was over, Amanda's arms wrapped around him, and they held each other cheek-to-cheek while the room exploded with tears and cheer. Any thoughts of ever letting Amanda go were far from Garry's mind, until he glimpsed his mother's hauntingly pale features over Amanda's shoulders. Of course Mariam was proud of her son for what he'd accomplished just now, yet it was the fear and betrayal in her eyes as she stared ghostly at his arms so lovingly around Amanda; it said Mariam was losing him and he was destroying an important Jewish value she had taught him.

His arms tightened about Amanda's waist then, the moment suddenly like hours as his mind filled with every horror story Mariam had ever told him. He suddenly wished it was Grampa sitting in her chair. At least Grampa never scared him with stories of Hitler and World War II. Grampa had an open view of life. When Grampa told a story, he made everything sound like a great adventure. Grampa, his greatest hero, who'd always say, "Look Garry, look at us today! Great assets we, to this beautiful country! *Nu?*" Knowing Garry's interest in the music world, Grampa would talk of the great Jewish people who brought America outstanding entertainment such as singer-comedian Fannie Bryce, Jack Benny, George Burns, and the Marx Brothers; great composers like George Gershwin, who wrote jazz/pop and symphonic compositions for productions like *An American in Paris*; the popular, classical composer Leonard Bernstein, who wrote the music for shows like *West Side Story*, and what of the many arrangements of Rodgers and Hammerstein? Not to mention the film producers of such greats as *Gone with the Wind*, the *Wizard of Oz*—Mayer and Shoznick, Spielberg, Woody Allen.

Sweet Grampa. Garry missed him. It wasn't the Jewish and Hebrew schools Garry attended that taught him courage and perseverance, how not to be ashamed of who he was. It was Grampa. He owed it all to Grampa.

Garry wondered what that old man would think of Mandy if he were still alive today. How he might accept her. Would he accept her? He knew Grampa would have to do a lot of thinking first. He'd get back to Garry… in an hour, a day, a week. Then he'd tell Garry the wisest answer he'd ever heard, and afterward say,

"But fast and pray, *boychikel,* then follow your heart."

Miriam suddenly stood and left the table. Garry loosened his hold on Amanda and watched Miriam depart from the room. The room was a shrill of noise, people still cheering and carrying on. "Way to go Garry!" they were shouting. "Now, all you have to do is kiss the girl!" His attention moved on Amanda's lovely face and he saw concern written there. He cupped her chin and kissed her worry away. Standing back, he shouted, "Champagne for everyone!"

Dan grabbed one bottle bucketed in ice from off the table. He uncorked it, its *pop* sending a roar from the crowd. A couple of waiters brought more bottles and handed out glasses. They even brought one for Robbie, filled with 7-UP and cherry juice splashed in behind it. Robbie had rolled in just after Melissa had presented the sheet music to Garry, not about to miss the duet. He was all smiles, and just as loud as the rest of the gang around him. He sat beside Melissa, who now wore a teal colored gown as lovely as Amanda's. Amanda slung her arms around Robbie as soon as she returned to the table. Garry was full of compliments to the boy who could play some mean beats on a drum. They took their seats next to Robbie.

"Mandy, I want you to meet Frank," Garry said. "Frank, Amanda Fields, my nurse."

"Would've never guessed," the older man teased, his aquamarine eyes shining with their usual luster. "If nurses come this pretty, I may need a little sick time."

"Don't think Mom would appreciate that," Garry warned. He glanced at the now empty seat beside Frank.

"No, you're right, son. Your mother would kill me and give me to a caretaker before she'd hand me over to a pretty nurse. Besides, her beauty is more than enough for this old body to handle. Amanda, you must be one angel of a nurse. I don't think I've ever seen Garry looking so good."

Amanda smiled and shrugged. "My job wasn't easy by any earthly means." Everyone laughed. "I hear you're a big jazz fan, Frank. Melissa says you've actually met some of the great jazz giants in your lifetime… Louis Armstrong, Billie Holiday, Benny Goodman."

"And 'Fats' Waller, 'Jelly Roll' Morton, Duke Ellington, Cole Porter… those to name a few," Frank said, grinning. "Garry keeps telling me he has a dream of singing with the big bands. I keep telling him to do it, but he's hesitant. Thinks he might be taking too big of a chance with his fans. Traditional jazz and big band arrangements just aren't as popular as they were back in the late thirties and forties, you know."

"But what would life be if one didn't take chances once in awhile?" Amanda said. "As long as it's not unrighteous and it's fun, I say do it! Sometimes, we just have to put our foot down and just follow our heart."

Amanda's hand took Garry's then and squeezed it. He met her gaze, amazed that she'd said the very words his Grandpa used to say... *follow your heart.*

*But Grampa, what if it's a mistake? What if...*

*Oy,* what if! What if you had no mind, there'd be no dream. And what is a man without a dream? *Nu?* A new Jerusalem without purpose. Even *Adoshem* has dreams, no?

"Garry, did you hear?" Melissa said. "Amanda has something special for you. And yes, I arranged things for you just like you told me to." She winked.

Garry's response was interrupted by a new stream of musicians taking seats at the orchestral platform, adding to the ones already there. A couple of faces he recognized were members of his own band back home in L.A. He looked to Frank beside Amanda, a giant grin on his mouth. But what totally took him aback was seeing Gerry Mulligan at the baritone sax, Warren Luening on the trumpet, and Buddy Morrow at the trombone! Garry's surprise aimed at his sister, and then Amanda.

"We had the best luck when we went shopping!" Melissa said. "You just wouldn't believe! Of course, we made a few phone calls too."

"Tell him about the guitar player, Amanda!" Robbie said excitedly, tugging at her arm.

"Oh, yes," Amanda said. "The 'musician's musician'—jazz guitarist Mundell Lowe. He's here at the Broadmoor! He's going to be a little late, but he promised he'd be playing guitar tonight."

"Hit it, boys!" Melissa shouted. Then the band began playing, "Happy Birthday To You," everyone in the room joining in, Amanda singing and looking a little perplexed for she couldn't fathom whose birthday it was. Frank's? Dan's? It wasn't Melissa's or Garry's. "Happy Birthday, dear Amanda, Happy Birthday to you!"

"What? It's not my birthday!" Then the cake arrived with entirely too many candles on it, which started her laughter. "It is not my birthday!"

"We had to celebrate somebody's birthday tonight," Dan said.

"Yeah, Amanda, what's a party without a birthday?" Robbie shouted.

"Make a wish, Mandy."

Amanda's stared at the enormous many-candled cake. She threw her hands atop her head, "Okay, okay, I'll make a wish." She closed her eyes for a moment, and then opened them to Garry. Her graveness swept through him like a storm for he knew without a doubt he was part of her wish. He tried to smile as she blew out the candles, accomplishing it only when she couldn't blow them out, no matter how much she huffed and puffed. "Trick candles. I might have known! Now what do we do? We'll burn the place down before we can get them off the cake! You all are so bad!"

A waiter came, taking the cake. Garry shoved two gold boxes wrapped in white ribbons in front of her—one half the size of a shoe box, the other much smaller. "From me," Garry said. He watched as her nervous fingers plucked at the ribbon from the larger box. She lifted the lid with one hand, the other reaching in to push away the tissue paper. Within a gold lining, lay the finest silk, scarlet ribbons money could buy. "For your hair," he said softly. He could see she was surprised that he'd remembered her childhood story—*and every birthday when I blow out the candles to make a wish, I wish for scarlet ribbons. I've always kept that a secret. I guess that's why I never got them.*

"There's seven of them, one for each day of the week, Mandy."

Amanda chewed on her bottom lip, as though she could hold back the emotion that threatened to break her. "I don't know what to say," her voice cracked. She quickly replaced the ribbons inside the box, else risk ruining them with those wet droplets falling down her face. She didn't bother to wipe them when she kissed him in appreciation. To Garry it was the most wonderful kiss a man could ask for. "Your turn," she said, Robbie helping her to lift a long oblong box on the table, her smaller present forgotten for the moment.

"For me? Hmmm," Garry mused. "The box is long and slim. A snake perhaps? Poisonous? A get-you-back gift for all that bad behavior I handed you as a patient, right?

"Close." Amanda giggled. "Just kidding! Open it. I promise it won't bite."

Slipping the silver ribbon from the box, Garry peeled off the shiny paper, slowly and carefully peeking inside. It was camouflaged by a load of tissue paper. He peered at Amanda who was urging him on and still promising no bites. Pushing away the paper, his hands stilled, as did his heart for what he found inside.

A walking cane. The most beautiful walking stick any man could ever own, its handle of ebony black, its long rod of ivory. And in between the two, at the base of the handle, was a plate of shining gold. And within the gold, a music staff engraved with notes, and above it, the words: "I don't want to walk without you."

"Do you like it?" Amanda asked excitedly. "See?" she said pointing, "The ebony and ivory colors represent the keys on your piano, and the gold rim, well, just because you're special. Do you recognize the notes it reads? I copied them off of that music you wrote. You know, the one without the words on your piano. Just think, every time you take a stroll, you'll have your very own traveling music!"

Garry was speechless. He stared down at the little sparkling chips inlayed in gold.

"I guess you're wondering if those tiny chips that fill the notes are real diamonds. Okay, well… they are. Now Garry, don't get upset. I know it looks as though I spent a fortune, but truly it wasn't all that much. I had a friend in Florida who thought he owed me a favor and…"

"She had the jeweler use the diamonds from the princess ring she got on her eighteenth birthday from her parents," Melissa blurted out.

"Melissa!" Amanda turned to Garry with a wry smile of guilt.

"Mandy, you sacrificed a gift from your parents for me. You shouldn't have."

"Well, if Melissa hadn't opened her big mouth!" She sent Melissa a narrowed glance. "But I wanted to. I was always misplacing the ring anyway. Now, I'll know where it is. I even melted the gold ring so it all could stay together. Smart idea, huh?"

Garry was so choked, he couldn't even smile. But he tried to jest. "I suppose when you want your ring back, I'm without a cane."

"Not a chance. It'll always be where I want it to be… with you."

His heart felt a twinge of pain then. *With you, Mandy… that's where I want to be.*

The orchestra was winding down, finishing its arrangement of *Green Eyes.* Garry stood, his handsome cane beside him. "It works," he said humorously. "Now if this fool could just learn to walk with it." The orchestra struck up another number, a composition based on an old Bunny Bennigan arrangement, the trumpet soloist Warren Luening leading the song with passionate skill. Garry moved his head around to Robbie. "Is there an instruction book in that box? I think Amanda is supposed to assist me to the dance floor, let me try this thing out."

Robbie sent him a big grin. "Yep. It's in the rulebook. I read it."

Amanda rose from her chair. "Guess I can't break the rules," she said taking Garry's outstretched hand.

Together they walked from the table, both glancing back at Robbie, then catching Miriam's empty chair as they stepped to the dance floor. Garry placed his free hand on her waist, brought her closer, welcoming her hands on him. He smiled and she smiled. And they danced, even though he couldn't step with any kind of grace. He began to sing softly in her ear as the band played an old Ira Gershwin title—*I Can't Get Started (With You)*.

His eyes held light humor, as did hers, until the end of the song. She'd joined in on those last words, harmonizing with his voice, feeling the extent of what they sang.

Applause echoed around them as the music stopped, but it was the clapping in his heart that caused him to grab Amanda and hug her with all of his might. Little did he know, his mother stepped in and quietly took a seat.

# 44.

# WE'VE GOT TONIGHT

MIRIAM HAD PURPOSE in returning to the table. Garry should have known. She'd gotten over being upset, determined more than ever to save her son from making the biggest mistake of his life. She spoke with Robbie for a bit, her conversation mellow and light, but then she commented how late it was for little boys to be up. She suggested that Sweetwater escort Robbie to their suite of rooms where Nicolas, too, had retired for the night.

The moment the boy was gone, Miriam played her cards nefariously while the cheerful smile on her face never wavered. She socialized with others about Amanda's brilliant ploy to deceive Garry—her nonchalant comments crudely degrading. And while she sent Amanda on a journey of shame, Miriam also approached the eligible men in the room to dote on Amanda's intellect and beauty. "And she's quite single, too," she'd say with a wink. Garry was clenching teeth when Miriam invited a flock of women to the table, bragging about her rehabilitated son. "And tonight, he's giving free autographs, ladies." That sent a dozen more women to the table, entrapping Garry between feminine bodies for a long while. Miriam had even baited him in taking a couple of women to the floor for a dance. Amanda was asked by several men to dance, one in particular who wouldn't take no for an answer. One who snuggled a bit too closely for Garry's liking. Before the night was through, Garry's and Amanda's relationship was tense.

Though Melissa had tried to help in situations throughout the night, she tended only to make things worse. Playing against mother was like playing in fire, mother's torch burning even as Amanda made her excuse to retire for the night. Melissa started to get up to follow.

"Melissa dear, no need to walk Amanda to her room. Can't you see she has an escort?" Melissa took note of the man at Amanda's heels, the one who had danced too close for Garry's comfort. Garry's gaze was aimed straight at him. He was trying to get up from the table himself, if only the two women at his arms would let go and stop smothering him with questions and flirtatious conversation. "Sit down, Melissa. Douglas will take good care of Amanda. He's been a gentleman all night. He'll make sure she returns to her room safely."

Douglas appeared to be no gentleman to Garry. He couldn't believe Amanda allowed the man to guide her away. She only just met him! That ancient green emotion ate at his gut. It was one thing to watch another man touch her, but if one should attempt a kiss, he'd—

"Garry, I say we call it a night, ole buddy!" Dan shouted over the noise. "Early day tomorrow. Melissa and I are beat."

Yes! His escape. He rose from the table, only to realize the band was motioning him over. "Dan, you and Melissa go ahead. I'll say a few words to the band and make my way out. Send me a hotel staff person so I can leave privately." He noticed his mother and Frank heading out themselves, the two retiring to their own room, separate from the large bedroom suite the rest of them were sharing.

Just when Garry thought he'd shaken the last hand and was finally on his way with his hotel staff escort, another hotel gentleman approached, informing him of an urgent phone call.

Reluctantly he took it after being led into a small conference room for privacy. He braced himself for a troublesome conversation with Daphne. It wasn't a good time for any conversation as his emotions were dangerously strained. The voice on the line was authoritative and male. There was no mistaking who it was. His ire ignited doubly.

"It's time for her to come home, Danzlo. Make tomorrow short."

Garry's hand shook on the receiver. He was weary, his right leg and hip burned with a dull ache, and he was damn tired of being antagonized at every turn. "Where the hell do you get off telling me what to do, Chandler! You don't own her, nor is she in love with you."

Eddie paused. "She belongs with me, Danzlo. She's not safe there. For more reasons than one."

Garry froze. "What are you talking about?" An anonymal fear surmounted in his gut. Something he heard in the voice. "If she's in some kind of trouble, I want to know. I'm fully capable of providing—"

"You need only know that Miss Dimont is up to no good. I've been able to hold her off, up to this point. She's your business now. She can't let things go. If you don't want Amanda hurting more than she's already going to hurt, I suggest you have her and the boy ready by late afternoon tomorrow. Tuesday will be too late. I'll be at your place. I'm bringing them home."

Garry had a million questions, yet one thought took precedence. "Over my dead body." His voice, stern and gruff, was just as menacing as Eddie's.

"Watch what you say, Danzlo. You might get your wish."

Garry's mouth pinched tight. "Is that a threat?"

Eddie chuckled. "I hate to disappoint you, bro, but it's not my threat. You've another enemy more ominous to worry about." He paused, his voice less intimidating. "Amanda loves you. Take that gift for what it's worth. I can appreciate your love for her. I'm asking that you do what's best. You can trust me to take care of her. I'll be calling her in the morning."

The phone clicked and Garry crumpled against a conference table, his cane dropping to the floor. He lowered himself into a chair and bent forward, his elbows on his thighs, his head collapsed in his hands. He felt tortured and drained, too many vampires sucking his energy, creating a hell he couldn't escape.

*Life without Mandy.* Nothing could hurt worse. Yet if she wasn't safe… for more reasons than one, Chandler had said. What the hell did he mean? It was one thing not knowing what Daphne had up her sleeve, but another to realize there was more he knew nothing about. He wanted to scream, tear something up. His fists clenched against his temples. He prayed for control, for grace, for some peace of mind.

But his mind played war games as he took the elevator to his hotel suite. He opened the door and walked slowly through the dimly lit room, nearly tripping over the two in the floor, Sweetwater Jones and Robbie, both asleep and lying on pallets, their bodies covered with blankets. What was Sweetwater doing here and why weren't they sleeping on the sofa sleepers in the room? Garry could only guess. They were "roughing it" indoors, part of the make-believe adventure Robbie thought he was on. And no doubt, Sweetwater, who'd grown fond of the boy and his zesty imagination, went along with Robbie's adventurous game. Garry was surprised no teepee was set up in the room.

He approached his bedroom quietly, hesitating at the door, his gaze on another one just beyond it. Unable to fight the temptation, nor did he want to fight it, he found himself facing it. He blinked back discomfort, the emotional kind, as well as the physical. He tried the knob, but it was locked. *I just want to see her that's all.* He reached into his left pants pocket to pull out the lock pick he always kept there. He suddenly remembered the gift—the small one Amanda hadn't opened yet. He'd taken it off the table, slipped it into his coat pocket right before their dance, forgotten in all the night's ruckus. He would quietly place it on the pillow beside her. She'd wake up to it and open it in the morning.

He opened the door, realizing instantly that Amanda wasn't in her bed. The lights were out and nothing stirred in the room. Dread, like he'd never known, gushed through him, just before he glimpsed her silhouette by the balcony doors. She was staring out at the night, the moonlight and the stars beaming upon her skin and the sheer, white negligee she wore. His palms began to sweat and he quietly took off his coat and laid it on a nearby chair. He advanced toward her. She never moved, her gaze unwavering from the moon.

"Not as beautiful as you are," he spoke softly behind her.

Her shoulders quaked at his voice, and she hesitated before circling to meet his face. When she did, it was only inches from his. They stood with shallow breath, waiting. "You shouldn't be here," she finally said.

His gaze fell to her lips. "No, I shouldn't," he whispered. She leaned forward in her weakened state, her nipples like pebbles against his chest; she pulled back with an intake of breath. Their gazes met. Then she moved to retrieve her robe from the chair where his jacket lay. "Don't," he pleaded, catching her by the hand. He urged her back. "Please, Mandy."

She trembled. "Garry…"

"Shh," he hushed her softly, bringing her close. He lifted her hair from her neck, and his lips descended there. His nose nuzzled beneath her earlobe. She grabbed his arms, lest she fall as his lips brushed her neck, her shoulder, his fingers delicately pushing away the strap of her gown and traveling down the side of one breast. His thumb circled it, balancing a nipple while his mouth and nose caressed the soft valley of both breasts. He went down on his knees, gently laying his beloved cane on the floor. His face nestled against the sheer fabric of her gown as he embraced her body with both his hands. He held her against his face, cherishing the moment, cherishing her. Then his shoulders began to convulse, like his heart was breaking.

Amanda was heart stricken. She cuddled his head against her belly, tears sliding down her face and sprinkling across her bare breast.

She closed her eyes as his arms moved about her, enfolding her body more tightly, her own hands molding him closer to her warmth. And he reveled in that warmth until all her tears subsided, and he kissed her hands, her arms, bringing her down on her knees before him. He cupped her face in his hands, smiling down at her. "My pretty brown-eyed girl," he said, his thumbs grazing her bottom lip, "your mouth too sweet and luscious not to kiss." His lips took hers tenderly, tasting their delicious nectar. He released them and spoke words so close, they tickled her lips. "You're amazing. Have I ever told you that?"

Amanda swallowed his breath. "I don't think so. Maybe so. I don't remember."

He smiled at her innocence. "You've got me on my knees, woman. What now?"

She stood on her own bended knees musing over his question. "What options do I have?"

"Are we playing naughty or nice?" he asked. "Naughty means you'll help me back up, and then politely ask me to leave."

"Oh?" she said with a lift of a brow. "And nice would be?"

"Throwing me down on the floor and having your way with me."

"Ah… and I suppose there aren't any more options?"

He sighed heavily. "I cannot tell a lie. There is one more. We could sit here on the floor and let you open the other present I got you. It's in my coat pocket."

"My present? You have it! I thought I'd lost—"

"Uh-oh, I see the third option is your choice. I should've never opened my big mouth. I could be lying on the floor right now…"

She eased him down to sit, his attention on that bare breast she had yet to cover. But his pleasure was short lived as she sat on the floor beside him, adjusting her nightgown. Catching his intent look, her cheeks heightened in color. He smiled at her, and then stretched back to retrieve his jacket off the chair. "Alright, here it is. I'm afraid it's not as creative as the cane you gave me, but it's the thought that counts."

"Ha! I have a feeling it's the present that counts by the sly look on your face. If this jumps out and—"

"I beg you, throw me on the floor and have your way with me!"

"I'll more than have my way with you," she promised, removing the ties from the box. She opened the lid slowly, peeking teasingly, and there within lay a dainty gold necklace. Dangling from it was a small gold heart, a key, and a musical note.

"Allow me," he said, taking the necklace from the box. He unlatched its hook and placed it around her neck, his cheek against hers in the process. Then he looked into her eyes and began to tell her what his gift to her represented.

"This is my heart," he said, picking up the dangling gold that hung about her neck. "The heart you touched and healed." His eyes didn't waver from hers as he felt the shape of the key between his thumb and forefinger. "This the key, Mandy, that let you in. And the musical note," his eyes smiling into hers while grasping it, "represents the wild and crazy music we played together. How's that for a representation?"

Her voice came out no more than a whisper. "Th-The best. Thank you." She leaned forward to place a chaste kiss on his cheek, but he was too fast, catching it swiftly on his lips. "Gotcha," he teased with a wink of an eye, reminding her he'd played the same stunt last night in front of Robbie. But that reminder only led to another—the beautiful feeling she felt when the three of them were together. *Gotcha*, it sang in her mind. "Do you, Garry? Will you keep me?" she asked seriously. She watched his smile disappear.

He then grabbed his cane, lifting himself off the floor. "Mandy, it's late. I need to go."

"That's not how you felt five minutes ago. You were ready to be ravished on the floor."

His gaze met hers uncomfortably. "It was just play, Mandy. I came to bring you your present, nothing more."

"Just who are you trying to fool? Me or yourself?"

"I said it's late. Goodnight."

"Oh, I get it," she said, rising, taking hold of his arm before he stepped away. "Tonight, you walk out on me. By week's end, I walk out on you. It's all in the game." The muscle in his arm corded beneath her hand. He realized she thought she had a few days left. If only she knew what he did. "Why don't you just tell me now, Garry? Get it over with. Say you don't want me. You've said it before."

He seized her waist and brought her body hard against his. "You know I want you! Do you think this is easy for me?" She whimpered as his groin hardened against her. "See, I'm hot and ready for you, baby." She started to struggle against him, but he held on fast. "Yes, my body wants you. It keeps remembering our first night together, remembering the beauty of becoming one with you, Mandy. But it's my heart that loves you, girl, and the memory it keeps that guarantees I always will." Amanda was no longer fighting him; she was clinging to him. "You read me so well, Mandy. You know I'm going to send you away. And you know it's not because I don't want you. You only said it so I might be honest with you, and with myself. It's true I have doubts in your marrying a musician and the hectic and sometimes lonely, though very public life it entails. It didn't seem to matter to me until it was you who I realized I wanted to spend my life with. I love you too much to see you hurt. And Mom will always be there to taunt you. You're wrong if you think she'll stay out of our lives. And Daphne's not giving up so easily either."

She was about to say something, but hesitated.

"Go ahead, Mandy, tell me I have another reason. You know I do. And you understand. Perhaps more than I do myself. I'm a Jewish boy at heart. It was drilled in my young head what to believe, and what not to believe. I've an obligation. Somewhere it says we should marry our own kind. And what is the reason for keeping us separate? So that we would not stray from Him and bring more sin in our lives? Yet all I see is that it was you who brought me away from my sins and closer to the Man upstairs. I've been blessed with skillful hands and a talented mind, and I'm just now realizing who I need to thank. And I thank Him for you, Mandy. I thank Him for this one chance, this one moment I can touch you and tell you how I really feel. In my heart, you are my bride and always will be. I love you and I cherish you, for better, for worse, for richer, for poorer, in sickness and in health, all the days of my life."

Tears streamed down her face—happy tears, sad ones. "And I love you, Garry," she said, clutching his arms steadfastly, "and I cherish you, for better, for worse, for richer, for poorer, in sickness and in health, all the days of my life."

"Again, Mandy. Tell me again."

Her arms went around his neck. "I love you, Garry. I love you with all of my heart and more." She kissed him, and he kissed her. Then he tossed his cane upon a pillow on the bed. He bent down and lifted her up into his arms.

"May God bless us," he said against her lips, and then carried her to the bed, barely limping. He placed her gently down upon the covers beside his jeweled cane, throwing off his shirt, unzipping his pants. Then he sat on the bed on his knees, straddling her legs, tugging at the string that unloosened her gown. It slowly opened to reveal her voluptuous breasts. He touched them with his hands, watching his fingers walk down her soft skin, across her slim belly, spreading wide to the V-strapped lace panties. His gaze lifted. She was watching him avidly. "Oh, yes, Mandy, I want you. The magic... *everything.*"

She lifted her shoulders and reached for him, bringing him down upon her body.

"Ah yes, sweet girl. Show me. Show me, baby."

She wrapped her arms around his arms, her legs around his legs, and she kissed his lips, his face, touching him, loving him. "Mandy... oh, Mandy," he whispered upon her soft skin, his moistened lips traveling down her body to places he'd never been. "I love you, I love you," he said a thousand times, or though it seemed when she turned him over, his cane placed upon the floor so she might climb atop him. And she kissed his skin, suckling him with moistened lips that traveled down his body to places she'd never been. And he welcomed it, every touch of her hands, every touch of her tongue, her mouth. He swam in its praise till he could stand no more, and he grabbed her up and made her his—his flesh within her flesh—and they drank each other's tears, becoming one in mind, and one in spirit, their silent screams swelling within to orgasmic peaks, crowned and glorified in their names.

Tonight they had each other. Tomorrow they'd say goodbye.

# 45.

# PUT YOUR DREAMS AWAY

"Amanda, you awake?"

Melissa had tried knocking on the door, but there was no answer. Finding it unlocked, she walked in, halting as Amanda sprang up in bed, her ample breasts bouncing free from the sheet. Her eyes searched the bed as if she expected someone beside her. Snatching the sheet, she covered her nakedness and sent Melissa a wry smile.

Melissa shut the door with her back, her gaze riveted on the pink silk cravat lying on the floor, Garry's white dinner jacket atop a sheer robe on the chair. "I see you've been busy." Melissa smiled, and then her expression turned grave. "You have a phone call. It's Eddie."

"Eddie? But why... how—"

"I don't know. He said everything was fine."

"Alright," she said, plowing through the covers as though looking for her clothes. She pulled out Garry's sock instead.

"Looking for these?" Melissa plucked a pair of white lace panties off the bedside lamp. Here, you take this, I'll take the sock. Garry's in the other room with only one sock on... talking to Eddie."

Amanda was scrounging through her suitcase for her rust-colored robe, the sheer one inappropriate to wear with other guests in the suite. "*What?* Garry's talking to Eddie? What on earth for?"

"I don't know. We got to the phone about the same time, even though I was standing next to it. I barely got a chance to hear Eddie's voice before he jerked the phone out of my hand. Garry rushed to the only room the cord would allow, shutting the door behind him."

Amanda was out of her room in seconds. She spotted the telephone cord, a tight trail to the bathroom.

She banged her fist against the door. "Garry? Don't I have a phone call? Let me in!"

"Amanda, we have another bathroom," Robbie said behind her.

She turned and leaned against the bathroom door, taking in Robbie's adorable face. He was still in his pajamas sitting in his wheelchair. Nicolas stood behind him, his forehead creased in severe lines. "Morning, sweetie. I just need to use the phone." Then the door opened behind her. She fell in, the phone dropping to the floor as Garry tried catching her. But like a caught rabbit, Amanda capered in his arms, attempting to escape so she could catch the phone from dropping on the ceramic tile floor. "Eddie, you still there?" she said gasping, reeling in the cord and bringing the receiver to her ear. "Hold on a sec, okay?"

The curly phone cord bounced like a slinky from her hand as she tried maneuvering in Garry's arms. She was suddenly staring into his face, her neck stretched back to accommodate his height. Her breath caught as their night of lovemaking came flooding to her mind and body. She could tell that Garry was affected likewise—the sultry gaze, the rigidity in his pants that felt so hot against her. But then he suddenly let her go, allowing her to find her own way of salvaging a fall. "Yes, Eddie's on the phone," he said. Then he limped away, leaving his cane against the tub. She watched him disappear. He shut the door behind him, leaving her enclosed with the telephone. She placed it on her ear. "Eddie?"

"Amanda…"

There was something eerie in the way he spoke her name. The timbre of his voice was different somehow, lacking its usual smoothness and strength. Something in his deep, masculine voice wasn't quite Eddie. She waited patiently for him to speak again, allowing the seconds to tick by until he was ready to continue.

"You're coming home."

His voice chilled her to the bone.

"Eddie, are you okay? Talk to me."

An awkward silence fell, seeming to confirm her suspicions, but then he began to speak rather frankly, though with some compassion. "I'm fine, Amanda. It's you I'm worried about. Listen to what I'm saying… it's time to come home."

It was a warning. He would never tell her everything, not if he thought it would protect her from hurt or harm. It used to make her so very angry. "Eddie,

I'm not ready yet. I'm not ready to—"

"Danzlo and I have already made arrangements. He's concerned for your welfare as much as I am. I'll have to remember to thank him one day."

"What are you talking about? What arrangements?"

"I want you to enjoy your day. I'll see you this evening."

The click on the line was like a rattle through her body, shaking her senselessly while her skin grew numb. *I'm leaving this evening?*

Amanda sprang from the bathroom, colliding with Melissa. She slung the phone in Melissa's gut and vaulted for Garry's bedroom, slamming the door behind her.

Garry turned with a calm face, unaffected by her abrupt intrusion. In fact, he expected it. He stood with nothing on but a pair of boxer shorts and a towel hanging about his neck. "I was going to take a shower, but if you'd like to join me..."

"Start talking, Garry!"

He contemplated how much he should tell her, not too sure he could tell her anything while she stood in front of him with her robe coming undone. He'd swear she wore nothing beneath it. His eyes must have given him away, for she quickly readjusted her robe and tightened the belt. "Nothing much to tell, except that Eddie will be escorting you home."

Amanda blinked. Astonishment, fear, and panic on her face. "And just whose plan was this? Yours or his?"

"I think I can safely say the plan is his and mine. His first; it was a little harder for me to settle on it. But I don't want you going home alone. Eddie will take care of you. You and Robbie. And who knows, maybe the three of you can..." he swallowed uncomfortably and turned to the suitcase on his bed, "you know."

"*You're giving me to another man?* How chivalric of you! And I didn't even get to choose. Ah, shucks!'"

He turned at her sarcasm. But it was hurt he saw on her face. And angst, evident in her trembling form and varying voice tone. She knew as much as he did that there time together was coming to an end. "It's time to be honest with each other, Mandy. You don't really know me, not outside of this safe little world we've created here in Colorado. Outside it, in L.A., I live a hectic life. It can be exhilarating at times, but very busy. And what do I know of you? Visibly, you've a past with Eddie. You nearly knocked me down, trying to get to him on the phone. What am I to think? I'm starting to wonder if I know you at all. What are your secrets, Mandy?

Besides the phony glasses and makeup you've been hiding behind for weeks?"

This was it. Amanda's breath caught. She swallowed back her pride, her fear, but couldn't stop the tears from slipping down her cheeks.

"It wasn't just the glasses and makeup, Garry. But all of the clothes as well. I never dress that way. I'd never wear…" she glanced down at the rust-colored robe, "… these horrid colors and—"

"What the *hell* are you telling me?" Garry's face grew ashen, the scar on his right cheek shining like glistening silver. "Good God! I thought you were going to confess a bit of your past with Eddie. Not to find out you've been lying to me from day one!"

"Garry, I'm sorry! I never meant to…" She attempted to step toward him, but he abruptly stepped back, nearly tripping over himself.

"Don't!" he said, holding up one trembling hand, his other latching onto the window frame behind him for support. His head lowered, she knew he couldn't bear to look at her now. "Seems my role is always the fool," he said. "What did you do? Go in cahoots with my father before he pulled the trigger, so you might carry on his legacy?"

"What an awful thing to say!" she cried, causing his gaze to shift uncomfortably. But even then, he looked past her shoulder and toward the door. His eyes were glassy and she knew he was hurting deeply. "I didn't know your father before I came to you. Had I known, things may have happened differently. I thought it was for your best and highest good at the time. I came not knowing that I would love you. That you would love me back. It's still me, Garry, that woman inside. Please, please look at me."

His eyes fused with hers then. But he couldn't say anything. Doubt, confusion, and love all abiding there.

"I tried to tell you many times, Garry. I wanted to so badly. Even last night, I had good intentions to, but I was selfish. The night was too special. I didn't want to ruin the memory we were sharing together and—"

"I thought you were special," Garry broke in, and she knew by his solemn tone that his words had nothing to do with last night. She sighed deeply, allowing him the moment, for she knew he had other words to say. "I accepted you for all the things I thought you were. Your wit and charm blew me away, and it didn't matter how varied and eccentric your taste in clothes, or how many times you got under my skin with your zany ways and annoying harassment. I learned to love it all. But now…"

"But now?" she bit down on her lower lip.

Garry saw the gesture and blinked. "The truth? I don't think it would matter if you were red, green, or blue. Whoever you are or how much I might try not to love you, I'd still want to kiss those lips of yours and wrap your body next to mine."

With one intake of breath, Amanda flung herself toward him, her lips on his face, his chin, his mouth. And for a brief moment Garry gave in, but just as quickly pushed her away. "The plans haven't changed, Mandy. Eddie will take care of you."

She stumbled back. He may as well have slapped her in the face. He was still giving her to Eddie. Her face grew hot as she tried to blink back the hurt reeling inside her. "I can take care of myself, thank you very much!" She straighten, raised her chin.

"And Robbie? If you plan to adopt him, he needs a father. I should know. Eddie can be that father."

Amanda began to panic. "What happened to... *loving* me? And you know nothing of Eddie. For all you know, he could be—"

"I know as much about Eddie as I probably know about you now."

Her eyes flittered, painfully so. His fingers lifted and brushed her cheek warmly.

"I'm sorry, Mandy. I didn't mean that in a hurtful way. But something's terribly wrong here. Your friend Eddie isn't willing to share with me all that he knows, and what he says you're unaware of yourself. I have to trust this and what I'm feeling in my gut. I know that Eddie showed up when you were in danger of drowning. How did he know you were in danger? How did he know you were here? It makes me wonder how many other times he's been there for you. No, don't tell me. Your eyes speak the answer. But then, so did your voice that day of the accident when you called out his name. If I'm wrong, Mandy, tell me now, but Eddie would never hurt you. Am I right?"

Amanda hesitated, her eyes misting with tears. She shook her head. "No. Not on purpose."

Garry weighed the uncertainty on her face. "If he's hurt you in the past, Mandy, he must be sorry. Any man who loves you would have to be. Guess Eddie and I have some things in common. Only, I've never had much luck on white steeds. He's got me on that one."

Amanda stepped forward. "Garry, you'll always be my hero. You hold my heart in your hands. Eddie can't say that. And what's a girl without a heart?"

Garry looked down at his empty hands. "A man without the rest of you?" His gaze lifted to her face, she felt the hurt of his words. "Don't cry, Mandy. I'm doing this for you. Respect that. You did what you felt was best for me. Now it's my turn. Only, maybe this is best for both of us." He tried to smile. "We got a bum deal. Too many complications. According to Eddie, Daphne's up to no good and my mother will always try to come between us. I'm one of those crazy musicians who loves his work and has little privacy in his life. And you're a marvelous healer and teacher who needs to focus on a little boy who loves you and is depending on you to be his mother." Garry wiped at her tears. "We still have today. Now quickly, go dress. Our time's too precious to waste."

"But Garry, you can't expect me to leave tonight. Eddie said tonight. Please tell me it's not true. I'll be too upset. I'll—" he took hold of her arms, escorting her backwards to the door. "I'm not going with him, Garry. I tell you I'm not."

"Read my lips, Mandy. You are and you will."

"You can't make me! You can't make me do anything!"

"Watch me." He pushed her out the room and shut the door in her face.

Outraged, Amanda turned and confronted an audience. Five anxious expressions revealed they were all waiting her next act. Robbie's lips were pursed, his head tilted to one side in total confusion.

"Are we gonna have fun today or what?" she burst out ecstatically. "I can hardly wait!" Melissa stood nearby still holding the phone against her gut with one hand. Amanda snatched her free hand. "Come, Melissa, help me pick out something to wear!" Melissa flew in one direction, the phone snapping from her hand taking flight in another. The phone clanged to the floor.

# 46.

# IF YOU LOVE ME,
# REALLY LOVE ME

*THIS IS JUST a dream,* Amanda thought as she placed her suitcases upon the rose silk coverlet on her bed. She was back at the log home in the room she loved—or so it seemed like home these past weeks. After the morning episode, Garry had taken Robbie aside and had a long talk with him. They both came out of his bedroom red-eyed and smiling, and ready to make the best of their last day's mini-tour of Colorado. And though the day seemed much too short for Amanda, they did manage to take in some breathtaking sights as they traveled along a scenic route. Garry had forgiven her deceit, yet his hurt was still new, so their moments together felt different, strained. She was glad that Robbie was having a great time, though, particularly during their stop at America's only mountain zoo on beautiful Cheyenne Mountain. They'd returned home late afternoon, the house now morbidly quiet.

*He'll tell me to stay. He won't let me go. Or at the least, he'll say our parting is only temporary. He'll call me. We'll meet.*

But even as she thought the words, she knew she'd be out of his life within the hour. Eddie was on his way.

A knock sounded, and Amanda spun on her heel, her sight on the brass doorknob. It didn't turn. Melissa would've tried the knob. Garry, too.

"Amanda?"

*Miriam.* She hesitated, and then warily opened the door. She expected the woman to smile in triumph with one glimpse of the open suitcases on the bed. But she saw no smile, Miriam's eyes dim, her face somber. "Can I come in?" she asked.

"Of course," Amanda said, moving aside.

Miriam took a few steps in, and then turned. She stood poised in front of

Amanda a long moment without speaking. "You're doing the right thing, Amanda," she finally said. "I know it's hard for you to understand right now. You're a good woman, a natural healer. One needs only to be in a room with you. You're kind and loving. Believe me when I say, I don't knock you for not being Jewish. I can respect you for who you are. But," Miriam brushed a tear from her eye, her voice dragging shakily, "I don't want you changing my son anymore than you already have. I see good changes in him, yet you're such an influence, I'm afraid he'll forget who he is, what he is. What he's been taught to believe in."

Amanda stepped forward. Miriam stepped back. The gesture shocked Amanda as well as disheartened her. "I'm sorry, I didn't mean to. I've never tried to take your son away from his birthright, nor sway his beliefs in any way. I—"

"No, you don't have to!" Miriam said a little too harshly. "Because you're an example sitting atop his pedestal, and every moment he sits and admires, he learns from you, drinks from you, only to love you even more."

"I'm no idol," Amanda said. "We're only two people in love. I admire him as well. I learn from him, only to love him even more. We make our own choices because we have free will. We don't always make the right ones, but that's how we learn. Sometimes we have to do what we feel is right. Sometimes, that's all we have to follow."

"Then I'll leave it as that, for my son has followed his heart and has asked you to go." Miriam's words struck painfully. She turned and walked to the door. Hesitating, she looked back over her shoulder. "I'm sorry, Amanda. If my son hadn't asked you to leave, then I would've asked you to. I do appreciate everything you've done for him. I thank God for you actually. Unfortunately, life doesn't always have happy endings."

Miriam left, and Amanda felt overwhelmed with loss. She forced herself to the dresser, crying all the while she emptied the drawers.

GARRY'S FINGERS LIGHTLY weighed upon the keys of his piano, playing an occasional melody as he sat alone in the music room. Robbie was in the kitchen with Nicolas baking cookies, so that he and Amanda could take them on his trip back home.

Garry thought about helping Amanda pack, just to be with her, but she'd probably take it the wrong way. He didn't want her thinking he was rushing her out the door.

He lightly struck a couple of ivory keys and a black one consecutively. He rocked back and forth on a few, checking out their sound, creating a melody to suit his mood.

His fingers ceased their melodic walk as he sensed someone behind him.

"I've got papers for you to sign," Dan said.

It wasn't whom he had hoped.

"You're looking pretty bad," Dan said, his head tilted. "Want me to fix you a drink?"

"I'll be okay. I just want this over with. And then I'm going back to California."

Dan sighed, tossing some papers on the bench beside him. "Robbie's adoption papers. A lot of money you're giving away. Have you told Amanda yet?"

"No. I want to make sure everything goes through first. I don't want her upset just in case something goes wrong."

"I wouldn't be too worried. Dr. Conyers has given Amanda an excellent reference, not to mention the pull he has as chairman on their committee. And it's not every day a famous celebrity puts out the money for an adopted son for a woman he's not even going to marry."

Garry winced at the remark.

"Sorry, I didn't mean to rub it in."

"They had better keep my dealings with this adoption confidential," he said, picking up the papers. He took the pen Dan had ready for him. He began signing.

A loud commotion stirred from the hallway. He and Dan exchanged a curious glance before setting their sights on Melissa who was suddenly leaning against the threshold gasping, her expression full of warning. Then Daphne barged her way through, the tall blonde taking up space in the room.

Garry grabbed his cane and stood. He watched as Daphne's staunch manner changed before his eyes, shock plastered across her beautiful features.

"Garry," she said breathlessly, a genuine tear forming in her eye. "Darling, you're standing. That's wonderful."

It was an awkward moment for Garry. For the first time in a long while, he sensed authentic happiness in those sapphire eyes of hers. In that one moment he could believe she actually did love him. Somewhere beneath all that haughtiness and selfishness she wore was a woman with a heart that could love like everyone else.

She came at him so quickly, he nearly stumbled, unable to stop the kiss she planted on his mouth, his hand grasping her waist to keep his balance. As he tore from the kiss, he saw Amanda's disheartened face in the doorway watching, the hurt in her eyes slicing right through him. Daphne turned and saw her too. She took in the slim-fitting jeans and red button-down shirt Amanda wore.

"Well, well, if it isn't the little miracle worker. No longer in your Cinderella rags, I see. So what role are you playing for Garry this week?"

"That's enough, Daphne. If you're here to talk, talk to me and make it quick. This is between you and me. *Only.*" His gaze caught Melissa's and Amanda's, his head gesturing a nod, urging both women to leave. But then Daphne pulled a folder from her large, shiny gold pocketbook, throwing it to the floor. Its contents spilled out and scattered in front of Garry's feet.

"What do you think of her now, darling? She's never been who you thought she was."

Garry stared down, at first angry and annoyed. A couple of dozen newspaper clippings spread out before him. He hadn't realized how involved Amanda had been in her husband's murder case. One headline revealed she'd actually been a suspect. But the most taunting news was the fact that Eddie Chandler's name seemed to be everywhere hers was. He'd served as her defense lawyer, and apparently, her lover. To his chagrin, more than half the pictures portrayed the two of them together, intimately.

"What the hell are you trying to pull, Daphne?" Dan said, bending down to gather up the papers. "This is bullshit. Garry of all people would not believe such scandalous articles." Dan attempted to scoop one last clipping off the floor, but Garry tacked it down with his cane, his gaze glued to it.

"Get out, Daphne!" Garry commanded, never raising his face, else he chance a look at Amanda. And he wasn't quite ready to deal with that yet. "Get out," he said again, "I think you've done enough damage for the day."

"Of course," she said. "You need time to think. But I really believe you need to reconsider—"

"Amanda's leaving within the hour and won't be back." His face lifted then, sending Daphne affirmation that his words were true. He had to question his motive in telling her this. Was he protecting Amanda from any more harm that Daphne may have planned, or was he trying to punish Amanda for the lies she had told him?

He was suddenly looking at that woman he'd grown to love, drawn to her face like he knew he would be. He hated that he could feel so much intimacy, even now. Affected by the confusion on her face, some hurt, and some guilt—surely that's what he was seeing behind the pursed lips, the wide eyes that turned down at the corners.

He lowered his eyes. "Everyone leave, please." He waited as footsteps receded from the room, his hand shaking on the cane while his eyes bored a hole into the black and white photo lying on the floor. Amanda in Eddie's arms, embraced in a passionate kiss. DEADLY AFFAIR, FATHER OF BABY, the headline read. According to the article, they'd been having an affair for years. There was speculation whether the child she lost the year before was truly her husband's.

"It's not what it seems, Garry," Amanda said, entering the room.

Her voice vibrated like a volcano inside him. He pivoted on his cane as she made her way beside him. He gazed into her worried eyes. "Pictures say words, Amanda. They don't lie... like you evidently have." He mocked her with a feminine tone. *"I don't know what's wrong me. I've only had one man in my life,"* he mimicked. *"I was a virgin on my wedding night, can you believe it?"* He loomed over her. "Why the hell would you tell me something like that? Did you want me to think you so innocent, feel sorry for you because the only man you'd ever bedded was dead? Did you think I might love you more? Or were you trying to cover your other lie. *We're just friends, Garry.* Only thing is, you forgot to mention you were *fucking* friends!"

His breath swept across her hot face. Her feet trembled in her shoes. Angrily she said, "I don't have to listen to this. I've got packing to do."

She started for the door, but he grabbed her wrist. "Oh, now you're ready to go," he hissed, pulling her back to him. "Maybe I should get one last quickie before you jump into bed with Eddie tonight."

She slapped him hard across the cheek, her eyes sharp with anger. He adjusted his jaw, and rubbed the sting from his face.

"If you believe that, then you don't know me at all."

"You're right. I've never known the real you, have I?" He stood back and raised his arms to an invisible crowd. "Will the real Amanda Fields please stand up?"

Disappointment and hurt stood clear in her eyes. "If you don't see her now, Garry, then maybe you never will."

She walked away.

AMANDA RAN TO her room, so tired of feeling hurt and shedding tears. She was focused too much on what she couldn't have. So that's all she got. More tears, more insecurity. More hurt. She'd given her all to Paul and received nothing in return. From Garry, she'd thought she'd received everything. Only, she was wrong. She hadn't received his trust.

Okay, so pictures rarely lie. She *was* kissing Eddie in the photo, a very passionate kiss, one he'd stolen at a very trying and emotional time during the court trials. She knew Eddie loved her and he'd respected her space up to that point. He'd been so caring and thoughtful of her feelings all through those long months. True, there were things about him she didn't understand, behavioral changes she'd begun to see, strange reactions that seemed almost beyond his control. But she'd given into his kiss that day. She had needed it. If for just one moment. A moment that had cost her yet another scandal in the newspapers. And now, Garry's distrust.

She grasped the handles of her suitcases and looked around the rose colored room one last time. She closed her eyes, grateful for the memories—the good ones she could take back home with her.

A knock sounded on the door. Melissa peeked in, and even though it wasn't the person she had hoped to see, she was happy that she was looking at the friend who'd made all her memories possible. "I see you're ready," Melissa said. "Eddie's here. Robbie's keeping him busy with stories of his Colorado adventures."

Amanda nodded, attempting to smile. "And Garry?"

Melissa moved closer toward her. "He's in the great room with everyone else. I think he found the courage for Robbie. I'm sorry Daphne spoiled your last hour with him. Eddie said she wasn't supposed to come until tomorrow, the reason he was getting you tonight. Eddie missed seeing her, just short of minutes." Melissa sighed sadly. "We're all upset that you're leaving. Poor Nicolas, he's overwrought."

"Nicolas," she said, choked with emotion. "I'm going to miss him so much, Melissa." She broke into tears. "Like I'll miss you." Amanda dropped her luggage to the floor, the two women flinging their arms around each other.

"I'll call. You write, okay? I want the best adventure stories ever!"

Amanda sniffed through her tears. "I promise to throw in some mystery. I know you like mystery," she said. Melissa nodded and released her, grabbing the handle of one of the suitcases. "Oh wait, Melissa. My ribbon. I left it in the bathroom on the towel rack." She rushed to get it, wiping her eyes, checking her face in the mirror. Fluffing up her hair, she tied the red silk in her hair at the base of her neck. Returning into the room, she halted just beyond the bed, for Melissa had gone, and in her place was Garry. He stood handsomely against the closed door, his right hand leaning on his cane. Their gazes locked immediately.

"You're here," she said, advancing a step.

"I'm here." And he stepped forward too.

They stood for a long moment just staring at each other. "I guess I'm ready to go now." She waited with baited breath, hoping he'd say something like, *sorry, you can't. I won't let you.*

"You look nice," he said.

She smiled graciously, though what she wanted to do was hit him for not saying, "Mandy, don't go" or "come, run away with me" or just, "shut up and kiss me."

But she realized he was tense. She was tense. "I thought about leaving my old clothes here, but I got this idea for a barn fire. You wanna come?"

He grinned. "You make me smile when I least feel like smiling. I'll miss that, Mandy."

An awkward moment passed. And then he took another step toward her. "I'm sorry, Mandy. I was angry. I was jealous. I wanted you selfishly and—"

She flew into his arms, smothering his face with kisses—her hands in his hair, on his face, upon his shoulders. He grabbed her up into his arms, cane and all, holding her against him with all of his might, relishing every wet and wonderful kiss she was giving him.

"I want you to have a sweet life," he was telling her. "A treasure of memories spent with Robbie. If your happiness includes Eddie, then so be it. I'll accept it and be thankful for all the memories you gave me. Your reasons for lying no longer matter. Perhaps you did it for me. Maybe somehow you thought—"

Her kisses ceased abruptly, replaced by hurt-filled tears and fists that pummeled against his shoulders, her body struggling for frantic release. "Get your hands off me, Garry! I want to go home. I want to go home now."

"Mandy…" he breathed, his arms pinioning her close. He tossed his cane on the bed. "Don't do this, baby. I said I was sorry. What more do you want from me?"

"Your trust, Garry! I want to be loved by someone who knows who I am. Yet since I've met you, I feel I've been lost in some crazy maze, and I keep crying out to you: 'Find me! Find me, Garry.' And I'm tired. I'm so very tired."

She fell limp against him and he caught her, grasping with hands that held her tightly. His eyes penetrated her, as though he were seeing her for the very first time.

*Déjà vu?* No. A dream? Dear God, his Eve… *was she his Eve?*

His lips were suddenly crushing hers, fervently, wildly, and she collapsed against the heat of his passion. It threatened to consume her. His arms wrapped around her, his hands kneading the fabric of her clothing as he drank in her tears thirstily, his tongue in her mouth with great depth and urgency. It was like he was searching for her, and almost finding her—though not quite.

*Not quite.*

Somehow she found the strength to push away. She was suddenly out of his grasp, their lips prickling from the heat of the kiss, weathered from his stormy onslaught.

She looked at him one last time. "Good-bye, Garry," she said.

And then she was gone. She'd closed the door and left him with only the ghost of her body in his arms, and the ghost of her kiss simmering on his lips.

Garry stumbled back against the bed, eased down on it and buried his head in his hands. With elbows on his knees, he stared down at the floor with blurred, burning eyes. It was like replaying last night, realizing he was losing her. Only tonight, he really had.

He sat on the edge of the bed for a long while, unmoving, barely breathing as realization sliced and mangled him mercilessly. Minutes ticked by miserably while his torment became a harsh melody of muffled voices that droned in his head. The indistinct sounds of car doors opening and shutting, slammed in his chest. But it was the crunch of tires receding down the graveled driveway moments later that threatened his sanity. He realized he'd finally made true his word. He had sent her away. Only this time, she'd really left, and she wasn't coming back.

His head lifted then, to the spot where he'd last held her in his arms. A scarlet ribbon lay ruffled on the floor, only inches from his feet. He leaned over and slowly picked it up, tumbling and interlacing its delicate softness through his fingers. He brought it to his face, his eyes closing to the honey fragrance that clung from her hair. "Oh, Mandy," he whispered, allowing her scent to careen through his body. "You taught me how to smile again… but what good is a smile without you to share it with?"

# *Finale:*
## THIS ONE'S FOR YOU

IT WAS THE last song of the evening, the Los Angeles audience roaring with cheers and begging for more. And though Garry would normally leave the stage and return to grace his fans with at least one more song, he couldn't bring himself to do it tonight. Tonight marked ten weeks since Amanda had walked out of his life.

When he got up from the piano, he carefully lifted his cane from the sleek shiny grand. He rarely needed his walking stick these days, for he'd mastered a stride that barely revealed any disability in that right side. Yet the cane had become more than just an occasional need after a long hard day; it was his connection to Mandy. It was always in his right hand when he left a performance. And he'd raise it in the air as though it were a gold Grammy he'd just won, the audience heightening their level of noise and excitement. Tonight was no different.

The exhilarating crowd should've lifted his spirits—and for the most part, they had over the past few weeks, his fans regarding him with new affection and admiration that bespoke their appreciation for what he'd accomplished physically, as well as musically. His comeback to the stage had seasoned his ambitions, and he'd made broader plans for his music career.

He approached the backstage curtain, signaling to his stage manager to make the night a cut, no matter that the crowd was growing louder, stomping for more. Appreciating their honor, but desperately needing some quiet, he entered his dressing room. He closed the door behind him, anticipating peace.

"Darling, you look a little out of sorts tonight. Anything I can do to help?"

His step faltered at Daphne's voice. His jaw hardened. "How did you get in here?"

"A silly question, don't you think? Everyone here knows me."

"Just what I said. How did you get in here?"

Daphne lifted from the couch, gracefully ironing her fingers down the sides of her shimmering gray, skin-tight dress. "Surely you're not still angry about that little interview I had with the local news. It's been weeks now, and—"

"It was uncalled for, and hardly local. It's one thing to take your spite out on me, but you had no right to—"

"It's always about her, isn't it?' Daphne's lips tightened. "I think what it really boils down to is that you just can't take the truth, Garry. You realize that Amanda is not so innocent. And you can't stand the thought that she could possibly be, at this very moment, in the arms of another man. Or for that matter, perhaps many men."

His shoulders grew rigid. His jaw twitched. "Get out!"

"What's the matter? You've not heard from your precious little nurse after all these weeks? Not quite the Amanda you thought she was, huh?"

His face grew hot as he pointed to the door. "I said get out!"

A burly bodyguard suddenly appeared in the doorway. Garry held up his hand, holding him back momentarily. Daphne grabbed her silver purse from off the dressing table. She stepped forward, only a couple of feet from Garry's face. "I came to give you warning. It's not over yet, darling. Not by a long shot. It was one thing to be humiliated in front of the whole world when you announced that you had broken your engagement with me, but quite another to be confronted by reporters day after day who want to know about the playmate nurse who took my place—the one you couldn't keep your hands off while you sent me on a supposed engagement present vacation!"

"I told you I was sorry, Daphne. I never meant to hurt you."

"Sorry isn't enough."

She flew past the bodyguard and out the door, her perfume trailing behind her.

"I don't know how she got in the room, sir. I'm sorry. I suppose I'll need to—"

"Later, Kirk. Right now, I'm thankful we're in L.A. and close to home. Find out if the limo is ready. I need five minutes, *alone*."

"Yes, sir," Kirk said. He shut the door on his way out.

Garry stood in the middle of the room, his hand tight around his cane. His throat felt constricted, his chest so tight he could barely breathe. What was wrong with him? Where was the positive in all that had happened these past weeks? He'd gotten his career back—a miracle in itself. He was back with the fans who loved him, and whom he loved. They brought such life into his lonely world. Nothing could mean more when the music was right. It was one of the reasons he'd never married. The music was all he'd ever needed. *Until Mandy.*

Tonight he could barely get through the songs. They all reminded him of her. He shouldn't have tried to call before the show. He didn't know what was worst: Daphne's threats hanging over his head, or the fact that Amanda had yet to allow any communication between them. What exactly had he said to upset her so much? He could only remember the kiss, and how she felt in his arms, and how empty they were when she walked away.

They felt empty now. He reached inside of his lined jacket and pulled from the breast pocket the scarlet ribbon he carried wherever he went. He held it to his lips and closed his eyes. He saw a vision of her on top of a chair, telling him he was the sweetest scoundrel of all scoundrels, and then singing, *How Sweet It Is (To Be Loved by You)*.

Although the memory brought a smile to his lips, a deep void settled in his chest as he rode home to his Bel Air estate. When he came through the front entrance door, Nicolas was waiting, anticipation marked on his face.

"She called?"

"Yes sir, but—"

Garry crossed the floor to the phone on the foyer table. He jerked it up and began dialing. Nicolas placed his finger on the hang-up button.

"Two things, sir—it's 3 a.m. in Florida, and secondly, she called with the request that you stop calling her."

Garry slowly placed the receiver down on its hook. "I missed her call," he said dejectedly.

"As was intended, sir. You keep her well informed of where you are. She says you 'hog' her phone and leave no room for other callers to leave their messages."

He noted the gleam in Nicolas' eye. "As is intended," he countered, walking into the parlor with his cane. He laid it against a couch and went to the bar, grabbed a bottle of Grand Marnier and poured himself a shot glass. He drank the amber liquid in one swallow, the burning sensation radiating down his throat and limbs. Then he did a little shimmy with his body. "*Woo!* A sweet imitation of how she warms me, Nic—a blast of heat, straight to my loins. Makes my feet tingle."

Nicolas cleared his throat. "Yes, sir."

He capped the bottle. "She adores my messages. Why disappoint her now by stopping?" He limped over to the couch and lounged back, stretched his feet out in front of him and rubbed the soreness from his right hip and thigh.

"The serenades, sir. I believe they intrigue her most. She seemed to particularly enjoy yesterday's song with the ukulele accompaniment—*Don't Sit Under the Apple Tree (With Anyone Else But Me)*. She said your version was quite entertaining. Had her smiling when she least felt like smiling."

"Yeah," he said, lowering his eyes. "I know the feeling well." His gaze then moved behind Nicolas, and he stared unseeing at the empty foyer for a long moment. "I ache for her, Nic. You think she's with him?"

"She loves you. I think that's all that matters."

"Of course the debonair billionaire is sure to rescue her from all that matters. Did you know he was a billionaire, Nic? The newspaper is quite an informative tool these days, isn't it? If Daphne hadn't put her two cents in to stir up the reporters, I may have been spared that bit of news. Chandler was already intimidating enough. The ultimate hero—tall, dark, and handsome with the four *B* attributes—big, brawny, brave, and billionaire. What woman would pass that up? It makes me wonder why she even bothered to take the job as my nurse when she needed only to turn to the one man who could make all her dreams come true."

"Yes, why would she, sir?"

Garry met his gaze; it was genuine and all-knowing. He watched as the older man slowly retrieved an envelope from his pocket.

"While you ponder that answer, sir, perhaps you'd enjoy reading the letter I received from Robbie today." Garry reached for the envelope, catching a hint glinting in the elder's eye. "Maybe you'll decide that actions do speak louder than words, sir."

Nicolas exited the room.

Garry stared down at the boy's handwriting on the envelope. It was addressed to *Mister Nicolas*. He'd not received a letter from Robbie for more than two weeks, but he supposed there was no need since he called the Children's Home regularly. He talked with the boy at least every other day. He opened the letter and read:

> *Dear Nicolas,*
> *I am sworn by galactic honor not to tell Garry that Amanda and I will be honored guests at the Children's Hope Fundraiser next Friday night. If Garry*

*happens to be at the Breakers Hotel in Palm Beach for the event, I DID NOT TELL HIM. I hope you get the hint and know that I miss you and Garry a lot. My friend Sarah is helping me with this letter and she says hi. Yesterday I helped bake cookies in the kitchen, but they did not taste as good as yours. Eddie gave me a real arrowhead last week. He says I have to keep Amanda from being so unhappy and lonely as he is very busy and cannot be with her. So I came up with a plan of action. This letter is it. What do you think?*

    *Love, Robbie*

Garry reclined his head against the sofa, the letter clutched in his hand across his chest. He grinned. "I think you're a brilliant boy after my own heart," he said.

### Palm Beach, Florida...

AMANDA THREW CAUTION to the wind. She'd never spent so much on a dress in her life, but it was one of the most beautiful creations she'd ever seen—a satiny, red A-line evening dress, its deep V-neckline elegantly outlined by a ruched bodice and back, with delicate beading along the waistline. It had a polished look that made her feel slim and beautiful. And she wanted to feel beautiful tonight. Losing Garry had taken a great toll on her, not to mention all the work and time she'd placed into the Children's Hope project. Upon returning home, she'd been distraught to find out that the Disabled Children's Home was in deep financial trouble. There was even talk about closing its doors in the spring if things didn't turn around. All the children would be relocated, including Robbie.

Though she'd applied for adoption once she returned home, she was told that her application would be on hold for months as an anonymous source had come forward. Her case was suddenly under investigation. She'd been devastated by the news, though it came as no surprise, for her name appeared in the newspapers only two days after her arrival in Florida. Old news dug up, new news revealed. She had suddenly become a celebrity, reporters trying to get the real story concerning her relationship with and her stay with renowned singer Garry Danzlo. Her *no comment* response was finally accepted by the press and for a few days, she'd gotten some peace. Only someone reported her sudden involvement in the fundraiser—a project she had planned and organized on her own.

The fundraiser kept her from falling completely apart. In less than two months, she alone had managed to raise nearly 250,000 dollars for the cause. Her status in the newspapers as the woman who nursed Danzlo back to health and back to the stage had people from across the nation calling in for her local cause. For all of her work and dedication toward the project, she was being honored tonight, along with Robbie. She'd gotten him involved from the start. He had come up with most of the creative ideas to raise the money.

What started as a small project of hope became something quite different. It had grown into something so grandiose that she finally conceded to Eddie's offer to pay for the banquet—she hadn't allowed him to help throughout the fundraising. She need only ask, and he would've purchased the entire Children's Home for her. From past experience, he knew better than to do any such thing, particularly behind her back. However, since she didn't give any special instructions as to where to have the banquet, he chose a grand meeting room at the prestigious and legendary Breakers Hotel in Palm Beach.

Amanda rocked in her shoes with nervousness after she entered the Mediterranean Ballroom, an astounding room of more than 6,000 square feet with a soaring 29-foot ceiling. It was lined with magnificent floor to ceiling windows, and contemporary pillars overlooking a Mediterranean courtyard. Rich blends of turquoise, peach, and beige filled the room, which held a swarm of elegantly dressed people. A grand piano was situated at one end of the room, not far from the podium. Contemporary songs were being played by a middle-aged, black musician in a white dinner jacket.

"Amanda, you look stunning! Where *ever* did you get that dress? Honey, isn't she gorgeous tonight?" Sandra, the CEO and director of the Children's Home, glanced over at her husband who was lowering his glass of wine. "Close your mouth, Harold, you're drooling."

Amanda smiled. "She's kidding, Harold. It's just a dribble of wine."

Harold wiped the corners of his mouth with his thumb and finger, both coming up dry. "I think you're both trying to embarrass me," he said grinning. He adjusted the glasses on his nose, eyeing Amanda appreciatively. "Have to admit though… you *are* red hot."

Sandra punched him in the shoulder. Amanda laughed. "Thanks, Harold. You're looking snazzy yourself." Gazing about the room, she asked, "Is Robbie here yet?"

"Actually he is, but he's…" Sandra glanced at her husband.

"Exploring," Harold finished for her.

"Oh," she said, suddenly turning to greet other guests approaching from several directions. Before she could speak to all of them, she was informed by a hotel staff member that she had a phone call. She followed staff to a phone located in a private area.

Her first thought was of Garry, which was totally unlikely as he didn't even know where she was. It didn't stop the surge of excitement racing through her body though. To her dismay, he'd not called for three days. Even though she'd requested he not call any more, she didn't really think he would stop. He'd only tried to contact her a couple of times since her talk with Nicolas, and then… *cold turkey*.

Was she the only one having withdrawal symptoms? He'd spoiled her royally with all of his phone messages. She had felt it best they not communicate with each other, at least for several months. She knew that speaking with him would make her want to see him. And honestly, she knew she didn't have the strength to say no to him should he ask. Garry needed to focus on his career. Not her.

She was still a bit angry and disappointed that he believed that she had lied to him. That she was capable of sleeping with Eddie after all they'd been through. She may have deceived him by hiding behind clothes, but she had never actually lied to him. And she'd never had sex with Eddie, though it was nearly forced on her that one time. Too much past, too much about Eddie she wasn't ready to share yet. Some things were best left unsaid.

But Garry had never asked for an explanation, for just like always, he assumed. She was so tired of having to defend herself. She'd done it for years—with Paul, who was always jealous and possessive. And then after his death, to a jury who didn't even know her. In the public eye, she'd been condemned until proven innocent. Why did she have to keep proving herself to everyone? Although Daphne initiated Garry's actions for doubt and accusation, it was Garry who had hurt her most, disclaiming her worth. He'd spoiled their last moments together, though the memory of his kiss still burned on her lips.

She realized that the only person in the world who truly knew her was Eddie. Robbie had been her comfort on the way home on the plane. Eddie had respected her space, knew she needed it. At the door of her apartment that night, she had collapsed into tears and he'd lifted her, carried her inside. He had sat on her bed and rocked her like a baby in his arms, whispering all the while, "He loves you, remember that, *mi querida*, as I do. He loves you. Let that be your strength."

It was then she knew just why Eddie was still her friend. Even after everything they'd been through in the past. She'd awakened the next morning and heard the click of the door, the deadbolt locking. She'd fallen asleep in his arms and he had placed her in bed with her clothes still on, a wicker chair pulled up next to the bed. She knew he'd sat there all night beside her. Just in case she would need him. Strangely, the next time she saw him, an entire week had passed. It was so like him, and yet it wasn't at all. He hadn't even called. At the very least, she'd have expected a note in her mailbox, or a message at the hospital. She'd been frantic with worry when he did finally call. She was at the children's home at the time. He always knew where she was.

Tonight was no different.

"Eddie, where are you? Are you on your way?"

"Miss me that much, huh?"

"You're not coming, are you? What if I say I do miss you? That I want you here? Would you be here?"

"Don't."

Silence. "I'm sorry. I'm just concerned and I'm trying to understand what's happening. I do miss you, Eddie. I miss the man you used to be. My friend. I feel something is wrong, dreadfully wrong and you won't—"

"You'll have a great time tonight. You'll be the prettiest one there."

She paused. There was a time when he used to tell her everything. "And you know this, huh? So what color dress am I wearing?"

"Who do you think I am? Nostradamus? Goodnight, my little red bird."

"Eddie…"

But he had already hung up. She placed the receiver back on its cradle, feeling a sense of loss and helplessness. All she could do was go back to the ballroom and try to have a good time.

That good time started the moment she approached the entrance door to the Mediterranean Ballroom, for Robbie was there, greeting her with his smiling face. After his big "woo-hoo!" and a dozen compliments that had her blushing in front of several dozen people that he just had to introduce her to, he was suddenly anxious to lead her to their seats. Their table was up front, close to the podium and next to the shiny black grand piano. The musician on the bench was just finishing "Can't Take My Eyes Off Of You," sending them a big smile with his pearly white teeth as they sat down.

"We've got the best seats in the house!" Robbie said, gleaming.

"Yeah, I wonder how that happened?" she said, looking at him suspiciously. Their table was much smaller than the others in the room, which tended to make theirs stand out. Quite profusely, she thought, suddenly realizing the space allotted them was twice the amount the other tables had in the room. The strangest part was, there was only one other place setting at their table. It was next to her own. "Are you sure we're supposed to be at this table? I'm feeling a little—"

"Good evening, ladies and gentlemen!" Sandra breathed into the microphone. "If everyone could please find their seats, we'll be starting our festivities in just a moment." Standing at the podium, Sandra paused to talk with one of her helpers. She sent a big smile toward Amanda, ignoring the questioning gestures and looks of confusion she was receiving back. Sandra proceeded at the mike.

"We are so honored to have this night of celebration here at the beautiful Breakers Hotel, something that would not have been possible without one very generous donation from—"

Amanda shook her head, a hushed finger against her lips. Luckily she got Sandra's attention.

"… someone who wishes to remain anonymous."

Sandra went on, naming off several people who were involved in organizing the night's event and those involved in the much-needed fundraising.

"And last, but not least, the dynamic couple who put their heads together and came up with the whole fundraiser idea to keep the Children's Home from closing its doors—Amanda Fields, and her keen-witted captain, Robbie Sterling."

Applause sounded from the crowd.

"And now, without further ado, it is my great pleasure to introduce to you… *oh, my gosh, I can't believe I'm doing this!*… Ladies and gentleman… our honored guest and speaker…" Sandra started flapping her hands in excitement, unable to quite get the words out. And then out of the blue Garry appeared from behind, wrapping his fingers around Sandra's on the mike and an arm about her waist to keep her from falling. "They call me Mr. Lucky," he said, lowering his head to the microphone, a loud roar of cheers and laughter sounding from the crowd. Sandra, obviously weak-kneed and her free hand now fanning her face, was finally able to announce breathily, "Garry Danzlo."

Amanda sat breathless in her seat, her gaze locked with Garry's. He smiled at her with that handsome smile she adored, and all she could do was try to smile back while her eyes bubbled with tears. She looked to Robbie with a bit of reprimand, but

Robbie just grinned his charming grin, saying, "I didn't tell him, I promise. I only told Nicolas."

Harold fetched his wife from the podium, for she had difficulty moving once Garry had taken the floor. Garry looked suave in his black tuxedo, a red silk hankie in his breast pocket. Everyone waited in suspense to hear what he had to say.

"I really like fundraisers," he said to the audience. "I particularly like that one sitting in front of me," he teased, glancing her way. "She's the reason I'm here tonight, if no one has guessed. No surprise to me that Amanda Fields played a big part in giving her time and devotion to a cause she believed in. When she does something, you can bet she's going to do it with all of her heart. I should know. She believed in me, and I'm able to stand here today when I thought I never would.

"It takes people like you and me to make a difference in another's life. That's what fundraisers are all about… *making a difference.* It's not just the dollar; it's the effort you put forth to make something happen, and that part you give of yourself that says you care. We have to care, for what a sad and lonely world we'd live in if we didn't, or if we didn't have someone to come along and make things right. Make things good again.

"I thank God I had someone to come along and make a difference in my life. And make it right again. Some of us tend to get stupid along the way. Think we can do it alone. But isn't it easier, better when we don't have to? When there's someone who cares enough to make that difference?" His attention moved to Amanda. She could barely breathe. Robbie took her hand and she squeezed it lovingly, unable to say a word.

"Ah Mandy," he said solely to her, "tonight I personally honor you, for doing what you so naturally do. Thank you for loving. Thank you for giving without taking. You once kissed me and stopped me from shaking, and I'll remember that all the days of my life. Because of you, I'm a different man. And a better one, I hope." He smiled and then looked toward the audience.

"Yes, I'm going to sing and play piano." The crowd cheered as he went and sat down upon the bench behind the piano. He leaned forward, placing the microphone in a holder. He placed his attention on Amanda and said into the mike, "This one's for you, Mandy."

An anticipating hush fell over the crowd just before his fingers touched the keys on the piano. They played briefly before his voice became a solo on the mike, singing a short intro to his song: *You gave me something my life can't forget—belief in myself, belief in you. And when you're not near, you're here in my heart. You still give me love though we're miles apart.*

It was a sighing moment for all, but for Amanda, it was so much more. Seeing him at the piano was heart swelling, and the greatest gift he could've given her. His voice played intimately inside her, and she couldn't stop the tears that kept falling down her face. His lyrics had clearly expressed his appreciation how she had touched him like no other, had changed him for the better, and how love was so very different now since he'd met her. She was his one chance to heal, and she was his moment to experience what love really was.

The entire room grew peacefully still as he finished his song, though one could hear a sniffle here and there. People waited on the edges of their seats as if to see what would happen next. To see what she would do next.

Amanda stood. Garry did likewise. He took a step forward. And then she ran. She ran straight into his arms, his hands taking hold of her, enfolding her warmly and tightly against his body while the crowd began cheering, whistling, clapping. "I love you, Mandy," he said against her hair. And his mouth took hers with a greedy need to taste what he hadn't tasted for too many long weeks. "Now is all that matters," he said against her lips.

"Now is all that matters," she said back. A tear fell down her face. "I love you, Garry. I've missed you."

He kissed her again, and then again. "We'll make it work, baby. Our love will find a way. I need you with me. I *want* you with me."

A spoon clinked on a glass nearby, bringing them to their senses. Robbie waved his spoon in the air. "Cool, I always wanted to do that," he said, clinking once more on a water glass. He had everyone's attention, particularly the two embraced on the floor. "Hey, since I gave the best of me for the both of you, I'm wondering where my kisses and hugs are." A sly grin curved the boy's mouth.

Amanda and Garry exchanged happy and mischievous glances. They both reached Robbie at the same time, Garry grabbing him up from his wheelchair allowing Amanda access to a load of hugs and squeezes. "You little devil you!" she said, plastering kisses all over his neck. The whole room was laughing and sighing while Robbie squealed, trying to take a peek at Garry. "Did I do good?" he asked through Amanda's onslaught of kisses.

"The very best," Garry said, feeling such gratitude of such magnitude, a tear fell helplessly down his face. Amanda saw it and attempted to kiss it from his cheek, but he moved too quickly, and she caught his lips instead. "Gotcha," he said, with a winsome smile.

And in that moment, they both knew… *he truly did have her, and he wasn't letting go.*

# Acknowledgements

ALL OF THE years, work and dedication I have placed into this one book would not have been possible without the support and love of many beautiful people who have made a difference in my life. The list is so long that I can't possibly name them all here. If you know me personally, your name probably belongs on this acknowledgement page, for it is through everyone I've met that my life has changed in some way, fashion or form. Also, for each and every one who is reading this book, I give my heartfelt gratitude, for what good or purpose have I accomplished without you?

Deeply appreciative of Mr. Manilow, who has been a great inspiration for this entire project and keenly moves my spirit with song, I wish to also give my heartfelt thanks to Inge Horowitz for her unforgettable kindness and friendship; to Mr. & Mrs. Fine for their hospitality (and my first Shabbat dinner); to Rabbi Creditor for his helpful words; and to the Jewish Community Center in Richmond, Virginia for all the information they provided me.

In loving memory of Lynda Allen and her motherly gifts & support.

In loving memory of Ann Peach—editor, writer and friend.

With loving acknowledgement to David Morgan, a literary agent and editor who encouraged me to see that "am I am inside" and taught me much about skillful writing.

My sincere gratitude to the 2nd Draft editors at Writer's Digest who were wonderful guides for me, as well as freelance editors Amy McElroy, Lauren Methena, and Destiny Just.

Love & gratitude to my oldest and dear friend of forty something years, Brenda Sale who is always supportive of all my creative endeavors. And not to forget my greatest supporter, friend and healer colleague Anita Snellings. I cannot forget the person who read the very first version of this novel via snail mail, chapter by chapter as pages were being typed—Judy Colyer. Thanks for your enthusiasm. It's quite a different story now.

Special thanks to my talented cover designer, Kari Ayasha, and the wealth of knowledge and help she provided me, and to Angela McLaurin for her creative interior design of this book. I also wish to acknowledge support from RWA, Virginia Romance Writers, my Intuitive Development Group, and others who have supported me in various ways concerning this book: Alexis Wingfield, Sandra Hughes, Lauren Wittig, Lori Dillon, Julie Keenan, Suzanne Smith, Sharon Dawkins, Lisa Conyers, Dorothy Berryman, Jamele Pope, and many more left unnamed.

Last, but not least, I acknowledge my daughters – Jenny, Chrissy, and Laurie – and my niece, Amie, who all have been supportive and guiding lights through the years. And then there's Michael, the one I chose for better, for worse. Thank goodness for my perseverance in believing in myself. I've finally proved that I'm not just "dreaming." Sometimes we need such challenges to give us more strength and fortitude in our projects. He's actually read this book twice (that in itself is a miracle, *and* that I dared to listen to a second critique). In truth, he's been an inspiration for a lot of my creative ideas. And his love, ever unwavering. For that, I am always grateful.

And to the Highest Power of All. Thank you, Dear One, for All That You Are and All That I Am. For the many blessings. And for each and every moment. *Selah.*